D0857221

Praise for *The Imperfects*

"A wonderfully structured multigenerational family drama woven with international intrigue, *The Imperfects* is a truly beautiful and truly American story full of unspoken history, loss, and hope. Absolutely winning."

—J. Ryan Stradal, *New York Times* bestselling author of *Kitchens of the Great Midwest*

"Both a gripping mystery and a family tale of imperfect people... Large gemstones have a certain magic of their own, and Meyerson expertly captures that fascination in her wonderful tracing of the origin of the secret brooch. I read this book morning and night until it was done, unable to break free of its spell. A sheer delight."

—Janet Fitch, bestselling author of *White Oleander*

"Amy Meyerson has created a captivating story about a hilariously dysfunctional family that comes into a shocking inheritance. *The Imperfects* is an absolute pleasure to read, guaranteed to have readers turning the pages late into the night."

—Angie Kim, bestselling author of *Miracle Creek*

"*The Imperfects* is a book that shines as brightly as the jewel at the center of its tale and will leave readers wondering what mysteries might be hidden in their own pasts, waiting to be revealed."

—Meghan MacLean Weir, author of *The Book of Essie*

"In this clever, meticulously plotted tale of secrets, family dynamics, and resilience, Amy Meyerson takes readers on a 'what if?' journey filled with equal parts history, tenderness, and intrigue."

—Cynthia Swanson, *New York Times* bestselling author of *The Bookseller*

Also by Amy Meyerson

The Imperfects
The Bookshop of Yesterdays

The LOVE SCRIBE

AMY MEYERSON

ISBN-13: 978-0-7783-8708-4

The Love Scribe

Park Row Books
22 Adelaide St. West, 41st Floor
Toronto, Ontario M5H 4E3, Canada
ParkRowBooks.com
BookClubbish.com

Printed in U.S.A.

To Adam, for our story so far and the many chapters to come.

The LOVE SCRIBE

For one human being to love another
human being: that is perhaps the
most difficult task that has been entrusted
to us, the ultimate task, the final test
and proof, the work for which all other
work is merely preparation.

—**RAINER MARIA RILKE,**
LETTERS TO A YOUNG POET

1

Gabby and the Love Pilgrims

It all started with Alice's best friend, Gabby, and a particularly potent bout of heartbreak. Gabby was one of those people who was always in love. She wafted from one long-term relationship to the next, her heart remaining open to the promise that something new meant something better.

Love was as vital to her system as breathing or sleeping, came as naturally to her as exercise and fashion. Gabby was both very fit and very stylish, unlike Alice, who was as averse to working out and chic clothing as she was to love. They'd been an unlikely pair since the third grade, Gabby outspoken and pretty. Alice quiet and gangly, her wild curls cut into the unfortunate shape of a bowl. So often, people speak of opposites attracting in love, but the same is true of friendship, perhaps more so. This was certainly the case for Gabby, forever confident that her one true love was out there waiting to complete her, and Alice, sure she was complete enough on her own.

That was what Gabby's ex, Brian, stole from her; the confidence she had in love. He did it not by cheating or neglect or abuse or any of the ways men tear down women they don't value. No, Brian just ended it. Out of nowhere. One weekend, they were jetting off to Hawaii, flying business class on miles he'd accrued from his work, and the next, a moving truck pulled up to their curb. Two burly men carted out their sleek sectional sofa and Amish dining table, leaving only the things Brian found garish. He wrote her a check for their purchase price, which Gabby tore to pieces the moment the moving truck drove away.

Brian offered her no reason for unceremoniously terminating their five-year relationship as one might cancel the cable subscription. It wasn't a matter of stark incompatibilities about wanting to have children, relocating for a job, or supporting rival sports teams. They both liked the Dodgers, wanted two kids, and were perfectly happy to spend their days on the West Coast. In the absence of logical reasons for their abrupt separation, Gabby blamed herself. Like the furniture and paintings he'd left in her condo, she decided she was too bold, too brash, too opinionated. Alice watched her best friend shrink before her eyes. Where before she'd laughed generously, she swallowed her joy, releasing little coughs of amusement in its place. And if anyone hit on her, she looked at them like they were a foreign species, as though she did not understand how they could desire her, someone so unlovable.

Alice had never liked Brian. He was rude to waiters—the cardinal sin to Alice, who worked in the service industry—and Uber drivers. Dismissive of homeless people. Condescending to women, particularly to Gabby, who insisted that he was only trying to help when he corrected her grammar and disparaged her grasp of current events. It seemed impossible that someone as emotionally astute as Alice's best friend would not see the way he spread rudeness like confetti over everything around him. But she was blinded by love.

That was how she described it when, after ignoring Alice's check-in calls for two weeks, Gabby finally announced herself ready to leave the apartment and meet her best friend for a drink. *I was blinded by love.* Eyes gouged, burlap sack over head, absolute darkness.

Alice had just finished her shift as a cater waitress passing around flutes of champagne and caviar on pastry puffs at the Carousel House in Chase Park when Gabby texted, asking if she was free to meet. Please don't make me drink alone, Gabby wrote, already at the bar. This left Alice no choice except to agree to meet her when she was done folding up chairs and breaking down tables.

Alice had been working for Cuisine by Caroline for eight years. While the job itself was routine—an hour of circulating trays of bite-sized food followed by the more precarious task of ushering larger trays laden with entrées between tables of increasingly intoxicated guests—each event was its own sociological experiment. Alice loved studying partygoers the way a biological anthropologist might study the habits of animals in the wild.

At the fiftieth anniversary party she'd just worked, she watched the attendees eye the couple of the hour, noting a mix of envy and awe as they tried to decipher their secret to lasting love. If Alice had not met them at the beginning of the evening, she would not have known they were a couple at all, let alone *the* couple the party was celebrating. There was nothing particularly notable about them, no sparks you could sense across the room, no covert handholding beneath the table to suggest they were as in love as on the day they married a half century ago, nothing to indicate why they succeeded where so many failed, nothing for their guests to emulate or extract from their good fortune. This was love, Alice thought. Random and unremarkable. Not worth the trouble.

Alice rode her bike straight from work to the bar, where she arrived slightly sweaty, her white button-down shirt splotched with béarnaise sauce. All she wanted to do was go home and shower. Her knees ached from being on her feet all night, and she could feel her curly hair frizzing in a particularly unflattering way. But Gabby did not trust herself to be alone at the bar. Alice didn't trust her either.

The bar was four blocks from Gabby's apartment, where they used to play trivia with Brian and his friends every week. Really, Gabby and Alice talked while Brian and his friends argued each other out of the right answers because none of them were willing to admit that one of their teammates might know more about college basketball or dead presidents than they did. Perhaps Alice should have suggested a place they were less likely to run into Brian, but she liked the small beach bar with its license plate collection and assorted Pop-Tarts for sale. Plus, on a Tuesday night, it was empty, giving Alice the space to drink in all her sweaty, frizzy-haired glory and Gabby the freedom to cry as much as she wanted.

Alice stepped into the bar and found her best friend lounging on the white leather couch in the back, dark circles under her eyes and an oversized sweater somehow making her appear even lovelier than usual. Gabby waved Alice over, wild floral wallpaper whirling around her as she sipped a cocktail that had turned her tongue turquoise. Behind the couch, bookcases filled with hardbacks, Tiffany lamps, and candelabra made the space seem like an old-time library. It gave Alice that Narnia feeling, as though she could push a shelf in and enter another realm.

Gabby lifted her drink to Alice, offering to buy her one. "It's called a blue lady." The inside of her mouth looked radioactive when she forced a laugh and added, "Like me."

Gabby wasn't normally prone to self-pity, and it wasn't like this was the first time she'd been dumped. She always insisted that it was easier to be rejected than to reject, a point with which Alice starkly disagreed. Alice could not endure even the idea of rejection let alone the reality of it, which was why she always ended relationships the moment nausea or insomnia hit her, her body's telltale sign that things were starting to get more serious than she could handle. By contrast, Gabby believed that the pain of realizing someone was not *the* one was more heartbreaking than the disappointment of someone failing to recognize your greatness. So why was it different with Brian? Why wasn't she shrugging him off like she did Jeff or Greg or Stella or Ryan or Tyler or all those other misguided souls who had walked away from the best thing that would ever happen to them? What was it about Brian that made his rejection a mark on her character rather than his?

Alice declined Gabby's offer of a blue lady, saying simply, "I'll keep my tongue pink for the night." She bounded up to the bar to order a tequila soda.

Alice hated seeing her best friend like this, all blotchy-faced and drunk over a man as self-involved as Brian, especially since she knew Gabby would find someone new in a matter of weeks. Every time Gabby became single, someone swooped in as though the city had put out a signal announcing her availability. She'd probably meet someone on the way home from the bar. Still, it was clear from the tears, and from the near incoherent rambling that Brian was the one and she'd never love like that again, that Gabby did not want to move on. So Alice sat beside her, letting Gabby drink those blue ladies until her lips looked like she had hypothermia and her words started to lilt.

When Gabby said, "Do you think I should call Brian?" and reached for her cell phone, Alice decided it was time to take her home.

On the short walk to Gabby's condo, Alice steadied her so she didn't trip on the sidewalks. By the time they got to her building, she was bawling, not caring about the glances from neighbors walking their dogs.

"I really thought we were going to be together forever." Her nails dug into Alice's forearm for emphasis. Alice wanted to tell her that forever was a fallacy even when the relationship was perfect, which clearly Gabby's was not. Someone who believed in love as much as Gabby did, did not want to hear this, even when heartbroken, so Alice nodded sympathetically and allowed her arm to be a target for Gabby's misdirected grief.

"I mean, we got a cell phone account together. We were talking about rescuing a dog. Who goes to the shelter with you and decides two days later you're through? Who does that?" Her nails threatened to draw blood, desperate for an answer Alice couldn't provide.

Gabby released Alice and ran her hand through her dark hair. "Sorry, I just, you're the only person who I don't have to pretend I'm okay with. I'm not okay. I'm heartbroken."

Alice searched through Gabby's purse and coat pockets, finally locating her keys in the right back pocket of her jeans. She helped her best friend up two flights of stairs and forced her to drink a pint of water, which proved a mistake, because as Gabby was gulping it down, she realized the glass was from Brian's favorite brewery. That started the waterworks again, and it took Gabby a good half hour to tire herself enough for Alice to get her into bed. If this was love, Alice didn't wish it on anyone.

Alice brushed the bangs away from Gabby's forehead. "You're going to be okay."

Gabby hugged her tightly. "I love you," she said.

"I love you too," Alice told her. This was the only kind of love Alice wanted.

Alice had never intended on being the type of person who avoided falling in love, but she'd learned long ago that she was not equipped for its emotional turmoil. At twenty, she had been on track for a very different life. She'd always planned to become a doctor, like her mother. The idea of any other career had never occurred to her. She wanted to help people, and medicine seemed the most logical way to do that. The other parts of adult life, a husband, some children, a mortgage, retirement funds, she assumed would naturally follow.

Alice did try for that life. In med school she felt self-conscious around her peers, who were simultaneously more focused than she was and partied more intensely than her body would allow. More significantly, unlike Alice, they never doubted themselves when they had a scalpel in hand or a diagnosis in mind. Alice's instincts were right. Headaches and vision changes were signs of migraines. Then she would start to think that they could also be indications of glaucoma, and if she mistook migraines for glaucoma, the patient might go blind all because she had leapt at the first conclusion that sprang to mind. At night, she'd toss and turn, imagining that blind patient who had lost his ability to see his children, to marvel at modern art—that blind patient who was not a patient or a person at all, merely a description on an exam. Still, if he *had* been a person, he would now be blind all because of Alice. She could make that mistake with a real patient. She could forever ruin a person's life. That risk outweighed the fact that she could save a person's life too.

Dating was no better. Her mind was equally acrobatic when she thought about the outcome of a romance. In fact, she did meet someone at med school. Taylor, with light brown eyes and cheeks that flushed when he was about to kiss her. Alice liked kissing him. She liked eating with him. She liked walking beside him. He was two inches taller than she, something to be appreciated given her six-foot stature. Alice would put her book down for Taylor when it was well established that she would not put her book down for anyone, not even her mother or Gabby. As soon as Alice realized that she preferred Taylor's company to Isabel Allende's or Agatha Christie's, the ambient tension she always felt in her body intensified in her chest as full-on panic. He was her favorite person, and at any moment she could lose him. He could decide he didn't feel the same way about her. Or, even if he did, something could still happen to him. One day, in some shape or form, their relationship would end.

Once this notion implanted itself in her head, Alice could not shake it. When they kissed, she couldn't feel Taylor gently biting her lower lip because she was distracted by the fact that for all she knew this could be their last kiss. As he slipped his fingers between hers when they crossed the street, she would remind herself not to get too comfortable. He could get hit by a bus right now, with their hands entwined. That fear kept her staring at the ceiling all night even as Taylor slept deeply beside her. She'd listen to the steady rise and fall of his breath, waiting for it to stop. It didn't help to point out to herself that the possibility of a healthy twenty-seven-year-old man dying in his sleep was exceedingly low. There were a million other ways to lose a person. His childhood friends, whom she'd been avoiding meeting, could dislike her. Or they could like her too much. His parents could decide she wasn't good enough for him. Or that she believed she was too good for him. She could lose her temper too easily or not be wild enough in bed and eventually he'd grow bored. She could start snoring or she could get after him for snoring, and he would decide that if they weren't compatible in sleep, they could never be compatible in waking life. These thoughts were the only ones that distracted her from the anxieties of blinding a hypothetical person on her med school exams, which wasn't exactly a comfort. She found herself constantly worried until she couldn't handle it anymore, med school or the relationship, so she quit them both.

After Taylor she dated Patrick, Bode, then Sebastian. The trajectory was the same even as the men were very different. As soon as the pain localized in her chest, she knew the end was imminent. With Sebastian, she'd wound up in her childhood bedroom with her mother administering sleeping pills because she'd been up for four straight nights, worrying not as much about him dying—he was of sturdy Eastern European stock—as what would happen when she woke up, if he would smell her morning breath, see her unruly morning hair, and realize that she was normal. Flawed. Wrong for him. As the fatigue set in, she became convinced that they'd be finished the second she drifted to sleep, so she pinched her cheeks, and clawed at her palms, forcing herself to stay awake until sleep was no longer a possibility and neither was the relationship.

With Patrick, she was so nervous that she spent three days without drinking water before she ended up with a stomachache from too much Gatorade when she tried to catch up on electrolytes. And with Bode, oh Bode, she'd forgotten the sound of her own voice, having grown mute for fear of saying the wrong thing. When she finally braved a sentence, her voice came out someone else's. After that, after insomnia, dehydration, and voicelessness, she decided enough was enough. She couldn't keep her body from its natural panic, its automatic aversion to love. It was easier to avoid romantic entanglements altogether since they would always end, even if Alice didn't manage to mess a good thing up.

Once she decided that love, like the field of medicine, was not for her, her entire body could relax. She remembered how much she liked herself when she wasn't consumed with wondering if someone else liked her enough. This self-love seemed healthier and more fulfilling than any affirmation she could get from a partner. As for the more physical aspects of a relationship, well, that was lust. Alice was fine with lust, so long as it ran clear of love.

Throughout her twenties, she taught herself to separate the physical from the emotional, which turned out not to be difficult if she chose the right partners. She began to identify the personality traits of those who would want more from her than she was prepared to give, those she in turn might want more from, the men who were too interested in her childhood or her life goals, those who told her they felt like they'd known her their entire lives. Others who were shy or wounded, whom she found herself wanting to fix. The men she pursued instead didn't have to be assholes or players, simply individuals with whom she didn't share that uncontrollable spark, that deeper connection. Even then, she had a fail-proof routine for keeping them at a distance. She never invited these men to her home, never stayed the night at theirs. If she decided she wanted to see them again, she always took their numbers, always texted, never called, met them for drinks, not meals, somewhere close to their homes.

Now, at thirty-two, Alice still believed in love—just for other people. Never for herself. Some people do not have the discipline to train to be a concert pianist. Others do not have the bravery to be a stunt person. Alice simply did not have the constitution for love.

After a few weeks, Gabby had not in fact found someone new. She was committed to mourning her relationship with Brian for as long as it took, which was proving to be a considerable amount of time. Alice needed to do something to shake Gabby, to make her understand how strong she was, how much love awaited her, how much love she had to give. She considered buying Gabby a collection of Yeats poems, but she wasn't trying to make her best friend even more depressed. Jane Austen felt too predictable, and besides, those were love stories Gabby had already memorized. No, Gabby needed something uniquely hers that would make her feel seen. So, as she continued to pair periods of isolation with heavy drinking sessions and public crying jags, Alice decided to write her best friend a letter.

Through the years, Alice and Gabby had established a tradition of writing to each other. In grade school, they passed notes. Rather, Gabby wrote little quips about the teacher's hair or whichever boy she liked, while Alice chided her, covertly hiding the notes for fear of getting caught. In eighth grade, after Alice's father died, she found among the cards of benign sympathies a tome from Gabby, complete with every kind and funny thing she remembered about Alice's father. In turn, Alice wrote to Gabby about all the ways she missed him, all the things she never wanted to forget. They never discussed these letters. Instead, throughout high school, they became each other's diary, chronicling their anxieties and grievances, their most personal thoughts. Knowing that their words were being read, that they weren't hidden in a drawer, deemed private and somehow shameful, made their feelings matter. It helped them trust their perspectives—Gabby quickly became a hopeless romantic while Alice hardened into something of a skeptic. In college, when their peers were embracing the ease and novelty of email, they sent pages of handwritten confessions by post. Gabby's letters always smelled like honeysuckle and jasmine, as though she sprayed the pages before she enclosed them in the envelope. Alice did not know what her letters smelled like. She didn't have a signature scent, at least not one that derived from a bottle. Still, she assumed her letters smelled like her, that their olfactory qualities comforted her best friend as much as her familiar handwriting. In those letters, they told each other everything from the mundane details of their classes, the small cruelties of cafeteria food, and the peculiar habits of their roommates to the travails of love and heartbreak. At the time, Alice was still trying to date. This was before she realized she was not prepared for the stress of pairing yourself with another.

As Alice biked home from a shift one day, making a mental list of all the things she wanted to tell her best friend about how amazing she was, how she deserved someone better than Brian, an image materialized so forcefully in her mind that it knocked her off balance. Her knee contacted the ground first, sending a shooting pain up her right leg. As she rubbed it, the vision crystalized in her mind, sharp and Technicolor. A red hummingbird.

When at last the pain subsided, she stood and walked her bike the remaining blocks home, confused by what had just happened to her. Her body buzzed with displaced energy from the fall, persisting as she locked up her bike, opened her front door, and settled before her computer to fill the screen with all the things she loved about her best friend. Except when her fingers found the keys, they did not write *My dearest Gabby*. Instead she began to describe the hummingbird, whose wings shed crimson hearts every time they fluttered, faster than a heartbeat. What followed from there was not a letter but a story.

Everywhere this hummingbird went it left a trail of love. Soon people were following it down State Street to the wharf. As they neared the Pacific, the crowd grew thousands deep, hundreds thick, like a protest. It was a love protest. A love march. A love pilgrimage. And when the hummingbird finally reached the ocean, it flew over the waves, carpeting them in red confetti hearts. All the people, all those love pilgrims, turned to the side to see if anyone else had witnessed the hummingbird too, and when their eyes locked with the person beside them, they found immediate and eternal love.

The letters to Gabby notwithstanding, Alice was not a writer. She'd never aspired to pen the next great American novel, to win a Pulitzer for exposing the nefarious dealings of political parties. Alice was not historically a finisher either. In addition to changing her undergraduate major four times and dropping out of medical school, she abandoned hobbies as quickly as she pursued them. Tennis. Beach volleyball, which despite her height she lacked the coordination for. Spanish, although Gabby's mother insisted on speaking the romance language to her. Pottery, because she found the teacher too attractive to be around. Knitting, gardening, running, even most televisions shows. In fact, the only thing Alice was certain to finish was a book. She never started reading a novel without seeing it through. Every story had some essential truth she could glean from it, some kernel of wisdom that made life a little brighter. But anything besides a book? She couldn't even finish a meal without leaving a few bites.

In short, it was as surprising that Alice had finished the story for Gabby as it was that she'd decided to write it in the first place.

It was a silly story, that hummingbird tale, but it left Alice with the tingling sensation of ice-cold air-conditioning on a sweat-drenched day. Even though she wasn't a writer or a finisher, Alice knew she'd finished writing something special, twelve pages of solid gold. She just knew. Before she could second-guess herself, she put it in an envelope, wrote *G♥bby* on the front, with a heart for the *a* like Gabby used to write her name in middle school, and left the story in her best friend's mailbox, hoping to cheer her up.

After that, Alice didn't see Gabby for two weeks. She figured Gabby was back in an isolation stage, which she would follow up with binge drinking before too long. Certainly her friend's silence couldn't have anything to do with Alice's story. Gabby had likely discarded the envelope in the bowl by her front door where it was destined to remain unopened. Surely the silence could not be because Gabby had met someone, since she was so committed to being heartbroken.

When Gabby at last emerged from her period of silence, she recounted the happenings of her last two weeks breathlessly over margaritas. No more blue ladies for her. No more crusted tears on pillowcases, no more untouched dinners. She attacked their order of guacamole, saying over a mouthful of avocado and red onion, "Your story. It worked."

"What do you mean it worked?" Alice scooped as much guacamole as she could onto her chip. On the best of days, she worried about getting her fair share of a communal dish, which was why she didn't share with anyone other than Gabby and her mother, who were both conscious of and accommodating to this hang-up. Usually, anyway. Not today. Not this bowl of guacamole. At least Alice hadn't agreed to share an entrée with Gabby too.

"I was reading your story at that French place I like on Arlington, the one with the really good croque madame?"

Gabby said as she mined a tomato from the guacamole. "It was really a stupid story."

Alice winced. She would be the first to admit the story was dumb, though it didn't feel great to have that fact confirmed by someone else.

"But it got me laughing. When the hummingbird turned the ocean red with love, it was just too silly, too on the nose, but it worked."

"I still don't understand," Alice said with a tinge of annoyance, miffed by Gabby's criticism of her story. "What do you mean it *worked*?"

"There was this guy sitting next to me. Oliver." She spoke his name like it was made of silk. "He heard me laughing, and he said, 'Anything that gets a reaction like that must be pretty good.' He's a stand-up comedian. I tried to explain to him that it wasn't actually funny, definitely not something that would garner a laugh at a comedy club, not that I'd ever been to a comedy club, and he said it was a crime I'd never seen stand-up and maybe he'd take me sometime. Then sometime became the following night, and we haven't stopped going out since." Gabby blushed. "Well, we occasionally stay in."

"Gabby!" Alice exclaimed, pretending to be scandalized.

"Oh, Alice, I'm in deep this time."

In deep, as though love was an endless pool to drown in.

The language we use to describe love never ceased to amaze Alice. Our crushes, our flings, our old flames. The way we fall. The way we break. The way we are struck, and that's supposed to be a good thing. Gabby was in deep, and instead of reaching to pull her out, Alice had apparently pushed her in.

"I trust him. I trust this feeling. It's just, well, it's easy. It was never easy with Brian."

Easy was good? Weren't we supposed to want someone who challenged us? Wasn't the whole point that the person pushed us to be a better version of ourselves? That we in turn pushed them? Looking at Gabby's face, the way she struggled not to smile, Alice could see that easy was indeed good. At least for the moment. With Gabby's track record, Alice was not inclined to assume this prelude would last, regardless of whether her story played a role in it.

"I'm really happy for you." Alice's voice faltered. Gabby was too giddy to notice.

"Here's the thing." Gabby pounded on the table for effect. "Don't be mad, but I may have given your story to Maria."

"Why would you do that?" Alice was more embarrassed than angry. As Gabby said, it really was a stupid story, and her sister, Maria, was the smartest person they both knew. Smart as in PhD in chemical engineering, calculus in seventh grade. Like many brainy people, she wasn't known for her sense of humor.

"I have absolutely no idea why I decided to give it to her. I just had this intuition, this instinct that if she read it she might meet someone too. And, Alice—" she drumrolled the table "—she did."

Part of what made Maria so smart was that she never wasted time. She listened to podcasts while she showered, dictated lecture notes while she cooked, darned socks while she watched TV. She wasn't about to devote time she could spend doing something more productive to reading Alice's story.

On a brisk afternoon, Maria skipped down the steps from Gabby's apartment building, eyes glued to a page of Alice's hummingbird tale, and smacked right into Claudia.

Claudia had taken the day off work because her dog, Claudia Jr., had eaten chocolate. Rather, her mother had fed the dog a Hershey's Kiss, not realizing it was like feeding the pup arsenic. Claudia had looked over in time to see Claudia Jr. funnel the kiss into her mouth but not quickly enough to stop her from swallowing it. Induced vomiting and several doses of activated charcoal later, Claudia Jr. was released from the vet. Claudia, feeling particularly sentimental from her dog's near-death experience, couldn't fathom teaching that day, so she stayed home with Claudia Jr., snuggling on the couch. When signs of the dog's typical boundless energy appeared, they decided to go for a walk. Two blocks later they rounded the corner, and bam—there was Maria, nose deep in the flutter of Alice's hummingbird.

Maria had always been a cat person, one of the few things she and Alice had in common. She had two at home. Claudia loved cats almost as much as she loved dogs. People always assumed you had to like one or the other, she told Maria an hour later when they were back at Claudia's apartment, naked in bed. Cats or dogs, vanilla or chocolate, wine or beer, apples or oranges, men or women. False dichotomies, Claudia insisted. Well, not the men or women, at least not for Maria and Claudia. They only liked women. On that, like everything else, they agreed. By the time Claudia Jr. had fully recovered, Maria and Claudia were deeply in love.

"You don't really think either of those instances was because of my story?" Alice asked when Gabby finished telling her about Maria. What she meant was, *You don't really think either of those are examples of love?*

Gabby shrugged, a knowing smirk on her face that made Alice's stomach drop, even before she said, "Well, Maria may have given it to Erica."

Erica was Maria's best friend, and after Erica met Dale when she rear-ended him at a red light, indulging her bad habit of reading while driving, she'd given the hummingbird story to Sal, her roommate. Sal then met Frankie at the library, where he took a break from his dissertation research to read the hummingbird tale. He became so absorbed in Alice's bird imagery that he didn't realize he was the last patron left inside once the library had closed for the day. Frankie, the head librarian, found him tucked away in the stacks when she was doing her final sweep of the premises. Sal then presented the story to his mother, Cat, who was reminded of a glass hummingbird feeder she'd purchased years ago. When she scoured her gardening shed for it, she discovered it shattered beneath a shelf of pots. She had bought the feeder while her husband was still alive and, at the sight of the broken glass, felt inexplicably overcome. She needed to replace it right away, so she headed straight to the plant nursery. Calvin was looking for a way to get rid of the starlings who were eating his strawberries. His wife had planted them the fall before she died. In their second year, their roots were deep, and they'd taken over an entire bed, producing enough fruit to make the jam and pies his wife would never get to taste. Calvin hadn't meant to tell Cat all this when they started chatting in line at the nursery. She'd cried at his story and the thought of strawberry rhubarb pie, which had also been her husband's favorite. She told Calvin that she couldn't eat strawberry rhubarb pie without thinking of her husband. "Maybe that's beautiful instead of sad," Calvin had proposed, holding out his handkerchief. It was embroidered with his initials, CL. "Those are my initials too," Cat told him, and they stared at each other, wondering where the other had come from, how they'd happened to be there in line together at exactly the right time.

Five single people. Five readings of Alice's hummingbird tale. Five encounters. Five instant connections. Easy. Deep. Drowning.

"I can't believe you shared my story without asking me first," Alice said. It was a novelty, being annoyed with Gabby. Vexed though she was, she was more hurt than angry. The story had been for Gabby. It had been their secret language, one that Gabby had now shared not only with her sister but with strangers too. It made Alice wonder if Gabby had let people read the letters she'd written to her, the passages where she bared her soul to her best friend, assuming no one else would be witness to it.

"Look, I'm sorry. You're right, I should never have given it to Maria without asking you first. Forgive me?" She batted her eyes in that *I'm too adorable for you to be mad at me* way that worked just as well on Alice as it did on Gabby's lovers. "Besides, you're missing the point. It's… I don't want to say it's magic, but it's something." Gabby motioned wildly, spilling clumps of guacamole on the table. "Your story, Alice. It *is* something."

At the time, Alice did not recognize this monumental news for what it was: the birth of her gift. At the time, she assumed that Gabby was letting her imagination run wild, seeing something fantastical in Alice's story when the results were nothing more than happenstance. She decided to prove Gabby wrong with a little thing called logic.

"Yeah, it's a jumble of not so eloquent words you all happened to be reading when you did something totally in character and met someone. I bet it was sunny too. Are you going to say that the sun caused you to fall in love?"

Gabby frowned. "It was cloudy, actually, when Maria met Claudia. And Cat hadn't thought about that hummingbird feeder in years."

"If she was the kind of person who had a hummingbird feeder, she probably cared about her garden, which means it wasn't unusual for her to visit a plant nursery even if her reason for visiting it that day was out of the ordinary."

"Why are you being intentionally obtuse?"

"I bet you were all wearing shoes too. Maybe it was your shoelaces that did it, maybe they were tied too tight and the pulsing in your arches put you in the mood for love."

"I wish you'd take this seriously."

"Gabby, there's nothing to take seriously. Coincidences happen. That's all this is. Maybe the story did manifest these connections," Alice conceded, "only because you were all looking for it. You wanted the story to lead you to someone and it did. That's the power of your will, not of the written word."

"Trust me, I was not looking to meet anyone. It was the farthest thing from my mind when I sat down to read your story." Gabby leaned forward like she was about to divulge a secret. "I'm telling you, Alice. There's something about that story. I can't explain it. It opened me up. Maria said the same thing. It was like being unfolded from the inside out, so the love could seep in." Seep in, like disease. Lovesick. Add that one to the list of ways love enfeebles us.

"So where is it now?" Alice asked, ready to be done with this conversation. "Where is my magical tale?"

"Sal's mom put it back in her bag as she was walking out of the nursery, but when she got home she couldn't find it. Do you have another copy? Oliver wants to give it to his sister. She's divorced."

"That's the only copy, I'm afraid," Alice lied. Alice was the type of person who saved everything. Trinkets, old clothes, her father's records, his books, every essay or lab report she'd ever written, even a silly story about a hummingbird.

"Well then," Gabby said with a devilish smile, "I guess you'll have to write another story."

Alice was not about to write another story. She had no idea where the image of the hummingbird came from, how it led to any story let alone one that had supposedly caused five people—Gabby and four others—to fall in love. She told Gabby that, when she thought about everything she wanted to write to her best friend, the symbol had simply hit her like a dump truck. It was not an experience Alice could replicate even if she believed her story had such powers, which she did not.

"We're going to have to work on your analogies if you're going to write love stories," Gabby said, her eyes sparkling as she saw the waiter carrying two plates of enchiladas to their table. "No one wants to be thinking about being hit by a truck when they're trying to find love."

They should, Alice thought. Love and death were two sides of the same coin. She shuddered at this analogy. *See?* She wanted to tell her best friend, *My mind works in clichés.* But Gabby was not looking for poetry. She was not asking for a gripping tale. She was looking for sorcery, something Alice had no interest in supplying.

"Gabby," Alice said, opting for reason. "I have no idea why that story helped you all find love. It's not something I can recreate."

"You don't know that."

"I don't know anything, that's my point."

"Maybe that's how your gift works. You don't try to control or understand it. You simply let it happen."

"My gift? Gabby, the only thing I'm gifted at is quitting. I have a preternatural talent for giving up."

Gabby frowned. "All the more reason not to quit now. And for the record, I've never believed that about you. It's just an excuse you've been telling yourself for years so you don't have to pursue anything challenging."

She was a clever one, that Gabby. If Alice turned her down now, she'd be proving Gabby right.

"Look, just meet Oliver's sister and see if inspiration strikes you again." Gabby shuddered. "It really is a horrible image."

They were at an impasse, eyes locked across the table, a little dot of guacamole at the corner of Gabby's mouth. She licked it away keeping her eyes fixed on Alice. Around them, pop music cloyed Alice's ears. The temperature in the room rose, intensified by Gabby's continued stare. Her insistence was too much, causing Alice to look away. Without seeing it, she could sense Gabby's triumphant smile.

Gabby always won. Alice had never been able to refuse Gabby, and historically this had been a good thing. Over the years, if she hadn't consistently said yes to Gabby, she never would have learned to ride a bike, never would have had her first kiss, never would have worn a bikini or Doc Martens, never would have gone across the country for med school, never would have left when it didn't feel like home.

"Good," Gabby said, scooping the last bit of guacamole with her index finger. "Her name is Rebecca, and you'll love her." She stuck her guacamole-laden finger into her mouth, making a popping sound as she wiped it clean. "This is the start of something big for you, Alice. I can feel it."

2

The Time Is Now

Alice did not love Rebecca. In fact, she found it difficult to believe Gabby did either.

They met at a bar Rebecca had chosen, a sleek bunker of blond wood and bare white walls, the absence of decor an ambience of its own.

Rebecca slipped onto the bench across from Alice. She did not say hello or make any polite attempts at small talk before presenting Alice with her situation.

"I'm thirty-eight," she said after ordering them each a glass of Malbec from the tablet left on their table. "My divorce finalized last month. Thank God I didn't have kids with him, only now, like I said, now I'm thirty-eight. I have two years to meet someone and get pregnant." She delivered her speech without an ounce of humor. She wore her black hair cropped behind her ears. Her fingernails were buffed and filed, and her neutral-toned clothing looked expensive.

"Lots of women have children in their forties," Alice said, sipping her wine. She had not seen the waitress deliver it, but there it was, a stemless glass on the table before her.

Rebecca took a microscopic sip from her own glass. "Can you help me or not?"

While she was cold, she wasn't rude exactly. She came off more as pragmatic than prickly. Could Alice help her? *No*, Alice reasoned. *You are going about this the wrong way if what you really want is love.* Although, love and a relationship weren't necessarily the same thing, not that Alice suspected she could write a story to help Rebecca find either.

Prickly or not, Rebecca was intimidating, so Alice nodded, afraid to say no, she couldn't help her, but unable to say yes either.

"Good." Rebecca slid an envelope across the table, took another small sip of wine and stood. "You have seventy-two hours. Anything can be done in that time. I'll be in touch."

Once Alice was certain Rebecca wasn't coming back, she poured the rest of Rebecca's wine into her own glass and drank it quickly, fearful that the stealthy waitress might disappear it while she was taking a breath between sips. Inside the envelope, Rebecca had enclosed enough money to pay Alice's rent for two months, all in fifties. She would have to work twenty catering shifts to make that much. Alice looked longingly at the money. Generally, she was not driven by financial gain, but it would be so much easier just to plop a few words on the page than to spend twenty nights smiling until her cheeks ached as she asked strangers if they'd prefer red or white wine with their entrée. She zipped the envelope into an inner pocket in her purse, certain she would be sliding that envelope back across the table when she apologized to Rebecca for being unable to help her. Maybe she would make Gabby do it for her. The woman really was terrifying.

Alice remained at that efficient, impersonal bar until she finished her wine. Sometime during that double glass, her perspective shifted. While her fear of Rebecca didn't go away, it morphed into pity. She felt for Rebecca, who mistook plans for dreams, who tried to control her future the way she'd controlled her meeting with Alice, through efficiency and determination. The more wine she sipped in the sterile bar Rebecca had selected, the more she thought about the type of woman Rebecca was, what she needed. A reprieve. A respite from her plans, a break from her watch, which had ticked away on her wrist the whole twenty-seven minutes they were together. Even if Alice couldn't find Rebecca love, she might be able to help the woman slow down. Lord knows, she needed that more than a partner or a pregnancy.

By the time Alice left the bar, the sun was beginning to set on the horizon, a small ball of fire dipping into the ocean. The sky was striated orange and red. Alice unlocked her bike and walked it down State Street toward the ocean, thinking of all the pilgrims in Gabby's story who had made the same journey. Along the modest strip of beach beside the pier, a few couples nestled on blankets, watching the sun disappear, the glorious colors it left in its wake. Seagulls lined the edge of the water as though they too were saying goodbye to the day.

Alice stood on the bike path until the sky lost all traces of the sun and blended into the dark ocean below. Without the glitter of the sun's reflection, the water looked thick and sludgy. An image came to Alice, one that hit her with that same clichéd rush of a barreling truck, one that had nothing to do with love. A tingling traveled up her arms, pins and needles like they'd gone numb, a dizziness in her head that was not entirely unpleasant. She hopped on her bike, took the path east, then turned north and headed home.

Her studio apartment was on the ground floor of a Victorian that had once been a single home, now subdivided into four apartments. She'd been living there since she left med school and returned to California. Over those eight years, she'd collected more belongings than the modest garden apartment could reasonably be expected to hold. Stacks of books migrated from the overstuffed bookshelves to the floor, competing for space with bins of her father's records. An impressive collection of afghans was piled on one side of the couch, an elaborate cat tree and condo for her shorthair, Agatha, was blocking the hallway on the other side. In the far corner, meticulously layered with more afghans, Alice's double bed was sandwiched beside an antique dresser that was too large for the area. While her apartment gave Gabby panic attacks, Alice liked living this way, cloistered with her stuff, cluttered but clean, cozy. Besides, it didn't matter how it might appear to anyone else. She rarely had visitors, certainly not the kind who might try to make themselves at home in her space.

On the desk, Alice rearranged her piles of pens and opened her computer to get to work, her body still buzzing with that image of muddy water. She had no idea what she was going to write, but as soon as her fingers grazed the keyboard, they became a life force of their own. She could not control them or the words that emerged from their patter across the keys, the scene that took shape on the screen.

The story was even less of a love story than the one she'd written for Gabby. It began with Rebecca lying in a pool of mud carved into the side of mountain. Steam rose from the surface, cloaking her in opaque mist. For eighteen pages, all that happened was Rebecca struggling to get out of the pool. She tugged at her legs. She tried to run. She flailed. Every effort pulled her further in. When at last she let go and submitted to the mud, she didn't sink. Instead, she floated. The mud was a soft bed she did not want to leave. Slowly, effortlessly, she wiggled her toes, and like a small motor, they propelled her to the lip of the pool. She tried to step out all at once and was unable to stand. Instead, she let the mud tilt her, leisurely, like it was pouring her out, until she landed on the hard ground, clean in an emerald dress, her bare feet nestled into a sea of rose petals. She lay down in the petals and fell asleep.

Alice wrote until the sky outside started to lighten. Her back ached. Her temples pounded. When she stood and stretched, her body cracked in places where she didn't realize she had joints. Every cell in her body felt drained, its energy removed and transplanted to the page, but she'd finished.

She stepped away from the desk, confused and a little scared of the words that had amassed on the pages, unsure what they meant yet certain Rebecca would hate it. Rebecca would probably make it halfway through the story before calling Alice to scream, "What the hell is this? Why are you wasting my time?"

And what the hell was it? Alice was not abstract or symbolic. She was rarely one to give advice, especially on how to improve one's life. Still, she couldn't shake the tingling that persisted, spreading from her arms to her entire body. Whatever these pages were, they were exactly what Rebecca needed.

When they met again, precisely seventy-two hours after their first appointment, Rebecca went to open the manila envelope with her story inside. Alice stopped her. She couldn't bear to watch Rebecca read it. More, the story would not have its intended effect if Rebecca rushed it. The whole point was to get her to slow down.

"Please, don't read it right now. I want you to wait until the voice inside you says, *Now. Now's the time.* Trust yourself."

Alice braced herself for an outcry, but Rebecca nodded as if in concurrence with a guru. Already Alice and her story seemed to be what the woman needed. She dropped the manila envelope into her briefcase and thanked Alice for her time.

Four weeks later Alice got the call.

On the phone, Rebecca spoke so deliberately it sounded like she had a drawl. She'd waited a week to read the story. "I've never waited that long to do anything," she said, "but I knew that was the point." Several times she'd considered opening it—

in line at the grocery store, while she was waiting for a friend at a café, at her therapist's office, in bed when she woke from a nightmare and couldn't fall back to sleep, at the office as she was waiting for a call—then resisted. Once, in the dressing room at her favorite boutique, she got as far as sliding her index finger beneath the sealed adhesive on the back of the envelope, stopping when the paper sliced her flesh. "It was fate punishing me for my impatience. I knew it wasn't the right time."

A few days later, as she was sitting in the mildewy locker room at the public pool where she swam four mornings a week, she felt the pull. The other swimmers scurried around her, slipping hair beneath swim caps and washing off as quickly as possible so they could claim a lane. Normally, Rebecca beat them all. First through the lobby doors when the pool opened, first into the cool expanse of saline water, first to flip-turn after a length, last to get out of the pool when the hour window for lap swim ended. That morning she found herself wanting an unprecedented moment of calm before she joined the bustle that surrounded her. Once the other early morning swimmers had exited for the pool, everything was still. Alone at last, it was time to read the story.

It wasn't reading so much as inhaling. She inhaled the story. "Does that make any sense?" she asked Alice, who confessed that that was what it felt like to write it too, as if she exhaled the entire story in one elongated breath. "I must have sat there for twenty minutes, like I was in some sort of trance. Then I put the pages back in my bag and went to the pool."

Normally, she jumped into her lane and immediately began to cut through the water, swiftly, fluidly, her body coming alive with the movement. Today, she found herself wading by the wall, unwilling to move. She took off her cap and began to swim the side stroke, slowly, decadently, relishing the cool water as it combed her short hair. It took her several minutes to span the length of the Olympic pool, and when she turned, a slender figure in a Speedo was dropping feet-first into the other end of her lane, his body vertically slicing the water.

"Normally, I don't like having to share a lane. Normally, I don't like Speedos," she said. "Normally, I don't like to be the slowest."

The man was a rocket, zooming up and down the pool, his body a fleeting apparition beside her. She mostly ignored him, luxuriating in the slow circular movements of her limbs. He was there and then gone, there and then gone again. When the lifeguard blew the whistle, warning that the pool would close in five minutes, he treaded water at the end of the lane, shooting liquid from a plastic bottle into his mouth. Rebecca did not speed up for her final lap. Instead, she tried to make it last as long as possible, wanting to hold on to that meditative feeling forever. When she finally reached the side of the pool, the man was still treading water, waiting for her.

He shoved his goggles to the top of his head, exposing deep indentations around his dark eyes, and smiled. "You're normally the fastest one here."

She held on to the cement lip of the pool, lifted her own goggles to expose the deep indentations around her pale eyes, and stared at him. "You've seen me before?"

"For the last year. I usually pace myself to you, but I can never keep up. You're too fast."

"Not today." She smiled.

"Not today." He smiled back. His name was Jonathan, and surprise, surprise, three weeks after they met, they were hopelessly in love.

"I guess your two-year goal isn't so far off," Alice said.

"We'll see," Rebecca responded. "Like you said, people have children in their forties all the time. Oh, Alice. I have to admit I was skeptical when Oliver told me about you. Consider me a convert. I hope you don't mind—I gave your number to a few friends. You should be hearing from them soon."

Rebecca hung up before Alice had a chance to tell her that she did mind. The story had been a favor to Gabby, a strong-armed one at that. She had no interest in writing additional stories for *a few friends* she'd never met. The notion caused her to panic. Already she'd lost control of whatever this social experiment was.

When Rebecca's friends called later that week, four very different people with very different issues holding them back from finding love, Alice intended to refuse them. She was not a lexical matchmaker—Rebecca's term, not hers. Her story did not make Rebecca fall in love. All Alice had done was teach Rebecca to relax enough to see the love that was already waiting for her. Jonathan had wanted to talk to her for months. When the moment presented itself, he made his move. Alice didn't create that moment. She didn't conjure Rebecca's attraction to him. She didn't give them a shared love of swimming. She'd just persuaded Rebecca to slow down.

Alice let the calls go to voicemail. She was still afraid of Rebecca, so she listened to the messages, planning to send polite texts of refusal. They'd been mistaken. Alice was not a matchmaker, lexical or otherwise. If they were looking for love, she could not help them.

"Is it true you can write a story that will make someone like me meet the love of my life? I'm not very special, I'm afraid," Rebecca's soft-spoken friend Jane had whispered into the phone.

"I don't usually go for this sort of thing," Crystal said plainly, "and I doubt it will work, but Rebecca said if I don't talk to you myself, she'll do it for me."

"If you could find someone who wasn't intimidated by Rebecca maybe you can find someone who loves me for my shortcomings too," Peter said near tears. "There are a lot of them."

"It's worth a shot," Beth said when she offered to pay Alice nearly four times her rent. "Don't worry, when it doesn't work out, I won't ask for a refund."

In much the same way Alice had diagnosed Rebecca upon meeting her, Alice identified what ailed these friends from their messages alone. Most people's problems, Alice was beginning to discover, were pretty obvious. Everyone thinks they're hiding their pain, their insecurities, their struggles. Really, most people are just so focused on their own issues that they aren't particularly observant of others. If you stop for a second and look, really investigate someone, they unfold before you like a book. Most people, at least. Who knows, maybe once Jane, Crystal, Peter, and Beth got out of their own way, once Jane believed in herself, once Crystal let go of her pessimism, once Peter trusted he was worthy of love, once Beth stopped self-sabotaging, maybe they would find love.

So Alice said yes to these four souls with no inkling of the stories she would write for them. Once again, as soon as she committed to the task, it followed a pattern: it began with a strong sense of how she wanted to help the reader, then a walk to clear her head, an image so fully formed that it hit her physically, a prickling from her arms to the rest of her body, a whirling mind, a sleepless night, a story she hadn't written so much as channeled.

Surprise, surprise. Four more stories led to four more couples madly in love.

After reading Alice's story, Jane was so struck by its beauty that she signed up for a creative writing class, having always dreamed of telling stories of her own but never quite summoning the courage to pursue it. In the class she met Dawn, who had confidence to spare. Dawn was not a gifted writer and didn't care. She wrote because she loved it. Her honest assessment of her own mediocrity made her belief in Jane's talent more trustworthy, so much so that even Jane could not deny it. To Alice, the truly astonishing part of the story was that Jane had seen beauty in Alice's words, so much so that they inspired her to write too.

After reading Alice's story, Crystal decided to purge her house of all the things she'd grown pessimistic about, the bedsheets that would never be new again, the lights that always seemed too dim. She boxed up the bulk of her belongings and brought them to a local charity, where Kiran, a volunteer, marveled at each of her donations as he registered them into their system. "Even his name," Crystal told Alice, "is a ray of light."

Peter had always known that his best friend, Trish, desired him, but he believed it was the unavailability she craved. He knew she would begin to lose interest the moment he asked her out. As he read Alice's story, which was not about a chase, a conquest, a game but an old mutt, scraggly and balding, too sweet not to love, he retraced the reasoning that led him to conclude Trish wasn't really interested in him and found little evidence to support this conviction. When he finally confessed his feelings to Trish, instead of retreating, she dove right in.

At first Beth was devastated by Alice's story about a doomed matriarchy, how depressing and hopeless it was. She wandered down to the train tracks and, unable to contain her sadness anymore, sat on the rails and cried. Distracted by how much worse she felt, she didn't hear the train approaching. In the background, someone shouted. It sounded far off, distant, until her body rose from the tracks just before the train rushed by. Her hair twirled around her face, and she couldn't see who had saved her. When the draft off the train settled, she saw soulful brown eyes searching hers, asking if she was okay. She understood that she was.

Alice had written six stories for ten people, all of whom had found love. Still, she was not convinced that her stories were responsible for the relationships that developed in their wake. She had a talent for making people see themselves a little more clearly—that much she believed. This was not supernatural, though, no more than a psychologist's ability to help her clients or a friend's talent for sage advice. All she did was encourage people to get out of their own way.

It wasn't until the eleventh person came along that Alice started to suspect that what she did really was magic. For the eleventh person was someone who had already had her one great love. Someone who did not want to find love again.

The eleventh person was her mother.

3

The Woman with a Man's Name

If it hadn't been for Alice's grandmother and a particular streak of not giving a damn, Alice's parents never would have met. Grandma Millie hadn't given a damn what her in-laws thought of their outspoken daughter-in-law, who had an opinion on everything from the Supreme Court's new obscenity test to puff sleeves. She didn't give a damn what her pupils thought when she doled out detention like seconds at dinner, didn't give a damn when their weak-willed parents pleaded that she was holding sixteen-year-old girls to impossible standards. She didn't give a damn what anyone thought of her, so she certainly didn't give a damn what the nurse on the maternity ward thought about the name she'd selected for her daughter.

"Bobby," Millie had declared to the nurse, holding her sticky newborn in the crook of her arm. "We're going to call her Bobby."

The nurse scribbled on the document fastened to her clipboard. "Roberta. What a lovely name."

"Not Roberta. Bobby. With a *y*," Millie said.

The nurse stared at her liked she'd proposed naming Alice's mother after a vegetable, Romaine or Zucchini, something that actors would call their children today. "Bobby is a nickname. Most often for Robert."

"Now you're catching on." Millie cooed to Bobby as the newborn began to awaken to the harshness of her new reality.

"What's going to happen to this beautiful little girl when people hear her name and expect a boy? She'll spend her entire life correcting them."

"Precisely." Millie sat up a little straighter in her hospital bed. "Why must a girl's name decide her fate? Make her ineligible for a job, a mortgage, a bank account?"

Millie was prepared to continue, but the nurse shook her head. "Bobby it is," she said and walked out.

While Millie had given her daughter a man's name to help her see herself as equal to a man, she had not expected her daughter to be confused for a man when she enrolled in college.

At eighteen, Bobby walked into her dorm room, expecting to find a pair of penny loafers beside the door. Instead, she tripped over a pair of men's tennis shoes. A fresh-faced boy with a smattering of freckles across his cheeks was napping on one of the two twin beds. He sat up at the sound of her body hitting the wood floor.

"Are you okay?" He rushed over to help her up.

Embarrassed and flustered, she pushed his extended arm away. "What are you doing?"

"Helping you," he said, awkwardly disappearing his hand into his pocket. "I'm Paul, Paul Meadows."

"No, what are you doing in my room?" She looked around to see an unpacked suitcase open on the floor, a Beach Boys poster already pinned to the wall.

"You must be lost. This is a men's dorm." Paul located a letter on the desk beside the dresser. "Says here this is my room along with a Bobby Klein."

"You're looking at Bobby Klein. In the flesh. As far as I know, I've never been a man."

The boy's cheeks turned a deep red, and Bobby laughed. "Don't worry. I've been dealing with this my entire life."

When she sat down on the bare twin mattress that was supposed to belong to the male Bobby Klein, the boy began pacing.

"We have to fix this immediately," he said.

"Are you afraid I might sneak a peek when you're in your boxers? You have my word." She raised her right hand. "I solemnly swear to avert my eyes the moment you disrobe."

He stopped pacing. Looked right at her, although he did not seem to see her, Bobby, the wide-faced woman he would love for the rest of his life. "You find this funny?"

"A little."

"There's nothing funny about it," he insisted. In time, he would find everything about their first meeting funny—the mishap, its fate, the ebullient woman who taught him to love life. In that moment, though, he could only focus on this young girl's honor, which he foolishly assumed needed protecting. "A man's dorm is no place for a woman."

"My delicate constitution just can't handle it."

"Don't worry," he said, oblivious to her sarcasm. "I'll take care of it."

"Thank you." She batted her eyes, waiting for him to get a clue. He offered her the hero's nod and carried her bags through the quad to the registrar's office.

The problem was resolved quickly, well before it could become a scandal or a blight on the university's reputation. Once Bobby was settled into another dorm with three girls who slept with rollers in their hair, she forgot all about the pseudo heroic boy with whom she'd shared a dorm room for an hour. He'd vanished from her mind, replaced by thoughts of cell structures and DNA and whether her roommates might burn down their housing by leaving those electric rollers plugged in all day.

A few weeks later, when Bobby was tucked into an oversized chair in the library reading about mitochondria, she heard a throat clear and looked up to see a lanky man fidgeting.

"I'm sorry," he said, plopping into the empty chair angled toward hers. A girl seated nearby shushed them, so he whispered, "I've been hoping to see you so I could say that. I'm sorry I made such a big deal about the whole roommate assignment thing."

Bobby studied the young man, trying to place him. He crossed his legs, bobbing a foot encased in a dirty white tennis shoe. The shoe she remembered. It took a few moments longer to recall its owner, Paul Meadows.

"Most men are excited at the prospect of sharing a room with me." Bobby returned her attention to her textbook, but not before she saw the horrified look on his face. "I'm joking. Really, what sort of woman do you take me for?"

"I didn't… I mean I wasn't thinking… It's just it was a rather unusual—" Bobby smirked, enjoying him squirm.

"Again, joking." She closed her textbook and stood. "Come on. We need to teach you how to lighten up."

From there, Bobby couldn't recall a lesson they hadn't learned together. Whether it was planning a route across Europe for a summer of backpacking after they graduated college or figuring out how to install a car seat in anticipation of Alice's arrival, they tackled everything as a team. Once they were a team, Bobby could not remember a time when they hadn't been united. Paul permeated all her memories, even those from before she knew him and those from after he was gone. At least that was how Bobby explained their love to her daughter. Alice wasn't sure how her father would have described their love because she never had a chance to ask him.

Still, Alice had always known that Bobby's life was configured around her love for her husband. After college, Bobby wanted nothing more than to be in love. For her, that meant abandoning her old, self-centered dreams in favor of new ones they could build together. They moved to Carpinteria because where else would you want to be in love but a quaint beach town on the Pacific and because Paul had grown up in the area and always dreamed of raising a family in a tile-roofed house with an ocean view. She found a part-time job in administration at a hospital, which she told herself was the next best thing to being a doctor. Every morning, Bobby would attempt breakfast for Paul before he made the short commute to UC Santa Barbara, where he worked as an admissions officer. Bobby was a terrible homemaker, even before she had the distraction of a colicky, sleep-averse infant. Eggs were forgotten on the stove so often that Paul left a fire extinguisher on the counter. And she never could figure out how to get coffee stains out of Paul's dress shirts, much less how to make a palatable cup of joe.

How ironic, it might seem, that Paul chose a profession so integrally connected to how he and Bobby first met. He imagined that when he granted students access to the university, he was setting them on a path toward love. As he read application files, he liked to predict which applicants might end up together, and surprisingly often he was right. With every student he admitted, he fell a little more in love with his wife, their life together.

They were so happy in that life that it took Paul longer than it should have to see how unhappy Bobby truly was. In fact, it took him thirteen years of marriage to realize that Bobby was living a lie she told to herself. At night, Bobby nestled into Paul, her fingers tracing his figure as she rattled off the names of more bones than he knew he had. In those moments, he understood she wanted more, even when she insisted she didn't. They had each other. And Alice. She didn't need anything else. She was happy. Paul finally recognized that you could be both at once, happy and wanting. In love and needing more.

One night, over petrified TV dinners—Bobby couldn't even effectively work the microwave—Paul plopped a pile of brochures on the kitchen table.

"What's this?" Bobby picked one up. It showed a group of students sitting cross-legged on a sunny quad.

"Applications for medical school."

"For you?" Bobby asked, genuinely confused. Paul had a lot of talents; the sciences weren't among them.

"For you."

"What?" Bobby laughed, spitting bits of fossilized mashed potatoes on the table. "I'm not qualified for medical school."

"Sure you are." Paul stared into the expansive face of the woman he loved. "You're the smartest person I know."

She stopped laughing. "It's been years. I wouldn't know where I'd begin."

"Where we'd begin," he corrected.

"Can we afford it?"

"Let me work that out."

"What about Alice?" They both looked at their three-year-old, who had outgrown her colic but not her antipathy to sleep. "Who will take care of her?"

"I will."

"Paul, it's sweet of you, really, but I love things the way they are. I like being here when you get home at the end of the day. I like taking Alice to the park. I like taking care of both of you. I don't need more."

"Yes, you do. I believe in you." That was all Bobby needed to believe in herself.

UCSB didn't have a medical school, so Bobby drove to LA for classes, a sojourn that took anywhere from ninety minutes to two hours. She'd drop Alice off at school on her way to the 101, returning home after Alice was already in bed. Those were Alice's childhood memories of her mother: banana nut muffins in the car on the way to school, soft lips on her forehead at night while she was half asleep.

Her childhood memories of her father were weeknights when he donned an apron and cooked one dinner more impressive than the last. Weekends when he would take Alice to the beach so Bobby could have a quiet house to study in. He'd let Alice bury him in sand, then toss her into the waves when he broke through and raced her into the ocean. It wasn't just Bobby who was born again when she pursued her dreams, it was Paul too. He discovered a passion for cooking, a dexterity with the vacuum, a penchant for starched sheets, a knack for taking care of the women in his life in ways no one had expected of him, not even himself.

When her father was still alive, Alice's memories of her parents were of them dancing in the living room when they thought she was asleep, their bodies nestled together, their faces buried in each other's hair. Of the look on her father's face when her mother walked across the stage to accept her diploma and at the dinner table when she would tell them about the children who came into her clinic, the ones she coaxed into shots with lollipops, the ones with bruises she could not ignore, the ones with tonsils that needed to be removed and crooked spines that couldn't be straightened. His eyes would spark as he said, "We are all so lucky to have you."

When her father was still alive, these were Alice's memories of love too, all the ways her parents were lucky to have found each other. All the ways she was lucky to be raised by them. That's the thing about luck, though. It's a streak, a roll, a spell destined to be broken.

Alice had always wondered whether her father would have had a heart attack at age forty-seven if they hadn't been quite so lucky. As the daughter of a physician, Alice understood that the heart, medically speaking, did not run on love, but she could not shake the suspicion that he had loved too much, driving that essential organ into overtime until it could not keep up anymore.

After her father died, her memories of love were her mother in black, handfuls of dirt on an open grave. The weight of her mother's body as it slipped into bed beside hers each night, the cold indentation it left in the morning when Alice woke and found herself alone. Love and loss became inextricable. She didn't know how to unweave them. She didn't know how to want one without courting the other.

A month after Alice turned sixteen and her father had been dead for two years, Bobby met Mark. He was widowed, like Bobby. A doctor too. An anesthesiologist. They had an easy comfort, a gentle admiration that gave Alice hope that love could take different forms, that the end of your great love story didn't have to mean the end of love itself.

A year later it was over.

"I thought I was ready," Bobby explained to her daughter. "Mark was ready. It just made us both realize that I wasn't."

Alice watched her mother's eyes well, uncertain if she was crying for Mark and the love that could have been, or for her husband and the love she wasn't ready to discard.

"I'm sorry," Alice said.

"I'm not." Bobby wiped a tear that had escaped. "I had my great love."

"Don't you think Dad would want you to—" She almost said *to move on.* There was no moving on, not from that kind of love. Still, her father wouldn't want Bobby to be alone, so Alice searched for the right words. "To be happy?"

"Of course. And he would like Mark. It isn't that. It's just, my heart is full. Every time I looked at Mark, every time he laughed or he hugged me, he just wasn't your father." Alice must have grimaced because Bobby added, "Please don't look at me like that. I've had all the love I want. Really. My memories are everything I need."

For Bobby, Paul had been part of the memories before he

was there and after he was gone. She didn't know how to make memories with someone new.

This was what Alice had learned from her parents about love—that it would end. Even great love. Especially great love. Something that perfect couldn't last forever. It would leave you worse off than you were before. It wasn't the lesson her mother had intended to instill in her. It wasn't even, it turned out, what Bobby believed herself.

As a result, she became the eleventh person who hired Alice, the one who, as always, made Alice realize she had a gift.

"What's this I hear about you writing poetry?" Bobby asked as she and Alice were attempting to cook dinner one Sunday in May. It had been three months since Alice had penned her hummingbird tale, and as far as she knew, all the couples that had met in response to her stories were going strong.

Bobby still lived in the house where Alice had grown up, a four-bedroom Spanish Revival in Carpinteria, down the coast from Santa Barbara. They'd purchased the home when Bobby added MD to her résumé. The house was too big for just Bobby, but Alice had not wanted her mother to put it on the market any more than Bobby herself did. "Renata told me something about a sonnet involving a dove that you wrote for Gabby before she met Oliver. Apparently, he's very funny."

In elementary school when Alice and Gabby became inseparable, their mothers had followed them into friendship, a fate both girls quickly learned was less than ideal. It eroded the separation between friends and parents, led to a lifetime of distorted gossip as the mothers swapped half stories they knew of their daughters' lives. The things Alice learned about herself from Renata Diaz, Gabby's mother, who always managed to get the details wrong.

"It was a short story, not a sonnet. About a hummingbird," Alice said as though that explained anything.

Bobby had recently signed up for a mail-order cooking service that delivered everything you needed—and not a pinch of oregano more—to cook a healthy gourmet meal. It was supposed to be easy, paint by numbers cooking that anyone could follow. Bobby's eyes widened as she surveyed the numerous plastic containers of spices, herbs, bread crumbs, and ground meat she'd laid on the counter.

"This was listed as simple," she said to her equally overwhelmed daughter.

As Bobby began to read the instructions, separating the basil and parmesan cheese to be added at the end, Alice's shoulders relaxed, assuming she'd successfully avoided a conversation about her stories.

Bobby dropped a spoonful of meat into Alice's palm for her to roll into the unnatural shape of a golf ball and casually said, "I didn't know you were a writer."

"I'm not." Alice worked the meat until it was only slightly lopsided and plopped it beside another asymmetrical meatball.

"That's not what Renata says." She dropped more cold meat into Alice's palm.

"Renata says a lot of things." In high school, Renata had told Bobby that Alice was trying out for cheerleading when the real story was that the head cheerleader had encouraged Alice to try out as a joke, knowing she wouldn't make the team. In college, Alice had learned from her mother via Renata that she'd gotten a tattoo of an eight ball on her lower back when it had really been Gabby who got the regrettable ink.

"But you wrote Gabby a story."

"That doesn't make me a writer."

"What would make you a writer then, two stories? Three?"

Alice averted her eyes, not wanting to admit that she'd already written six.

"Well, I for one think it's great that you're allowing your creative side to blossom. You were always such an inventive child." The stovetop knob clicked as Bobby pushed it in to ignite the starter. The kitchen smelled briefly of gas before the fire caught and hissed beneath the pan.

"You must be confusing me with your other child."

Bobby swirled olive oil into the pan.

Alice motioned toward the oil decorating the pan. "You're learning."

"And you're deflecting."

"We both have our talents."

"Yours apparently are of the narrative variety."

After that, browning the meatballs required all their attention.

"It looks good," Bobby said optimistically when they sat down to eat. She scooped a bite of pasta onto her fork, trying to hide the flinch as the sauce hit her tongue.

"That bad?"

"No, it's good. Maybe a little…peppery? Or salty? Too acidic? Or bland? Maybe it just needs more cheese." She grated enough cheese into her bowl to feed a starving writer.

Alice twirled her own pasta onto a fork, piercing the meatball with its tines. "What are you talking about? It's fine. Good, even."

"Oh, how you flatter me," Bobby said. "So, how's work?"

"Good," Alice said, relieved that she'd managed to weather the inquisition into her stories. "I did that event for the mayor's office. Two engagement parties and the biggest baby shower you've ever seen. It was a baby monsoon." Funny how when you put it in exaggerated terms it no longer sounded appealing. Then again, the whole celebration had been unappealing. Often, there was a direct correlation between the grandiosity of the party and the pretensions of the people throwing it. The bigger the wedding, the more the couple seemed to have to prove. The grander the baby shower, the clearer it was that the couple was both terrified and ambivalent about becoming parents, not that Alice worked many baby showers.

In turn, Bobby told Alice a story about a new family who

had visited her practice, how the parents came in distressed that their teething son hadn't defecated in ten days. "I explained to them that anything between ten poops a day and one every ten days was perfectly normal."

"That's a one-hundred-poop differential and also not a great topic of conversation for dinner."

"See," Bobby said. "You've always been funny. I bet that comes in handy as a writer."

"I'm not a writer." Alice sighed. She was not going to get out of this conversation. "I'm, I don't know what you would call it. An intuitor, I guess."

"As a writer, you should know that's not a real word."

"Do you want me to explain it or not?"

Bobby gestured that she was backing off.

"It started with Gabby. She was so sad." Alice told her about Gabby and Maria and the hummingbird tale, Rebecca and her friends, how she'd discovered something essential about each of them that they couldn't see in themselves and how, in exposing it to them, they felt ready to embrace the love they'd always wanted.

Alice waited for Bobby to laugh. She waited for her mother to suggest therapy. She waited for her mother to offer reason, arguing it was all coincidence. Bobby did none of these things. She stared intently at Alice.

"It's not inexplicable," Bobby finally said. "You were raised in a household of love. It makes sense that you'd be able to impart some of it unto others, especially since you never want to keep any for yourself."

They'd had this conversation too many times to count. Bobby constantly worried about her daughter being alone despite having seen firsthand the toll Alice's past relationships had taken on her body and ministering her back to health. If Alice let herself be fully vulnerable, Bobby knew her daughter would experience a love like she and Paul had. A love that ended, Alice had contended. A love that persisted, Bobby had insisted. It was the only thing they argued about regularly.

For the moment, Bobby seemed to have no more desire to repeat their tired refrain than Alice did. Instead, she said, "Tell me how it works."

Alice explained that it started with an image, one she didn't understand until she finished writing and the metaphor revealed itself. The stories seemed to run through her rather than out of her, like she was the pipe rather than the spout. The medium, not the oracle.

"And you don't believe that's magic?" Bobby asked. Her face softened, and she stared at Alice with an expression of awe that seemed strange coming from someone who had borne her. "Can you write one for me?" she asked without an ounce of sarcasm, possibly even with hope.

"What? You don't want to fall in love again."

Bobby shrugged. "It turns out you can always use more love."

Ever since Alice dropped out of med school, Bobby had tried to encourage her pursuits. Whether it was training for a marathon she never ran or fostering kittens until it became clear that Agatha was not willing to share Alice with another cat or learning the very practical language of Latin because she wanted to recognize the roots of the words she loved to read, Bobby always supported her. And when Alice inevitably gave up Latin or knitting or quit skiing after one awkward fall, Bobby didn't urge her to keep trying, to persist. Instead, she told her that knowing what you didn't want brought you one step closer to knowing what you did. Bobby had always known what she didn't want—someone to replace Paul. Thus, Alice concluded that her mother was asking for a story not because she wanted to find love but because she wanted to encourage her daughter.

Instead of saying that she could see what Bobby was up to, she said as forcefully as she could, "I don't think it's a good idea for me to write something for you."

"Why not?"

"Because you're my mother."

"And that's a problem because?"

"Because everything." Because what if she didn't like the story? Because what if she did? Because what if it reflected an unflattering image of Bobby? Because what if Alice could summon no story at all for the person in the world most important to her?

"Just consider me like anyone else. I'll even pay you."

"I'm not going to take your money." In truth, Alice took her money all the time. Even this bowl of semi-edible spaghetti and meatballs, this tannic table wine, it wasn't like Alice chipped in for them. "Why now? Why are you suddenly open to love?"

"For so long I wasn't ready. Lately, though… I still feel your father with me all the time. He makes me strong. I'm emboldened by his memory. Maybe it's getting older—"

"You aren't old," Alice said with familiar panic. She couldn't bear the idea of her mother gone too. Every time the thought crept in, when Bobby took too long to return Alice's call or rescheduled plans because she was tired, that intense pain localized in her chest. She was terrified by all the ways she could lose her mother. It was as bad as when she recognized she was falling in love.

"I didn't say I was old," Bobby said with mock indignation. "I just, every time I meet someone, at some point or another, it hits me: he isn't Paul. He will never be Paul. I'm realizing that's an impossible standard. At my age, I'm tired of impossibility. I want to believe in the possible. Your father taught me how to love. It would be a shame to squander that."

This was not how love worked. You couldn't compensate for one love with another. You couldn't honor a soul mate by loving someone new. What did Alice know? She ran the moment a relationship crossed into territory that was remotely intense or even possible.

"I'm sorry." Alice focused her attention on twisting and untwisting her pasta. "I don't know how to write something for you."

Bobby was not like the others, not simply because she was Alice's mother. Alice's stories weren't magic, but they did help people change. Bobby didn't need to change. She simply had already experienced her great love. Alice couldn't write her mother a story because she was truly convinced that Bobby was complete as she was.

Bobby did not get through the dismissiveness of her peers and instructors in medical school without building a strong resistance to pushback. If she didn't bow in the face of that rejection, she wasn't about to take no from her daughter.

"Look," she said. "If you write something and decide you don't want me to see it, we'll never talk about it again."

"You really want this? It isn't just your way of being supportive or whatever?"

"I really want this."

"Okay," Alice said, wanting to be done with the conversation. "On two conditions. First, if I decide I can't go through with it, we never discuss it again."

"I already agreed to that. What's the second?"

"You promise never to make this spaghetti and meatballs again." Alice dropped her loaded fork into her bowl.

Bobby laughed. "It's terrible, isn't it?"

"It really is," Alice agreed.

Bobby held out her hand. "So, we have a deal?"

"We have a deal." Alice shook on it, knowing full well that there would be no story, that like her previous pursuits endorsed by her mother, this too would quietly fade.

4

Worth the Wait

Alice proceeded with her week, having no intention of sitting down to draft her mother a story. Sure, this deception brought about a reciprocal guilt, but ultimately no good could come of writing something she did not believe would aid her mother. With the others, she really wanted to help them become better versions of themselves. This certainty of purpose was what prompted an image for the story that poured onto the screen as though she had no control over the words she committed to the page, not even as she was composing them. Even if she'd wanted to appease her mother, she had no idea where to start.

That Saturday, Alice had a wedding at the courthouse, her favorite venue in Santa Barbara. Whenever she had an event in the gardens, she made a point of arriving early to spend some time at the top of El Mirador, the clock tower. On afternoons when Bobby had needed a quiet house, Alice and her father often climbed the tower, joining hordes of tourists scaling the steep steps to the open air above. The winding staircase was narrow and musty, like a portal to the past, like they were ascending an ancient tower in Bruges or Palermo. When they arrived at the top, Santa Barbara became somewhere just as far away. Paul would look out over the vista and ask his daughter if she could see the dragons flying above the tiled roofs, the mermaids diving in the waves, the golden chariots carrying soldiers made of chocolate. Paul had a sweet tooth, even in his imaginings. "They're princesses not soldiers," Alice would tell him. "Mermen, not mermaids." They would make up stories for the princesses, their one great weakness a tendency to melt, and for the mermen, who wished they could come to land.

As Alice scaled El Mirador alone, it was as clogged with tourists as ever. Eighty-five feet below, couples milled about the lush grounds. Paul and Bobby had planned to renew their vows in that very garden on their fortieth wedding anniversary. The first time around, they'd eloped. Millie, Bobby's mother, hadn't approved of their union, and Paul's parents hadn't approved of Millie's disapproval. The whole thing had drama and unpleasantness written all over it, so Alice's parents decided to dispense with the wedding part of marriage. They went to a courthouse—not this one—got a license, and that was that. When Alice had asked why they planned to wait until their fortieth anniversary, her father said that they would be sixty-five—the age Bobby was now—older but not so old that life could not begin again. They'd still have the time and energy to do all the things they'd never gotten around to earlier in life.

Alice's vision blurred as she felt the physical impact of an image consuming her mind. In fact, it was not one image but two: a very long aisle and a butterfly. She leaned against the wall of the tower and breathed to steady herself. The dizziness and the brilliance of the colors along the butterfly's wings intensified. Her epidermis electrified, calling her to sit down and write even as she tried to fight the impulse. Alice did not want to draft the story for her mother. Glorious as it was, she did not want to see the intricate pattern of the butterfly's wings that had invaded her mind. But the only way to clear it was to write.

"Are you okay?" she heard someone ask her.

"I'm fine," she asserted as she breathed deeply. Her vision was narrowing, and she feared she might faint. The story needed to come out of her. There was no fighting its force.

Alice raced down the winding stairwell, bumping into several tourists huffing and puffing their way up. When she reached the ground floor, she sprinted outside and plopped down on an empty step leading to the sunken garden. At the bottom of her bag, she found a crumpled menu for an event the previous week. She smoothed it out and started writing.

The story began with a detailed description of her mother in a white dress she'd never worn, walking down a very long aisle. Bobby might fall in love, but she would never marry again. That part of her life, a vow, betrothal, was over. This was not the wedding Alice was giving her.

This was a wedding for one. No relatives, no rabbi, no friend ordained by an internet church, not even Alice. Her mother needed to be alone. Bobby couldn't feel like she was being unfaithful to Paul if the only person she was promised to was herself.

At the end of the very long aisle, a butterfly landed on Bobby's right ring finger. It was the largest, most resplendent butterfly she'd ever seen, with gold-tinged wings. Bobby watched as it tiptoed from her ring finger up her arm, across her shoulders and down her left arm to her other ring finger where it reached the tip and flew away.

This was Alice's shortest story yet, fitting on the back of one piece of paper. Like the others before it, Bobby's story came to her in a mad rush. The moment Alice placed the last period on the page, she knew she had reached the end. Once it was done, it was done. No editing. No amending. It simply was what it was.

Misspellings, homonyms, and all. The butterfly might be too prosaic or too much like Gabby's hummingbird. She was going to have to start coming up with imagery that did not involve flying animals. For now this simple and perhaps hackneyed story was just what her mother needed. Alice had told Bobby what she already knew. It was time to let go. Time to vow to herself that she would tend to her own needs. Time to let someone else care for her if not take care of her. As soon as Alice folded the menu and returned it to her bag, she understood that she'd been wanting to tell her mother this for a long time. In the end, Bobby was just like the others. Someone Alice could help.

During the wedding reception she worked, Alice continued to feel that buzzing through her body, even though she'd finished writing her mother's story. When she returned home, unusually high on the adrenaline of rushing around on her feet for the last five hours, the tingling sensation persisted. It would not go away until she unleashed the story. She settled before her computer and typed it. Revisiting it, she found the symbolism less trite, more true. When she was finished transcribing the page, she printed it, sealed it in an envelope, and drove down the coast to her childhood home. It was late enough that her mother had turned off the porch light. Alice looked up at the dark window of her mother's bedroom.

"I hope this is really what you want," she said before tiptoeing up to the door and slipping the envelope through the mail slot. When the slot clanged closed, Alice began to panic. It was too late to reverse whatever she'd just set in motion.

By the time Alice returned to her apartment, her limbs were so tired she could barely move to unlock her door. Inside, a few glasses and empty plates decorated her desk and living room, but they would have to wait until morning. She flopped face-first onto the couch, her cat, Agatha, gently nudging her, concerned.

"I'm okay, Aggie," she managed to mutter before falling into a deep sleep that lasted fourteen hours.

When she woke up the following afternoon, she expected to find a message from her mother. Certainly by dinnertime there would be a text indicating that she'd received the story. When one day became two, Alice started to worry that something had happened to Bobby. She left voicemails and text messages, getting no response. Quickly, the panic shifted to anger, for surely after forty-eight hours, if something had happened to her mother, someone would have alerted her. Had Bobby read Alice's story and hated it? Or been confused by it? Maybe it really was trite. Maybe Bobby had simply felt nothing, which seemed the worst possibility of all.

All week, Alice was distracted by the suspicion that her mother had hated her story and was too afraid to tell her the truth. At a fortieth birthday party hosted by the birthday boy's older wife, she dropped not one but two trays of mini crab cakes. At a launch party for a lipstick brand, she spilled a glass of wine down the front of the CEO's dress. Fortunately, it was white wine, not red. That did little to quell the anger of the sticky, sodden woman, even though her cherry red lips looked perfect.

"What's with you this week?" Alice's boss, Caroline, asked. "You better get your head on straight before you drop scalding soup into someone's lap and we end up embroiled in a lawsuit."

Alice was mindful to take trays of salad rather than soup for the first course, careful to place the plates of oil-dredged lettuce evenly on the table. Caroline was right; Alice's head was askew, twisted and contorted with worry that her mother was avoiding her. Of all the reasons Bobby had not contacted her, the possibility that her story had worked did not occur to her.

She was biking home when at last she received a call from her mother.

"You're alive," Alice said as she picked up.

"Sorry, dear. I didn't mean to worry you. I've just been…well,

I've been wanting to tell you… I wanted to know what it was first and I guess I've always known but I've been scared. Now I'm finally starting to realize—" As Bobby continued to ramble, hedging her words, Alice realized her mother was in love. "Your story was beautiful. Even if you weren't my daughter I would have loved it."

"Really?" Alice said.

"Of course. The way you described the lace on the dress, the way you evoked the motion of walking down the aisle, its uncanny quality—it was all very effective. I read it the morning after you dropped it off, while I was eating a croissant. I'd bought one at the bakery the day before when I picked up bread for the week. I don't know why I even got a croissant. I never eat croissants. All that saturated fat." Bobby had become obsessed with fat content since Paul's heart attack. "So I'm eating this croissant and reading your story and a memory hits me of this time I was eating a croissant and a butterfly landed on it. I hadn't thought about that moment in so long. Or the person who shared it with me."

As Bobby read Alice's story, her chest seized and her heart began to beat too fast. Although she worked with children, she was still a doctor and knew what was happening to her body was not a heart attack. When she managed to slow her heart rate enough that she could think again, her mind drifted to the memory of that croissant and the butterfly, and the man who had sat across from her witnessing that simple but beautiful moment.

"Your story," Bobby continued, "it made me realize how much I miss Mark." Since they broke up fifteen years ago, Bobby had never mentioned Mark to Alice again. Alice assumed that her mother had tried to forget about her one attempt at romance after Paul.

"Really?" Alice intended to write her mother a story to let go of the past, and instead had unlocked a repressed memory that might live again.

This wasn't a case of the unconscious shaping the work of the conscious mind. Alice had never heard her mother's story about a butterfly landing on a croissant. The coincidence was nothing short of magic.

"I didn't overthink it. I just picked up my phone and called him. I hadn't spoken to him in fifteen years, but I remembered his telephone number. Oh, Alice—"

Oh, Alice. It was what they all said when they told her what had happened to them after reading her story. *Oh, Alice.* So much emotion in those simple words.

"He could have remarried. He could have been in a relationship. He just plain could have not wanted to talk to me. I wouldn't have blamed him."

Of course Mark would talk to Bobby. When Alice moved back to Santa Barbara after dropping out of med school, she'd run into Mark at the farmers market on State. He was the kind of man who gave his ex-girlfriend's daughter a hug. The kind of man who could ask Alice what she was up to and make her comfortable telling him the truth about being adrift. The kind of man who offered to set her up with a job at his niece's catering company to tide her over until she figured out what she wanted to do. The kind of man who followed through and actually called the niece, the kind of man who would not judge Alice, eight years later, for still working that temporary job. If he was the kind of man who would do all this for his ex-girlfriend's daughter, he was certainly the kind of man who would give his ex a second chance.

He'd answered after the first ring.

"Bobby," he'd said as though he'd been waiting for her call.

"Mark," she'd said as though she'd been planning to call him all along. "I'm eating a croissant. I don't think I've eaten a croissant in the last fifteen years, not since that time with the butterfly."

"How is it?"

"It was worth the wait."

She could sense him smiling through the phone.

They met that afternoon at the beach in downtown Carp, where they took off their shoes and walked along the water's edge. When they dusted off their feet and scrubbed the tar from their heels to put their sandals back on, Mark held out his hand to stabilize Bobby. The contact was warm and familiar. It reminded her of the feeling of returning home.

"Oh, Alice," her mother said again. "I don't deserve Mark's time. I've already wasted so much of it."

"You deserve everything," Alice said, meaning it.

"You do too, my love. You have a gift. Share it. Share it with everyone, everywhere you can. Be a beacon of love."

A beacon: a warning, a signal, a guide. Alice could do that.

"But, honey?" her mother added. "Just remember to keep some love for yourself. It can take its toll, giving yourself away like that. Don't forget to hold on to love for yourself."

After they hung up, Alice continued her bike ride home, mulling over what her mother had said. Maybe she was able to give people the love they wanted because she didn't want to hold on to any of it herself. Whatever the reason, Alice knew she was gifted. She shut her eyes as the wind brushed her face. She had the power to help people in a way no one else could, a way, unlike medicine, that she didn't have to fear could incidentally harm them too. She was special. She was magic for sure. This feeling was better than love.

5

Love Scholarship

Now that Alice believed in her gift, the question was what precisely to do with it. Over the past four months, she'd written seven stories for eleven people all deeply, passionately in love. Eleven devotees of the church of Alice, all of whom had friends.

Kent was the twelfth person to contact Alice, a studio musician, who had gotten her number from Jane. It took Alice a moment to remember that Jane was Rebecca's friend. Kent *needed* love. That was how he explained it. Like it was a narcotic.

Then Lily got her email address from another of Rebecca's friends and wrote to inquire whether Alice could draft her a story to help her fall back in love with her husband. *I don't want to divorce him*, she wrote, *but I can't be in a loveless marriage. I just can't.* Alice felt for her, even though she wasn't sure her powers extended to helping people fall back in love with each other. That seemed to require an alchemy of its own.

Nora texted next, then Tristan and George, followed by Jon, Stefanie, CeCe, and Raul. Some folks were deferential—Dear Ms. Meadows, I'm writing to inquire about your services. Others were embarrassed—I'm not normally the kind of person who would do this. A few were demanding, clearly used to having people work for them—I need you to take care of this immediately. They were all looking for the same thing—love. Real and lasting. Eternal. Could she find that for them?

The sheer number of requests, not to mention the stories of heartbreak and loneliness and perseverance, overwhelmed Alice. She'd never be able to get to them all. There were only so many hours in a day, so many stories she could write in a week, a month, a year, a lifetime. Meanwhile, the requests kept coming. They paralyzed her. She needed a plan. So she told everyone the same thing—she'd get back to them.

Some were indignant—What do you mean you'll get back to me? Don't you know who I am? She didn't. Others were too polite, apologetic, fearful that Alice was their last chance at love—Of course. Take your time. I understand you're busy. I'm just so, so appreciative. Did I mention how much I appreciate you considering taking me on as a client?

Was that what these people were, potential clients? Was this the start of a new profession? What would she write on her taxes, *magical love story writer*? Or was it more of a hobby? A vocation? Could she be so bold as to consider it a calling? This was definitely the start of something, but what?

Alice could certainly use the extra income. The springs on her mattress no longer sprung. Her television had a curious stripe down the screen that only went away when she watched the news. The engine to her aging Honda coughed like a lifelong smoker when she drove it above forty-five miles per hour. She had no qualms about charging the individuals who barked orders at her. What about the others, though? What about Jackie, who was nineteen and so heartbroken because her boyfriend had dumped her for her roommate that she'd started sleeping in her car, not having enough money to move into another apartment? What about Phil, who was seventy and had loved so many women but never one who loved him back? What about Tammy, a single mother who wanted someone to love her children as much as they loved her? Could she charge people who were lonely and sad and would likely pay any price she named for a chance at love? Was there something morally corrupt about charging people for the most basic human desire? Shouldn't love be free?

No, Gabby argued. It should not.

"Forty-seven," Gabby said, holding Alice's phone and scanning her emails. "Forty-seven people want you to help them."

"There are twenty more voicemails," Alice said. They were sitting by the pond in Gabby's favorite park, feeding the ducks and turtles despite the signs expressly forbidding it. It was that special, expectant time of morning when the June Gloom had almost burned off, giving everything an ethereal look, like they were sitting inside a painting. Alice tore off a piece of bread and tossed it to the ducks and turtles congregating at their feet. "I'm not sure how word spread so fast."

Gabby sipped her latte while she read the messages. "This guy's been single for a decade since his fiancée left him at the altar. This woman has a horrible scar on her face from a fire when she was a child and thinks no one will ever love her because she's deformed. This guy was an orphan, bounced from one foster house to another where no one wanted to keep him so he's spent his entire adult life convinced he doesn't deserve love."

"It's like they're writing personal essays for college admissions."

"This guy has outlined specifications for bust size and waist. Well—" she swiped "—let's just delete that one." Gabby gave Alice back her phone. "Can you believe it, all these people wanting you to help them?"

"It's overwhelming," Alice said, trying to lob a piece of bread to a turtle at the back of the huddle. It always felt like a small victory when the turtles were able to best the ducks, snagging a piece of soggy dough. A fable, like she used in her stories.

"It's empowering," Gabby corrected, kicking out her legs and leaning her face toward the sky, where the sun was becoming visible.

"I don't know what to do." Alice mimicked her friend's posture, face aimed at the sun. It offered an ambient warmth, comforting if a little thin.

"You write stories for them," Gabby said like it was obvious. "Well, not for everyone, not for Mr. Bust and Waist, but everyone you want to help. You should write for them and charge aggressively for it."

Alice nodded, not quite convinced. She glanced around the lawn. At this early hour, it was sparsely populated. Everywhere around her, she saw inspiration—the couple seated on the bench on the tiny island at the center of the pond, the tall skinny palm tree that loomed above them, a rabbit that hopped among the daffodils. Now that she'd opened her world up to the stories, symbols were everywhere. She wondered if she'd ever see life the same way again.

"First things first," Gabby said, interrupting the moment with a dose of reality. "We need to come up with a business model and get you incorporated."

"Incorporated?"

"An LLC or better yet, for your situation, an S Corp." Gabby was an accountant at the largest firm in Santa Barbara. She loved numbers the way chefs loved chanterelles.

"But it's not really a business. I mean, I've made a few months' rent, only because Rebecca and her friends insisted on paying me, which was more like a tip. I didn't charge them. What do you charge for love?"

"A lot," Gabby said.

"What if people can't afford to pay? Is love just for those with big wallets?"

"Certain kinds of love," Gabby said seriously. "You mentioned college, right? Think of it that way. Some people pay full price. Others get scholarships or loans. Maybe we should set you up as a nonprofit."

"A love scholarship," Alice said, pleased by her cleverness.

Gabby smirked and reached into her attaché for her tablet. She typed, clicked, and scrolled, then tilted the screen toward Alice. It showed a picture of a bride and groom kissing in front of a wall of bougainvillea. *Elite Matchmakers* was scrawled over the background of pink flowers in bold sans serif. Beneath the picture were several photographs of buxom women in red tank tops looking longingly at men in wire rim glasses. Beside the photos were testimonials about money well spent and lines like *Your time is too valuable to waste on bad dates. Let us take care of the lemons so you meet the gems.*

"Do people actually pay for this BS?"

Gabby clicked on a button that said *Packages*, which led them to a pricing list for consultations, image construction, and mixers. One thousand dollars for every face-to-face date. Five hundred for a pre-date makeover.

"That's highway robbery," Alice said. "It's predatory."

"It's smart business. It says, 'We know our services work.' It says, 'You won't regret spending money on us. In fact, you'll feel better about it because we're so expensive.' It's like a luxury car or luxury designers. Luxury dating."

Alice bought her clothes from the clearance racks at department stores. Her car was thirty years old and not a classic. The only jewelry she wore was a thin gold chain with a small swallow charm her father had given her. Nothing about her was *luxury*.

"This all feels dirty. It's so not me."

"Alice, it's beautiful what you can do. I'd drain my bank account for it. In fact, for the rest of our lives, I'm never letting you pay for another drink again. Seriously, you've given me something priceless."

It was true, something intangible yet obvious had changed in Gabby in the three months since she'd met Oliver. With the others before him, she would veer the conversation toward them whenever she got together with Alice, as if trying to convince herself the relationship was real, incessantly checking her phone in case they called, too jittery to do anything other than pick at her food. Now she ate greedily and left her phone in her bag because she trusted that Oliver would still be there after she and Alice were finished hanging out. In the past, she'd pursued kayaking, swing dancing, poetry, even fishing, abandoning her own interests. With Oliver, she had gone to one stand-up show and declared it not for her, letting him have that part of his life for himself. In fact, she'd never even seen him perform. It wasn't like she expected him to be into taxes or *The Bachelor*. Yes, Alice had given Gabby something priceless, a love that allowed her to be herself.

In addition to how he treated Gabby, Alice liked Oliver. They'd met for dinner at a Mediterranean restaurant with little fires at the center of every table. When Oliver sat down, he remarked, so quietly that Alice almost didn't hear him, that he was relieved he'd decided against his polyester suit. Alice laughed reflexively before she decided whether she found the joke funny. In fact, she wasn't sure it was funny, but his deadpan delivery made it so. For his part, he looked relieved that Alice had laughed, as though he was as surprised that he'd made a joke as she was. Through her stories, Alice was finding herself to be a good judge of character. Oliver was reserved, bordering on shy, something she would not have expected from a performer. While he didn't speak a lot, what he did say was thoughtful and curious. He asked Alice questions. He rubbed Gabby's back as she spoke, making sure she was warm enough. He was polite to the people who served them. It all added up to someone who was interested in those around him. If anything, Alice wished he'd talk more. She found herself curious what he thought, when in the past she'd wished she'd known less about Gabby's boyfriends' opinions.

"Everyone will feel the way I do when they meet their person," Gabby continued. "Don't feel bad for asking people to compensate you in return. You don't have to be selfless to help people, not with something as important as love."

The conversation was starting to give Alice that itching sensation on the inside of her elbows.

"As long as I don't have to create a website or a social media presence." Alice had tried to be on Instagram. She liked taking videos of the waves crashing onto the beach, photographs of cacti in bloom, but everything about comments and likes made her uneasy. What did it mean when college friends whom she hadn't spoken to in ten years tapped the heart icon on her photograph of the Pacific lapping at her toes? What did it mean when an old flame wrote, *Wish I was there!* on a photograph of Alice eating tacos on the train tracks in the Funk Zone? It was too intimate and too insincere at once, exposing these fragments of herself. It required its own set of social mores that made her overanalyze everything in an unpleasant way.

Gabby tapped a manicured finger against her pink lips. "Actually, it's better if you don't. Creates that air of exclusivity, of having to be in the know. Plus, you've already got forty-seven people who emailed you—"

"Plus twenty voicemails," Alice added.

"Right, and that's just from eleven clients. That's—" Gabby's eyes drifted toward the sky as she calculated "—that's a six-hundred-percent increase. At that rate, these sixty-seven people will produce four hundred more clients, which will produce twenty-four hundred clients—how long will it take you to write a story?"

"I think we're getting ahead of ourselves."

"We should get ahead of ourselves. Alice, my love, you're sitting on a gold mine."

An image came to Alice of her face transposed onto a goose's body, a giant golden egg beneath her. It wasn't one she enjoyed.

Gabby could sense Alice's distress. "Okay, let's step back. You've been charging what, a thousand dollars for a story?"

Alice nodded, embarrassed to admit that she had simply been accepting whatever people wanted to give her. Sometimes it was much more than a thousand dollars. More often it was less. From a monetary standpoint, it was never enough. At the rate it took her to write a story, she was making about five dollars an hour. She was going to have to learn to write faster. At least she still had catering, which offered her a steady if paltry income to fall back on.

"Make a list, first come, first served. If you try to determine who's more deserving or more urgent, you're going to have a serious headache on your hands. I mean, you should reject anyone who gives you an icky feeling or reeks of difficulty. Otherwise be egalitarian about it. It's the only way." Gabby found a legal pad in her bag and started outlining a plan. "I want you to keep a log of everything, the hours you spend with clients—including biking to meet them, gas if you drive—the hours of writing and editing. Any fifteen minutes you devote to a client, write it down. That will give us a sense of how long it takes you to complete a story, and we'll adjust the waitlist time and price from there."

"Will people really sign up for a waitlist?"

"If they'll wait for brunch, they'll definitely wait for love."

"I'm not quitting catering," Alice said.

Gabby mulled this over for a moment. "That's smart. Until we figure out exactly how to monetize this into a viable and steady income stream, you shouldn't quit your day job. It would be too stressful." She knew how Alice responded to stress, the physical shutdown of her body, the hibernation when life overwhelmed her.

"I don't like this," Alice said.

"Of course you don't. That's why you have me." Gabby sat up, a smug look on her face. "No more stapled stories though, okay? And I love Agatha, but no one wants to read a story with cat hair on it. You need to put them in a folder or something. On sturdy paper. Make them look professional and expensive." She sucked in her lips and made a popping sound. "And you need a name."

"What's wrong with Alice Meadows? You mean like a nom de plume?" Alice imagined herself in a trench coat and fedora, smoking a pipe that emitted heart-shaped puffs of smoke.

"A business name. Any ideas?"

Alice had one.

And so Oh, Alice Productions was born. Gabby wasn't sure about the name. It sounded a tad orgasmic, pornographic even, but Alice was insistent. She wouldn't budge on the comma either. Oh-comma-Alice. That pause was integral. It was deep enough to contain every manifestation, every type of love.

In a small spiral notebook that she now carried with her everywhere, Alice kept meticulous records, noting every fifteen-minute writing interval, every prewriting conversation with clients, in person or on the phone. The list of requests continued to grow. She did her best to be precise about when calls or emails came as well as when she responded. Love was inherently unfair, the way it showered some and starved others. The least she could do was make people's access to it as equitable as possible.

Still, inspiration was its own life source. It had its own timeframe, its own predilections, its own will, which was more obstinate than Alice's. The images did not always come to her in the order the requests were received. They simply bulldozed her when they wanted her to listen, abducting her body until she committed them to the page. Any effort to control her calling resulted in its revolt until Alice acquiesced. Despite her best efforts to be fair, she had to follow inspiration where it led, letting the stories unfold in the order they desired. Like love, her gift beckoned her to some over others. It wasn't rational. It certainly wasn't fair. Like love, its intoxication was impossible not to pursue.

6

In Which a Mysterious Envelope Arrives

On a crisp night amidst a fog thicker than smoke, an envelope arrived on Alice's doorstep, the first of its kind. All other requests had arrived via modern technology, emails and voicemails, the occasional text. Alice had not given her address to anyone. She was just returning from work, wanting nothing more than to sleep. Catering was hard on her body. Her lower back ached. Her temples pounded. She fantasized about collapsing onto her bed, but she had several stories that needed endings. Alice produced her best work in these nighttime hours when she was too drained to interfere with the muse as it poured through her. Outside her front door, she took a deep breath to collect herself and went inside to write.

Alice might have missed the envelope entirely if not for her shorthair cat, Agatha, who swatted it free of the doormat. It was thick stock, unblemished, not so much as a smudge of dirt from the mat, perpetually sandy from the wind off the beach no matter how often she swept it clean.

The back was sealed with a wax emblem, *MA* monogrammed in scarlet. Alice picked at the wax, careful not to break the seal, and slipped the cream card from the envelope. A five-hundred-dollar bill floated to the ground. Alice snapped it up before Agatha got her claws in it and ravaged it like one of her toys.

She held the card and the bill as she read the note, penned in practiced cursive.

Dear Ms. Meadows,
Word has reached me of your gift. I find myself in dire need of your assistance. It's best if I explain my circumstances to you in person. Join me tomorrow for high tea. My home is located on Stagecoach Road past the tavern. You can't miss it.
Please don't be late. I despise tardiness.
Regards,
Madeline Alger

As a dedicated mystery reader, Alice knew this seemingly simple letter was anything but. She'd practically memorized all of Sir Arthur Conan Doyle's Sherlock Holmes stories, devoured every Agatha Christie novel. She loved Daphne du Maurier, Patricia Highsmith, modern-day masters like Tana French and Ruth Ware. She'd read Stieg Larsson's Millennium series at least four times, never able to guess the ending or the twist, even upon rereading. That was a lie, actually. Alice never tried to guess the twist. Some readers might take satisfaction in uncovering the murderer before Hercule Poirot. Alice preferred to let the mystery unfold as the writer intended.

Right away, this letter intrigued her, the trail of clues it left for Alice to solve: exactly where they should meet and when; the formal high tea; the dire need; William McKinley staring up at her from the face of the five-hundred-dollar bill. Until now, Alice had never seen a bill larger than a hundred, which she was sometimes awarded as a tip at the end of a party. From bar trivia, she knew that this particular currency had been discontinued in 1969, which meant that it was in fact worth a lot more than its value as legal tender. Who was this woman who dealt in rare currency and lived in an isolated part of the Los Padres National Forest where red oaks and sycamores would be her only neighbors?

Stagecoach Road was forty miles of windy two-lane highway carved into the mountains between Santa Barbara and Los Olivos. The road was all edge on one side, all steep bluffs on the other. It had become obsolete more than a century ago when stagecoaches were replaced by the railroad and was now good for a scenic drive, a secluded hike, or access to Cold Spring Tavern. The tavern, once a coach stop, had been operating as restaurant and saloon since the forties and was a popular spot for bikers and tourists alike. Part of what made it so popular was its seclusion, the way it felt detached from the outside world, harbored by forests that stood in contrast to the ocean and beachside city below. There were no houses along the hairpin turns that led up to the tavern, no roads or driveways connecting to houses deeper in the national forest. Yet Madeline insisted both that she resided there and that her house was obvious from the road. Alice was certain if there was a house up there, she would have noticed it before, not that she'd been to the tavern in years. There was one way to know for sure—take her old beast of a car up the steep, looping CA-154 toward Stagecoach Road.

The other detail she needed to decipher from Madeline's letter was when precisely she was expected. A quick internet search revealed that high tea, unlike afternoon tea, did not involve cucumber sandwiches or scones. High tea was in fact a larger meal, consumed after the workday was over. While various etiquette websites said it started anywhere from five to seven, Madeline's letter had condemned tardiness. This was another clue, meant to indicate that Alice was expected promptly at five.

Alice had a time. She had a vague location. That left one mystery Alice could not solve from the comfort of her studio apartment. *I find myself in dire need of your assistance.* The line would have sounded melodramatic if the rest of the letter had not been so spare. *Dire* was the only adjective in the entire note. If someone who wrote in directives, in plain, unadorned language, chose to indulge in an adjective, it was important. It meant that Madeline truly regarded her need as urgent.

Need was a common emotion in Alice's line of work. All her potential clients declared a need for love, as though it was as essential as food or water, something they could not subsist without. Everyone deserved love if they wanted it. Alice wasn't quite sure that was the same thing as needing it, though.

Only Madeline hadn't said she was in *dire need* of love but of assistance. That meant she did not think she could find love on her own, that she believed Alice could help her access whatever she lacked. It meant that Madeline possessed an essential weakness, and essential weaknesses were quickly becoming Alice's specialty. She could sniff them out the way her cat, Agatha, could track a dog a block away. And once Alice located the blockage that stood in the way of her clients finding love, she could write them a story that would clear their arteries to let the love course through them. All she had to do was meet Madeline and she would know what ailed her—assuming she could locate her home somewhere along Stagecoach Road.

7

High Tea

The sky glowed as Alice's car lurched up the steep incline to Stagecoach Road. By a little after four, the sun had already fallen behind the mountains, its rays fractured by the lush green hills. She had forgotten the rise of that first turn into the forest, the way the brush obscured the road and everything that lay beyond it. While she was nervous about finding Madeline Alger's house, the real feat for her was facing the road itself, each curve tightening with the memory of her father.

When Alice's mother, Bobby, started medical school, her father, Paul, had decided to embark on a lifelong dream of his own to ride a Harley. "You're really going to pursue something life threatening when I'm off at school, learning to save lives?" Bobby protested. Paul reasoned that it was only dangerous if you weren't careful. Although Bobby disagreed, she could hardly refuse him, not after he had all but filled out the paperwork for her to follow her passion. They were not equivalent desires, being a doctor and riding a motorcycle, yet they stemmed from the same need not to let life pass by.

At first Bobby forbade Alice from riding on that death trap. Once Alice's legs were long enough to reach the footrests, the legal requirement for riding passenger on a motorcycle, her mother could not stop her. Every Sunday while Bobby was studying, Alice donned the brown leather jacket and glittery helmet her father had bought her, clutched his thick, warm body as he took the curves on 154 toward Cold Spring Tavern. The wind assaulted her knuckles and knees as she hid the rest of her body behind her father's. Each Sunday, when they returned home bloated on barbecue, ears ringing from bluegrass, but otherwise unharmed, Bobby grew a little less anxious, until the motorcycle trips to the mountains became as routine as Alice and Paul's beach adventures, their minigolf expeditions. Who knew the tri-tip sandwiches they'd eaten at the tavern would be more dangerous for Paul than the bike on the windy road?

Alice pulled her beastly car around another hairpin turn, her chest spasming as the tavern came into sight. Several bikes were parked out front. Men in leather pants leaned against a wooden fence as they blew cigarette smoke into the otherwise pristine mountain air. Light spilled from the tavern's open door where a couple was standing in the alcove waiting to be shown to their table. Alice pulled to the side of the bend and watched the happy hour crowd that spilled to the tables outside the bar, a wooden structure a short walk from the tavern. Her eyes stung. It was all exactly as she remembered. It hadn't grown grander or shabbier in her mind than it was in life.

Alice had been back to Stagecoach Road once since her father died, when Skylar, a musician with a lisp that came out when he sang, had wanted to impress her with an unsung piece of California history. When they began the drive toward the mountains, Alice assumed he was taking her to wine country until he hit his left blinker and his car took the sharp incline onto Stagecoach Road. At first her heart was beating too fast for her to tell him to pull over. When the car finally careened to a stop, they were parked across the road from the tavern. He smiled eagerly at Alice until he noticed the stricken look on her face. “What’s wrong?” he asked. It was their third date. He didn’t even know that she’d grown up in Carpinteria, let alone that her father had died unexpectedly when she was fourteen. As she looked at his imploring face, she had no interest in explaining it to him. Instead she said, “Please take me home.” They drove back to Santa Barbara in silence, and once he was stopped outside her apartment, she whispered, “I’m sorry,” before sprinting out of the car. After that, they never spoke or saw each other again. In Santa Barbara you always ran into people sooner or later, but miraculously she’d successfully avoided bumping into him.

A car door slammed, jolting Alice out of her memories. She watched as two women walked arm in arm toward the restaurant. One of them laughed as the other held the door open for her. They disappeared inside, and Alice wondered what would have happened if she’d followed Skylar into the tavern, if she’d allowed this place to have new memories, ones that could never replace those afternoons with her father but might make their legacy a little less painful.

She put her car into Drive and watched the tavern retreat in the rearview mirror as she continued on Stagecoach Road toward the stretch where Madeline’s house was supposedly located. Sometimes, when Alice and her father left the tavern, they would take the long way home, not wanting the afternoon to end. Paul would follow the windy road north, as Alice did now, under the highway bridge, until it eventually met up with the 154 again, farther from Santa Barbara. Like the rest of Stagecoach Road, the miles beyond the tavern abutted sandy bluffs on one side, the other a sheer drop to the forest below. There were no houses, no streets, no driveways carved into that part of the national forest, nothing except trees and rock.

Alice followed one curve and the next until she reached the highway bridge. Its arches cut diagonal lines across the darkening sky. She'd forgotten to look for a perpendicular road on the stretch between the tavern and the bridge, but she was certain she hadn't passed any turnoffs. The cliffs were too steep. As she wound deeper into the woods, the panic of her father's memory was replaced with a more visceral, immediate concern: What if she couldn't find Madeline's home? Her phone battery was dangerously low, not that she had a number for Madeline.

She kept her eyes peeled for a place to make a U-turn so she could revisit the stretch of road where the house must have been. This felt like a test, one Alice was already failing.

To her left, a flash of muted red appeared amidst the green foliage. Was that a chimney? A mirage? Alice craned her neck to see what it was, only to drive past an unmarked dirt road that might be a driveway. A mile later, she finally found a turnoff and swung her car around to inch toward the unmarked road, careful not to drive past it again.

The sky continued to darken as Alice followed the bumpy dirt road through the red oak and sycamore trees, only her dim headlights to guide the way. Her old sedan was not made for off-roading. It thudded in protest over every divot and root. The road seemed to go on forever with no sign of the brick chimney or the house Alice now despaired of finding. The farther she drove, the more the road narrowed, so much so that Alice would not be able to turn her car around if she decided to abandon this fruitless endeavor. She kept driving, fearful that if she gave up, she'd find herself stuck in the woods. She checked her phone, dismayed to discover that the battery had died. Why hadn't she left a note for Gabby or Bobby, alerting them to where she was going?

Moisture stung her eyes as it became clear how reckless this journey was. Alice wasn't scheduled to work again until a wedding that weekend. Although she'd never missed an event before, no-shows were common in the catering business. The manager would make note of it in her file and would not schedule her for another event until he got the go-ahead from Caroline, Alice's boss. While Alice and her mother often met for dinner, it wasn't regularly scheduled. And Bobby was back with Mark. A week might pass without her even realizing. These days it took several texts back and forth to nail down any engagement with Gabby. Alice's clients would assume she'd run away with their deposits, that she was a swindler when really she was a corpse behind the wheel of a beat-up car stuck along a forgotten strip of dirt road in the woods. Alice kept driving, tears welling, threatening to spill over. She was completely alone. Not just in this moment but in life. She had no one who would notice that she was missing, no one who prioritized her above anyone else in their life.

After a large divot sent her car thudding, Alice slammed on the brakes, causing the poor old car to screech in protest. If she made it out of these woods, she was going to have to give it a good wash or tune-up, something to show it the love it deserved. The tears began to fall. It was ridiculous, crying over her car and her own foolishness. Eventually, the absurdity of her situation caused her to laugh. It was not funny, but laughing comforted her more than crying. She concentrated on her breath, trying to decide what to do. In her rearview mirror, the road behind her car disappeared into blackness. There was no light pollution up in the woods, nothing other than the bright stars to punctuate the night.

She looked into the darkness ahead, and that was when she saw it, a light bleeding through the trees. It wasn't natural light but an honest-to-God manmade glow emanating from something in the distance. That must be the house. It must be the house!

It took Alice another ten minutes before the road ended at a clearing where an A-frame house sat perched between the trees, a single light illuminating the porch.

The mountain air pricked like needles against her cheeks and smelled sharply of soil. She breathed in deeply, the sting of the evening burning in her lungs. It was fully nighttime. She was late.

Alice clutched Madeline's letter and followed the stone walkway to the front door. The porch light offered hope that someone might be inside, even though the house behind it was dark. There was no bell, just a brass knocker shaped like a lion. The woods swallowed the dull sound of the knocker as Alice banged it against the door. She hadn't realized just how silent the forest was, how rarely she was engulfed in absolute quiet. She shut her eyes to absorb it, trying to hear noise in the void.

The only sound she heard was that of the door creaking open.

Alice met Madeline's voice first.

"You're late," she said as a rush of warm air from the house kissed Alice's face. Madeline's voice was deep and gravelly. When Alice opened her eyes, the house behind Madeline was so dark she could only discern the outline of the woman's small frame and mass of short white around her head.

Before Alice could protest that she'd gotten lost, Madeline added, "Come. Tea's ready." She started down the hall.

As Alice stepped into the foyer, the lights came on and she found herself standing in a cavernous hallway paneled in redwood, an antler chandelier dangling twelve feet above her. The floor was fashioned from the same redwood as the walls, making the hall appear boundless, except for Madeline's childlike figure disrupting the space. The halo of corkscrew curls around her head was starkly white as though it had never had any pigmentation to it. She was dressed in tapered black tuxedo pants, a silk blouse tucked in at the waist. Her feet were bare and alabaster, her exposed ankles covered in varicose veins.

"Are you Madeline, Madeline Alger?" Alice asked just to be sure.

She turned to face her guest, and Alice was struck by how beautiful the woman was. Alice had never before seen someone so old who was so beautiful. She scolded herself for this ageist thought. Society had preconditioned her to treat youth as beauty. Madeline did not try to look younger than she was.

Her skin was creased along her forehead and cheeks, so much so that Alice didn't immediately spot the scar carved into her right cheek, echoing the curve of her oval face. It was as deep as the smile lines on both sides of her mouth, its plump lips lavished in crimson. The lipstick was the only makeup she wore, other than equally bright red nail polish. Her cheeks were bare, with sunspots and hints of rosacea. Chunky gold and turquoise rings adorned every finger, even her thumbs, her knuckles so swollen that Alice doubted Madeline could remove the rings if she'd tried.

"Were you expecting someone else?" Madeline asked. Her eyes read Alice, and Alice tried to surmise what the woman saw in her own presentation, her ill-fitting jeans and loose T-shirt, her wild shoulder-length brown hair that she left unbrushed in hopes that people might mistake her for an artist. She wore no makeup, not even lipstick or nail polish. Looking at the cherry red on Madeline's nails, she reconsidered her stance on painting her nails. The charm of Madeline's Cupid's bow made Alice want to sketch two perfect peaks onto her own lips. The cut of Madeline's clothes made Alice want to invest in a wardrobe, to see her clothes not as something to hide behind but as an expression of how she wanted the world to see her, how in turn she might be able to see herself.

Madeline motioned for Alice to remove her muddied hiking boots. Obediently Alice bent down to take them off, aware the old woman was watching her. Madeline's eyebrow inched upward at the sight of Alice's big toes poking through her socks, so she took those off as well. She looked down at her own feet, bunioned from working so many hours on them, toenails ravaged, veins bulging from the tightness of her boots. People say our hands reveal the stories of our lives, but it's our feet that expose how we treat our bodies. Alice needed to take better care of herself.

The two women headed down a long narrow hall beside a staircase. From above, a clock ticked loudly. On the right side of the hall, an open door revealed a billiards room the length of the house. On the other side were three closed doors with dim outlines and fluted glass doorknobs to distinguish them from the surrounding redwood. Madeline stopped at the middle door and twisted it open.

The dining room was larger than Alice would have imagined from the hall, with a farmhouse table long enough to seat a dozen people, spread with enough platters to feed at least that many. A lanky Persian cat nibbled at a plate of whole small fish.

"Poirot," Madeline admonished, scooping up the cat and plopping him on the floor. "You know the humans get first pickings."

Poirot, Alice nearly exclaimed, telling Madeline that her own cat was named for Agatha Christie. She caught herself. This was not a social engagement. She had to exude an air of professionalism. There would be no bonding over felines or mystery authors. Instead, the topic of conversation would remain fixed on Madeline, how Alice could help her.

The cat trotted toward the door, nudging it open with his head and disappearing into the hall. Alice made a mental note to avoid the plate of fish, hoping that the cat hadn't also grazed the other plates on the table. She was famished, but not so hungry that she'd overlook fur in her food.

Madeline sat at the head of the table and gestured for Alice to sit beside her. Now Alice could clearly see the arced scar on the right side of Madeline's face. All scars tell a story. This one was long and deep.

High tea, it turned out, did not involve tea but wine. While Alice was wary of drinking since she had an arduous drive home, she accepted the glass Madeline poured.

Madeline raised her glass in a toast, so Alice did the same. The wine was a lush garnet that absorbed the light.

"To beginnings," Madeline said. "They're always the best part of stories. Or perhaps you prefer endings?"

"Endings are harder," Alice said, speaking from personal experience.

"Shouldn't they be? It's so much easier to know where to enter a story then where to leave it." Madeline brought the glass to her lips.

The wine coated Alice's tongue in robust cherry. It tasted expensive. She found she couldn't resist a second sip, then another.

"Slow down, my dear," Madeline said. "No one is going to take it away from you."

Embarrassed, Alice placed her wineglass behind her water so she would have to reach around to drink it.

"I got your letter," Alice said rather obviously. How else would she be here? "Can I ask how you heard about my services?" What she meant was, *How did you know where I lived?* Suddenly it occurred to her how intrusive the letter had been, how foolish it was to follow it into the desolate mountains.

Madeline laughed, seeming to read Alice's mind. "Relax, my dear. If you were in danger you would realize it already. Besides, isn't that the goal of a word of mouth business, that people hear about you?"

"Usually when new clients reach out, they mention who referred them, and they do it over email."

Madeline shrugged. "I'm not most clients. I assume you've already gathered that." She seemed in no rush to eat or to talk business. She took a full sip of wine and held it in her mouth a moment as she shut her eyes, swallowing appreciatively. "Let's just say that I was always going to hear about you. That's how fate works when it's destined to bring people together. And I'm a proud Luddite. Electricity is just about the most modern thing you'll find in this house."

Madeline watched Alice, gauging her response. While the old woman was cagey, Alice found she didn't mind. It complemented the general mystique Madeline cultivated. Alice just needed to determine what she was hiding, the fatal flaw that Alice would fix in a story. She patted her curly hair self-consciously as her host unapologetically continued to observe her.

"You shouldn't do that," Madeline said. "You're a pretty girl. You should let people stare at you without embarrassment." She angled her scar toward Alice as if daring her to ask about the story that marked Madeline's life as much as it marked her face. Madeline could have hidden the scar behind carefully positioned hair or concealed it with thick makeup. Instead, she let it define her without apology.

Even if Bobby had never taught her daughter how to cook a proper meal, Alice knew how to behave at one. She did not ask about the scar. She did not continue to press Madeline on how she'd heard about Alice's services. Still, having Madeline stare at her so baldly made her feel too large for her body, too clumsy for her chair. She reached around the water for the wine, took a sip, and placed it in front of the water glass. No use pretending she wasn't going to finish it and possibly another. She'd just have to wait a few hours before she drove home.

The discomfort Madeline aroused in her notwithstanding, Alice was intrigued. With her other clients, despite their varying reasons for wanting love, that first meeting unfolded in approximately the same way. The clients divulged too much too quickly, as if Alice was a new therapist they were seeing and they wanted to get right to the heart of what they believed their problem to be. Alice was learning to read between the details they shared, the way they tried to focus her attention on how they'd been unlucky instead of how they'd manifested that bad luck, the way past lovers hadn't understood them rather than how they misunderstood themselves. But Madeline—Madeline offered Alice nothing. She was going to make Alice work for her story.

Madeline reached for the closest bowl of food. It was filled with some sort of room temperature eggplant. Alice did not like eggplant. It was too slimy, too fleshy, but when Madeline held it out to her, she scooped some onto her plate, followed by cucumber slices in yogurt, roasted duck, beef tenderloin, smashed potatoes that were somehow piping hot, and green bean casserole. The only thing she declined was the whole fish.

Madeline ate deliberately, chewed pensively. When she finally swallowed, she shut her eyes, savoring the flavors before they disappeared from her palate.

"Did you make all this?" Alice asked. "It's delicious."

"I learned a long time ago how to be self-sufficient. Not just out of necessity, though of course living here as I do, one must be able to care for oneself. No, I choose to live this way."

"Why?" Alice tried to eat as slowly as Madeline did, but she was too hungry and the food was too good. When Madeline didn't reply right away, Alice added, "You don't have to answer that. I shouldn't pry."

"Is that what you were doing, prying?"

"Maybe?" Alice said uncertainly.

"How else are we to get to know each other if we don't ask questions?"

"Some questions are rude."

"And was it rude to ask me why I choose to live alone?" Madeline stared expectantly at Alice in anticipation of her response.

"Maybe?" Alice said again.

"My dear, for someone whose reputation as a decisive writer precedes her, I would have expected you to carry yourself with more certainty."

Again Alice was tempted to ask where she had heard about Alice's reputation. If Madeline hadn't told her the first time, she wasn't going to divulge a name now. It didn't really matter anyway. Alice was here. She wanted to be here. She wanted to know why Madeline had summoned her.

"I'm finding myself on unfamiliar ground," Alice admitted.

"By all means then, let us make ourselves more familiar." With that, Madeline wiped her mouth with a black linen napkin and pushed her chair away from the table. When she stood, her stomach was distended slightly below her waistband. "Shall we retire to the parlor?"

Alice reached to clear her plate.

"Leave it," Madeline said.

"Please, let me help you," Alice insisted, holding on to the plate.

Madeline rested her hand on Alice's wrist and gave it a gentle squeeze. Her fingers were alarmingly cold. "You will, dear, but not with the dishes. Besides, Poirot and Ripley would be furious with me if I didn't let them have last grazing privileges."

Alice followed Madeline through a hidden door beside the banquet into a parlor. There, she saw Poirot, lounging on a settee beside another Persian; she assumed this was Ripley.

"Believe It or Not?" Alice asked, pointing to the fat white cat. Madeline looked confused until Alice added, "Ripley's?"

Madeline laughed. "Tom Ripley. Quite possibly the best character in fiction."

Of course. Alice loved Patricia Highsmith's Ripley novels. How could she have made such a silly mistake?

"You're a reader?" Alice said excitedly.

Madeline sat in one of two armchairs beside a fire that was already blazing when they'd entered the room. Alice plopped into the other.

"You have to be a reader, living as I do." Madeline followed Alice's eyes around the spacious room, which was covered in oil paintings of landscapes more pastoral than the dense woods that surrounded Madeline's home. The room was sparsely furnished, just the settee and the two armchairs, a large Persian rug covering the expanse of the redwood floor. Alice saw no books other than one on the coffee table entitled *Cabin Life*, resting beside a tray holding a pot of tea and shortbread cookies with jam in the middle. Alice's favorite.

"You're wondering where my books are. Always judge a person by their books, isn't that right?" Alice shrugged. She didn't want to appear snobbish. Madeline laughed again. She had a glorious, airy laugh. Like a child's. "The library's upstairs."

Alice waited for Madeline to offer her a tour. Instead she poured Alice a cup of tea. At last, the promised tea.

"So, Alice." Madeline leaned back, nearly disappearing in the tall, voluminous chair. "Tell me a story about your childhood."

"My childhood?"

"Your clients don't ask you about yourself? How are you to get to know me if I don't get to know you? How we describe our childhood reveals more about us than our present selves."

Alice took a sip of tea, discovering it too hot to consume. It scalded her tongue. She forced herself not to flinch. She set the cup down and selected one of those jam-filled cookies, nibbling on a corner as she asked, "What does your childhood say about you?"

Madeline tsked then took a sip of tea, evidently unafflicted by its temperature. "Nice try, but we're talking about you."

Alice almost protested. This wasn't about her. It was about Madeline. Only she found herself wanting to make Madeline understand what it meant for Alice to be here, to have confronted that stretch of road.

Alice swallowed the last bite of cookie and told Madeline, "My dad used to take me to Cold Springs Tavern every Sunday as a kid. He wasn't a biker, really. A weekend rider, real bikers would call him. My mom said it was his midlife crisis. I think it was more something he'd always wanted to do and he got to a point where he couldn't remember why he hadn't done it. I don't know, maybe that's the definition of a midlife crisis. I used to love riding on the back of his bike. Anyway, this is the first time… I haven't been up here in years."

"When did he pass away?"

"How do you know he's dead?"

"The way you talk about him. That kind of loss charges language." Alice waited, but Madeline did not elaborate.

"I was fourteen. Some days it feels like it happened so long ago. Others it feels like he's still here." Alice watched her hands wring in her lap. It was not the sort of thing she admitted to anyone, even herself. Some days she would wake up and his death would hit her anew. Others it seemed like he'd always been an apparition. She wasn't sure which scared her more.

Madeline smiled in commiseration. "It's been over ten years since Gregory died, and some mornings the realization that he's gone is enough to keep me in bed all day." She didn't say who Gregory was. She didn't need to.

"What happened to him?"

"An accident." Madeline stroked the scar on her cheek.

"My dad had a heart attack. My mom was in the kitchen. I was clearing the plates, but he was at the table. He was a big eater, so even though he ate quickly, it always took him longer to finish than me or my mom. We'd start doing the dishes while he was still eating because we didn't want to wait. When I walked back in, he was slumped over his plate. I always thought, I always wondered, if I'd been in the room when it happened, if maybe I could have saved him."

"Do you know CPR?"

"Not at the time."

"Did you have a cardiac board for resuscitation?"

"Of course not."

"So what exactly would your being in the room have done?"

"I could have called 911 sooner. My mom could have helped."

"And a minute or two would have made a difference?"

"If I'd been there, he wouldn't have died alone."

And there it was. The essence of her guilt. Alice and her mother had been laughing over something that had happened to her at school that day, something she'd long ago forgotten, while death had seized her father's body, refusing to let go. Did he hear their laughter? Did it fill him with one last moment of joy before he was gone? Alice would never be able to ask him.

"Blame is its own form of grief." Madeline scratched at the scar on her cheek. "It's easier to feel guilty than to admit you're helpless. We're all helpless when it comes to love and to death."

"You blame yourself too," Alice said.

"I would have done anything for Gregory." Madeline held her frail hands out to warm them against the fire. "I mean that literally. I would have died for him. I would have had children if that's what he wanted. I would have moved anywhere to be with him, even here, to the woods. It didn't scare me to be that devoted to him. What scared me was my suspicion that he didn't love me with the same intensity that I loved him. I couldn't shake it. One day he might wake up and decide we were over. No matter how often he told me he wasn't going anywhere, words were never enough. Flowers felt like a ruse. Passion was just passion. I never doubted that he craved me physically, but desire isn't the same as love. I could feel him in my blood, pumping through my body, keeping me alive. I didn't believe it was the same for him. So I'd test him. I'd say, 'If you love me, you'll walk across the highway blindfolded.' 'If you love me, you'll jump into this freezing pond.' 'If you love me, you'll eat a pot of dirt.' Sometimes, the tests were silly. Other times, they could be dangerous. Russian Roulette, knife throwing, fire walking. Anything I asked, he would do it. While it was fun for both of us, it never seemed to be enough for me to trust that his love was absolute. I didn't want anything less." Madeline sipped her tea, savoring it as she had the food, eyes shut, mouth pursed.

"You let him eat a pot of dirt?" Alice interrupted, horrified and struggling not to show it.

"It was a very small pot," Madeline said.

"And he really crossed the highway blindfolded?"

"It was the middle of the night, and I made sure there were no cars coming, although I didn't tell him that. It wasn't actually dangerous, just held the illusion of danger."

"What about the Russian roulette?"

Madeline shot the girl an incredulous look. "The gun was empty. I would never let anything happen to him. That wasn't the point. How can love be unconditional if you don't condition it? That's why I constantly tested him. Even that day."

It was a rare clear morning in the mountains, normally cloaked in fog from the ocean. Gregory had been jumping on the bed until Madeline could not ignore him anymore. She peeked open one eye. That was enough. He grabbed her hand and dragged her outside. They ran through the woods barefoot, Gregory in his boxers, Madeline in her long white nightgown. She dared him to scale a tree in the name of love. He climbed so high she made him come down, and when he did his palms and feet were bloody. They made love against the tree, the bark tearing Madeline's skin, cuts that outlasted Gregory. When even the contact of their bodies could not warm Madeline against the icy morning, Gregory carried her into the house and drew her a bath. Madeline bet him his love wasn't limitless enough for him to hold his breath underwater for a minute, and he held it for two. When they were famished, he made them eggs, holding his palm over the open flame when Madeline lamented that his love for her didn't burn. It was a perfect, aimless morning where they had nothing to do but enjoy each other. That was always when she tested him the most. Gregory said it was because Madeline didn't believe she deserved the perfection of their love. Madeline asserted it was because she did.

Gregory felt like taking a drive. They dressed in black. Madeline always insisted they match subtly. That way everyone who saw them would realize they were a pair. After Gregory died, Madeline wished they'd picked different outfits that day, stripes or paisley, anything other than black.

They barreled down the dirt road in Gregory's old truck. Madeline played with his hair. He had thick wavy hair that he grew long because she liked to comb her fingers through it.

He turned up the music and drove faster, the truck bouncing

with every root along the road. He swayed his head, tapping the steering wheel as he shut his eyes and sang.

"Deer!" Madeline screamed. "Gregory, deer!" Even in moments of panic she called him by his full first name.

He opened his eyes and slammed on the brakes. The truck continued to lurch toward the petrified deer, staring at them from two feet, then one.

Madeline thrust both hands against the glove compartment. She screwed her eyes shut, bracing for contact. The truck thudded to a stop, sending pain through her body from the shock of motion curtailed too abruptly. When she braved a glimpse, the deer stared at them indifferently, antlers mere inches from the unbroken windshield, before huffing and sauntering away.

Gregory peered at her, exhilarated, wild-eyed, laughing. Madeline clicked off the music, before he clicked it on again, louder. This went on for a bit, Madeline switching the radio off, Gregory switching it on again.

"Gregory!" she yelled when she'd had enough of the little game. He left the radio off, but he laughed again, sliding his foot from the brake to the gas pedal as they resumed their drive toward town. As he sped up, undeterred by their near collision, she realized that he was a thrill seeker. A daredevil. Of course he would do anything she asked. Daring him was not the way to test his love for her.

The forest thinned as they approached the paved road. Its smoothness beneath the old truck did little to calm Madeline. She angled her body toward the window, and the pale bluffs beyond, refusing to look at him.

"Oh, don't be mad," Gregory said.

"You could have killed us," she said.

"But I didn't. Let's not start worrying about things that didn't happen." He brushed his finger across her smooth cheek, an affection she found hard to resist.

In town they feasted on crab and sea urchin and local wine.

Satiated, they walked along the ocean, naming the waves so they belonged to them. She decided not to test him. She simply let them exist in the moment, not worrying about the past or the present, whether he loved her as much as she loved him, whether he would continue to love her as they grew old. They watched the sun set over their ocean. Gregory kissed her knuckles, and told her for the thousandth time that he loved her.

It was dark by the time they headed back to the mountains. Madeline rolled down the window, letting the wind ruffle her short hair. In the past she wouldn't have trusted how perfect the moment felt. She would have corrupted it with a test. Covered his eyes and made him drive them home based on her instructions. Or made him tightrope along the guardrail. Her mind devised a dozen different tests, only their whole day together had been a test, the kind that could actually prove his love. She just had to let them be, and in her letting them be, he'd done nothing but love her. At last she accepted that his love was absolute. Limitless.

At first Madeline assumed her eyes were watery from the wind against her face. She was not a crier. When she closed the window, the tears intensified rather than dried. She found herself overcome with happiness. Each tear that trickled down her cheek was warm with love.

"What's wrong?" he asked, his face a kaleidoscope of worry.

"I'm just so happy. This was a perfect day. I love you."

There are infinite meanings to "I love you." *I appreciate you. I want you. I need you. I resent you. I'm afraid you'll leave me. I'm afraid I'll leave you. I am used to you. I am used to our love. I think you're special. I think you're clever. I am glad you're here. I like our routine. I like our life together. I want everything to stay this way.* In their time together, Madeline had exhausted every meaning except the simplest one: *I love you.* No qualifiers. No distrust. Just pure, mutual love.

"I love you," she said again, and laughed like the meaning of the phrase had just struck her.

Gregory glanced over at her, dubious until he read her face and understood what she really meant. *No more tests. At last, I trust you.*

She leaned across the console and rested her cheek on his chest. He bent to kiss the crown of her head. She shut her eyes and clung to him hard. His breath was hot across her scalp. It was only a second. Between life and death a second is enough. One moment the smoothness of the road beneath them disappeared as the truck became airborne. The next, it thudded as it hit the valley floor below.

Her head had missed the steering wheel, which had crushed Gregory's sternum. A piece of glass from where his head had broken the windshield was embedded in her cheek. Otherwise, she was uninjured.

"He saved me," Madeline said to Alice. "His body protected mine." It was a test she hadn't meant to initiate, one that proved for the last time how absolute his love for her was.

It took all of Alice's energy to remain still through Madeline's story. Her back muscles were so tense they vibrated. The story had taken hold of her body and refused to let go. That was what she feared most, even more than loving someone who did not love her back. From the moment you treasured how perfect your love was, it could disappear.

"It was an accident," Alice said, wanting to deny the essential truth of Madeline's story. "You can't blame yourself for an accident."

"I don't. I just wish I'd allowed myself to trust his love. If I had, if I'd believed all the times he showed me how absolute his love was, maybe he'd be alive today."

The tension rose to Alice's shoulders. This was why Madeline had summoned her, to rewrite the past, to reconcile her loss.

"I can't bring him back," Alice said. "Once someone you love is gone, nothing can replace that, not a story, not even another love."

Tears welled in Madeline's eyes. "True love is never gone." To Alice, that seemed more a curse than a blessing, the way love outlasted the body, the way it forced you to want something you could never have again.

"Why now?" she asked. "You've been living like this for ten years. Why are you ready for love now?"

"I don't have much time left," Madeline said so plainly that Alice could not determine whether this prospect scared her. The flames flared against her skin, and in the burst of brightness Alice saw the woman she once was, a woman in love. "I need to forgive myself before it's too late. Not for his death. For distrusting love."

Madeline hugged her body as though trying to protect it from whatever disease was moving through it. Sure, she was old, small-boned. To Alice's untrained eye, though, she looked like one of those old women who subsisted off loneliness more than food and lived to one hundred just to prove the world wrong. Looks lied all the time. Her father ran every morning. Except for sunspots on his arms and cheeks, he presented as a decade younger than he was. He appeared strong and energetic, while his heart was slowly giving out.

"Do you… How much longer…did the doctors give you an estimate?"

"None of us know how long we have," Madeline said. The soberness of her face sent a chill through Alice. "I have to let go of this guilt while I still can. I've been afraid of it for so many years. I can no longer live in fear of myself. Of love."

"And a new love will bring you forgiveness?" Alice asked.

"Only I can forgive myself. You can help me though. I know you can help me."

A loud crash sounded beside them as a cat—neither Poirot nor Ripley, but a lithe black Siamese—skittered away from the porcelain plate of cookies that had just shattered on the floor.

"Ellis!" Madeline scolded the cat as she bent down to pick up the plate, split neatly into two pieces. "Look what you've done." She set the broken plate on the coffee table. The cat inched cautiously toward one of the jam cookies on the floor, and Madeline poked at her with a painted red toe. "Off, you. Go find Currer and Acton."

Ellis slinked toward a windowsill where two lazy tabbies lounged as though warming themselves in the sun that would not rise for another several hours. Alice had lost all track of time. The sky outside was completely dark. It could as easily be nine at night as one in the morning. Alice had not seen a clock since she entered the house, although she could hear a steady metronome ticking somewhere above them.

She smiled at the names of Madeline's cats, Currer, Ellis, and Acton, references to the Bronte sisters' pen names. There was no denying she felt connected to this strange woman, a kinship that Madeline must have intuited before they met if she suspected Alice could help her.

Madeline collected the cookies from the floor and returned them to the broken plate.

"Well?" she said as she settled back into the chair. "Don't leave me in suspense. Will you help me or not?"

When Alice met Madeline's gaze, she saw something familiar in her expression, something it took her a moment to identify as hope. Madeline, like all of Alice's clients, believed Alice could assist her. Alice wasn't clear yet on how to aid Madeline, but she hadn't encountered a case she couldn't crack, a client who did not find love.

"I will help you," Alice said. "I'll write you a story."

8

A Love Scribe Is Born

It was strange the way life both changed and remained the same. Each Friday and Saturday, Alice still donned a collared white shirt, black slacks, and Dansko clogs to pass out trays of food. She returned home with achy knees and a sore tailbone, her body too tired for sleep. Only now, rather than scooping Agatha up and settling on the couch for a black-and-white Hitchcock movie or an episode of *The Twilight Zone*, she would plop Agatha on the couch alone and settle into her desk chair to write.

If her gift had its way, once an image seized her mind and the prickling sensation animated her skin, she would stay glued to her computer, not moving until the story was complete. That had worked when she wrote one story at a time, when each was a few pages, a wisp of a tale. Now she had to juggle multiple clients at once, their stories more nuanced and longer than they'd been before. She was finding that the more complicated the case, the more particular the client, the more extended the metaphor and hence the story had to be. Most of her tales now required more than sitting down for four hours and cranking something out. They were written over several sessions, a few pages a day. As a result, that tingling feeling never entirely went away. It energized her like an amphetamine. It also nagged her with guilt, a constant reminder that she needed to get back to the page.

Her vocation also required a wardrobe change. When they met to go over her financial records, Gabby took one look at Alice's ill-fitting polka-dot button-up blouse and said, "Please tell me you didn't wear that to meet a client."

Alice tugged awkwardly at the blouse, which she'd purchased years before at a thrift shop. "I thought it screamed artist."

"Starving artist maybe." Gabby stood from the sidewalk table of the coffee shop. "Come on."

Alice followed her across residential streets, past murals of swans and violet eyes that watched their every step, to a department store on State Street where Gabby made her try on low-cut dresses, stiff pants, and shirts that were sure to stain from deodorant.

"This is so not me," Alice said, trying to figure out how to tie the belt of a wraparound dress. She emerged from the changing room with the belt lobbed into an awkward bow at her back. Gabby stood behind her, untying the strange origami Alice had assembled the dress into, and rearranged it perfectly. As Alice stood before the mirror, she twirled, marveling at the fact that she had curves where she'd always assumed she was straight, at the way her body looked made for the dress.

"That's the point," Gabby said.

They agreed on three dresses, two pairs of tuxedo pants, and blouses that were not entirely unlike her catering uniform, although Gabby made Alice promise never to wear her work clogs with clients or her silk blouses to pass out trays of food. From there, they ventured to Gabby's salon, where the receptionist air-kissed both her cheeks and fit Alice into the schedule right away. Gabby and her hairdresser, a waifish man with spiky black dyed hair and eyeliner so thick it extended to his eye creases, leaned over Alice, talking about her as though she wasn't there.

"It's a little unruly," the hairdresser said, lifting and dropping a curl of Alice's hair. "But it has bounce. People would kill for this kind of body. Why doesn't she take better care of it?"

Gabby shook out Alice's mane. "Can you give it some shape?"

The hairdresser and Gabby agreed on fringed layers that would keep Alice's curly hair free-spirited but styled. After it was cut, the hairdresser angled her to face the mirror. Even Alice had to admit it looked perfect.

From there, makeup followed.

"If it's too high-maintenance," Gabby told the cosmetician, "she won't wear it." Alice wanted to protest, but her best friend was right.

"Fortunately, she has good skin," the cosmetician said.

They decided on a tinted moisturizer, some mascara, lip gloss, nude nail polish. Alice asked the cosmetician to apply cherry red lipstick, then balked when it came to purchasing the vibrant color. One step at a time, Gabby advised. When Alice returned home from their shopping spree, she discovered that Gabby had slipped a tube of the bright lipstick into her bag with a Post-it that read, *For whenever you're ready.*

The transformation did not end with clothes and makeup. It involved exercise, business cards, bindings to replace the report covers Alice was using. "I'm sorry," Gabby had scoffed when she spotted one of Alice's stories in her bag, encased in clear plastic. "I didn't realize you were writing a seventh-grade social studies paper. Presentation is everything. Can't you find someone to make them look like real books?"

Was this a possibility in the digital age? Were there still craftspeople dedicated to the lost art of binding books? She promised Gabby she would investigate.

In addition, she also purchased business cards. "And don't even think of using one of those services where they give you free business cards in exchange for putting the maker's name on the back. You need a thick stock, the kind that rests heavy in someone's hand."

Gabby had urged Alice to put *Alice Meadows, Writer* on her business cards. Alice did not feel like a writer, not in the conventional sense. She wasn't published. Wasn't writing stories or articles for mass consumption. Translator was more akin to what she did, but Gabby said that *Love Translator* was too confusing and Alice was inclined to agree. They settled on *Alice Meadows, Love Scribe*, which seemed apt to them both, someone the words poured through rather than someone who owned them.

Yes, with the aid of her best friend, Alice was learning to exude an air of professionalism she did not feel, no matter how committed she grew to the craft. The clients never seemed to notice how she tugged at those perfectly fitting silk blouses, how her back stiffened as she walked into the café or bar in a floral dress for their first meeting. When she stuttered, "I charge fifteen hundred dollars plus additional binding fees," they immediately agreed, even when she suspected they could not afford it.

"Plenty of people drive BMWs when they shouldn't," Gabby reasoned, plowing ahead of Alice on their now daily morning hike. Her legs were shorter than Alice's, but they moved with a deftness Alice had not yet developed. Each morning she struggled to keep up. "They make it work because they want to project a certain quality of life. And that's just about perception. For love, they'll find ways to pay."

Gabby stopped to let Alice catch up. They were on a trail that followed the hills above town, Gabby in matching geometrically patterned leggings and sports bra, Alice in an oversized T-shirt and jean shorts.

"Shouldn't you be making Oliver do this with you?" Alice said through labored breaths.

"He says that hiking is masochistic and he gets enough self-flagellation on stage." It was another point for Oliver that he did not like hiking and would not submit to Gabby's pressure, except for the fact that Alice was now expected to get up early and lug herself up a mountain so Gabby didn't have to go alone.

"Besides," Gabby continued, waiting for Alice to arrive at the top of the pitch, whereupon she started walking again. It was unfair how the slower hiker never got a break. The moment Alice caught up, Gabby would set off once more. It destined Alice to remain behind.

"He's in full prep mode. He has this big showcase at the end of the year where there'll be agents and everything. He's so determined. He even gets up before me, can you imagine? By the time I'm out of bed at the oh-so-late hour of six thirty, he's already sitting at kitchen table with his notepad, scribbling jokes."

"How's his routine?"

"I haven't seen it yet. I mean, I'm sure it's amazing. He's just really private about it. I guess he's one of those artists who doesn't want anyone to see it until it's done. Eventually he'll have to test out his jokes to see what lands, but he made me promise not to go to any of his shows before the showcase. He wants it to be perfect for me. It's actually really nice. We both have our own stuff. And every morning there's coffee already made by the time I get up. Plus, cleaning is his form of procrastination. When I get home from work, the house is spotless and the bed is actually made."

Something about the way she said *home* struck Alice. "Is he living with you?"

Gabby turned, glowing, and nodded. "He moved in last week."

"Isn't it a little soon?" Alice said before she could censor herself. They'd only been dating three and a half months.

Gabby stopped, seeming to consider the question.

"Normally I'd say yes, but it's different with Oliver. I would have moved in with him after our first date. When you know, you know." Alice resisted the urge to argue that Gabby had *known* with her last two boyfriends too. "I realize I've said that before. It really is different this time. Oliver is my person. He likes me for me. And I like him for him. We aren't trying to change each other."

Gabby stared out at the vista. Even Alice had to admit that there was something powerful about gazing down upon the city where you lived, about rising so far above it.

When Gabby looked back at Alice her face was resolute. "I have both eyes open, okay? It's fast, but I'm not rushing anything."

To her surprise, Alice believed her best friend. Besides she wasn't asking Alice for approval. Instead she chose to trust how she felt, chose to trust love. At its essence, this was what Alice had taught her.

As with the haircut and wardrobe change, Gabby was right about the presentation of Alice's stories. The report covers were juvenile, and the logo for Oh, Alice Productions that Alice had designed on her word processor was a little too DIY. Gabby connected Alice to one of her clients at a graphic design firm who created a sleek colophon of Oh, Alice in thick black lettering fashioned into the shape of a heart. It would look perfect debossed into the spine of a book.

Alice found a binder the way most people find a service these days, with the assistance of a little thing called Yelp. Not Alice's service, though. Her contracts stipulated that clients could not review or in any other way post about Oh, Alice Productions online. It surprised her that an artisan committed to an Old World art would not have the same policy, but that was the thing about Old World arts: they were dying and in need of customers. Still, Alice was not expecting a banner ad for Willow Bindery & Paper Goods at the top of her Google search.

She liked the name and the logo of—maybe it went without saying—a willow tree. It was one of two binders in Santa Barbara, and the only one with a website that looked like it had been designed in the last five years. Perhaps there was something to a good online presence, even if the internet was not the right venue for her gift.

Willow Bindery & Paper Goods was tucked on a residential street near the courthouse, a short bike ride from Alice's apartment. A bell rang as Alice pushed the door open and a rush of air-conditioning hit her face. She fluffed her new cut trying to combat the inevitable helmet hair that came from using her bike as a primary form of transportation. Inside, it looked like a stationery shop. One wall was covered with sheets of wrapping paper listed for staggering prices. Another wall offered more types of pens than Alice knew existed: felt tip, calligraphy, roller, ballpoint, fountain with vials of ink like colorful blood.

"Just a minute," a gruff voice called from the back.

Alice plucked a leather journal from the table at the center of the store. It was an achingly bright red, so much so that Alice was surprised it didn't stain her fingertips. All the journals were equally saturated, in every imaginable hue, the leather a natural grain that looked to be of high quality. The pages inside were off-white and blank. On the back, Alice traced a small etching of a weeping willow. This was the perfect journal. Whoever made it would bind her the perfect book.

"Those are all handmade by yours truly."

Alice looked up to see a husky man with a wide, whiskered face, its oval shape accentuated by his dark hair, the bulk of which was collected in a ponytail at the nape of his neck. From across the room, she could tell he was a few inches shorter than she. He was around her age, younger than she would have anticipated for a bookbinder. In the era of the artisanal, she wasn't sure why she'd expected the bookbinder to be geriatric, but the man before her defied her expectations. She studied him, trying to decide if that was a good or bad thing. There was something undeniably sexy about him, even though Alice was not normally attracted to men with long hair, men that were not as tall as she was. And she preferred a lithe, lanky body to one that was compact. Gabby often told her, "All the men you date look like birds." When Alice sniped back that she didn't date, Gabby amended her statement, "All the men you fuck, then," trying to be as vulgar as possible. That the binder was both good-looking and not Alice's type enabled her to marvel at his looks, appreciating his attractiveness without desiring it. She decided she liked the idea of someone sexy binding her projects. Maybe his mystique would rub off on the books, informing her love stories with a little extra spark.

"If you don't see a color or pattern you want," he said looking up at her, "I can make one however you like. It just will take about a week."

He had cloudy green eyes that made him seem far away even as he stared right at her with an intensity that caused her chest to tighten. Through her stories, she'd grown accustomed to categorizing people quickly. There was something guarded about this man, some distance he created between himself and the outside world.

"I wanted to see about some custom jobs. You do that, right?"

"Of course, although not as much as I would like." He motioned around the store. "Hence the stationery." He wiped his ink-stained hands on a canvas apron tied around his waist and held the right one out for Alice to shake. "Duncan."

"Alice," she said, extending her arm. He had a firm grip that seemed trustworthy, but appearances lied all the time. She understood that all too well; she was either dressed as the consummate professional she did not feel herself to be, the consummate waitress with crisp white shirts that would be stained by the end of the shift, or the consummate writer in her dad's old sweatshirt. Today, here in Willow Bindery, was a rare day where Alice was dressed like herself, in worn jeans and a striped T-shirt that Gabby would say made her look like a teenager in the nineties. In all fairness, it was an apt description of her style, even if Gabby would not have meant it as a compliment.

Alice continued to study Duncan, feeling hesitant about entrusting her stories to him. "Before we talk about the project, you should know my writing is very personal. I need to make sure, I need your word, that you won't read it."

A bruised expression materialized on Duncan's face before he could hide it. "I bind hundreds of books a year. I don't have the time to read them, let alone the interest."

"I didn't mean anything by my comment," Alice said, realizing she'd offended him. "It's just really important to me that my work remain private." She was belaboring her point, drawing more attention to it instead of less.

He held up his right hand. "Consider it my binder's oath. I solemnly swear that I will not read your book."

Alice pressed on with an unprecedented need to explain herself. "You see, the stories I write, they're a bit unconventional. People hire me to write them personalized narratives that help them fall in love." Duncan laughed, then quieted when he realized that she wasn't joking. "They aren't romances or for entertainment. They're more like fables, precisely calibrated to each of my clients' needs. After they read them, they immediately meet the love of their life. The stories are theirs alone, and they pay good money for them. It would be a betrayal of their trust if anyone else read them. I can't—" Alice interrupted herself. Why was she telling him all this?

Surprisingly, he laughed again, more heartily than before. "Well then, you definitely don't have to worry about me reading them. I want nothing to do with love."

Alice startled. She'd never met anyone else who so immediately and wholeheartedly denounced love.

"I'm divorced. We separated about a year ago. That's when I

moved here, opened this store. I was working for my father-in-law at his bindery in Portland—Maine, not Oregon. I never needed to make that distinction until I moved to the West Coast. Once she cheated, once it was over, I couldn't exactly work for him anymore, so I packed up and headed west." He tried to tell this like an upbeat story—westward expansion, manifest destiny—but his pain punctuated every syllable, making his words consonant and bitter.

Alice wondered if coming here was a mistake. Did she want someone heartbroken to bind her stories?

Before she could respond, Duncan added, "Sorry, I don't usually share that much. It's been hard, being so far from home. And I don't know many people here. Plus, I'm not the joining type. One of the many things my ex-wife couldn't stand about me." He blinked and inhaled deeply. "Anyway, that was a long way of saying you can rest assured. I have no interest in reading your love stories."

Duncan picked at the skin around his thumbnail, not meeting Alice's eye. She wanted to say that he had no reason to be embarrassed for sharing his past. She sensed that would make him more uncomfortable, though, so she shrugged as if it happened all the time. It did happen all the time. She'd made a profession out of it.

And like all the other backstories she'd heard from clients, it gave her an idea. Not for a story but for a test to prove he wouldn't read her tales, that he could be trusted to leave love alone.

"What if we start with one book and see how it goes?" she asked.

"That sounds reasonable," he agreed.

"Great," she said a little too enthusiastically. "I'll print it out and bring it to you later today so you can get started right away."

"Do you have any preferences on grain or color?" he asked. Alice hadn't considered the color or different finishes. She glanced over at the table and grabbed the first journal that caught her eye. It was a burnt sienna that did not remotely make her think of love. "How about like this one? I'll come back with the pages."

"It should take a week," he said. "I'm going to need an electronic file though. This may be a bookbindery, but it's still the twenty-first century."

Alice sped home and headed straight to her computer, a familiar energy buzzing through her that was akin to her usual ping of inspiration.

For 127 pages, she wrote **DUNCAN, I LOVE YOU. DUNCAN, I LOVE YOU. DUNCAN, I LOVE YOU. DUNCAN, I LOVE YOU. DUNCAN, I LOVE YOU. DUNCAN, I LOVE YOU. DUNCAN, I LOVE YOU. DUNCAN, I LOVE YOU. DUNCAN, I LOVE YOU.** All caps in Times New Roman boldface. She tried underlining it, but that made it harder rather than easier to read. She typed those four words repeatedly until they lost their meaning. It was the opposite of the stories she wrote for her clients, steeped in imagery and deeper meaning. Alice added a title and a copyright page, a dedication as well as an epigraph and an author's note at the end of the file to hide the message. Then she saved the document and sent it to Duncan. The rest was up to him.

A week later, Alice got a call that her book was ready.

When she returned to the bindery that afternoon, it was empty again. It held a staticky silence like no one was ever there. Not lonely, exactly. More like undiscovered.

When Duncan presented the book to her, his expression remained neutral. He did not even comment on that slightly pornographic *Oh, Alice* she'd asked him to deboss on the spine. The book itself was as elegant as the journals for sale, textured leather pulled taut across the cover, that lovely little tree on the back.

"Is there a problem?" Duncan said, sounding more offended

than concerned. Alice had been standing at his desk for too long, inspecting the book.

"Of course not," she said. He watched her, waiting for her to explain why she was lingering, and she realized that he was expecting praise. "It's perfect. Really, the artistry is just…perfect." It was indeed a work of art, so much so that Alice felt guilty it harbored meaningless professions of love.

Duncan nodded, smiling for the first time. Certainly pride in craftsmanship was important, but Alice now realized how strange it was that he hadn't smiled at all during their first meeting. He was truly guarded. Or perhaps just cold. Either way, she wondered again if he was the right person to bind her stories.

"What?" Duncan asked, brushing his chest with his ink-stained hands. "Do I have ketchup on my shirt or something?"

"Well, now you have ink."

"Never trust a printer with clean shirts."

"Never trust a writer who tells you a true story," Alice said, remembering something her middle school language arts teacher used to say. "They're too good at making things up."

Duncan nodded but didn't laugh, and Alice appreciated that he didn't pretend her remark was funnier than it was. A false laugh was as bad as a lie. It was a small point. Combined with his disinterest in her stories, it was enough for her to trust him.

She handed him a flash drive with her most recent stories. It was shaped like a cat, black with pink ears. Duncan examined it, amused.

"I like cats," Alice explained.

"This looks more like an alien cat," he said.

"I'm not prejudiced against intergalactic felines."

"That sounds like the plot of a Douglas Adams novel."

"I'll write the novel and you can bind it with a gilded cat on the cover. Not that you would know what it was about because you wouldn't read it." Alice wasn't sure if she was still testing him. The sober expression on his face indicated that he was not amused.

"These stories are a little shorter than the first one I gave you. Can you bind something that's only like twenty pages?"

"I'll have to make some accommodations. As long as it's one-sixteenth of an inch thick it should be fine with a thinner cover and thicker paper. I may have to put the colophon on the back instead of the spine."

"You're the artist," Alice said.

"And you," he said, bowing, "are the writer."

Normally she flinched when anyone called her a writer. It felt not only inconsistent with her gift but overly bold, like calling yourself a chef rather than a cook, a visionary rather than a boss. Yet she found herself liking the way Duncan said *writer.*

Alice nodded before waving goodbye. When she got to the door, she paused.

"Just one more thing—" She motioned toward the flash drive. Now that she was making hardcover books for her clients, she'd given them the option of having their books bound in any color they'd like. Without fail, all seven had chosen the same color. While the clients were as different as their stories, no matter how cynical and disenchanted some were, or how bubbly and generic, they all wanted the same thing, an unironic, unapologetic kind of love. There was only one color for that type of love.

"This time," she told Duncan, "I'd like them bound in red."

9

A Visit to the Library

Alice sat at her desk and opened her computer, stretching exaggeratedly to wake her body up. It was time to get to work on Madeline's story. Her fingers spanned the keyboard, ready to create. As she stared at the screen, the cursor blinking steadily, her mind went blank. Her body felt none of the tingling sensation that she had learned to recognize as the muse summoning her to the page. She stared at the screen, waiting for an image to appear in her mind's eye. All she saw were vast swaths of emptiness. There was no color. There were no thoughts to grab on to. No images from which to milk a story, not even tumbleweeds.

Motion usually helped spur the muse, so she gave Agatha a quick pat and set out into the thick fog of morning. She wandered through her neighborhood past Victorian and Craftsman houses, beyond the courthouse to the beach, where she stopped to watch the skateboarders race up and down the cement ramps, wheels whooshing. Alice shut her eyes, trying to absorb the satisfying sound. Still nothing came to her, no crash of inspiration, no flurry of chills up her arms. Eventually her stomach rumbled in a way that seemed promising until it revealed itself to be hunger. She walked home to prepare breakfast. Perhaps a little sustenance would do the trick.

When she sat at her computer for the second time, her apartment was so quiet she could hear the refrigerator buzzing. Its steady hum taunted her. Her cluttered apartment taunted her. So she did something she almost never did—she cleaned. Organizing her father's records and dusting her books led to washing the dishes led to mopping the floors led to sanitizing the bathroom. Still no image materialized. When the toxic smell of disinfectant was almost enough to make her faint, Alice flopped on to the couch and turned on the television. She flipped through the channels, but watching other people's stories unfold reminded her of the one she couldn't write. And why couldn't she write it? She understood that Madeline sought forgiveness. Though it had to come from within her, Madeline needed Alice to guide her to a place where she could let go of her guilt. This was Alice's role with all her clients, identifying the change required in them, then nudging them down a path of self-discovery. So what was different this time? Why didn't an image present itself? With the others, the pattern had unfolded swiftly. As soon as Alice knew what her story needed to accomplish, she saw the vehicle for it. With the image in mind, a current coursed through her, an adrenaline that carried her through to the end of the draft. She'd come to recognize each of these stages, to embrace them as her process, only here she was, with a clear sense of what she wanted the story to say and no idea how to say it. Not yet.

Without second-guessing herself, Alice hopped into her car and drove toward the mountains. Along the 154, the fog had dissipated, giving Alice a clear view of the ocean below. The aquamarine waters blended into the horizon, making everything beyond the road a uniform blue, as though neither ocean nor sky existed, nor the city below, its beaches, the stories Alice was neglecting in favor of one particular old woman in the woods.

On Stagecoach Road, the unmarked road to Madeline's house was more obvious than Alice remembered. Once she dipped down beneath the highway overpass, she found it easily. Her old car kicked up plumes of dirt as it bumped down the path, partially obscuring her vision of Madeline's house ahead. While the surrounding forest was thick, there was never any doubt that the redwood house was waiting for her.

When Alice pulled up, Madeline was sitting on the front porch, wearing cargo pants that could be unzipped above the knee and a wide-brimmed hat. She held two canteens of water. Maybe it was the bright light of early afternoon, but she looked paler today, thinner too.

"Ready?" Madeline asked, offering Alice one of the canteens.

"How did you know I was going to come back today?"

Madeline shrugged. "Frankly, I'm surprised it took you this long to realize you had to come back."

Alice smiled awkwardly. She took a long pull from the canteen. The water was so cold it stung her teeth.

"Also, your car is very loud. Are you sure the engine's okay? I heard you as soon as you turned off Stagecoach." Madeline motioned her around the side of the house where they walked past a stone patio. On the table, a carafe of lemonade and croissant sandwiches were laid out. Alice looked longingly at a croissant, realizing she'd skipped lunch. Madeline caught Alice staring and wove her arm through her guest's.

"That's our reward. First, we walk."

They stepped over fallen trees, now decomposing, their guts filled with ants, and wound around tall thin oak trees and squat ferns that all looked the same to Alice.

"Don't you get lost out here?" she asked. There was no trail stamped between the trees, no cairns or ribbons tied to branches marking the path.

"The first thing you'll learn from the forest: one step west and the terrain is born again." Madeline bent down to pick up a felled branch and used it as a walking stick. "Every day I get lost on purpose. Turning right and left until I can't tell one tree from another, until I'm convinced that today will be the day when I won't find my way back. Every day, when I fear I'll never find home again, I look up and there's the chimney. That's why I built it taller than all the trees that surround it. It will always guide me home."

An image came to Alice swiftly. Madeline lost to the woods, her white hair grown long, a nightgown trailing her as she ran with no destination, unafraid. No. That wouldn't do. It was an allegory Madeline had already fashioned for herself. Alice couldn't steal it.

As they walked farther, the forest condensed, groves of sycamores tightening. They twisted and turned until Alice had no idea whether they were walking toward or away from the house. The arches of her feet began to ache, and the sun was high in the sky above them. She was famished. She drank from the canteen, hoping water would distract her from her hunger. The teal metal insulated the water, keeping it painfully cold. Her mouth grew numb, but that did nothing to quell her all-consuming desire for that croissant. Her brain was no good to her until she fed it again.

Just when Alice thought she could not walk another step, the chimney appeared in the distance. Madeline clapped in delight.

"See," she said, "it's so much more satisfying when you get a sign that it's time to return rather than making an arbitrary decision."

They followed the chimney until the redwood siding of Madeline's house became the backdrop to the trunks.

When they returned to the patio, the sandwiches and carafe were still laid out on the table. Madeline poured each of them lemonade. The ice, somehow not melting in the day's heat, clinked as it fell into the glass. The croissants were warm, as though they'd just been pulled from the oven, and the chicken salad sandwiched inside was perfectly chilled. Alice let the layers of croissant melt in her mouth. She shut her eyes, holding her face up so the sun could kiss her cheeks. The moment was calm and perfect. Alice felt completely at ease. This was it. She waited for an image to rise in her. The moment was ripe for it. Her body was ready to be inspired. But the blankness persisted, white and vast, thick as morning fog.

When Alice opened her eyes, Madeline was watching her. She waited for the old woman to ask if Alice had made any progress on her story. Madeline continued to observe her with an indecipherable expression.

"What?" Alice asked.

"I was just thinking how nice it is to have company. I love my solitude. I've cultivated it. When you spend so much time alone, it's easy to forget that sharing time with others has its merits."

"I spend a lot of time alone too," Alice admitted. Since she began writing, she was spending even more time sequestered in her apartment. Only it never felt like she was alone because she had her stories, their imagery and characters, to keep her company. "It's easier to appreciate spending time with people when you don't need them to be happy."

Madeline nodded pensively. "And are you happy, Alice?"

It was such a simple question, one Alice rarely stopped to ask herself.

"Of course."

"Why of course? Is it so obvious?"

"I embrace the life I've chosen. Like you."

"You say that as if we always make the best choices for ourselves."

"And you," Alice said, "are you happy?"

"There are as many ways to be happy as unhappy. They aren't mutually exclusive." Alice waited for Madeline to elaborate, but the woman sipped her lemonade, watching the shadows the trees cast on the ground. "I was thinking that perhaps you would like to visit my library? There's nothing like a person's books to let you see into their soul."

With the offer, Alice understood. Madeline had not asked about Alice's story because she knew that she had not volunteered enough of herself for Alice to begin writing.

"I'd like that very much."

They left the remains of their lunch outside and slipped into the kitchen. Alice followed Madeline down the hall and upstairs, where the floorboards creaked with their weight. The grandfather clock that Alice had heard on her first visit grew louder with each step until they reached the second floor and Alice's temples pulsed from the intensity of every tick.

The hall upstairs was painted white. There were three closed doors, white like the walls and paneled. Madeline explained that the one down the hall was to her bedroom, the one facing the woods behind the house to a guest room and the other to the library. The library door did not have a crystal knob like the others. Instead it had an elaborate brass doorplate with a heart-shaped metal knob, worn smooth from touch and glistening in the dim light.

Madeline reached into her pocket to retrieve an antique brass key. The bow was monogramed with *MA*, identical to the initials on the wax seal from the letter Alice had received in the mail. The doorplate did not appear to have a keyhole. A three-dimensional image of a woman in a voluminous dress and laced boots covered most of the plate. In profile, it was impossible to tell if the woman was young or old. She carried a parasol tucked under her arm, the tip of which pointed to a numbered dial with a filigreed heart at its center. The dial was currently set to sixty-seven although it went up to one hundred. Beneath it was a passage in cursive that Alice couldn't quite read from behind Madeline's shoulder.

Madeline pressed on one of the raised buttons on the bust of the woman's dress, and her right leg kicked up, exposing a keyhole beneath. The key slid effortlessly into the hole with a satisfying click as the dial rotated clockwise, the tip of the parasol now pointing to sixty-eight. Madeline turned the heart-shaped knob and pushed the door open.

Inside the room was floor-to-ceiling shelves filled with hardback books, a fireplace already blazing, the ticking grandfather clock, and a small safe that broke up the space. Recessed lighting complemented the Tiffany lamps scattered around the room, lamps that added more atmosphere than light. Each of the two oversized chairs was draped with a cashmere throw, the floor covered in overlapping Persian rugs. Alice glanced at the clock to check the time. The pendulum swung back and forth, but there were no hands on the dial. It ticked at an even cadence, signifying that time was passing even if Alice could not be sure of how much. She stepped toward the shelves, prepared to look into the soul of Madeline Alger. Books had always been an inspiration to Alice. She read to understand herself. She read to understand the world around her. Surely she could look to Madeline's books to understand her too.

As Alice surveyed the collection, she couldn't make sense of what she was seeing. Several copies of the same book sat together, although they were not alphabetized or arranged by author. *East of Eden* was nowhere near *The Winter of Our Discontent.* Sometimes, as with *A Farewell to Arms*, all the copies were of the same edition while the many copies of *Little Women* all had different covers. Most titles had a single copy, including each of Shakespeare's late romances, the only Shakespeare in the entire library. And every shelf had a copy of *Wuthering Heights*, Alice's favorite book. In her cursory examination, she spotted no books that seemed out of character, no bodice rippers that would have been too scandalous for someone like Madeline, no books like *Gravity's Rainbow* or *The Sound and the Fury* that were displayed almost always for appearances. More peculiar still, despite having cats named Poirot and Ripley, Madeline had no works by Christie or Highsmith, no mysteries at all.

As Alice continued to walk around the room, scanning all the books she'd read, those she wanted to read, some she'd forgotten about and must read again as soon as possible, she thought, Where is he? It didn't seem possible that Madeline could have loved a man who didn't also love books.

"Are all these books yours?" Alice asked. "What about Gregory? Did some of these belong to him?"

"He never kept books. Don't misinterpret me. He loved books possibly more than I did, but it was different for him. He liked to imagine the life his books had once he gave them away. Me, I'm selfish with my books. I want to know that they belong to me alone, as if the stories belong to me alone too. Henry James is mine. Octavia Butler is mine. Dorothy Parker is mine. Even Virginia Woolf. My Virginia Woolf does not belong to you or anyone else. Whatever books Gregory left behind I gave away. I have plenty of other ways to remember him." Madeline laughed. "He used to get so frustrated with me for having so many books. Our former house was small. I didn't have enough space for all my books, so I'd pile them on the floor, on end tables, in the linen closet. One time he told me that hoarding books is still hoarding. That got to me. I don't think I talked to him for three days after that."

Madeline walked over to the shelves and ran her finger along them, checking for dust that hadn't gathered. Like the rest of the house, the library was meticulously clean and orderly. No cat hair, no scuffs on the wood floors, no throw pillows even slightly askew.

Madeline leaned against the shelves, facing Alice, as though posing for a portrait. "You know, we met because of a book."

Alice sat in one of the chairs, and Madeline joined her in the other. They watched the fire crackle, flames like figures summoning spirits.

"Gregory and I met all because of a book," Madeline said again, fidgeting in her seat until she found an angle that seemed to suit her. "I found it in the park. A beat-up hardcover, so well loved that I knew I needed to return it to its owner. People leave their marks on books, even when they don't underline passages or write in the margins, even if they don't dog-ear pages or leave behind receipts. Spines get broken. Ink gets smudged. Books bruise like any other body."

Alice thought of her own books, which she kept pristine. The suggestion of dog-earring a page made her queasy. An intentional mark on the page, be it from a ballpoint pen or, God forbid, a highlighter, was like nails on a chalkboard for her. Don't get her started on food. Eating while reading should be regulated as strictly as drinking and driving. Tea was a necessary evil, for any book was enhanced by a strong cup of Earl Grey. She couldn't imagine finding a battered old book and assuming it was loved rather than taken for granted.

"I saw the owner all over its pages." Madeline held her wrinkled, turquoise-adorned hands toward the fire. More liver spots dotted their backs than on their previous encounter. Madeline also looked like she'd lost weight, even if she hadn't had weight to lose. While the changes were subtle, the panic they aroused was not. Alice was running out of time.

"Even before I met him, I was in love with him. I needed to find him. Only how? It's not like his name was written on the inside of the cover. I knew where he'd let his thumb linger on the page, where he'd dripped coffee—" words that sent a chill down Alice's spine "—these facts could not lead me to him. It's funny how we can know someone intimately without knowing them at all and how we can think we know someone but not understand what makes them tick. I knew his ticks. I didn't know his name. That left me with one option."

Alice inched to the edge of the chair, eager for more of Madeline's tale.

"You see, the book wasn't new. The edition was out of print and too old for him to have purchased it when it came out, so he had to have bought it used. And there was only one store in town that sold used books. I wasn't sure I was right, but I didn't have another avenue to find my love.

"I brought the book to the store and asked the bookseller if she could locate the person who had purchased it. As sympathetic as she was, she wasn't about to divulge information about a customer, not a name, not even a confirmation that the copy I showed her had been purchased at her store. She assured me that the book was one that could be replaced easily. It was a very common edition. In fact, they had four copies on the shelves. She pointed me in that direction. I left a note in each copy with my telephone number and a brief explanation that I had the reader's original copy.

"Then I waited. I waited so long I feared the copies of the book had sold and he would never find my notes. I went back to the shop and all four copies were still there with my notes inside. Then I got mad. How could he just lose the book and not replace it? It didn't occur to me that he might buy it elsewhere. Eventually the anger shifted to sadness. I became certain that the owner of the book was my soul mate. I kept returning to the store to check on my notes like they were plants I could watch grow. And then one day there were only three copies. I was so excited I rushed straight home. I sat by the phone and waited. Day turned to dusk turned to starry night. The phone didn't ring. Not the next day or the day after. I grew despondent. I couldn't eat. Couldn't sleep. I couldn't even read the book, which I'd been doing ceaselessly since I found it, imagining where his eyes might linger, where they sped up, where he had to step away to absorb the magnitude of the story. I was completely beside myself, unhinged, until I saw the absurdity of it all. I was so in love and I'd never even met this person."

"I can't believe he didn't call," Alice said involuntarily. She hadn't meant to pierce the bubble of Madeline's story with such an empty comment.

"Of course he called," Madeline snapped. "I was in the middle of ironing when the phone rang, so I picked it up, resting it between my ear and shoulder as I continued my task. He kept hemming and hawing, 'I'm sorry to bother you, this might seem strange, you see I never normally do this but'—I thought he was selling something. I tried to get him off the phone, until he said, 'I got your note.' I felt his words in my heels, grounding me in place. The sourness of burning silk filled the room, and I quickly reached over to set the iron upright. My blouse was ruined, but I didn't care. He found my note. It was all I could do to say, 'What took you so long?'

"His laugh was like spun sugar. I was entirely serious though. I asked again, more forcefully this time, 'What took you so long?'

"'You left your note toward the end,' he explained.

"'I left the note where your bookmark was,' I corrected. 'The exact page.'

"'I couldn't just pick up there. I had to start again at the beginning.'

"Right away, I knew what he meant. It was the same story but it was a new book. He had to ingratiate himself with the pages. He had to love it the way he loved the copy he lost. He had to give it its due time, and it was a very long book. It wasn't something he could sit down and read in a day."

"When he found my note, he rushed back to the store. The three other copies were there, and he found my notes in those ones too, so he bought them all. Then he waited for the right time to call.

"'And why was the right time now?' I demanded. I was annoyed. He made me wait too long. I was ironing. I ruined a perfectly good blouse for him.

"'Because the idea of not calling you finally scared me more than calling you.'"

Madeline picked up a bookmark resting on the small table between them and tickled her palm with its tassel. "We met up later that afternoon, and for the next three decades we didn't spend a day apart. It was worth it. All of it, even the loss."

In Madeline's story, Alice heard all the reasons she didn't want to fall in love. No matter how much time Madeline had had with Gregory, the time after was infinite. Alice didn't want infinite loneliness when she was perfectly happy being alone. This was their great disconnect. Madeline still wanted love after the worst had happened to her. Alice did not want love, even though nothing had happened to her, not directly. No wonder she couldn't write Madeline a story.

Madeline stood and stretched. "It's getting late."

While the library had no windows, its clock had no hands, Alice could smell the night air wafting down the chimney. She had so many questions, but when Madeline said good night, tiredness hit her all at once. Her limbs felt like they might snap off if she tried to use them. She was brittle tired. Immobilized.

Madeline pointed to the wall of books that led to the hall. "I had the guest room prepared for you."

Alice was relieved by the offer, as she didn't want to drive in her sleepy state. When they left the library, she asked, "What was the book? The hardcover you found in the park, the one that belonged to Gregory. What was the title?"

Madeline yawned. "That's a very intimate question. It's between me and my love."

"And the book," Alice said. "It's between you, your love, and the book."

Madeline smiled. "And the book."

She pulled the door shut behind them. The clock continued its ticking, hardly muted by the thick wood door. Madeline twisted the brass key she'd left in the keyhole, and the dial rotated once more, to sixty-nine. She plucked the key out of the lock, pressed the top button on the woman's dress, and her leg sprang back into place, obscuring the keyhole as though it had never been there.

"Why do you lock it?" Alice asked.

Madeline slipped the key back into her pants pocket. "Did you lock your car when you arrived?"

"Of course."

"You're very fond of that phrase, *of course.* Of course you're happy. Of course you lock your car. Why are these things so obvious? Why is it a given that you would lock your car here in the woods where it is just you and me? Do you think I'm going to break into your car and steal something?"

"Of—" Alice stopped herself. "No, I don't think you're going to steal anything from my car."

"Perhaps you fear the bears will try to force their way inside, although if they're determined a measly lock won't stop them. No, not the bears? The deer then? Or perhaps a fox? They are pesky little fellas."

Alice's face grew hot. "It's just habit," she said feebly.

Madeline shook her head adamantly. "Habits are built from patterns that are built from active decisions. If something becomes a habit, it's because you cultivated it. So I'll ask you again. Why did you lock your car?"

"Because I love my car," Alice said reflexively.

Madeline nodded. "You love it, and you want to know it's all yours, that you're the only one to touch it, even when it's irrational to think anyone else would." She gave Alice's shoulder a squeeze before reporting that she would see Alice in the morning.

As the old woman shuffled down the hall, Alice retreated

into the guest room across from the library. She kept the door open a crack and watched Madeline disappear into her own bedroom, the space beneath the door growing dark moments later. Alice remained poised in the doorway as the house descended into silence except for that steady clock. When she was confident Madeline was asleep, she creaked open her door and tiptoed across the hall to the library.

Her fingers grazed the heart-shaped doorknob, feeling its smoothness. She did not dare try to turn it, although if she did it wouldn't budge. When she pushed the button on the woman's dress, her leg sprang up just as it had for Madeline. Alice leaned toward the keyhole, the sliver of library beyond. All she could see was darkness. She stepped back and read the quote etched into doorplate at the bottom: *Two solitudes that meet, protect and greet each other.* The words sounded vaguely familiar, but Alice could not recall where she'd read them before.

She continued to stand outside the library, staring at the doorplate, listening to the grandfather clock inside tick away. Those books were more than just a library, Alice was certain of it. *Active decisions become patterns*—Madeline had said as much herself. In that library were patterns, arrangements that Alice did not yet recognize. Somewhere among those ordered shelves was the hardback book that Madeline had found in the park, the one that had led her to Gregory. Even if she'd gotten rid of Gregory's books, she would never cast away the one that had cemented their love. Alice needed to discover why this particular title had the power to bind them together. Once she understood that, she might begin to identify what Madeline required from another love, another story.

Alice stepped away from the library door, pressing the button on the woman's dress so her leg sprang back into place. The keyhole disappeared once more, but Alice knew what lay beyond it. She had to find that book.

10

Teachers

In the morning Alice awoke in a panic, uncertain where she was. She didn't recognize the white room, the eyelet comforter pulled snugly over her body, the diaphanous curtains rustling in the wind from the open window. The air smelled sharply of pine, absent of the salt and brine that normally greeted her each morning. It was unforgivingly cold. When she exhaled, her breath rose in a plume. She sat up, and her head pounded from too much sleep or not enough. She looked down at her bare arms, goose pimpled, her body hidden under a cotton nightgown that did not belong to her. A shiver seized her, and she rose from the bed to close the window. Then she dressed in the clothes she'd worn the previous day and followed the smell of butter downstairs to the kitchen.

Madeline's back was to the doorway as she stood over the stove, which gave Alice a moment to watch the old woman undetected. Perhaps it was the cavernous kitchen, but Madeline looked even smaller than she had the day before, childlike from behind, despite her sleek tuxedo pants, this time in emerald with a matching satin top. Her halo of white hair swayed slightly as she attended to something cooking over a high flame. The varicose veins along her ankles and bare feet ebbed and flowed like streams.

Madeline turned to find Alice watching her and smiled. She clicked off the burner and deftly tossed two sandwiches onto plates resting on the counter. "I was beginning to wonder if you'd passed in your sleep, and I was going to find a corpse in my guest room."

"What time is it?" Alice asked.

"Lunchtime," Madeline said as she swept past Alice with the plates. "You missed the morning walk. Fear not, the woods will be there tomorrow and the day after that."

The two women ate lunch in the dining room where they'd first broken bread.

"So, my Alice," Madeline said, taking an enormous bite. "Do I have the pleasure of your company today, or must you be getting back to your other stories?"

Alice had nearly forgotten about her other stories. When she was with Madeline, the others all seemed pedestrian in comparison to the challenge that lay before her here in the woods.

"I can stay for a bit," Alice said. "Could we, would it be possible to visit your library again?"

"I suppose." Madeline smiled, exposing bits of parsley caught between her two front teeth. "But one of the great indulgences of growing old is requiring a siesta. Can you entertain yourself for an hour while I recharge?"

Madeline hoisted herself from the table and stood shakily. Her eyes were glassy as she stifled a yawn. Alice let the old woman lean against her as she guided her upstairs to her bedroom.

Inside, the walls were decorated in poppy wallpaper, a mix of blooming orange flowers and buds not yet opened. Alice pulled back an eyelet comforter identical to the one in the guest room and lifted Madeline onto the four-poster bed, surprised at how light she was. Madeline rolled toward Alice, her eyes tightly closed. Her skin looked deathly pale against her bright red lipstick, which had not smudged or faded during their meal.

"I'm so lucky to have you," she said then rolled away, and immediately began to snore.

On the mahogany nightstand beside the bed sat a shallow ceramic bowl holding two gold wedding bands and the antique brass key. Alice slipped the smaller of the two bands onto her ring finger where it fit snugly. Madeline's hand rested on top of the comforter, her fingers adorned with gold and turquoise, knuckles too large to remove those rings, too large ever to wear her wedding ring again. This seemed more final than Gregory's death, the way Madeline's body had aged without him.

Alice returned the ring to the bowl and reached for the antique key. It was heavy in her palm. She stared at the monogrammed initials on the bow, the long stem. It would have been so easy for her to abscond with the key and let herself into the library, but she had no reason for subterfuge. Madeline had promised to take her there later that day. Alice returned the key to the bowl and pulled the comforter around Madeline's frail body. As she brushed the old woman's hair from where it had matted against the side of her head, she noticed wrinkles along her forehead Alice hadn't spotted before. She fought the urge to bend down and kiss Madeline's temple.

Alice tiptoed out of the room, stopping at the library door, giving the heart-shaped knob a quick brush of her fingertips. While she desperately wanted to go inside, not so much so that she was willing to betray Madeline. Their trust was nascent and delicate, not yet solid.

Instead, she ventured downstairs to clean up the remains of their lunch. When she entered the dining room, their plates had been removed, the table wiped clean. In the kitchen, the pan Madeline had used to grill their sandwiches was drying in the rack. The splatters of butter had disappeared from the stove. It was as though Madeline had never cooked the meal to begin with, and Alice wondered if she really had. This house had a way of serving itself and its occupants. She didn't understand it, and no amount of questioning would allow the house to make sense. It existed by its own rules, was governed by its own reality. Alice decided she was happy to bear witness to it.

With nothing else to do, she wandered into the parlor where she let Currer hop into her lap, stroking the sleek black fur that was silkier than Agatha's. The grandfather clock ticked away above, each minute dragging on as she waited for Madeline to rise. Eventually, as it became clear that waiting was nothing more than stalling, she stood and braved the threshold to the guest room to write.

On the wicker desk a stack of paper and ink pen awaited her. Alice preferred to write on a computer. The keyboard could keep better pace with her mind. But a notepad was all she had, so it would have to do.

Hand poised above the cream stationery, she tried to concentrate. Her mind remained vast and empty. She willed herself to get something down, even a single word. But writing one word required some intuition of what might follow. Something as simple as *the* was not just an article. It had to be complemented by a person, a place, a thing. Alice pestered her brain to come up with anything at all, a rambling stream of consciousness that might guide her into Madeline's story. This was not Alice's way. She needed an image, and before that a clear message, a lesson her client needed to learn. Alice wasn't sure what she had to teach Madeline. She was beginning to suspect that instead the old woman had much to teach her.

Frustrated, Alice lifted the pen from the page, where it had left a blue blot, spreading like blood into the shape of a heart.

Even the page itself was taunting her. She threw the pen across the room, where it skidded against the floor and hit the wall with a gentle thud. The sound echoed, collecting intensity as it vibrated through the room and down the hall, as though she'd dropped a dumbbell or a hammer, something much heavier than a pen. When the banging quieted, the floorboards creaked and a steady patter of feet approached the door.

"Alice, is that you? Is everything alright?"

"Yes," Alice said, embarrassed. "I just—I dropped my pen."

She opened the door to find Madeline rubbing her scar as she stared into space, hair askew, like a child who'd just woken from a fitful nap.

"I was having the most wonderful dream and—" Madeline stopped. Alice watched the dream wash over her, brightening her eyes, as she continued to stroke her scar. Alice understood that the dream was about Gregory, that it was a gift and a curse to get to see him again.

Madeline excused herself to freshen up. When she reemerged a few minutes later, she was wearing a pale blue paisley blouse and navy pants. It was at once the outfit of an old woman and timelessly fashionable. Anything comparable would look absurd on Alice, not so much because of her youth, but because the confidence of the woman wearing the outfit made it exude style. Alice tugged at her own ill-fitting shirt, wondering if it was the hunched body beneath it that caused it to gape and pull.

Madeline headed for the library, producing the key from her pocket just as she arrived at the door. Alice did not realize that she was hovering until the old woman turned and her face was mere inches from Alice's. That close, Alice could see just how deep the scar was, how it collected dry skin in its red crevice. It was still raw, even though the accident had happened a decade ago.

Madeline held Alice's gaze until the girl motioned toward the quote on the doorplate.

"It's Rilke," Madeline explained. "*Love consists in this, two solitudes that meet, protect and greet each other.* Some translations have it as *solitudes that border, protect and greet each other.* I prefer a meeting to a border, even if I suspect *border* is more accurate to Rilke's intention. It was Gregory's favorite quote."

She slipped the key into the lock and twisted as the number on the dial shifted to seventy. She turned the heart-shaped knob and pushed the door open. "After you."

The air in the library hit Alice, both stale from closure and warm from the fire, already blazing. It smelled piquantly of paper and sweetly of wood laced with a hint of cinnamon and clove.

Madeline settled into her chair in front of the fire and lifted a copy of *Great Expectations* from the table, flipping to somewhere in the middle of the thick book. As she read, Alice wandered around the library. She let her fingers graze each title, noting that Madeline had every D. H. Lawrence novel and yet the six copies of *Women in Love* were nowhere near the fourteen editions of *Lady Chatterley's Lover*, the third most repeated book, as far as Alice could tell, after *Little Women*, for which Alice counted eighteen copies near the fireplace, and *Wuthering Heights*, a copy gracing every shelf.

"Searching for something in particular?" Madeline glanced up from her book.

"Not really." Even to Alice, these words sounded like a lie. "I'm just wondering, it's a very peculiar collection."

Madeline slipped her bookmark into the Dickens novel, set it on the table, and crossed her arms. "It's idiosyncratic to be sure. Shouldn't a library be particular to its owner?"

"Yes, but why, for instance, do you have so many copies of *Little Women*?"

"Not a fan?"

"I'm a fan. I have one copy at home." Her father had given her the book when she was ten, and they'd read it together each night. Alice laughed as he put on different falsettos for each of the sisters. When they finished the book after a few months, Alice insisted they start over again. This lasted until she outgrew bedtime stories. It was the only book they read together. After he died, Alice never read the novel again, although she had every scene memorized.

"You have eighteen copies. Why does anyone need so many copies of *Little Women*? Of any book, really." It wasn't like they were first editions, collector's items.

Madeline studied Alice, who suddenly felt ashamed for her brashness. "It's correlative," Madeline said at last. "The more copies I have, the more the book has seeped into my bones, the more it has taught me about love."

Some shelves were packed with obvious romances like *Pride and Prejudice, Emma, The Princess Bride*, some held books like *Anna Karenina* and *Madame Bovary* that were more about heartbreak than about love. Others that didn't seem to be love stories at all.

Alice lifted the single copy of *The Plague* by Albert Camus off the shelf, waving it at Madeline. "How is *The Plague* about love?"

Madeline barely glanced up from her novel, as though she was bored by the line of questioning. "Every story can teach you something about love, for what is life without love? But you must not confuse the love in books with love in life. Books can prepare you to love, but they aren't the same as loving."

Alice had no response, so she returned *The Plague* to the shelf and kept searching. "Why don't you keep authors together?"

"All of my Margaret Atwood books are together," Madeline said. Indeed Atwood's books, everything from *The Robber Bride* to *Oryx and Crake*, occupied two shelves in the middle of the library.

"Sure, but why aren't they by the door, filed under *A*? Why aren't your books alphabetized?"

"Why should they be?"

"It makes it easier to find what you're looking for."

"I can always find what I'm looking for. I know where every book is filed."

"How?"

"Because they are arranged chronologically."

This was patently untrue. *Atonement* and *Remains of the Day* appeared just before *Vanity Fair.*

"Perhaps we have different definitions of chronology."

"They are chronological to me, to how I read them." Madeline sat back in her chair and picked up *Great Expectations*, seemingly finished with the conversation.

The shelves suddenly told a story Alice had not seen before, Madeline's evolution as a reader, insight into how her mind worked. She had gone through phases: magical realism, gothic and southern gothic, briefly noir. It was such a perfect way to arrange a library that Alice couldn't believe she hadn't thought of organizing her own books that way.

Which just made clearer to Alice the one book she needed to find, the book every other book gravitated around.

She continued to walk around the library, letting her fingers linger on each title, wondering if she would feel the energy of the book when she encountered it. When nothing sparked, she asked, "And is the book you found in the park, Gregory's book, is it somewhere in here too?"

Madeline did not look up from Dickens. "I already told you that's private."

"Why?" Alice asked.

"Because love is always a private conversation between the people in it. You cannot read the book and understand us. You will never understand us."

"If I don't understand the love you lost, how can I understand the love you want now?"

"Alice, you're the writer. You should have confidence in your gift. You should not be afraid of a challenge."

"I'm not," Alice said, annoyed. "But I don't know how to help you."

It felt surprisingly freeing to admit this until Alice saw the expression on Madeline's face. It was cold and stern.

"A book will not assist you with that. You can't read our book and understand us. That's not why I asked you here." Madeline stood and brushed at her pants. "I think that's enough for one day." She walked to the door, and held it open, forcing Alice to follow. From there, Madeline whisked her down the hall, down the stairs, and toward the front door, which she also held open, expecting Alice to leave. Alice hesitated. It would be so easy to storm off, to take her beastly old car down the mountain, to forget about this place, about Madeline, her love library, the story Alice couldn't write. Instead Alice's feet remained fixed to the floorboards. Madeline cleared her throat, motioning with her eyes for Alice to leave. The old woman's frustration just made Alice more resolute.

"No." she said. "You asked me here to write you a story, and I'm going to do it. But you need to help me. You need to make me understand why, after everything that has happened to you, the tragedy, why you want to fall in love again."

The frustration fell from Madeline's face and she looked sad suddenly, sadder than Alice had seen her. "I don't know if I do," she confessed, "I want to believe that I still can."

This was the source of her problem, why she'd been unable to write Madeline a story.

"Well," Alice said, "let's figure it out together."

11

International Stationery Day

In late June, when Alice arrived at the bindery to collect her first batch of finished books, there were real live customers in the store. On her past two visits, she'd never seen another patron. Now four people browsed the paper goods, their arms full of journals, wrapping paper, and overpriced pens. One woman twirled a strand of blond hair as she asked Duncan if he could bind her a journal in gold-plated leather. Another interrupted them to see if he had any chartreuse ink. "It's my favorite color," she giggled, although Alice couldn't tell what was funny.

"Did you put an ad in the paper or something?" she asked when Duncan finally found a moment to retrieve her books from behind the counter.

"Maybe it's international stationery day?" Duncan posited.

"Is that a thing?"

"There's a day for everything else, why not stationery?" He

handed her one book to inspect. Alice turned it over. Her customers were right to want red. Everything about this book screamed love.

"It's perfect," she said, causing him to blush. The pride he took in his work made him someone else, someone bashful, someone he'd been before his heartbreak. Alice felt a pang of sympathy for this version of Duncan, for his loss, for how much happier he must have been.

Duncan piled the books into a Willow Bindery tote bag. "Figured you had graduated to the VIP clients who get their books delivered in a tote. Just bring it with you when you come back to get the next batch. VIP or not, I only have so many totes to go around."

"I will guard it with my life," she teased.

"Let's not get dramatic," Duncan warned, raising an eyebrow.

Alice held out the flash drive with the next batch of books, four this time. She'd cut back to one catering shift, which allowed her to complete two to four stories each week. With the steady income from her stories, she did not need to keep catering, but she wasn't prepared to quit. She felt indebted to Caroline, who had given her a job when she desperately needed it. And it was a good safety net so she didn't have to rely entirely on her writing, which seemed reckless to Alice, even though the requests kept coming, the stories kept pouring from her, most of the time anyway.

Even if she committed all her energy to writing, she could not keep pace with the waitlist. Each story, she was coming to learn, had its own timeline. Some were swift, the entire process, from meeting the client to uploading their story for Duncan, occurring in the space of an afternoon. Most took longer, even when the clients were not evading her. The more she studied her clients, the more she realized that while people's problems were obvious, they were also nuanced. Not all low self-esteem was the same. Not all loneliness had the same tenor. Often weaknesses were also strengths; they just needed to be reimagined. As with any skill, she was honing her craft.

After twenty-nine stories, she was getting better at plot and characterization, at writing stories that were uniquely suited to each of her clients, so much so that she was fairly certain they would not be able to share the stories with anyone, even if they wanted to. Alice never questioned the visions she got for her stories. She followed them wherever they wanted to go, across as many words as they needed to arrive at some unpredicted conclusion. Once she reached the end, she never read over her stories, which truly made her feel like the vessel, not the architect.

The woman who had asked for the chartreuse ink held up a note card and waved it at Duncan. "Can I order a box of these?"

Duncan nodded at Alice as he excused himself to see which cards she meant. Alice watched for a moment as he inspected the card and told the woman that if she wanted to order them in bulk, he could give her a discount.

The woman giggled as though he was making her a different kind of proposal. "I'm a party planner, and I think I need you on speed dial."

"Isn't everyone on speed dial these days, with numbers saved to cell phones?"

This got her laughing even harder. Duncan looked over at Alice, who shrugged.

"Happy Stationery Day," she called as she headed toward the door. This caused him to smile. He had an array of smiles, she was coming to learn. This one was new, wider, exposing deep dimples on both cheeks.

"Same time next week?" he called to her before she walked out. It took Alice a moment to realize that he meant to pick up her books. While she was touched that he was turning their exchange into routine, it disappointed her that the routine was solely about other people's love stories.

As Alice stepped onto the sidewalk, she glanced back through the picture window and watched the woman continue to chat with Duncan. He looked up and saw Alice, rolling his eyes quickly before returning his attention to the customer. Alice wasn't aware that she was smiling until her cheeks started to hurt. Her chest tightened. Her stomach grew nauseated as she recognized her body's cautionary responses to getting in too deep. Much to her dismay, she found herself desiring Duncan.

This discovery should not have been so alarming. She was attracted to men all the time and knew how to detach desire from relationships. What alarmed her was that since she'd begun writing her stories, she'd unconsciously divided men into two categories, clients and potential suitors for her clients, leaving herself no room to be attracted to any of them. Now, here she was, her body warning her to back off. Their fingers hadn't even grazed as Alice's books exchanged hands, much less intentionally touched. She was getting completely ahead of herself, something she never did, yet she felt it clearly throughout her body, the need to be protective.

"Well?" Gabby asked, leaning up on her elbows on the massage table. Her bare torso and perky breasts were exposed when she looked over at Alice, who remained supine, her body tightly cloaked under the sheet, only her head angled toward her best friend. "What's so bad about getting ahead of yourself?"

Gabby subscribed to a weekly massage the way women in the fifties got their hair done every Friday. It was her therapy, spiritual as much as physical. Alice got a massage once a year, just enough to remember why she didn't like them. Her body always stiffened as she anticipated where the masseuse's hands might land. Once they were rubbing her, every inch of skin animated like a pressure point. *Relax*, the masseuses would tell her, shaking out her arm to make it go limp. Alice had assumed she was relaxed. The fact that she wasn't only made her tense up even more.

"That's half the fun of falling for someone," Gabby continued, "letting your mind get ten steps ahead, imagining everything that could happen between you. Occasionally it happens in real life, and then it's glorious." Gabby lay back down, nestling into the headrest. Obviously she was not the right person to talk to about Duncan. She was too in love.

"I'm not falling for him," Alice protested, wishing that their masseuses would arrive already and put an abrupt end to the conversation. They were at a salt cave spa, Gabby's latest obsession. In addition to walls fabricated from large rocks of pink Himalayan salt, sandy granulated salt covered the floor. The air was infused with microscopic salt particles that Gabby insisted she could feel breaking down the toxins in her lungs. Oliver was supposed to be getting this couples massage with Gabby, but inspiration had struck him that morning and he couldn't tear himself away from his jokes. "Who knew I'd have so many artists in my life," Gabby had said when she called to ask Alice to take his place at the massage table.

"You mean you won't let yourself fall for him," Gabby corrected. "Okay, let's imagine a hypothetical scenario where you and Duncan date. What's the worst thing that could happen?"

Alice was about to remind her of all the times her body had revolted during a relationship. It was too much stress for her system. Her constitution wasn't made for it. It was like a food allergy. Gabby hated this analogy. "You aren't allergic to love," she'd argue, "you're afraid of it."

Alice did not present this familiar refrain to Gabby. Instead she positioned her head into the cradle, which offered her a view of the sandy salt floor. She breathed in the iron- and calcium-rich air and thought of Duncan, his array of smiles, how he seemed to be two men at once, cut in half by the kind of heartbreak Alice never let herself experience.

"He's still getting over his ex-wife," Alice said. She told Gabby what she knew about the ex's cheating, about how he had to leave his work, his home, start over somewhere new. "Even if I wanted to, he isn't ready. He's too broken."

"Okay, so maybe it's a rebound thing. That's more in your wheelhouse anyway, isn't it?"

Alice didn't want to be his rebound, a fling, a diversion. The knots in her stomach intensified. So much for the calming powers of halotherapy. The massage hadn't even begun yet, and already every tendon in her body clenched. Besides, she wasn't even sure Duncan was attracted to her.

"Well, that's easy enough to figure out," Gabby said, sitting up and exposing her entire body, indifferent to her nudeness. Alice wondered what it was like, being that comfortable with your body. She was fine being naked in sexual situations. Otherwise, she'd made an art of taking off her clothes without showing an inch of skin, even on a massage table where she was conspicuously naked.

"Take a pen—" Gabby mimed bringing a pen to her lips, chewing on it slightly as she smiled and giggled. "Just flirt with it a little and see what he does."

That was what the customers in his shop did, and Duncan found it inexplicably strange. Plus, knowing Alice, she'd probably bite on the pen too hard and end up with a face covered in blue ink.

"Or casually mention that you're hungry. If he suggests grabbing a bite, then you know he wants to spend time with you."

"He's not going to leave his shop to have lunch with me."

"Why not? Even sexy bookbinders have to eat."

"You're really enjoying this, aren't you?"

"That goes without saying. Or, Alice? Maybe you could just go with your intuition here. You've gotten good at understanding love. If you're this nervous about it, there's something there. For both of you." Gabby lay back down, burrowing into the table. Before Alice could respond, the large wooden barn door slid open and two masseuses walked in, their feet crunching audibly on the salted floor.

During the massage, Alice was more relaxed than usual. She was too distracted by Gabby's comments to pay attention to the digging into her flesh. Sure, Alice was learning about love, the relationships that grew out of it. Those relationships weren't merely attraction or longing. They were about a mutual desire to be together. Alice knew, as certainly as she recognized the recoiling in her stomach, the acid in her throat, that neither she nor Duncan wanted what came with love.

When the massage was over, she leaned up from the table and said, "It's not going to happen."

Gabby opened and closed her mouth, wanting to argue but realizing when to stop. "Come on," she said, standing up and finding a robe beside the table. "My body's too depleted of toxins. Time to restock it with wine."

Alice followed her friend out of the cave into the dank hall, the air heavy with minerals. She could sense disappointment emanating from Gabby, from herself too. It was terrible, feeling this way. Her desire for Duncan was out of her control, but it wasn't something she could act on. She believed what she'd said. Duncan was too fragile. Even if she was ready, he wasn't. She needed to protect both of them.

12

Meet, Protect, and Greet Each Other

Alice returned to Madeline's a few days later with a newfound determination to figure out what Madeline needed in a story. The women spent the morning strolling among the trees. Madeline's legs looked spindly beneath her hiking shorts. Alice was surprised they could hold her up let alone endure the long walk.

Upon returning to the house, they had a continental breakfast on the back porch, followed by an extended visit to the parlor downstairs, where their conversation faded as they settled into their respective books, *Great Expectations* for Madeline and *The Portable Dorothy Parker* for Alice because Madeline could not believe, was borderline disgusted, that Alice had never read Dorothy Parker. At lunch Madeline swallowed a fistful of pills that made her nauseated. Alice helped a queasy and sleepy Madeline to her room for a nap before retreating to the guest room, where she tried in vain to write. Part of her still hoped that inspiration might strike before she knew why she was writing, but even if Madeline was different from her other clients, Alice's gift was not. She could not trick or cajole it into submission. Without recognizing what Madeline needed, no image—and thus no story—would come to her.

When Madeline roused again, her hair was matted in some places, frizzed in others. She looked pale and was confused that she'd fallen asleep even though it was part of her daily routine. They took to the woods again, where the mountain air added color to Madeline's complexion, energizing her enough to make it through the rest of the afternoon until dinner, a meal as resplendent and overabundant as the first one they'd shared, followed by Alice's favorite jam cookies in the parlor until Madeline absolutely could not keep her eyes open a moment longer and Alice helped her upstairs and into bed. Again, as Alice lifted the old woman's body, frailer after just a few days, she lingered over the ceramic bowl with the two gold bands and the antique key. Throughout the day, Madeline had said nothing about the library, so neither did Alice, although it was constantly on her mind. She could not understand why Madeline, who otherwise seemed eager to talk about Gregory and their love, would not divulge the title of the book that brought them together.

Alice watched the rise and fall of Madeline's chest beneath the eyelet, listened to the gentle snoring that accompanied it. Was it her imagination that the orange poppies on the wallpaper were closed more tightly now than they were before, that they were all buds? The grandfather clock ticked away, reminding Alice that time was passing while everything around her remained still. Her eyes flitted to the key, so unassuming on Madeline's bedside table. In the hour Alice sat with her, Madeline did not stir. Her sleep was heavy and deep. Absolute.

Alice stared between Madeline and the key. Before she could

overthink or lose her nerve, she leaned over and lifted it out of the bowl.

She walked down the hall, hand extended with the key. In her brief perusal of antique locks, she learned that Madeline's was a Victorian detector lock, designed to be impenetrable with a complex series of levers and trips that made it impossible to pick. The woman gracing its front was no mere decoration, her parasol pointing to a dial that was no mere marvel of Victorian technology. It was carefully calibrated so that each time the lock was turned, the dial shifted up one number, announcing that the door had been opened or closed. In short, if Madeline was keeping track of the number on the dial, she would know that Alice had been inside her library without permission.

Fortunately, strengths were also weaknesses. The counter that provided confidence that the door had been undisturbed could also lie—if it was reset. The dial went up to one hundred, then started again at one. All Alice had to do was flip the key one hundred times, and the parasol would return to the original number. Madeline would never realize that the door had been unlocked, the library infiltrated.

Alice pressed the button on the woman's dress, slipped the key into the hole then hesitated. Could she really do this? The clock seemed to tick louder, as if urging her to be decisive. She took the key out of the door and pressed the button that kicked the leg shut. She could not betray Madeline, but as she walked toward Madeline's bedroom to return the key, with each step it felt less like a betrayal than a necessity. To Alice, the true betrayal was promising to deliver a story and being unable to finish it in time. She simply had to find the book Madeline was hiding from her.

Standing before the library door once more, her heart pounded so forcefully she could feel it in her temples. Her hands were the wrong combination of clammy and shaky to unlock any door, particularly one with a finicky antique detector lock. On her first attempt, she didn't even get the key into the lock before it fell to the floor with a clang. Alice froze. When the house remained quiet, she tried again, her entire arm wobbling as she aimed for the hole.

"Relax," she chided. She shut her eyes and counted her inhalations and exhalations, encouraging herself that she was doing this for, not against, Madeline. The peachy darkness of her eyelids calmed her nerves in a way looking directly into the keyhole did not, so she kept her eyes shut as she slipped the key into the lock. Then the real journey began.

One, two, three... She locked and unlocked the door until the dial was ninety-nine rotations ahead, just short of the full one hundred it took to reset the device. That way she'd only need to turn the key once when she left. With the woman's parasol pointing to seventy, she reached for the heart knob. Before pushing the door open, she scanned the Rilke quote inscribed on the brass plate. *Two solitudes that meet, protect and greet each other.* It was from one of his letters to Franz Xaver Kappus, the titular young poet. In the letter, Rilke spoke of love as Alice had never heard anyone speak of love before, as a product of solitude and work. He condemned young love as false, a surrendering of one's loneliness. The point of love was not to meld into one but for both to maintain their solitude, and then to meet, protect and greet each other.

At first all Alice did was stand in the doorway, breathing in the intoxicating scent of paper and fire, which was blazing in the empty library. Alice wondered if there was a mechanism on the door that triggered an igniter to light the fire the moment it was opened. She would not put it past Madeline.

She braved a few steps into the room, stopping at its center, twirling her feet in tiny circles, and staring, awed at the presence of Madeline's books. Part of her did not expect the library to exist without Madeline in it, yet here it was, all her books, all their lessons on love, including the ultimate love story, the one that connected Madeline and Gregory.

Alice did a lap, running her hands along each book until she was certain she'd touched every spine on the shelves. Then she sat down by the fire and waited. It happened almost instantly. A warm flood through her body. A homecoming.

Once the rush calmed, Alice investigated the books. When none of the editions of *Jane Eyre* set the house on fire, when *Their Eyes Are Watching God* did not call down a hurricane, Alice grew confident that she was meant to be here. She began to look for Madeline and Gregory's book, certain that she would recognize it when she saw it.

One of the earlier shelves in Madeline's library contained *As I Lay Dying*, *A Very Easy Death*, *The Painted Veil*, and several other books that at their core were stories of death. Alice gasped. Was this when Gregory died? Several shelves over to the left were rows of what could only be considered eternal love stories. This must have been the period when Madeline met Gregory. She searched the titles, waiting for one to announce itself.

There was a single copy of each title on this shelf. In Madeline's story of how they met, she'd mentioned five copies of the book that connected her and Gregory—the one she found in the park and the four she left notes in—all of which Gregory had bought. It would stand to reason that she would have those five copies in her library, even if she'd given away all of Gregory's other books. Those copies didn't belong to him but to them as a couple. So, Alice was looking for a book with five copies. And not just five copies—five of the same edition, a detail Madeline had noted in her story. Madeline had also mentioned that Gregory could not reread the title in a single day. Somewhere on these shelves, were five copies of a long book, all the same edition.

Five was a common number. In science. In the Bible. In Madeline's library. She had five identical copies of several lengthy books. Alice picked up one of the five copies of *Tinker Tailor Soldier Spy*, wondering what the novel had to do with love. John le Carré was her father's favorite author. When Alice was in middle school, the family had created their own book club. Paul chose *Tinker Tailor Soldier Spy* for his month's pick. He'd read *The Bridges of Madison County* and *Even Cowgirls Get the Blues*. The least they could do was humor him with the very foundation of modern spy novels. Maybe Alice was too young. She really did try. More than her mother anyway. At the end of the month neither had read more than a few pages. "It's just so dry," Bobby complained. "It's complex," Paul protested. Then her father said something about how he thought Bobby was more sophisticated than that and things erupted from there. It was one of the few times Alice could remember her parents fighting. After that, the family book club unceremoniously dissolved. They each settled into their reading preferences, medical journals and romances for her mother, fantasy and coming-of-age tales for Alice, and spy novels for her father. Alice still had her copy of *Tinker Tailor Soldier Spy*, the one her father had bought her for the book club, on a shelf in her apartment with the rest of his favorite books.

When Alice cracked open one of the five copies in Madeline's library, she was immediately struck by how engaging the prose was, how the narrative consumed her from its first moment. Yet it did not seem to fit with the story Madeline had told Alice about how she and Gregory first met. Reluctantly Alice slipped it back onto the shelf.

Sandwiched between seven copies of *Of Mice and Men* and two of *Flowers for Algernon*, Alice found five copies of *The Heart Is a Lonely Hunter*, all the same edition. Alice had read McCullers's novel in high school and had found it to be…sad. This was not a particularly astute reading of the novel, but it was how she'd felt. She had a hard time imagining that something so maudlin could bind Madeline and her beloved to each other. Plus, while hardly short, it wasn't a particularly long book. She kept looking.

In the far corner, a shaft of sun hit a gold-leaf mosaic design on the spine of a maroon book. Alice approached it, discovering five of those gilded spines, all reading, *The Wings of the Dove.*

She traced the embossed title on the spine of one copy, then the next, stopping on the spine of the third book, which was broken in a few places, the edges of the pages yellowed from time. *People leave their marks on books*, Madeline had said, *more so when they love them. Spines get broken. Ink gets smudged. Books bruise like any other body.* When she took the book from the shelf, it was warm to the touch, as though it had just been held. It smelled like love. Alice didn't realize love had a smell. It was sweet and musty, ink and paper.

Alice had tried to read the novel twice but had never owned it. When she'd first attempted it in middle school, on the recommendation of her language arts teacher, she was far too young, the book far too long. When she confessed that she could not get through the first hundred pages, her teacher told her it was supposed to be difficult. This did not entice a fourteen-year-old girl devoted to books that were silly or suspenseful. In college, when she approached the text again, she still found it dense although not inscrutable. It was one of the rawest portraits of ruinous love she'd ever read.

Despite the ominous ticking of the grandfather clock, Alice was in no rush to leave the library, to stop reading. She was completely absorbed by "the game" as Henry James called it, the way the three protagonists were entangled, how Milly died but was forever there. Alice read so long her knees started to ache, so she leaned against the shelf, accidentally knocking over a candelabrum. She froze expecting it to make a crashing sound that would wake Madeline.

Only, the candelabrum didn't fall. It remained tipped at a forty-five-degree angle. The edge of the bookshelf was no longer flush with the bookshelf beside it but ajar. A seam of darkness appeared behind it. Alice dug her hands into the crack between and pulled the bookshelf door open.

13

The Library Within the Library

The hidden door opened wider as Alice tugged on it, emitting a plume of stagnant air. The enclosed area behind the bookshelf was completely dark. Alice reached for her phone in her back pocket. She had reception, although the screen did not display the time, just a strange error message. Alice tapped the flashlight on, its beam swallowed by the space. She pulled the door as far open as she could, using her hip to get her weight behind it. The door scraped the floor as it inched wider, swollen from time. Alice slipped through and stepped into the hot, breathless unknown. There was just enough light to see the shallow dimensions of the room, a closet really. It had no windows. The entirety of its walls was lined in books. Alice had never heard of a library within a library before. Would there be a book in here that led to another secret door, a library within a library within a library, until the libraries were so small Alice could not fit her pinky toe inside?

A string dangling from the ceiling made itself visible in the modest light. Alice pulled it, illuminating a spherical glass ball with one extremely bright bulb, blinding if you looked directly at it. The room erupted into a tapestry of color. Every book was a hardcover bound in bright leather. The books were all the same height, the same depth, varying only in width and hue. There were no titles etched into the leather spines, no names debossed along the cobalt, emerald, sunflower, violet, and crimson. The consistency of the books' sizes gave the shelves the orderly look of a decorative library, the kind where the pages of the books were blank or harbored secret compartments. Alice scanned the shelves looking for signs of age, violet faded to mauve, crimson gone cherry at the edges, cobalt frayed cerulean. All the books were in mint condition, seemingly new despite the mustiness hanging in the air.

Alice stepped further into the room and ran her fingers across the spines, expecting their tips to be coated in color when she pulled them away. They remained the peachy pink of her flesh, tingling with anticipation of all the stories behind the covers waiting to be read. Carefully she tilted a red book from the shelf, afraid a cage might fall from the ceiling and imprison her in a trap. Instead the book slipped forward like it was any other book.

At first Alice didn't understand what she was reading. The font was clear enough. Garamond, one of the most common. The story was about a woman whose job it was to feed the skeleton of a horse spread across a plush velvet blanket. Each day she offered the bones apples, hay, and carrots. Slowly the bones began to gather bits of decomposing flesh that formed muscles and tendons, eventually a coat. The mane was the last to grow, and when it did, it was thick and golden. Fully reformed, the horse stood and bowed its head so the woman could climb onto its back. Together, they galloped away.

It went on for pages, lengthy descriptions of the mane, the sensation of the wind in the woman's long, shiny hair as they ran. Alice slipped the book back and selected another at random, a blue book about a carpenter who was building a house on a hilltop for the woman he knew would find him there. He built and built and built, hoping that once he had the perfect house, the perfect woman would follow. He kept building until the house was too big for its foundation and it toppled. Rather than giving up, he built again. And again. And again. The same thing continued to happen. Bigger and bigger until the house was nothing more than debris.

Alice flipped through a yellow book and a green. Another red. Two purples. She consumed the words like a silky wine. The stories all had the same lofty tenor, the same generous prose. Prose that was so much better than Alice's writing. Prose that simultaneously made her feel like she should never try to write again and like she had to race back to her desk. The stories were bolder than Alice's, the metaphors both more obvious and more significant. The lessons wiser. As Alice compared these stories to her own, overwhelmed by an intoxicating mix of impostor and aspirer, she realized—Madeline had the same gift Alice had. She was also a love scribe.

Alice sank to the floor, staring at the colorful shelves. This was why Madeline hadn't told Alice the title of the book that united her and Gregory. It would lead Alice to her hidden library. It would expose her secret. Every thought returned Alice to this bald fact: Madeline was a liar. Alice could not write an honest story for a liar.

There were too many questions coursing through her, none of which she could answer from the cold floor of a secret library. Her knees cracked as she stood. She scanned the shelves a final time, making sure everything was returned to its exact position. Then she slipped through the crack in the wall and carefully pushed the door shut, surprised that the library outside felt and looked the same as it had before she discovered Madeline's secret, right down to the blazing fire.

In the hall, she could see that it was still night. She turned the key once to reset the detector dial, clicked the woman's leg back into place, and made her way to Madeline's bedroom to return the key. Alice had no idea what she was going to do about her new discovery. Part of her wanted to storm into Madeline's room and start screaming, but this would not be productive. Madeline would not be cowed by an attack. Besides, there was the unfortunate truth of the key Alice had taken, the act of betrayal it signified. How quickly Madeline would shift the conversation to Alice's deceit rather than her own. No, the only way to deal with someone like Madeline was to play on her terms, to continue to visit her and get to know her, acting as though she had not discovered the secret library. Except now, Alice would have the upper hand. Now she would be in control. Alice could lie too. They could both be liars. Maybe their lies would cancel each other out, leading Alice to the truth. Maybe then she could write Madeline a story.

14

Cassoulet

Now that Alice knew Madeline's secret, she watched her like one would watch a spider, inching too close. She wasn't sure what she was looking for, so she studied Madeline's every gesture, every word. Madeline did not seem to notice, which confounded Alice. How could someone so insightful on the page, someone whose allegories were as unique as every walk through the woods, not intuit that something had changed between them? It charged the room. Raised the temperature. Echoed in the ticking of the grandfather clock. The presence of Madeline's secret sat heavy on Alice. Each moment Madeline did not confide in Alice, she continued to make it impossible for Alice to write her a story.

Over cassoulet, as Madeline prattled on about the first time she had tasted the dish in Paris, Alice's lingering hope soured to anger.

"You never forget your first cassoulet," Madeline said, swallowing a mouthful of beans. This was Alice's first cassoulet, and she was entirely certain that as promised, she would not forget it either.

Madeline continued to eat greedily. "Gregory and I were in Paris. It was one of those biting nights when winter's fingers massaged the cold into our skin."

Winter's fingers. No matter how many stories we tell, no matter how many sentences we wield, we rely on the same words woven together in new patterns, familiar phrases that reveal the truth. Everything new is old. Every phrase we assemble we've already spoken. Or written.

Winter's fingers. A green book, about a man who tries to capture the sun for his frozen love. Instead of thawing her, it incinerates him. It was one of Madeline's more violent stories.

Madeline continued to detail her first cassoulet, oblivious to Alice's watchful eyes. "Finally I couldn't take it anymore. The cold was too much—" She pounded her stomach. "A hunger that needed to be satiated."

A hunger to be satiated. A yellow book about a man who could not be satiated, he just ate and ate and ate until the entire world was subsumed by his stomach.

Each time Alice recognized one of Madeline's phrases, she felt a tremor of rage, as if Madeline was taunting her.

"You could see the Eiffel Tower from the windows of the café, so I asked if we could sit in the front, even though the cold bled through the windows."

A cold that bleeds through the windows. A purple book. A girl whose lover is the cold and she follows him from south to north, chasing winter the way the elderly chase the sun.

"Alice, are you listening?"

Alice smiled. "More than you know."

Madeline held her wineglass up to the light, and Alice could see her own reflection contorted in the crystal. "I shivered through the wine. My teeth chattered through the pâté. It wasn't until the oversized porcelain bowl was placed at the center of the table, cooled just enough to eat, that I finally warmed up. I remember the porcelain was a milky white without any stains, which contradicted the boiling red stew inside. Surely the tomato, the duck confit, would leave some remnants on that blank canvas of a bowl, but they hadn't. It was defiantly clean."

Defiance. A blue book, a red, a green. Everything was defiant. The sun, memory, shadows, love. Love was the most defiant act of all, at least in Madeline's books.

"I'm sure my memory has made the dish grander than it was. It was my first cassoulet. And it was the only time we went to Paris." Madeline brought a bite of beans and duck to her mouth and shut her eyes as she slurped it from the spoon. The corners of her mouth twitched, and Alice could see her eyeballs moving behind her closed lids as the cassoulet brought her back to that first one in Paris.

"When was that?" Alice tried to sound merely inquisitive, but she could hear the tinge of accusation at the end of her question. "When were you in Paris?"

Madeline chewed indulgently, savoring the memory of each bite, in no rush to answer Alice's question. "Our honeymoon," she finally said, and Alice realized that she'd already known this would be the answer.

"I didn't realize you were married." Madeline had never described Gregory as her husband, though it explained the wedding bands.

"We weren't." Madeline tilted the bowl to extract the remaining beans congealed to the side of the porcelain. "Not in the conventional white dress and chapel sort of way. We made vows to each other, but they were our own. You have to write your own love story. You can't borrow someone else's."

Alice laughed despite herself. The gall of this woman.

"Isn't that why I'm here?" she asked, emboldened. It was a

glorious feeling. One largely unfamiliar to her. "To write you a love story."

"And how is that going? You've been to see me what, five times? You've said nothing of your progress."

"You can't rush inspiration," Alice said.

"Procrastination by any other name is still stalling. I don't have all the time in the world, you know."

"What exactly, may I ask, is wrong with you?" Was Madeline even sick? Had anything between them been honest or real?

"You can ask." Madeline wiped her mouth. "That doesn't oblige me to answer."

"Why wouldn't you tell me?"

"Because you'll see me differently when I do, and I don't want that."

This Alice believed. But she was already seeing Madeline differently.

"Now, shall I continue my story, or do you have any other loosely veiled accusations you'd like to lob my way?" Madeline spooned the very last of the broth from her cassoulet. "Gregory's family was quite religious and never would have settled for anything other than a church wedding. We didn't want anyone telling us how to consecrate our love, so we chose to do it in Paris, a city that had already heard every type of love story. It was perfect, even if Gregory's mother didn't speak to us for a year."

"Our families will never understand our love, so it's best that we save it for ourselves," Alice said, reciting Madeline's words back to her. They were from a blue book about a couple whose mothers were battling to create the perfect wedding for them, so they absconded with their love, marrying in Vegas with an Elvis impersonator crooning in the background. Alice had liked that line about love and families.

"There are all sorts of reasons to be greedy with love." Madeline wiped the orange residue from the cassoulet off her lips, evidently not recalling her own words.

"I've never wanted to save love for myself." Alice had not meant to divulge something quite so true, but she was angry, and anger was its own energy source. It made us say and do things we shouldn't. Much like love.

Madeline's eyes softened. "How can you do what you do if you don't want love for yourself? A chef must try her own food. A teacher must first be a student. A writer needs to read. You need love to give love."

You need empathy, sure. Compassion. Intuition. Those qualities could be cultivated without love.

"Love is a distraction from what I do," Alice told her, meaning it.

The pity on Madeline's face suggested that she was not convinced. How could she be? Love was her gravitational pull. Her life revolved around Gregory. He fueled each of her stories. Perhaps Alice's and Madeline's gifts were not so similar after all.

"Oh, child," Madeline said.

Alice did not want to be pitied, especially not by a woman who was lying to her.

When Alice helped Madeline to bed that night, she did not plan to return to the secret library. What would she gain? She had already discovered the book that linked Madeline to Gregory. She already knew that, like Alice Meadows, Madeline Alger was a love scribe.

Alice pulled the comforter around Madeline's shoulders, watching her disappear beneath its pillowy white. The old woman's hair was thinner than it looked. Alice let her fingers lace Madeline's corkscrew curls before traveling down to her cheek, the deep impression of her scar. Madeline murmured at the touch but did not stir.

Alice shifted her gaze toward the poppy wallpaper which looked different than she remembered, the orange petals falling from the stems and collecting by the baseboards. There was no denying that Alice cared for this woman, that despite her secrets, her perplexing house, Alice wanted to help her.

Just then, a bright light struck Alice's eye, refracted by the brass key in the bowl on Madeline's bedside. It seemed to be coming from the window even though it was dark outside. Alice shifted the bowl to angle the reflection away from her face. Before she could question whether it was the right thing to do, trespassing not just into Madeline's private space but her private thoughts, she clasped the key and made her way down the hall. The library, Madeline's stories, was the only way she could get to know the woman better.

Alice tugged at the candelabrum, dislodging the hidden door, and slipped inside. She spun on her feet deciding where to begin. As she twirled faster, the colors began to blur into an exotic landscape. Purple valleys. Green skies. Blue deserts. Red lakes Alice wanted to dive into. When she was sufficiently dizzy, she stopped spinning. She was facing the thin strip of empty space where the door remained open. She decided to start reading there, on the set of shelves beside the door. Tall as Alice was, the top two shelves were out of reach even when she rose to the tips of her toes. The swelling of the door prevented her from opening it enough to bring in a chair, so she let those books be. There were plenty of other stories to occupy her time.

On the third shelf from the top, Alice pulled down a blue book about a man who grew blueberries that brought people love. As word got out, his crop could not keep up with the demand, and the poor man found himself surrounded by people who resented him for the berries he had not produced. The tale was stylistically and narratively simpler than the red book about the pile of bones that turned into a horse or one across the room about a child whose soulful voice made everyone fall madly, destructively in love with her. It terrified her, so she never sang, not until she met a woman she wanted to love in return, and at that point her voice was so rusty it cracked on the first note, making the woman recoil in disgust. The books in this library, Alice realized, were organized similarly to those in the larger library, by when they were written.

The evolution of the stories from one bookshelf to the next confirmed her hypothesis that they were in chronological order. As she made her way through the library, there was a notable transition in the writing from novice to proficient to expert.

One story in particular, about a woman and a gold-braided necklace, was so heart thumping Alice could not put it down. The necklace was a birthday present from the boy who grew up next door to her, the boy she had always loved. While they were too young to call it love, that didn't stop it from being limitless. Then his family left abruptly one day. She never discovered what had happened to him, and she felt his loss acutely. She cared for others, but not as purely as she had for that boy from childhood. The necklace remained clasped around her neck, a noose of hope that one day she would see him again. When one lover removed it, her head fell off. He quickly hooked the necklace back on again, and her head reconnected. She searched for the boy, now a man, to release her. She needed to be able to remove the necklace without falling apart. So she returned to the beginning, to the day he left, searched her memory for clues until she located something he'd said that morning, how if anything happened to him she should—

A chill like a feather tickled the back of Alice's neck. The words before her bled together. She remained focused on the page, hoping her body was playing tricks on her. When the feeling didn't go away, she slowly spun around to find Madeline standing at the threshold of the secret library, watching her with a twisted smile.

"Alice, Alice, Alice. I didn't think you had it in you."

15

A Million Dollars

"I can explain," Alice said. She was still holding the green book about the woman cursed by her childhood love. She desperately wanted to know what happened to her, if she ever found the boy, if this was a tale of love restored or heartbreak.

The old woman crossed her arms, leaning back against a wall of books. "By all means."

Alice clutched the book to her chest. "I didn't… I wasn't trying to… I never thought when I started looking through your library that I would discover… I only wanted to discover the title of the book you found in the park that…" Sentences began and ended, blending into each other until Alice landed on the truth. "I just wanted to understand you."

"So it's my fault that you decided to sneak into my private space without permission? That you stole my key to do so?"

Holding the book against her body gave Alice strength, Madeline's strength. "I wouldn't have needed to take the key if you'd just been honest with me."

Madeline nodded, seemingly pleased that Alice had not backed down. She began to walk around the room, stopping occasionally to survey the shelves.

"I haven't seen these in a decade." She pulled a book down, pet the smooth blue cover. "They've changed since I last saw them."

"What do you mean, changed?" Alice asked.

"Most of them were red, for one thing." Madeline returned the book to the shelf, walked over to a thin purple book, went to pull it down, then hesitated before touching its spine. "None of the books were purple." The word sounded as bruising as its color.

"Books don't change color," Alice said.

"Just like they don't make people fall in love?" Madeline walked toward the break in the wall. "Come. I can't stand to be in here." She shuddered and retreated to the main library, expecting Alice to follow.

Alice put back the book she was holding and scanned the shelves wistfully, fearing this might be the last time she would be in this space, this house, these woods. There were so many more books for her to read, so many more ways for her to learn from Madeline.

In the main library, Madeline was already sitting in her chair before the fire. She motioned to the secret door. As Alice pushed the bookshelf shut, she felt the finality of the act. She leaned against the wall, bracing herself for the old woman's wrath.

Madeline studied Alice with an indecipherable expression on her face.

"I'm sorry," Alice said when the silence became too much.

"Are you?" Madeline asked, genuinely curious.

"Yes?" Alice said.

"Alice, you shouldn't apologize for things you aren't sorry for."

"I betrayed your trust."

"True, but if you're honest with yourself, you don't regret it. You would do it again."

"I would," Alice said quietly, her gaze fixed on one of the overlapping Persian rugs, its geometric eight-point flower heads vibrating slightly like they'd caught hold of a gentle wind. She braved a glance at Madeline. "Are you mad?"

"On the contrary, I'm impressed. Although your stealth could use a little work." Madeline laughed. "Did you really think I didn't notice you leaning over me in bed? And, Alice, the door to this library is mahogany. While you may assume a light wood is quiet, it whistles. The detector lock is not the only way I know if my library has been infiltrated."

"If you wanted me to find your books, why didn't you just show them to me?"

"I never said I wanted you to find them. I wanted to see if you were capable of it. Now I know that you are."

"So you were testing me?"

"Oh, don't look so put out. Life tests us all the time. That's how we learn who we truly are."

Alice walked across the library to the empty chair beside Madeline's and sat down. The fire danced wildly. The flowers on the rug continued to sway. She had so many questions about this house, how a fire was always blazing the moment they stepped into the library or the second they walked through the door from the dining room to the parlor downstairs, how the grandfather clock set the beat to the house but didn't keep time, how the flowers on the rug had suddenly started moving, how the dishes were surreptitiously cleared, the fridge always stocked even though Madeline never appeared to leave her home, how the food waiting on the patio could still be hot after it had been outside for longer than Alice knew, the drinks still cold, how the poppy wallpaper ebbed in and out of bloom. These were practical curiosities. Alice had something essential to ask her.

"So you're a love scribe too?"

"I've never heard it called that, but yes, I have the gift."

"Are there others?"

"You're the first I've learned of. That's why I had to find you, to get you to stop."

"Why would you want me to stop?"

Madeline's eyes remained fixed on the fire as she lifted her bony index finger to point to a shelf on the far side of the room. "When Gregory was alive, I used to store my stories there. I was so proud of them. I wanted them displayed beside the books that had inspired me. The books that taught me to write. The stories that taught me to love. When I first wrote them, I bound them all in red leather. It was a little trite maybe, but I liked seeing all those crimson books, all the love I'd spread to others. At the time, I thought I had so much love I could give some away."

When Gregory was alive, Madeline was drunk on love. It was easy to believe that everyone deserved to be as happy as she was. Surely if everyone could love as much as she did, it would solve all the world's problems. When Gregory was alive, she was convinced she was doing something holy, something vital. Her clients reaffirmed this. The way they loved. The way they praised her. The way they sent her more people to help.

After Gregory died, there was emptiness. Unending swaths of time. Isolation so complete it became her companion. Still, the requests for stories persisted. People wanted love, even if Madeline knew she could no longer manufacture it for them. She had no love left in her to give.

When Gregory was alive, she could control her stories. Her love was so strong that it held a firm grip on others'.

After Gregory died, her hold on her stories weakened. The stories were only beginnings. As Madeline let go, they started to have their own endings.

"I'll never forget that first call. Maggie Sims." Madeline tapped the small end table between their chairs. "I had a phone back then. I was sitting here when I answered it. She was so hysterical I could barely make out what she was saying. There was only one reason for that kind of despair. If I'd known why she was calling, I wouldn't have picked up." Her husband, Luke, was forty-two. A marathon runner. A pescatarian. The paragon of vigor. His heart had a congenital defect that was not diagnosed until, walking hand in hand with Maggie after a particularly satiating dinner, he fell to the sidewalk never to stand again.

"I wasn't sure what she wanted from me. I don't think she was either. I'm not sure she wanted anything. So I cried with her. I told her about Gregory. We shared our grief.

"When I hung up, I stared into the fire, collecting my thoughts. I glanced over at my books, hoping they could offer me a modicum of comfort too. Amidst the crimson spines, one was a deep maroon, so dark it nearly looked black. It was swollen, like it was waterlogged, and it began dripping down onto the books beneath it, the dark red collecting on the floor like a small puddle of blood. I didn't dare touch it, didn't dare wipe the blood or whatever it was off the floor. I knew it was Maggie's."

Madeline shivered despite the warmth from the fire.

"After that, there were a few more calls. The endings they told me were as different as the lovers the stories had summoned. Not all were deaths. John found his wife in bed with his cousin. Rachel came home to discover her husband's closet emptied, a note on the kitchen counter saying, *I can't do this anymore.* Jean suddenly and irreversibly could not look at her partner of twelve years without being completely repulsed. And Liz, Liz simply felt nothing anymore. She no longer cared about her husband enough even to hate him.

"I watched each of their books change. John even showed up at my door, called me horrible names, cursing at me like I was the one who had cheated. In a strange way it felt good to be punished like that, to feel something besides grief. When I returned to the library, there was one emerald spine amidst the red.

"Rachel's book turned while I was on the phone with her. I watched it fade from crimson to rose to quartz then to blond, canary, lemon, until it became a bright sunflower yellow. Her voice was so calm. Reasonable. If I could write a story to make her husband fall in love with her, couldn't I also write her something to make him pay for abandoning her, a hex so he would regret every day he spent without her? I told her that if he was willing to give up on love, he was already cursed. She seemed to accept this, but I'll never forget what she said after that. 'Still. I'd like to see him pay for wasting so much of my time.' She'd been one of my earliest stories.

"With Liz and Jean, their books turned before I found out what had happened. I walked into the library to find another yellow book, a second green, and I spent the day waiting for the phone to ring. After that I stayed away from my library for a week. It was torturous to abandon my books like that, but I was afraid to look at them, to see how they were shifting. Sure enough, when I grew brave enough to return, even more books had changed color. And there was a new shade. Blue.

"I don't know what I was hoping to accomplish. At the sight of all that color I panicked, grabbed as many books as I could carry, and stuffed them into the alcove Gregory had built behind the wall. I kept carrying armload after armload, feeling some of the books warm to blue and others cool to yellow while they were in my hands. I didn't look at them. Just kept stacking them, shelf after shelf, until none of them remained here in the library." She pointed to the secret doorway. "I shut them up and haven't looked at them since. I thought, if I didn't see them, if I didn't hear how the relationships they spawned had ended, I could pretend everyone was still happily in love."

"Maybe they are," Alice said. "Some of them at least."

Madeline shrugged, unconvinced. "It doesn't matter. Even if some of my couples are blissfully happy, I brought pain into people's lives. I should have known better than to interfere, especially when it came to love."

Alice wanted to ask Madeline about her gift, about how she could give it up, lock her books away, pretend none of it had ever happened. Only Alice was stuck on one detail that seemed monumental to understanding what had happened to Madeline's gift.

"What do you think it means, that they changed color?" she asked.

"I don't know, and I don't care to find out. And I don't want you setting your sights on investigating it either."

"Then why tell me this story? Why let me find your books?"

"What we do isn't magic, Alice. It isn't even a kindness. It's madness. A curse. I can't let anyone else get hurt."

"Well, I've never been in love, so you don't have to worry. I can't lose control over my stories like you did. They can't change."

"Can't they? If you've never been in love, how can you be certain that's what you're giving people?"

Alice hesitated, having not fully formed the thought before saying it aloud. "You never wanted me to write you a story, did you?" The disappointment in her voice surprised her more than it did Madeline. "I can't believe you lied to me."

"I did no such thing," Madeline said. "I never said I needed you to write me a story. I said I needed forgiveness, and I do. I brought you here because I seek forgiveness, forgiveness for all those people whose lives I meddled in, lives I made worse. I can't undo the harm I caused, but I can stop you from causing more harm." She walked over to unlock the safe in the corner of the library. Inside was a gold ledger and a check binder. Madeline pulled out the binder, extracted a pen tucked behind her ear, and began writing. "How much will it take to make you stop? You charge what, five thousand a story? Four? Three? Oh, Alice, please tell me you don't charge less than three. The toll writing takes, the time. And what do you write, a story a week?

Would a hundred thousand cover it? Two?" Madeline continued to rattle off absurdly high numbers until she landed on, "A million? Will you put an end to all this for a million dollars?"

"Madeline, stop. That's ridiculous. I'm not going to take your money."

"Why not? You take your clients' money."

"In exchange for a service. You're trying to pay me off. I'm not going to stop helping people. Not for a million dollars. Not for any amount of money."

"Weren't you listening to my story? You aren't helping people, Alice. You're playing God. That never ends well."

"All I'm doing is writing people stories that make them see themselves in a new light so others can see them that way too. So they can be loved for who they truly are." This was perhaps her most succinct characterization of her gift. She'd have to remember it, to employ it in the future. "Besides, so many of the books in your library are still red. They didn't change color or have whatever metamorphosis you think destroyed their love. They are the same as you left them."

"You don't know that."

"Well, let's see then." Alice jumped up and bounded toward the candelabrum. As she tilted it down to spring the door open, Madeline shouted, "Alice, don't!" Alice stormed in, reached for a red book at random, and returned to Madeline's side, plopping the book in the old woman's lap. "Open it."

Madeline gripped the chair's arms. "I'm not going to touch that book."

"Fine," Alice said, reaching for it. She flipped to the first page and began reading. *"Low tide was her favorite time of day. When the water retreated, the beach exposed its secrets. Starfish—"*

"Stop!" Madeline cried. "Please don't make me listen to that crap."

"Do you remember this story?"

"Of course I remember it. I remember all my stories. That

was Abigail—" Madeline walked over to the safe and retrieved the gold ledger. She scanned pages, ran her finger down a list until she arrived at the name she was searching for. "Abigail Herkowitz. Such a lonely girl. I didn't imagine she'd ever find love, even with my story."

Alice typed the name into her phone and found a Facebook profile for the woman. She aimed it at Madeline. "Is this her?" Madeline nodded, so Alice scrolled through the profile. "It says here she's been married to Tom Walker for the last fourteen years. They have three children. And she's an immigration lawyer. That doesn't sound like someone who has time to be lonely."

Madeline grabbed the phone from Alice's hand and looked at the profile. "That's the man she met after reading my story."

"See, her story didn't fail."

"Just because she's still married doesn't mean she's still in love. A loveless marriage can be worse than one that ends," Madeline said.

Alice rested the red book on the table. "Let's find out then. Abigail lives in Santa Monica. We can be there in two hours. Let's go see her, find out if she's in love."

"What's your master plan, to knock on her door and ask if they're happy?"

"No." That had indeed been Alice's plan. More or less. "When people are in love, you can feel it. It charges the air. If they're in love, we'll know."

"Why does it matter to you anyway? Why is it so important to you that my stories didn't fail?"

"Because there are people I care about that I've written stories for. I need to believe, I need to know that I've given them something pure. Lasting."

"And barging into Abigail's home and finding out if she's in love will somehow prove that?"

"No, but it's a start."

"A start to what?"

"To proving to you that you brought goodness into people's lives. That you don't need forgiveness."

Madeline studied Alice, who did her best to look confident. In truth, she wasn't clear about what it would accomplish to meet Abigail, but Madeline needed to see that not all her love stories had ended badly.

"Fine," Madeline said. "But I'm driving."

They barreled down Stagecoach Road, past the tavern onto CA-154, where Madeline spun the steering wheel and pumped the gas pedal along the bends like she was playing a video game. Seventy-five minutes later, they pulled to a stop in front of an orderly ranch house with a lawn too green to be real grass.

"Well, what's the plan now?" Madeline said.

They could pretend to be going door to door, collecting signatures. Or Alice could feign looking for her lost dog. She could pretend to be a graduate student doing a study on households in the area. As she debated whether any of these scenarios were believable, a minivan pulled into the driveway. From the back, three preteens tumbled out and barreled toward the door. A woman climbed out of the passenger seat and shouted to them, "Shoes off. I don't want to see any mud on my new rug." They waved her off as they raced inside.

Madeline gasped. "That's Abby." She slunk down in her seat so as not to be seen. Abigail hadn't noticed them. A man stepped down from the driver's seat and threw an arm around her shoulders. She looked up at him, her eyes softening as he leaned down and kissed her. Their steps perfectly aligned as they walked to the door.

Once they disappeared inside, Alice turned to Madeline. "Okay, you can't tell me that couple is not in love."

"Because they kissed? Kisses lie all the time."

"Eyes don't lie. And I saw hers. They were practically sparkling."

"Look who's suddenly a hopeless romantic."

"Shouldn't you be excited?" Alice pointed toward the house. "That is a successful love story."

Madeline nodded in a way that intimated acceptance, if not the relieved satisfaction Alice was hoping for.

On the drive back, Madeline's chaotic driving was no match for the formidable traffic. As they inched toward the mountains, Madeline spoke first. "I appreciate what you're trying to do, Alice. Really. But I saw the pain I brought into others' lives. I know the pain I brought into my own. A hundred love stories aren't worth a single broken one."

It took them over three hours to return to the house. By that time Orion and Gemini were watching over them from the cloudless sky above. Madeline said she was too tired to eat and disappeared into her bedroom. Alice scavenged the fridge for a plate of leftovers and carried it upstairs to eat in bed. When she arrived at the top of the stairs, she hesitated. The door to the library was ajar. For the first time Madeline had left it open.

16

The Wager

"Didn't I make myself clear yesterday?" Madeline asked when she found Alice sitting cross-legged on the floor of the secret library. Piles of red books cascaded around her. Her limbs twitched from lack of sleep. Madeline's eyes surveyed the shelves, her expression turning from irritation to horror as she saw how Alice was rearranging her books.

They were organized by color, a few shelves for red, a wall each for blue, green, and yellow, a mere shelf for purple. The only exceptions were the top two shelves, which remained out of reach, and thus a random pattern of color. There were 2,398 books in total: 207 red, 734 yellow, 834 blue, 596 green, and 27 purple—at least for the moment. Every time Alice assumed she had them all organized, a book would turn. Red to yellow. Green to blue. Blue to green. Yellow to purple. Alice couldn't deny there was something ominous about those few purple books. Their rarity, for one. Also, they emitted a sorrowful moan every time she touched one. The other books had an energy to them too. The blue books were slightly warm like a tepid bath. The yellow were chilled like a window on a winter morning, but nothing compared to the purple books. To the best of her ability, Alice kept her distance from them.

"What have you done?" Madeline whispered.

"Don't worry, I'll put them back exactly where I found them. I want to show you something." Alice hopped up and pointed to the shelves of red books. "I've started to go through them one by one and find the couples in them." Alice tossed Madeline a red book, forcing her to catch it. "That's Sarah and Rickie D'Angelo. They just renewed their vows after twenty years. And—" she tossed another book "—this is Lydia and Marvin Winterson. They moved to Hawaii, where they surf every day." The pile Madeline was holding continued to grow. "This is Emmalee and Vincent Brown. They're cowriters in Hollywood. In their Oscar acceptance speech, they said that they don't know where one of them ends and the other begins."

Madeline stroked the cover of Emmalee and Vincent's book. "They were one of my favorite couples. Vincent had been in a fire as a child. His arms were badly scarred, and he had trouble using his left hand on account of the keloids on his skin." Madeline absentmindedly stroked her own scar. "He thought no one could love him because of what he viewed as his deformity. He was a lovely man, inside and out. I knew he was wrong. So I wrote him a story about a woman with a birthmark on her shoulder blade in the shape of an archipelago. That way he'd always have a place to live. They met at a wedding, under a full moon. Emmalee was the bride's sister, and Vincent worked with the groom. He almost didn't go. He was tired of celebrating other people's love when he never seemed to find love for himself. During the ceremony Vincent noticed Emmalee in the same distant way he noticed all the pretty bridesmaids, dressed in unflattering gray satin and diaphanous shawls to ward off the night chill. As she was walking up the aisle at the end of the ceremony, the shawl slipped. Vincent caught it. When he looked up to give it to her, he saw a birthmark on her back, a series of spots arranged like tiny islands."

Madeline looked longingly at the book, and just as she seemed to accept that some of her stories had brought people the love they desired, the book started brightening, turning lime green before darkening to the emerald of so many other books in the library. Madeline screamed and dropped it. Unthinkingly, Alice clutched the old woman as they darted out of the library together, thudding the door closed behind them.

"Did that just happen?" Alice asked, panting as she leaned against the bookshelf beside Madeline.

"I told you." Madeline hugged herself.

Once Alice's breath slowed, she pulled the candelabrum from the shelf.

"Stop that!" Madeline said. When Alice tugged the door back open, she begged again, "Please, Alice, don't."

"I refuse to be afraid." Adrenaline coursed through Alice. When she stepped back inside, the now green book sat on the floor as quietly as any closed book. She lifted it and brought it out into the main library, where Madeline had traversed the room, standing as far from the hidden door as she could. Alice shook the stubborn green book. "We need to find out what it means that it changed color."

"Why? If their love has changed in some way, we can't change it back."

"Maybe not," Alice said, "but that's like saying if someone is sick with an incurable disease, we shouldn't try to understand what's wrong with them."

"I'd rather be living in ignorant bliss."

"That's not fair to the people you'd leave behind."

"Haven't you learned by now that there's no one? I wouldn't be leaving anyone behind."

"You'd be leaving me behind," Alice said with emotion in her voice that surprised her.

Alice moved away from the shelf and found her phone on the table. Madeline watched her from across the room as she typed, tapping the screen a few times before she read, "*The Hollywood Reporter* just announced, 'Longtime writing partners and spouses Emmalee and Vincent Brown are divorcing. Emmalee is returning to her maiden name, Weiner, and is starting her own production company as a solo writer. *When the talent in a partnership is imbalanced, it inevitably leads to jealousy and irreconcilable differences. The same is true of a marriage*, Weiner explained about her decision to leave her husband.' Yikes." For some reason, Alice couldn't help but chuckle.

"You find this is funny? They were so in love. To see it come to this, there isn't a thing funny about it."

"I know." Alice fell silent. She didn't consider Madeline responsible for the end of their relationship. Still, there was no denying that the relationship was over, that this was an example of a love story that ultimately failed.

"Why green?" Alice asked.

"What?" Madeline glared at her like she had asked a very obvious question.

"Why do you think the book turned green? Why not yellow or blue or—" Alice could not bring herself to utter *purple*. "Or orange even? Why aren't there any orange books or white or pink? You don't think it's strange?"

"Alice, have you not noticed that everything in my house is strange? I like it that way."

Since she first arrived, Alice had been questioning the uncanny ways of the house, wondering how everything worked, suspecting secret mechanisms she couldn't see, possibly even magic. It had not occurred to her that the house responded to

Madeline. That it was strange because its matriarch was strange. That it could not be any other way. These were questions for another time, distractions from the root of what she had to prove to Madeline.

"The green must mean something," Alice insisted.

"It hardly matters. If it's green, brown, if it ignited in flames. Their love is gone."

Alice's eyes widened. "You think a book could do that, spontaneously combust?" She wondered what that would do to the love inside.

"A book can do anything."

At last they were in agreement.

Madeline snatched the green book from Alice. "These are not your stories to peruse however you'd like." She disappeared briefly into the secret library, returning with the gold ledger. "Did you break into my safe?"

Alice couldn't tell if the prospect infuriated or impressed her. She wanted to say yes, just to see how Madeline would respond, but Alice was done lying.

"You left it out."

Madeline sat down by the fire and flipped through the pages. "I remember when Gregory bought this for me. I was so proud of my stories, all those people I was helping. As I entered each name, each completed story, I thought I was committing them to the eternity of the page. Now I look at this and it's a different kind of record."

Alice stood beside her and leaned down, looking at all those names neatly scribed into the book beside the first line of the story. Like Alice's tales, Madeline's books did not have titles.

Alice motioned to the ledger. "May I?"

To her surprise, Madeline consented, relinquishing it like a pliant student. Alice slipped into the chair beside Madeline's and paged through the large gold book.

"There are hundreds of books that are red, so I figured I'd

look into those couples and see if they were still together. So far, all of the ones I've found are."

Alice flipped to a page in the middle of the ledger, settling on a name. "Jane Janvey, for instance."

Madeline's eyes flitted toward the ceiling. "Everything about her was an alliteration. She wore blue blazers. Plaid pants. Neon-painted nails. A Wisconsin woman. A lustful lover. I could never tell if she did this intentionally or if she couldn't help herself. Either way, it was genuine. I had to help her find someone who was genuine too, someone free of affectation."

"Well, you must have," Alice said, "because she and Philip Lipson are still together."

Madeline smiled at the consonance of his name.

Alice read from the list of names, rattling off other clients' that she'd located online. "They are all in lasting relationships. I know that doesn't mean they're happy or madly in love, but they're still together and they're still red."

"A few red books are hardly representative."

"Then let's make them representative. We can find each of these couples, every book in your library."

"And what will that accomplish?"

"You said you're looking for forgiveness, right? Well, you assume that you've done something that requires you to be forgiven. I don't think you have. I think revisiting the people you helped will show that."

"And what about all those books that have turned, the ones that aren't red?" Madeline insisted, obstinate as ever.

"That's what we need to find out," Alice argued. "The colors must mean something. We can go through them and figure out what each color means. Then we can see which stories failed and why. If we understand why they failed, maybe we can learn to write better stories. Stronger stories. Fail-proof."

"You make it sound so easy."

"It won't be easy, but we can do it together."

As Madeline continued to stare warily at Alice, something shifted in her posture. She sat up a little taller, looked a little more robust. "If I go along with this madness, if I help you, will you make me a promise? If we look through these books and see how much more sadness than happiness I've brought into the world, will you vow to stop writing your stories? If I prove to you that it's a curse not a gift we cast upon people, can you give it up?"

"If it comes to that, then yes. I will stop writing. And what about you, will you make me a promise? If we realize that there's still so much love in these stories, will you help me write one for you? Will you let yourself be loved again?"

"Oh, Alice." Those two small words, flush with their infinite meanings. "I never wanted to find love again. I'm not worthy of it."

"You are," Alice said. "And I want to give it to you. I want to help you believe in love again."

It felt a touch silly, but she held out her hand for Madeline to shake. The old woman paused a moment, then slipped her palm into Alice's.

17

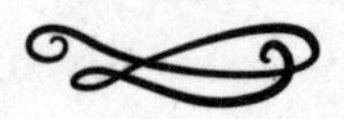

Same Time Next Week

It became their mantra. Their parting phrase. Their tradition. Also, their boundary. When Duncan motioned goodbye, voicing those familiar words, Alice heard a door shutting to remain closed until she returned to his shop the following week. She trained herself not to think about him during the time between, as though he only existed within the walls of Willow Bindery & Paper Goods. Since she'd never seen where he lived, never witnessed him interacting with cashiers at the supermarket, waiters at restaurants, bartenders, it was easy to imagine that he never did these things, that he was just a bookbinder. Easier anyway. The brain was a powerful muscle, one Alice couldn't control as well as she hoped.

She found her mind drifting to Duncan at inopportune times. With clients. At her desk. When she was asking guests if they preferred red or white. By late July, Santa Barbara's wedding season was in full swing. With Alice's cutbacks to make time for her writing, she was exclusively working those events. Often she didn't even realize her thoughts had wandered from the demands of these over-the-top receptions to Duncan until she stood a moment too long at a diner's side with a bottle of each.

"I said white," a man corrected as she began to fill his glass with red.

"I told you I don't drink," another snapped when he saw a full glass before him, as though she was intentionally taunting him.

As she sat across the table from a client who was delineating a very long and very unsuccessful dating life, she found herself visualizing Duncan's strong, ink-stained fingers, wondering what they might feel like if they stroked her hair.

"Alice? Did you hear me?" her client asked.

"What?" Alice sprang back into the present. "Sorry. I just started to get an image for your story. Do you mind repeating yourself?" That was proving to be a good lie.

When she and her mother watched a movie they'd rented, Alice saw Duncan's emerald eyes, during a close-up of green eyes on screen. This made her think of Duncan's hair, the way its deep brown accentuated those eyes, which made her wonder what his hair would look like if it wasn't fashioned in a ponytail, how it might change his face, which made her think of his mouth, his voice, the way he said his own name, *Duncan*, and the way he said hers, *Alice*, until the credits rolled and she had not registered anything else about the film.

Bobby clicked off the TV and looked over at her daughter, misty-eyed. "Wasn't that wonderful?"

"It was." Which happened to be true, even if Alice wasn't talking about the movie.

After the film, Bobby walked Alice to the door. In the past, Alice might have stayed over in her childhood bedroom, not wanting to make the late-night drive back to Santa Barbara. In the past, they would have driven down the hill the next morning to their favorite Mexican bakery, where they would have been in no rush to part, no rush to begin their day. But Alice had stories to finish, and Bobby had plans to meet Mark for a sunrise beach walk.

"You could join," Bobby offered.

"I've got a lot of work to do," Alice said because it was easier than admitting she felt an unfamiliar, inexplicable distance from her mother, one she'd created by bringing her love.

"I'm proud of you," Bobby said, tucking one of Alice's curls behind her ear. "I hope you know how much I admire what you're doing." Alice waited for another lecture about saving some room for her own heart, the *I just wish* preamble, followed by all the ways Bobby hoped Alice would open herself up to love. Instead she smiled at her daughter and nodded encouragingly. This seemed to be all she wanted to say, all she expected of Alice.

Each week Willow Bindery was a little busier, customers breeding like flies. When the bell on the door rang, Duncan glanced over annoyed until he saw that it was Alice and his face opened into a smile that she'd come to interpret as his smile just for her. He gestured that he'd be a minute.

She waited by the register, watching as a brassy girl held a pen too close to his face.

"Is there any way you can have these pens inscribed with my name? I'm a writer—" she brushed her red hair off her shoulder as she said this "—and the other writers I share an office space with are always stealing my pens. I want them to say, *Fuck off unless you're Jenni Malone*."

"That's a lot of words to put on the side of pen," Duncan said.

She guffawed, a laugh that bordered on hysteria. "You're funny," she said. "How about just my name then?"

Duncan went to his desk for a pad of paper. "If you leave me your number, I'll call the company and see if they do special orders."

She blushed as she wrote her number down. "You'll call?"

"Either way," Duncan promised. Jenni waved each finger individually as she said goodbye.

When Duncan turned his attention to Alice, something in her chest caught, a subtle nausea roiling in her gut.

"Do they put something in the water in Santa Barbara?" he asked. "People here are too much. Maybe it's the sunshine?"

"You know you're not actually funny. She was flirting with you," Alice felt compelled to explain.

Duncan picked up the pen Jenni had left on the desk and rolled it in his palm. "Nah, she was just being California."

"Yeah, California flirting."

Duncan began crooning an off-key version of "California Dreamin'," with the substitution of *flirtin'*. Alice covered her ears, which had the opposite of its intended effect, encouraging Duncan to sing louder. She expected everyone in the store to look embarrassed for him, if not mildly disgusted, but they must have been hearing a different octave than she did. Faces of all complexions flushed with desire, lured by Duncan's pitchy siren song.

From across the room they heard a loud crash as a bespectacled man collapsed on the floor, a plastic rack and a bevy of cards threatening to bury him. Apparently he'd been leaning against it too forcefully, trying to eavesdrop on the conversation between Alice and Duncan. When Duncan skipped over and reached out to help him, the man looked away bashfully. He insisted he was fine, flustered, not letting go of Duncan's hand, and began to apologize profusely, offering to pay for the broken card rack. It wasn't broken, just dislodged from the shelf, and Alice helped Duncan reattach it. Once it was fixed and the cards restacked, the man nearly sprinted out of the store.

"You sure they don't put something in the water here?" Duncan asked.

There were too many bodies in the small space, raising the

temperature to slightly above comfortable. The majority of the customers were female, covertly eyeing Duncan as he wiped a sheen of sweat from above his upper lip. One girl locked eyes with Alice, looking disappointed, then turned away.

"They do. It's called love." Alice winked, reaching into her tote bag for the familiar cat thumb drive.

Duncan took it and placed it behind the counter, filling his arms with a stack of her red books.

"Your stories, milady." He bowed as he presented them to her. A stray piece of hair fell from his ponytail into his face.

Alice's face warmed as she took the books. Her stomach growled, loud enough to be audible above the ambient chatter in the store. Duncan raised an eyebrow.

"Did you skip breakfast this morning?"

Alice shrugged and her stomach growled louder, causing him to laugh.

"We'd better get you fed." He looked around the crowded store. "Can you give me ten minutes? I'll finish up in here and close for lunch."

"Oh, you don't have to do that," Alice said, even though the prospect of being outside the store with him excited her.

"Ten minutes." He followed her to the door, where she indicated that she'd wait at a bench across the street, before he flipped the sign on the door to closed.

Alice sat on the bench, remembering what Gabby had said about testing Duncan to see if he was interested in spending more time with her. Was that what her stomach was doing, unbeknownst to her, gauging his interest? Her hunger was quickly overshadowed by nausea. She wasn't ready for whatever this lunch was.

The customers slowly trickled out with their bags of journals and pens. It was a veritable meat market, if you could call it that when everyone was eyeing the same piece of meat. A half hour later Alice was so famished she'd grown lightheaded. At last Duncan skipped out of the store, exhilarated.

"Sorry," he called as he jogged across the street. "I know they say people on the West Coast are friendlier. Personally, I'd take a curt, genuine East Coast exchange over an insincere but cheery conversation any day."

"Well then, you shouldn't have moved to Santa Barbara." Alice meant this teasingly, but the smile fell from his face. This move hadn't been a choice, not entirely.

They walked a few blocks to a deli in silence. It was the first moment of awkwardness between them, one Alice had created. Perhaps this was a sign that she and Duncan weren't suited for each other, one that should have enabled her body to relax.

After they ordered at the deli counter and settled outside at a white plastic table with matching chairs, Alice broke the silence. "Why did you pick Santa Barbara?" she asked cautiously.

"Well, I wanted a city similarly sized to Portland, and I've lived my whole life in smelling distance of the ocean. I couldn't imagine not seeing the water every day. Anywhere on the Atlantic just reminded me too much of home." Home was Portland, a place he couldn't live anymore. Everywhere else was somewhere to harbor him. He'd been displaced by love. Alice was right to be cautious with him.

Inside, the cashier called Duncan's name, and he leapt up to get their sandwiches. He returned to their table on the sidewalk and handed Alice hers. She carefully unwrapped it.

"What about you, have you lived your whole life in Santa Barbara?" Duncan asked, taking an enormous bite of his baguette.

Alice shook her head, realizing how little they knew of each other. She pulled off a piece of her sandwich and tossed in into her mouth. "I went to med school on the East Coast."

Duncan coughed in surprise, spitting a small piece of ham onto the table. To Alice's dismay he picked it up and threw it into his mouth again. "You're a doctor?"

It was funny the way you could understand a person, their humor, their smiles, while knowing almost nothing of their biography. "No, I dropped out at the end of my first year. It was too much pressure."

"I dropped out of college when I was a sophomore. I've always liked to learn, but the institution, I hated the way it expected nineteen-year-olds to know exactly what they wanted to do with their life. The only thing I knew I wanted to do at nineteen was party. Hence the dropping out. Do you always eat sandwiches like that?"

"Like what?" Alice was not aware she ate sandwiches in any particular way.

"Like you're afraid of them. Like that—" He pointed to the piece she'd ripped off and was about to eat. "The entire point of a sandwich is that you can just take a bite." He gnawed at his baguette like it was a turkey leg at a Renaissance fair.

Alice popped the bite into her mouth. "I like eating this way. It's neater."

"Actually it's not. Look at that glob of mayo on your finger." She wiped it off, then tore off another piece. "I can't watch," he said, covering his eyes. "Tell me when you're done."

"I literally just watched you eat a piece of regurgitated ham off the table."

"I didn't do that."

"Trust me, you did. I watched it arc from your mouth onto the table. And then you ate it. Plus, you have mustard in your hair."

"No I don't," Duncan protested, running his hand through his ponytail until he located the dab of mustard. "Fine then," he said, holding out his sandwich, expecting her to tap her bread to his. "Cheers to us both being disgusting."

Alice laughed and made a point of taking a bite straight from her sandwich. Duncan nodded, impressed.

"I wouldn't have taken you for a party guy," Alice said, steering the conversation back to their pasts. She found herself wanting to know more about him outside the bounds of the bindery.

"Back then the prospect of free beer was enough to make me social."

Alice could tell there was a lot more to the story than he was telling her. Then again, there was a lot more to her story too. He hadn't pressed, so she wouldn't either.

"How'd you end up a bookbinder?"

"Well, I started off a carpenter. I mean, it's not something you stop being. I still am a carpenter. I was doing custom jobs when I met Maryanne. My ex. She had bought this hundred-year-old wood frame house. Gorgeous bones. Everything else about it needed to be refinished. It took me the better part of the year to fix it up. When she moved in, so did I." The expression on his face changed as he recalled the beginning, the glorious start before everything was ruined. "Her dad was a bookbinder. When I proposed, I wanted to hide her ring in her favorite book, but I've always loved books, and I just couldn't bring myself to cut one up. So I asked him if he could make a fake one for me to use, with the name on the spine, the cover image, except blank inside. I guess it was my way of asking for his approval. He said he wouldn't do it but he'd show me how to do it myself. After we were married, my father-in-law got Parkinson's and there was only so long he could keep binding. His sons weren't interested in taking over, and I just kind of fell into it from there. Now, after everything, I wish I could give it up, go back to restoring houses, but it's different. Carpentry was a craft. Binding books is an ethos, a lifestyle. For me anyway. It's just too much a part of me to stop, even though I'd probably be a lot happier if I did. Or maybe I wouldn't. I don't know."

"You still love her." Alice's stomach sank. She could convince her mind to lie, not her body.

"I don't think you ever stop loving people, not really. It'd be easier if you did. Even for Maryanne. She grew to hate a lot about me, but that's just another form of love. A tortured one." Duncan took the last bite of his sandwich and balled up the wax paper. "You done?"

Alice looked down at the massacred remains of her sandwich, and she nodded. He scooped it up to discard it. As he started walking toward the bindery, Alice trotted to keep up.

She didn't know what he was thinking, what she wanted him to be thinking. "I've never been in love," she admitted. "Not really. At least I don't think I have."

"It's kind of one of those things you know," Duncan said.

"I'm not good at relationships. I prefer to be alone."

Duncan looked pensive. "Those who can't do, teach. Or in your case, write."

It was such a perfect response that she wanted to hug him. Instead she nudged him with her shoulder.

When they arrived at Duncan's shop, there were a few people waiting outside. They looked up from their phones optimistically when they saw that he had returned before their eyes shifted to Alice with a mix of suspicion and derision.

"Well," Duncan said, "same time next week?"

Alice nodded and gestured goodbye. Before she could get very far, he called to her. "It's nice to have made a friend here."

Alice forced a smile. Even though this was all she could handle from him, having him declare it so definitively—it made her realize that all her angst over the last six weeks was in her head.

"Friends," she said, committing it to memory and to heart.

As she biked back to her apartment, she waited for her body to relax the way it did when she extricated herself from a relationship. The knots in her stomach, the poker in her chest, persisted. It wasn't fear she was feeling, it was disappointment.

18

The Divorcees

Together, Alice and Madeline tackled Madeline's books, finding the couples, determining their fate as best they could. They continued with the red books, which Alice had already been parsing her way through. Red seemed the safest place to begin. These were the stories that hadn't changed color, the ones they suspected were still full of love, the ones that could convince Madeline of all the happiness she'd brought into this world.

The two women investigated one book at a time, locating the client in Madeline's ledger based on the first line of the story, then finding out what they could from social media profiles, newspaper and website articles, public records. They were unable to reach the top rows of books, including Madeline's earliest stories, so they let those shelves be. Alice would have liked to peruse those earliest works, but since Madeilne did not begin to catalogue her stories until several shelves lower, when Gregory had gifted her the ledger, they had no way to cross-reference those clients anyway.

Among the red books Madeline was relieved to see her magnum opus. If a magnum opus could fail, there was no hope for any other story.

Madeline had loved the man for whom she'd written the story almost as much as she loved the story itself. Walter was a muralist, which meant he painted houses for money. He specialized in Victorians, their trim like lace that needed to be detailed by a careful hand. Most house painters did not dare touch Victorians. They were too complicated, too time-consuming, not worth the money, the clientele as fickle as the houses themselves. Walter had the focus. It was part of his problem when it came to love.

As a lover, Walter attended to women like he did to those delicate old houses, lavishing attention on their every aspect. It was too intense for most of the women he met, who did not want every inch of themselves explored, every comment they made dwelled upon. "Can't you just relax?" Walter was often told. He didn't want to relax. He didn't want a relaxed love. He wanted one that was complex and detailed. He wanted someone who needed care and maintenance, like the houses he painted. Unlike most people unlucky in love, Walter knew what he wanted. He just couldn't find it. That was where Madeline came in.

"Working with him was the closest I ever came to being unprofessional. I always fell a little in love with my clients, even the ones I didn't particularly like. You have to, to write them stories. Walter was different, though. The feelings were more real. It shouldn't surprise you that I would relish being explored." Madeline unconsciously petted Walter's red book while she recounted his story. "But I was already in love with Gregory. Since I couldn't have Walter, I was even more determined than usual to find him the exact right match."

It was fitting that he would meet that kind of woman on a job. At a house he walked by daily, one that caused him physical pain. The taupe paint along the fish scale shingles was chipping, the blues and purples of the stick work and garlands were so faded they retained nothing more than the suggestion of color. It was heartbreaking, seeing that kind of neglect, especially on a house so deserving of love.

When the call came in, Walter recognized the address. He happily accepted the job despite the owner's numerous specifications, which were not limited to the hues of paint he wanted for each balustrade and gable, the columns along the turret. Walter was to speak to no one in the house. If anyone should try to speak to him, he should ignore them. "We're a private family," the owner explained. So private that he would not give Walter his name, just wired him the money in advance from an untraceable account.

"I just have to ask," Walter said. "Why now?"

"Because the house deserves to be beautiful again," the man said. That, and the complaints the neighbors had filed with the city.

The job was as challenging as promised, requiring thin paintbrushes usually reserved for canvases. The wood needed to be sanded by hand before the paint would adhere to each beam, each stick. Every shingle required its own love.

At first it was easy to honor the owner's request not to speak to anyone, for no one ever appeared inside the house. As the days stretched into weeks, he felt the presence of someone within, saw shadows but never the person who cast them. Then, at the window along the turret, he caught a glimpse of blue-black hair just as it whirled out of view. Walter realized he was being watched. He liked the feeling that he was performing for the woman with the shiny black hair.

He left messages for her across the house, painted words onto the panels below the eaves. When at last he saw her, she was even more beautiful than he'd imagined with her opaline eyes offset by that straight jet-black hair. Each day she watched him from the turret. When he waved, she disappeared. The next day, she was back again. Slowly she grew bolder, unabashedly monitoring him first from the turret, then the bay window, then the front porch. She never spoke, and he said nothing in return, obeying the owner's rules.

When she finally did speak, her voice was bolder than he anticipated. He expected it to be willowy, that she would ask for help, that she needed a savior. Instead she was the one to rescue him.

"Her father found out that they were interacting and was furious." Madeline hugged the red book to her chest. "He was not a man to make furious. He had connections, if you catch my meaning. He devised a plan—one day when Walter showed up at the house, his henchmen would be waiting—but Esther got wind of it. She intercepted Walter a block from the house and they ran off together. As far as I know, they're still running."

"Only one way to find out," Alice said as she whipped out her phone and began typing with her thumbs. She stared at the screen, confused.

"What? What is it?"

"They're divorced." Alice let her phone drop at her side. Her eyes traced the shelves of red. "I thought the red books were stories that hadn't changed, that the couples were still in love."

"Let me see that." Madeline reached for the phone and read the divorce record. She began typing on Alice's phone, quickly growing frustrated and handing it back. "I don't understand how you all rely on these things. They're too disobedient."

"What are you trying to find?"

"An address."

"Why?"

"This is my magnum opus. I refuse to believe it failed."

It took Alice three clicks to locate two addresses in North State, one for Walter Peabody and another for Esther Peabody.

"They live across the street from each other," she said, noting the consecutive numbers of their addresses.

They were in the car and on the Peabodys' street a half hour later, passing several murals painted on the sides of commercial buildings, on garage doors, the cement bases of fences. Whirls of black hair. Braids woven into swans. Collections of blue eyes lined in violet that could only be described as opaline.

"Esther," Madeline said as her eyes lingered on an image of the woman's face painted on the side of a little free library.

Alice pulled up to the curb outside Walter's house. They needed to hear both sides of the story, for the full truth was likely buried somewhere in between. They decided to start with Walter because he was the one who had hired Madeline.

When they knocked on the door, Esther, her jet-black hair now streaked with white, answered.

"Yes?" Those opaline eyes blinked eagerly as she smiled at the two women at her door, one old, one young, both unknown to her.

"I'm sorry." Alice checked the addresses she'd found online. "I thought this was Walter's house."

Esther called over her shoulder to the dim hallway behind her. "Walt, there's someone here to see you."

He was slighter than Alice had imagined, with dark eyes and the strong forearms of a craftsman. He reminded her of Duncan, of his arms, his hands, muscular in places where Alice didn't know people could be strong. Walter gently massaged Esther's shoulders as he popped his head over her shoulder to see who was at the door. His face lit up.

"Madeline!" he exclaimed. "Is that really you?"

"Who else would it be?" she said acerbically but not without affection.

"Come," Walter said, "we were just about to make lunch. Essie's garden is bigger than mine, but she can't grow nightshades like I do."

Esther gave him a light shove. "Now you're going to take

credit for the angles of the sun? It's amazing," she said to Alice and Madeline, "what difference a stretch of road can make. My yard is always overcast. Here it's blinding."

The backyard was awash in warm sunlight, raised beds lining a stone patio. Alice and Madeline sat at the table, watching as Walter and Esther debated which tomatoes to pluck from the plants, which cucumbers were fully ripened. Once they'd collected their bounty, Esther carried the vegetables inside, using the apron tied over her skirt as a basket.

Walter sat beside Madeline, locked his hands behind his thick head of salt-and-pepper hair and leaned back on two legs of his patio chair. "This," he said, "is the good life."

"Aren't you divorced?" Alice asked.

"I am indeed." Walter smiled and picked up his feet, his chair thudding as it steadied on all four legs. "Going on fourteen years now."

Esther came back outside and placed a large bowl of salad, a loaf of home-baked bread, and four plates at the center of the table. Walter reached for a piece of tomato, but Esther swatted him away.

"You think I'd want to be married to someone with these table manners?" she said.

As Esther said grace, the four of them tilted their heads down, shutting their eyes. Alice peeked at Walter, who was nodding along as Esther conveyed gratitude for the meal. She thanked Demeter and Helios, the worms that kept the soil rich.

Alice's eyes flicked back and forth between Walter and Esther, as she tried to comprehend how they could be so happily divorced.

"Everything was perfect until we got married," Esther said, poking at her lettuce, deciding which piece to pierce first.

"Essie eats like she doesn't trust her food, even when she makes it."

She elbowed him. "If he'd said that when we were married,

it would have been mean-spirited. Now that we're divorced, I can hear it as the gentle teasing it is."

"Oh no," Walter said, "I meant it as a full-fledged criticism."

"See what I mean? This just wouldn't do in a marriage."

"Why not?" Alice asked. Certainly married couples teased each other. Surely married couples could endure jokes steeped in truth.

"Because marriage loads everything with contrived significance. Oh, he doesn't like the way I eat, so my options are either to annoy him for the rest of my life or change myself in ways I don't want to change. In marriage everything is a question of what this will mean for the future. Will we last? The second we got married, as soon as that gold band—" she raised her bare ring finger like she was flipping them off "—was locked around my finger, we started fighting. Incessantly. About everything. Often we lost track of what we were fighting about. Marriage is a death sentence for a relationship."

"Not all marriages," Walter pointed out, seeing the concern across Alice's young face. "Essie has a way of assuming our truth is everyone else's too."

"Well, we're happier than all our married friends, I know that much. We aren't together because we're legally obligated to be but because we want to be."

Madeline smiled in agreement, and Alice remembered that she and Gregory were not married, not in the conventional sense of a signed license, an oath ordained. They were married by their word, something they renewed each day they were together.

"So why do you live separately?" Alice asked.

"There was a time after we divorced when we needed to be apart, to reset," Walter explained. "We needed the distance. We also couldn't bear it. So I bought the house across the street from ours so I could watch her."

"So I could watch you," Esther corrected.

"Your love began by watching each other," Madeline said.

"After, when you didn't need distance anymore, why didn't you move back in together?" Alice asked.

Walter shrugged. "We like our own space."

"People talk about being in love, but that's passive, inactive. Love is a choice. Every day we choose each other. It's work. It requires effort." Esther rubbed Walter's knee.

"It's the effort that makes it worth having," Madeline said so quietly only Alice could hear her.

After lunch, Walter and Esther walked the two women to the door.

"Oh, Madeline," Walter said, reaching out for a hug. "It really is good to see you."

Madeline wrapped her arms around his torso, a hint of desire grazing her face before she let go.

In the car, as they circled back toward the freeway, Alice counted the glimpses of Esther painted across the city. Her eyes. Her mouth. Her hair. All the ways Walter had immortalized her.

As they drove past a painting of Esther's ear resting in a field of daisies, Madeline said, "They're as happy as ever."

When they returned to the house in the woods, Madeline trotted toward the door like she might hop into the air and click her heels together. Alice trailed her, relieved. While Alice had never met Walter and Esther before, she could not imagine a happier state for them than being divorced. Certainly that was an active choice, yet they made it look effortless, being that connected. They'd written their own terms for love, a love that grew out of Madeline's story. It was not a failed story. Although there wasn't an official tally to their wager, Alice mentally put a check mark in her column, one point for continuing scribedom.

19

Sea Glass

Same time next week remained their parting phrase, now uttered after lunch. Neither had acknowledged the establishment of this new routine. When Alice arrived to Willow Bindery the week after she and Duncan had ventured to the sandwich shop for the first time, the closed sign was already turned on the front door. Alice waited as the last two customers paid for their journals and pens, waving goodbye to Duncan with manicured nails. Duncan nodded indifferently.

"How's the fan club?" Alice asked as the women disappeared down the block.

"As bewildering as always," he said, reaching for Alice's books beneath the register. She opened her tote bag for him to drop them in like Halloween candy. "And where shall we dine today?" he asked. Alice suggested her favorite taco shop.

Since then, they'd journeyed to a wine bar with great paninis, the tourist crab shack at the end of the pier where the food was delicious, exorbitant prices notwithstanding, a brick oven pizzeria, a burger stand, and back to the deli counter. She liked being his guide to Santa Barbara, introducing him to the eateries she'd come to love.

Being around Duncan seemed to bring out a superpower in her, one more confounding than her writing gift. He always had something clever to say about the food and she always had a quip in return. Everything she said was well-timed and funny, like they were playing verbal tennis and she knew how to keep the volley going. She wasn't this way with most people, but she felt unusually comfortable around Duncan, a feeling that stemmed from their pact to be friends, nothing more, nothing less. Soon she found herself forgetting his perfectly straight front teeth, the way she wanted to tuck the piece of stray hair that didn't quite reach his ponytail behind his ears, his cloudy eyes with their sad beauty. He was just Duncan. Her binder. Her friend.

When Alice was invited to the wedding of her client Coco, she knew she had to go, and to bring a date, so she decided to ask Duncan. While Alice was about as excited to go to a wedding where everyone would gawk at her, the love scribe, as she was to go to the dentist, she had to attend. It would send the wrong message not to celebrate the love she brought into this world. As bad as it would have seemed to decline the invitation, it was worse to go alone.

"What are you doing in two Saturdays?" Alice asked, leaning against the counter in Willow Bindery. Duncan stood on the other side of the register, close enough that she could see the whiskers on his cheeks, could smell the mix of his musty deodorant with the metallic scent of ink, the sourness of the rawhide glue he used, which Alice was dismayed to learn was literally named.

"That's, what, the first weekend in October? I'll have to check my busy social calendar." He ran her credit card through the machine with a flourish.

"I have this thing. For a client. I don't really want to go alone. I kind of have to go though. It would look bad if I said no. I totally get it if you aren't interested—" As she fumbled for her invitation, she saw Duncan watching her, amused. "What are your thoughts on weddings? Are you morally opposed?"

"I'm opposed to marriage," he said, "but who doesn't like an open bar and a dance floor?"

Coco's story was one of the first Duncan had bound for Alice nearly two months before. When she met Coco at her Parisian-style perfumery, Coco provided her with a list of things she did not want in a partner, everything from a passionless job to curly hair. "I don't trust men with curly hair," Coco explained. "If it's too well kempt, they're vain. If it's too wild, they lack awareness of how the world sees them." Alice patted her own curly hair as she read the list of nonnegotiables: men estranged from their families, men who lived with their parents, men who ran marathons, men allergic to dogs, men who drank too much, men who didn't drink at all. The list continued in ways that seemed both arbitrary and pointed.

"What *do* you want in a partner?" Alice asked.

Coco looked up from the small vial of liquids she was mixing and said, "Someone who loves me." She continued to combine clear liquids until the vial was full, then used a tester to put some of the perfume on the underside of Alice's wrist. "Rose, mandarin, and pink pepper with a touch of marigold and oakmoss." Alice brought her wrist to her nose. The perfume smelled floral without being cloying, the pepper giving it just enough bite. "It's my gift, knowing what works for someone. Kind of like you." Coco winked, plugged the vial, and gave it to Alice.

As Alice stepped out of her sweet-smelling shop, an image came to her straightaway. Sea glass. She didn't know what it meant, but she didn't need to understand. She simply needed to follow where it led.

The story that unfolded on her screen was about a vial of love potion cast overboard by a lovesick sailor. Over time, saltwater eroded it until the potion imbued the glass itself. The vial traveled the Atlantic and the Pacific, the Adriatic Sea. Unlike most sea glass, it was colorless, not eye-catching. If someone happened to notice it and rub it, a bit of the potion would rub off on them and they would instantly find love.

It was a story that could teach Coco to erode all the things she didn't want, to let herself believe in the goodness of someone who wanted to love her.

When Alice finished writing the story, she felt an inexplicable and potent melancholy. The story was decidedly upbeat. It took her a few minutes of unfocused staring at the screen to discover that it wasn't the story but the image of sea glass that evoked the sadness in her. Often little parts of Alice's life found their way into her stories, details from the physical world around her, memories repurposed from her past. She didn't realize she was borrowing from her own life until it was on the page, now part of someone else's story.

Alice had forgotten how at low tide she and her father would search for the ocean's treasures, inventing stories for each piece of sea glass they found on the beach. A pirate shipwreck. A mermaid's chalice. A glass castle on an underwater island. Sea glass had a story to it, weathered and tumbled by the ocean, its edges smoothed, its color frosted. Once Alice and her father uncovered the story, they'd toss the glass back to sea so someone else could find it. That was what she'd loved most, how their story became part of the ocean's lure. Now, in Coco's story, she was giving away a bit of herself she couldn't reclaim. Alice didn't want to relinquish any moments of her father, even the ones she'd forgotten. She had a finite pool of memories of him and each time she used one in a story, she was one memory closer to having nothing new to rediscover about him. Still, this story was what Coco needed. It was her job to offer it to her. That was the sacrifice she made to her gift.

Because Duncan had bound Coco's story, it seemed fitting that Alice invite him to the wedding as her plus one. To her knowledge, Coco and Tomas were the first couple she'd linked who were taking the plunge. That was marriage, a leap into a cold and dark unknown, especially for these two. They'd only been together for three months. When Coco told Alice she'd met a man without a single negative from her list, she said, "We hate all the same things." This seemed like an odd bonding point. For a woman who knew exactly what she didn't want, perhaps it made sense.

"I'd tell you which story was theirs," Alice said, signing the credit card receipt, "but you wouldn't know because you don't read them." He startled. "I'm joking. Relax."

He didn't respond and Alice wondered if he was more sensitive than he seemed.

"Anyway, given what I know about Coco, it should be top-shelf." She slipped her credit card and the receipt into her wallet. "I won't know anyone there, so we won't have to talk to anyone. We can sit at our table and drink vodka and make fun of the bridesmaids."

"You had me at shelf, top or bottom. As for making fun of people, I'm always game, and—" Duncan moved his limbs stiffly in an impressive robot dance "—who would want to waste these dance moves?"

"Okay, please don't do that at the wedding."

"No? What about this?" He moonwalked from behind the register into the shop. "Or this?" He proceeded to do the Running Man, the Sprinkler, the Macarena.

"You're going to make me regret inviting you, aren't you?" Alice said laughing.

"Oh, definitely."

When Duncan started to do the MC Hammer shuffle, Alice said, "Alright, let's settle down before you pull something."

He followed her onto the sidewalk. "All this dancing piqued my appetite. Where we headed today?"

Alice pointed toward State Street, and they started walking. "How do you feel about Indian? They've got a biryani with uni that will literally bring tears to your eyes."

"Uni's not the first thing that comes to mind when I hear Indian, but color me intrigued."

"This is Santa Barbara. If there's a way to incorporate uni, we'll find it. I've even had uni ice cream."

"Now you're just being gluttonous," Duncan said as they turned onto State Street. "So, will there be uni at this top-shelf wedding?"

"Do you really think I'd take you to a wedding that didn't have uni?" Alice stopped in front of the Indian restaurant. "Wedding's at four sharp. Please tell me you own something that isn't plaid."

"So you're saying I shouldn't wear my kilt?" Duncan said, holding the door open for Alice.

Alice shot him her best death glare as she stepped inside, unable to shake a flurry of excitement at the promise of attending the wedding together.

20

To the Lighthouse

After the visit to Walter and Esther's, the changes in Madeline were both immediate and profound. She buzzed around the house with a newfound vitality, dusting mantels that were already spotless, rearranging furniture to capture the afternoon sun, talking at a higher octave about their plans for the day. These plans grew more extensive too. Longer walks, more hours in the secret library poring over the red books. Every love story that persisted invigorated her, and soon Alice began to wonder if the fatal illness that had seemed so imminent was really just a loss of hope. Madeline's skin grew rosier. Her muscles engaged. It was as if she'd shed ten years.

The house itself began to change. The orange poppies across the bedroom walls were all in full bloom, bathing in a brighter light that poured through the windows. The hallways, once dark, now glittered with sun dust. The grandfather clock did not tick so much as chime. Every piece of furniture grew softer, fluffier. Even the food, which Alice would not have imagined could be any tastier, became sweeter, more complex.

In her spiral pocket notebook, Alice sifted through her records on other clients until she found a blank page to draft a new list, a color key beginning with *Red = lasting love.* There was something satisfying about seeing the meaning so plainly displayed. Those 206 red books were the easy cases, though. There were another 2,192 books in the library that were not red. This was where Madeline and Alice's journey truly began, with the books that had switched color. Alice didn't know what she feared more: discovering what the changes might signify about the couples united by those stories or how they might affect Madeline.

Still, she remained steadfast. She and Madeline had a gift. They helped people find the love they wanted in their lives. In their own way, the other books would show this too. They had to. Alice was not about to lose their bet, not about to stop writing.

On the day Madeline returned the last red book to the shelf, she giddily asked, "Which color shall we explore next?"

The room was daunting. So many books. So many colors. So much unknown. Alice could feel the uncertainty twisting in her stomach. She willed herself to exude confidence.

"Yellow," she said without hesitation. Yellow was her mother's favorite color. After she became a doctor and was able to buy her husband the house of his dreams, the first thing Bobby did was hire painters to brighten the white stucco facade to yellow. She wanted their home to greet the sun each morning, to welcome it in, to be its own energy source when the fog shrouded it. "Let's explore the yellow books next." Madeline grinned, exposing teeth that Alice was certain were whiter than before.

They worked through the afternoon into night, Madeline pulling a yellow book from the shelf and reading the first line for Alice to cross-reference in the ledger. Then, they searched online to locate Madeline's clients. Many were happily married, some were single, others gone from this world. The single consistent thing Madeline and Alice discovered about the clients from the yellow books was that none of them were still involved with the people they'd met after working with Madeline.

"What do you think it means?" Alice said, scrolling through the profile of an advertising executive who had hired Madeline fifteen years before. Her social media account went back that far, and Alice found several photographs over the course of four months showing her with the man she'd met through Madeline. Then he disappeared from her account, replaced by other men. This kind of fleeting romance accorded with the experiences of the other clients from the yellow books, who had short-lived attachments to the people they met through Madeline's story before moving on. "Were they all just flings?"

Madeline frowned, peering over Alice's shoulder at the smiling woman now in her midforties. "Or maybe the stories had no effect on them? Is it possible that our magic might not work on some people?"

"There are people who are immune to everything," Alice said.

"But there are so many of them. That's not immunity, that's ineffectiveness."

Nearly a third of the books were yellow, the second most popular color after blue. Madeline walked away from Alice, shoulders drooping. Was her conviction so fragile that a little doubt could crumble its very foundation? Perhaps she was not as strong as Alice considered her to be.

As Alice debated how best to rally Madeline, one yellow book caught her eye, blinking like a lighthouse beckoning her. She walked over to it, pulling it from the shelf. The flashing intensified, its light too bright to confront directly.

The story belonged to Ingrid Olsen, who emigrated from Norway to sunny Santa Barbara when she was eleven. As she lost her native language, she'd told Madeline, she lost a part of herself, so she went looking for relationships that might make her whole again. When they didn't, when the men she thought were godlike proved themselves all too human, rage consumed her. Generally she was mild-mannered, and this streak of passion scared her. It would have been welcome, if it was channeled toward a career or talent, but we can't choose what overwhelms us. For Ingrid, it was a failed relationship. Whether she or the suitor was the one to end it, she'd transform into an irrational, angry beast before squandering three days in bed eating ice cream, desolate over all the energy she'd expended on someone who was not the person she'd wanted him to be. After a decade of this cycle, she was ready for a change. For her thirtieth birthday she bought herself a love story, hoping Madeline could send someone to complete her.

"That's not what she needed," Madeline said as she and Alice drove toward the harbor in Ventura. Ingrid worked as a ranger on the Channel Islands, so they'd booked a day trip to San Miguel, where she was scheduled that week. They needed to find out what the blinking yellow meant, why hers was different from the other books. "Ingrid was already complete. She was looking for the wrong thing out of a relationship."

Madeline wrote her a story about a woman whose arm kept getting cut off only to grow back stronger. She'd discovered this by accident during a freak mishap involving her brother and an axe. When the arm grew back, she had her brother chop it off again. Sure enough, they watched it grow even thicker. Again and again they chopped, each time requiring a little more effort to cleave it from her body. Eventually it grew too strong to be amputated, and the woman knew she was complete.

The story, however, was not finished. It needed a translation. Madeline found a Scandinavian studies student at the university to translate it to Norwegian. When Madeline gave Ingrid the red book, Ingrid was taken aback.

"I can't read Norwegian," she protested.

"You can," Madeline encouraged her. "Just try."

Reluctantly, Ingrid brought the book home and tried to decipher the sentences on the page. They were a code to be broken. Frustrated, she tossed the book aside. Each time she walked by the end table where it rested, it beckoned her like a powerful magnet, until she could not withstand its pull. She continued to approach it like a puzzle, locating the most common short words to deduce their meaning. When the language continued to evade her, she considered hiring a translator but knew that if she couldn't read the story herself, its magic would never work on her. She wondered if she could read it without trying to comprehend it, instead embracing each word like the indecipherable, unpronounceable hieroglyphic it was. If she just treated it like a pretty picture to linger over, maybe the message would wash over her.

When she stopped trying to determine what the words meant and simply observed them on the page, the language flooded her all at once, a dam broken. She read the story repeatedly. Like the woman's arm, Ingrid's command of her native language grew stronger. She began to dream in Norwegian, to think in her lost tongue. At last she understood: she didn't need someone to complete her. She was complete on her own, if she allowed herself to be.

"That's when she met Mel. He didn't complete her, but he did complement her."

Ingrid went to the library, looking for Norwegian-language novels to read. In the bank of public computers, she spotted one that was free. When she went to sit in the chair, a man bumped her aside and nearly knocked her over. He pretended not to notice her as he logged onto the computer. He'd been waiting for an hour for a free computer and was not about to allow this pale blond woman to skip ahead, pretty though she might be. His lunch hour was almost up, and he needed to check his personal email before he headed back to work. Normally Ingrid would have given up, muttering under her breath that he was an ass, but now she was willing to take a stand.

At first they fought in whispers, which quickly escalated into shouts, too loud and passionate for something as minor as a fifteen-minute window on a public computer. Finally the man at the computer next to them offered his, shaking his head as he walked away. They worked side by side, keenly aware of the scandalized looks the other patrons gave them, and of each other.

"They had this way," Madeline said as Alice pulled into the parking lot at the harbor, "of talking without speaking, of knowing each other's thoughts. I was certain they would last."

"Maybe they did," Alice said unconvincingly.

The yellow book on Madeline's lap continued to flash sharp bursts of light, on and off, like a flickering light.

"What do you think it means, that it's blinking like that?" Alice asked.

Madeline shrugged. "Not sure I want to know. I don't imagine you'll just let it be?"

Alice gently nudged the old woman. "Just admit it, this is the most fun you've had in years."

"That says more about the years past than about now."

When they boarded the boat to San Miguel, Madeline insisted on sitting inside, claiming she did not want the sea air to upset her carefully coiffed hair. The boat backed away from the dock and began its journey into open waters, which quickly grew rough. Madeline clutched both sides of her seat as the boat thudded against the solid water, her face paling.

"It might help to get some fresh air," Alice pointed toward the stairs leading to the open deck above them.

Madeline nodded and latched onto Alice's arm. Unsteadily they made their way to the stairs and up to the main deck, where Madeline fell into an open seat. Alice rubbed her back as she watched dolphins arc above the waves, then dive below.

At least a dozen dolphins swam beside the boat. Each time one appeared above the water, Alice was caught by surprise. It was magical, how the ocean hid all this life.

When they stepped off the gangway onto the thin strip of beach, Madeline looked up at the steep sandy bluffs above them. The austere beauty washed over her. When she looked at Alice, her face was radiant. Though she would never admit it, Madeline was excited to be here.

They followed a small crowd toward the highlands, the other hikers speeding up to claim the best campsites. The dry brush greened and thickened as they went. They didn't see the ranger's station until they were almost upon it. It was a redwood ranch house that blended into the hills surrounding it. Outside, a pale blond woman in a ranger's uniform sat writing in a notebook. When she looked up, she smiled and said, "Madeline."

They waited at a splintering picnic table while Ingrid disappeared inside to retrieve a French press and three speckled camping mugs.

"I can't believe you're here," she said as she poured them each a cup of strong coffee.

"How did you find me?"

Madeline motioned to Alice. "This one here fancies herself an internet sleuth."

"It didn't take sleuthing," Alice said. "Unless you consider Google some sort of underground resource."

"I find the whole thing invasive," Madeline said, sipping from the tin mug.

"Well," Ingrid said, "however it happened, I'm glad you're here. I think about you more than you know."

"And how is Mel?" Madeline asked. "You two must have a gaggle of babies by now."

"Mel might have a few babies. I wouldn't know."

"May I ask what happened?" Madeline delicately inquired.

Ingrid shrugged. "It ran its course. We were together—" her

eyes drifted to the cloudless sky "—ten months maybe? It was so long ago. And there have been so many since." She glanced at her watch and stood. "Care to accompany me to the grounds? You wouldn't believe some of the fire hazards people bring to the island. It's like they want to burn it all down."

Madeline and Alice followed Ingrid down a path to where the shrubbery opened into a small field. A group of church kids were playing soccer while their chaperones set up a lunch station.

"So it just ended?" Alice asked the back of Ingrid's head.

Ingrid could not see who had spoken. "Oh, Madeline," she said, "it was perfect. More perfect than the relationship I assumed I wanted. Before Mel, everything ended in explosives. I was all fireworks and stomach acid. I never even stopped to consider whether I liked the guy, I just was so outraged that it was over. With Mel, one day we both knew that we'd gotten whatever we needed from each other and underneath that need there wasn't any love to keep us going. The magic just faded. It was magical, for a time, but its time was up. Afterward, I felt betrayed, to be honest, that you brought me someone whose love didn't last. Then I realized that wasn't what I needed from you. You gave me something more. I've been with so many other men, and whether it's a month or a year, when it's over, it's over. No fanfare. No fighting. It's glorious."

"Really?" Alice asked. How could a relationship that inspired nothing when it ended be worth anything?

"Listen, it's not going to work out with most people. When it comes to the long term, so few people are suited to be together. That's the simple truth of it." They wove between campsites where couples were pitching tents and groups of friends were laying out food. "The more energy you exhaust on someone who isn't right for you," Ingrid continued, "the less you have for the person who is." Her eyes caught Alice's; it was the first time she'd really looked at her, the comment directed at the young woman instead of the old. "You should date people who are wrong for you. It helps you realize what you don't want, which makes it easier to discover what you do want. And it's a reminder that a breakup won't break you. If you embrace the end instead of making it into something ugly or angry, then you can learn from it. If you're angry, you can't see anything else."

A man jogged up to Ingrid and asked her where he could find potable water. She pointed him in the direction of the facilities. The campsites were full of couples, both on their own and in groups. Statistically, half of these couples were destined to fail, even if it was hard to see that now as they laughed, working together to light fires and pitch tents, all happy memories being constructed. If or when these relationships ended, stained with anger or hurt, what would happen to these memories?

After Ingrid made the rounds, they took the long way back to the station, hiking along the bluffs. The bay looked calm below. The ferry had disappeared beyond the horizon, and the empty dock bobbed with the waves invisible from so far above. They were trapped on the island until the next boat docked. Everyone here was.

"Why did you want to become a ranger?" Alice shouted over the wind as she took big strides to keep up with Ingrid. Her hair was swirling around her face, and she kept having to pull strands from her mouth.

Ingrid turned around but kept walking. She looked as if she was floating, stepping backward with her hair electrified around her.

"Mel, actually. He took me here once. I'd never seen anything like it. I was immediately taken. I started volunteering, completed my ranger's certification, and, when a position opened, I made sure I got it." She stopped walking, and Alice nearly bumped into her. Madeline, trailing behind, was walking with her head down, communing with the grass instead of Ingrid and Alice.

"If I hadn't dated Mel, I wouldn't have all this." She twirled around, claiming the land, the ocean, the wind. "I could write Mel off as a fling, or I could remember him as the man who brought me the Channel Islands. Everyone gives you something. It's up to you to take it and move on."

The boat ride back to the mainland was smoother than the ride out. The modest waves did little more than sway the boat. Alice searched for dolphins, but she didn't see any, just dark green waters stretching to the horizon. She tried to decide if Ingrid was right, if everyone you dated gave you something. She always regarded her exes as giving her insomnia, dehydration, paranoia. They'd given her other things too. Restaurants that were now her favorites. Little-known hikes. Preferences for light roast coffee and Meyer lemons. So many things about her came from the men she'd been with, the relationships, however brief, that she'd seen as evidence of what was wrong with her rather than a part of who she'd become.

"What'd you think?" Alice asked Madeline.

"I think that was never love."

"Maybe not, but isn't it heartening to know that even when a story doesn't work out, it can be life-affirming?"

They walked to the back of the boat, where the crew was lowering the gangplank. The wind caught Madeline's short hair, lifting it vertically a few inches from her head.

"And that's what that little performance proved for you? Trust me, when it ended with Mel, she wasn't that calm. And I doubt she's that Zen when relationships end now. She's constructed a story that makes her feel better about being alone. I suppose that's more commendable than wallowing. It doesn't change the fact that I wrote her a story filled with false promises."

"Maybe you just promised something else."

"That's not how this goes." Madeline brushed past Alice onto the gangplank. "Ingrid said as much herself—the magic worked for a time, then that time was up. The story didn't keep its power."

They stepped down onto the dock, and Madeline surveyed

the vast ocean before them before she spoke again. "We're not trying to play God here, Alice. We do a very specific thing. And since we can't do it effectively, we shouldn't do it at all."

Alice watched Madeline walk away, trying to decide if the old woman was right. She'd been so inspired by Ingrid, who'd forged a life on her own terms, one that grew out of a failed connection. There was beauty in that, but Madeline was right too. She had not delivered on the promise she made to her client. The relationship Madeline had brought her had ended. The same was true of the other yellow books too.

Alice found her notepad in her back pocket. Beneath *Red = lasting love*, Alice wrote *Yellow = flings, quickly faded.*

It was impossible to tell from the records they'd uncovered if these brief romances had felt like love at the time. Either way, they weren't lasting. They burned bright then died, the magic petered out.

It made Alice wonder if the same thing could happen to her stories, if they could lose their luster.

21

The Bridesmaid

"Sit still," Gabby said, holding an eyeliner pencil inches from Alice's eye. "If you keep blinking, you're going to end up looking like a raccoon."

"I'm trying," Alice said, her eyes fluttering involuntarily. "Can't I just wear my everyday makeup?"

"Gabs," Oliver shouted from inside the condo. "Are you torturing Alice again?"

"No," Gabby shouted back.

"Yes," Alice shouted over her.

Oliver popped his head out to the balcony, where Alice was sitting on one of their wicker chairs, Gabby looming over her. They'd already taken a straightening iron to Alice's hair. Gabby then insisted they apply her makeup in natural light, since the wedding was outdoors.

"Do I need to alert the authorities? Is there some law about friend abuse?" Oliver said. He had a few days' worth of stubble, and wore faded sweatpants that gave Alice the impression he hadn't changed his clothes that morning. Normally that would infuriate Gabby, the slovenliness, the lethargy, the fact that he hadn't even bothered to get dressed when her friend was coming over. Today she hardly seemed to notice.

Gabby stood, clamping her hand to her hip, pretending to be annoyed. "Do you really want to wade into the waters of female friendship?"

"No," Oliver said, tapping his trusted memo pad against the balcony door. "No, I do not." He disappeared inside.

Gabby surveyed Alice's face. The makeup was caked into her cheeks uncomfortably. "Try shutting your eyes," Gabby said.

Alice obeyed, feeling Gabby's pencil across her eyelids.

"So, are you nervous about today?"

"Why would I be nervous about today?" Alice asked too quickly.

"Maybe because you're going on a date with Duncan."

"It's not a date." Alice opened her eyes, and Gabby's pencil slipped down the side of her face.

"Gabs, you heard the woman. It's not a date," Oliver echoed from the kitchen.

"Well, now you've done it. You officially look like a melted clown." Gabby picked up the pencil. "And you," she shouted to Oliver. "Stop taking her side."

"It's my duty as the boyfriend of Alice's best friend to take her side over yours. Them's the rules of navigating your friendships. There are landmines everywhere. Hey, that's a good line."

Gabby leaned against the exterior wall, facing Alice. "When you spend time with a comic, you'll quickly learn not to say anything that you don't want warped into a joke."

"I heard that!" he shouted.

"Of course you did," Gabby sniped. She found a makeup

wipe and smoothed it across Alice's face. Right away, her pores could breathe again.

"Seriously, though," Gabby said. "You're good about today?"

"I wouldn't have invited him if I didn't want him to come with me. We're friends, Gabby. I know it seemed like there might be something more there, but I'm happy with how things are. Honest."

Gabby didn't look convinced. "Well, I officially give up. Do with your face what you will." She wandered inside, leaving Alice alone on the balcony, a table of makeup before her. Alice carefully applied a bit of concealer to the red spots on her face, coated her lashes in mascara. She could hear Gabby and Oliver talking, Gabby laughing, but couldn't make out what they said. The rhythms of their conversation were natural, comfortable. Gabby was completely herself around Oliver, something she'd never been with a partner before. Alice had given this to her best friend. It reminded her of all the good she brought to her clients' lives.

"So?" Alice asked when she slipped into the apartment.

Gabby clapped in delight. "You're wearing the lipstick."

Sure enough, Alice was wearing the cherry red lipstick Gabby had surprised her with four months before, though she feared it would end up having the opposite of the desired effect, making her feel more exposed than polished, like everyone would be able to see just how uncomfortable she was.

"You look perfect. Olly, doesn't she look perfect?"

Oliver looked Alice over. "Oh no, I'm not going there. If I say she does—which you do by the way, Alice—then it'll seem like I'm harboring secret feelings for your best friend, and if I give anything less than complete approval—well I won't even go there. Like I said before, ladies, landmines." He scribbled something on his notepad.

"I'm not sure the landmines thing is really that funny," Gabby said. "And the whole poke fun at your girlfriend and her friends, it's a little sexist, don't you think?"

Oliver looked up, wounded. "The whole point of comedy is to go to the edge without going over."

Gabby went to him and cupped his head against her chest. "My sensitive artist, I've offended him," she said to Alice.

"I'm not sensitive, I'm just not going to take my cues from someone who considers *Friends* the height of comedy."

"I know you didn't just disparage *Friends*."

Alice watched them volley back and forth over the merits of their very different senses of humor. They seemed to have forgotten she was there.

"I'm just gonna—" She motioned toward the door, but they were lost to her. She needed to get back to her apartment to change for the wedding.

As she was about to step out, Oliver called, "Hey, Alice? You really do look great. Knock 'em dead." He winked at her before she whispered, "Thanks," and slipped out.

The courthouse where Coco and Tomas were getting married was a short distance from Alice's apartment, so she and Duncan had agreed to meet there and walk over together. At the time the plan had seemed so inconsequential, so natural. Now, as he knocked on her door, she panicked. Was he intending to come inside? Alice had not prepared for that. She was not ready for him to see how she lived, her sagging couch, the Georgia O'Keeffe and Frida Kahlo posters on her walls, the record and book collections that spilled from their cabinets onto the floor. This was her private space, no dates allowed, even if this wasn't a date.

The knocking persisted. Alice opened the door a crack and slipped out sideways. If Duncan noticed her awkward exit, he didn't let on. He smiled as he looked her up and down, not lasciviously but perhaps with a bit of desire.

"You clean up nicely," he said, burrowing his hands into the pockets of his suit pants. The accompanying navy blue jacket accented his muscular shoulders.

Alice patted her now-straight hair self-consciously.

"I like the lipstick," Duncan added. Alice waited for a joke. Apparently that was all he wanted to say.

"You'll tell me if it ends up on my cheeks or teeth?"

"Probably not." He held out his elbow, and Alice wove her arm through his as they headed toward the courthouse. To outsiders they probably looked like a couple, mismatched as they were, Alice a half foot taller in her high heels. This was why she didn't date shorter men. They made her feel lankier, more awkward, merely by existing at her side. Not that she and Duncan were on a date.

As soon as they stepped down the stairs to the sunken garden behind the courthouse, Alice sensed the eyes on her, heads tilting covertly, mouths whispering. At this point, everyone seemed to know someone who had made a call to the love scribe. While Alice had expected attention, she wasn't prepared for it to start so quickly. She tightened her grip on Duncan. It was only four in the afternoon, but the autumnal days had grown shorter and the sky was already darkening with the suggestion of sunset. Alice hoped she wouldn't be so obvious once the night arrived.

"You okay?"

"Everyone's looking at me," she whispered.

"I'm pretty sure they're looking at me," he said, deadpan, so that it took Alice a moment to realize he was joking.

The string quartet began to play, signaling that the ceremony was about to commence. Alice was relieved; it would take a celebrity much bigger than her to distract the crowd from the procession of groomsmen and bridesmaids. The groom emerged, flanked by his parents, his complexion bronzed with too much makeup. Coco followed, her train requiring four people to help it down the aisle. By the end of their vows, which they'd written themselves, both bride and groom were crying as well as several attendees. Duncan's eyes glistened, which made Alice's eyes well, something she wouldn't have expected. When the officiant pronounced them husband and wife by the powers vested in him by the internet, everyone hooted as Tomas dipped Coco and kissed her. There were a million cynical thoughts Alice could have had about this marriage, the same ones she'd had at the many comparably over-the-top weddings she'd worked where she hadn't known the bride or groom. Those weddings always seemed like a charade, all the fanfare, the couple overcompensating to drown out their doubt. She realized she'd been wrong about those weddings. What she'd considered a spectacle was in fact a spectacular celebration. While no one else could understand the contours of the couple's love, the couple invited the people in their lives to share in a night of celebration that mirrored what it felt like for them to be together. Alice was glad she'd decided to attend.

Alice and Duncan followed the attendees toward the reception. "That was a—"

"A lot," Duncan finished her sentence. "Oh yeah. But I bet they'll have a raw bar."

A raw bar indeed, as well as a cascading cheese table, a top-shelf bar, trays of hors d'oeuvres, which Alice was relieved to see were not being delivered by her colleagues, if she could continue to call them that. She hadn't picked up a shift in weeks. It would have embarrassed her to see them here, on the other side, even though everyone went to weddings, even caterer waiters.

Duncan suggested they divide and conquer, ushering her to the bar while he waited in line for oysters and cherrystone clams. The line at the bar was shorter, and Alice had ordered two gin and tonics before Duncan was anywhere close to the towers of oysters. As she waited for their drinks, a man sidled up to her. She held her breath, waiting for him to ask in that starstruck voice if she was the love scribe. On the rare occasions when strangers worked up the nerve to approach her, they all used the same voice, like they were inquiring if she was the tooth fairy.

"Hey there," he said, leaning against the bar with false nonchalance. "Here alone?"

He was tall and thin with stubble shadowing his jawline. His suit was obviously tailored, and he'd paired it with Converse sneakers now crossed at the ankles. There were so many conclusions Alice could draw from his appearance, not the least of which was that normally he'd be just the type she'd take home from a wedding. She could see each step that would lead to his apartment, her coy smile to suggest she was available followed by some benign conversation about how they each knew the couple, a toast to Coco and Tomas, then a series of toasts that kept them drinking swiftly until they were dancing, hands all over each other, when at last he would ask if she wanted to get out of there, as though this had been his plan, not hers, all along.

Alice glanced over at Duncan. His back was to her, talking to two women in line behind him. They giggled at varying intervals, as if the end of one's laugh prompted the other to begin. To Alice's surprise, Duncan laughed too, so engaged in their conversation that he didn't notice the line ahead of him speeding up.

When she returned her attention to the man at the bar, he was watching her. It all felt so predictable, not safe so much as disappointing. She held two gin and tonics up to him and headed across the grass toward Duncan, stopping at a distance as he continued to chat with the pretty women in line. This was not a date, she chided herself.

"Alice?"

Alice turned to see a woman smiling at her. She was of median height and build with symmetrical eyes, clear skin. Pretty, generically so.

"Carrie," Alice said, thankful she could recall the name. Carrie was one of Oh, Alice's first three clients once she'd officially become an S Corp. When they met, Alice had been surprised at how average Carrie was. In Alice's mind this observation was not an insult; most people were by definition average. To Alice, Carrie looked like the kind of person who would have no trouble finding someone as completely average as she was. But looks lied all the time. There were as many reasons that people did not find love as there were reasons they did. For Carrie, it had just never happened. She'd dated a lot in her twenties when she wasn't looking for anything serious. Then, when she was ready for something lasting, everyone around her had partnered already. Her mom told her she just needed to wait a few years until everyone was divorced, except she didn't want to wait, didn't want to be someone's seconds. It was a rare case where Alice agreed with Carrie's assessment of her own situation. She'd simply been unlucky. Luck was something Alice could bring her.

Carrie stood on tiptoes to give Alice a hug. "It's so good to see you. How do you know Coco?" Her eyes widened. "You're responsible for this, aren't you?"

Alice shrugged.

"I should have guessed. Someone that perfect for Coco, I should have realized it could only come from you."

A sturdy dark-haired man approached them, handing Carrie a glass of white wine. As she took it, she said, "Thanks, babe." He enveloped her, kissing her temple. "Alice, this is my boyfriend, Cal."

"Alice? *The* Alice?" he asked. When Carrie nodded, his arm fell from her shoulders and he reached over to enclose Alice in a bear hug.

"Cal," Carrie said, tugging at him. "You're suffocating her."

He let go, apologizing. "I forget my own strength when I'm excited. I can't believe I'm meeting Alice Meadows in the flesh."

"Cal thought you were a myth."

"Like the Easter Bunny or Santa Claus," Cal laughed.

"Just flesh and blood," Alice said, and they both laughed a little too heartily. Alice glanced over at Duncan, who was still holding court in the raw bar line. "It's Cal?" Alice asked. She remembered Carrie telling her about someone she'd met when she visited the wind caves to do some soul-searching after reading Alice's story. Toward the end of the trail, up to the highest caves, the path faded, and a man named—Alice was certain—Emiliano had shown her the way. The metaphor was too obvious to ignore.

"Oh yeah," Carrie said, interpreting the confused look on Alice's face, "I told you about Emiliano. He was sweet and all, but as soon as we went on a date that didn't involve hiking boots, it was clear we had nothing in common. Then—" she batted

Cal's chest territorially "—Cal was our waiter at the one meal we tried to have together. If I hadn't gone out with Emiliano, I never would have met my Cal."

Alice watched them embrace before Carrie added, "It's so funny to see you. We were just talking about you yesterday. Cal's sister was complaining that she's having such a hard time meeting someone, so I suggested you."

Alice wanted to ask why. Clearly her story for Carrie hadn't worked if she was now with someone other than Emiliano. That was how her gift functioned, the client read the tale Alice had prepared, then, like all those pilgrims who had followed the hummingbird, they looked to their right or left and found love. It was immediate, direct. It wasn't one degree of separation, the waiter at a failed date. But the expression on Carrie's face, the way she clung to Cal, made it apparent that she wanted Alice's story to have brought her to Cal. The question was, why? Why did she need to regard their union as the result of a story? It suggested to Alice that Carrie still lacked the confidence to believe she, on her own, was worthy of love. And if she didn't feel worthy of real love, only one that was magic, what had Alice really given her?

"Her name is Lily Harting, so if someone by that name calls, I sent her. She could really use a little good luck."

Cal placed his hand on the small of Carrie's back, offering Alice a nod as they walked toward a circle of people she didn't recognize. Carrie spoke for a moment before everyone in the circle looked over at Alice. She pretended not to notice, scanning the raw bar line until she spotted Duncan almost at the front.

Duncan introduced Alice to the two women he'd been chatting up. They were overly friendly in a way that was not meant to be friendly at all. He frowned at Alice when he detected the serious expression on her face. "You okay?"

She nodded and handed him his clear effervescent drink.

"I'm surprised they didn't do a signature cocktail. Like Love

Potion Number Nine or something." He started humming the melody of the song. Alice laughed politely, but she wasn't really listening. "You sure you're okay?" he asked.

Alice nodded, glancing back at Carrie. The sun had disappeared, but it was still just light enough for Alice to find Carrie and Cal, now standing alone beneath a bougainvillea. As Carrie adjusted Cal's tie, he leaned down to kiss her on the cheek. They were obviously happy together, so Alice tried to put the encounter out of her mind. The magic of Alice's story may have faded, but her former client was in love.

Alice returned her attention to Duncan, who was watching her, concerned. She held up her cocktail then tipped it back, finishing it in one long gulp. "Just haven't had enough to drink to be at a wedding."

"Well, there's an easy fix for that," he said, shaking his glass.

At last they reached the front of the line, where Alice took three oysters, two clams, and one piece of uni, while Duncan piled his plate until it could not possibly hold another shell.

"You know it's tacky to load up on the raw bar," Alice said as they found two empty chairs beneath a bougainvillea bush.

He slurped an oyster greedily from its shell. "You know what's worse than being tacky? Having to wait in that line again."

Throughout the early evening, every time Alice left Duncan's side to get them another drink or to chase one of the waiters down for a wonton with tuna tartare, she would return to find him surrounded by a small group of women, who quickly dispersed when she appeared at his side, casting her cool glares.

"Seriously, do you wear catnip or something?" Alice said as she offered him another gin and tonic.

"If I did, I would attract cats." Duncan's voice turned dryer when he joked. It was his only tell, and it always took Alice a moment to notice.

The band started playing a Whitney Houston cover, and Duncan's eyes sparked as he grabbed Alice and dragged her to the dance floor. Alice loved to dance, usually in the privacy of her apartment, where Agatha remained indifferent to her offbeat moves. To her surprise, beside Duncan she had both rhythm and grace. She let herself get lost in the moment. When a ballad came on, he pulled her close and counted off steps as they waltzed around the floor.

"Where'd you learn to do that?" she asked when the music stopped and they were all directed to their tables for the salad course.

"You forget, I was married. Dance classes were a prerequisite for the wedding, at least for my ex."

At the table he pulled out her chair, and she looked at the faces of the envious women surrounding her, finding she didn't mind that they were jealous.

Salad was served. Wine was poured, then poured again. Alice tried to keep track of how much she was drinking. Part of the waiters' job was to make the guests lose count. Salad was replaced with filet mignon and Chilean sea bass until the table was emptied of everything except teacups, spoons, and wineglasses to prepare for the dessert course. Alice excused herself to go to the bathroom.

When she came back, Duncan was not sitting at their table. She scanned the dining area but did not find him. In her periphery, she glimpsed string lights lilting above the dance floor. She spotted a familiar suit and ponytail at the center of the floor, gyrating to the music. As she approached, Duncan's back was to her, and when the music slowed, he reached for one of the bridesmaids and pulled her close, his legs disappearing into the violet satin of her skirt.

Alice's chest tightened as she watched them dance. The woman rested her head on his chest. He leaned his head onto hers. Alice did not want to keep watching yet found herself unable to pull away. They looked natural together, as though they were already a couple, so much better than Alice and Duncan would have seemed had they been slow dancing together. When the song ended, the woman drew Duncan's head down to kiss him.

It was not a gratuitous kiss. It was gentle, prim. Alice's knees buckled. As she glanced around, she was not the only one staring. Some guests pretended to be indifferent while others outright glared at the bridesmaid as the kiss continued. They all seemed entranced, bewitched. This was not normal. Then something Duncan had said earlier sprang to mind, something she'd barely heard, distracted by thoughts of Carrie and Cal.

I'm surprised they didn't do a signature cocktail, like Love Potion Number Nine or something. It had seemed like one of Duncan's corny jokes, except it wasn't. Coco's story was about a love potion in a vial turned to sea glass. Had Duncan read the story? As she pictured the giddy women at the bindery and eyed the besotted ones watching him now, she realized that this romantic attention was the cumulative effect of her stories. Duncan had read them all.

Alice rushed over to the table for her purse. She grabbed it and headed toward the street.

"Alice," she heard Duncan call out. She walked faster, unsteady in her heels. "Hey, Alice. Wait up."

He caught up with her quickly, and Alice silently cursed Gabby for making her wear these ridiculous shoes that gave her height she didn't need and a lack of coordination that made her vulnerable. He reached for her arm, but she shook him off.

"Where are you going?"

"Home." She bent down and slipped off the heels.

"You sure you want to walk barefoot? Santa Barbara's clean and all, but these are still city streets."

"I'm fine." She started walking faster. Duncan darted in front of her, blocking her path.

"Alice, stop. What's going on?"

"You tell me." Her voice was steadier than her heart, which was beating violently.

Duncan laughed. "What, that bridesmaid? That was nothing. Just got caught up in the moment. I know, bad form for a date, even if we aren't on a date." He slapped his hand in mock chastisement.

She'd been the one to insist this was not a date. Still it stung, how easily he dismissed the possibility. She'd been lying to herself, she now recognized, about not wanting more from him.

"I don't give a shit about that *bridesmaid*," she said, masking her hurt in anger. He flinched. Who was he to feel injured? Alice's eyes stung and she searched for another reason to be hurt by him. "You read it."

"Read what?"

"My story. For Coco. About the love potion and the sea glass."

He pulled on his ponytail, collecting his thoughts. "Not on purpose," he finally said. "It's not like I sat down with a cup of coffee and flipped through the pages. I didn't even realize I was reading them."

"You read all the stories, didn't you?"

His face was conflicted, and she saw that their whole relationship had been misaligned. Here she was, believing they were friends, when he'd been overcompensating for his betrayal with friendliness. "I'm not sure I read them exactly. It was more like I was breathing them. Like they were airborne."

"So it's my fault? You just couldn't help yourself?"

"I'm just saying I didn't mean to break your trust." He braved a step toward her. Across his face a film of sweat glinted in the light from the streetlamps. "It felt like the stories found me. They knew I needed them."

Alice's throat had gone dry, and she was suddenly dizzy, like there was no oxygen even though they were outside. She had nothing else to say to Duncan, so she shoved past him and continued to walk toward her home. The gritty pavement felt good under her feet. To her surprise, Duncan watched her go. She wouldn't have wanted him to chase after her, but she grew angrier that he'd given up so easily.

By the time she reached her driveway, the bottoms of her feet were black. They left prints on her doormat. She brushed them on the coarse fibers until they burned. When she inspected her left heel it was still filthy.

Inside, Agatha was tearing at the pages of one of her red books.

"Stop that!" She rushed over and picked the cat up. Several red books had been knocked off the shelf, the distinct odor of cat urine emanating from the pile. As she was about to scold Agatha, she noticed that the book Agatha had been clawing was Carrie's. She never reread her stories once they were bound. She kept copies as records, physical objects that reminded her how much love she'd brought into the world.

After sixty-two stories, Alice did not remember most of them in detail. She had no recollection of Carrie's story. The imagery was evocative and foreign to her. The prose had a gentle cadence that seemed the pattern of someone else's mind. It did not sound like Alice's voice. It wasn't Alice's voice. She was merely the channel through which the story had poured. In every syllable she could see that the story was effective, yet it hadn't worked. Carrie was not with Emiliano but another man entirely. The fact that she had met Cal through Emiliano was happenstance. It was not a result of Alice's story. Carrie was happy, she reminded herself. That was the important part.

Alice sank to the floor, leaning against her front door, holding the clawed book. Her mind kept returning to Duncan on the dance floor, his lips locked with the bridesmaid's, the expression on his face when he saw Alice, as if he'd been caught. He didn't owe her anything. They weren't dating. They were hardly friends, really. Just work acquaintances, and they weren't even that anymore. Duncan had bound fifty-five of her stories and he'd read them all. She felt foolish for trusting him. One thing was certain. She would have to find someone else to bind them, someone truer to their word, the binder's oath, which like any oath was irreparable once broken.

22

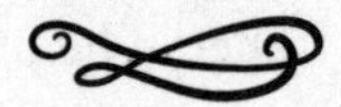

The Impossibly Tall Cake

Alice drove to the mountains, eager for the distraction only Madeline could provide. While she'd seen so much hope in Ingrid's breakup, Alice realized that Madeline was right, at least where the fate of their stories was concerned. They were designed to do a very specific thing, to bring the reader an instant and lasting love. Any other relationships or contentment their clients ultimately found was not a product of Madeline and Alice's stories. Of this, Alice was certain.

Alice was not convinced, however, that she must immediately stop writing her stories. She'd yet to see evidence that, when the stories failed, it had a negative effect on people's lives. And she still had 1,458 books left to explore, 1,458 books to persuade Madeline that even if some romances faded, they should continue being love scribes.

To Alice's surprise, Madeline was more determined than ever

to continue. Their quest had invigorated her once more. The color had returned to her cheeks. Her shoulders had unfurled. This time, however, Alice strongly suspected, Madeline was motivated to win their bet.

"Shall we move on to the next color?" Without waiting for an answer, Madeline scurried upstairs and initiated the ritual of opening the library door. As Alice watched the dial turn, she realized that the counter was not for detecting whether someone had tampered with the door but for enabling Madeline to keep track of her own visits. It marked the passage of time in a house devoid of time, with only a defective grandfather clock.

Again Madeline allowed Alice to decide which color they would explore next. The purple books continued to moan their terrible low-pitched cry. The sheer number of blue books was too daunting despite the calmness of their hue.

"Green," Alice decided. Green was the color of rebirth. It was also the color of envy. Still, it seemed more approachable than either blue or purple.

Madeline's fingers danced across the green shelves until she reached for a book that to Alice's eye looked like all the other green books that surrounded it.

"If I told you this was a true story, you would not believe me," Madeline read, *"so we will treat it as a fiction although each moment that follows is precisely as I experienced it."* She had a mesmerizing reading voice.

Alice scanned the ledger to locate the story. She loved identifying stories this way. A first line was like a first kiss. It embodied the promise of everything that could follow.

"Lulu Jones," she read.

Madeline cradled the book. "Yes, Lulu. She was passionate, that one. Her eyes had fire in them, green with little bursts of yellow that flamed when she spoke about baking. She was a pastry chef. Her lemon soufflé melted on your tongue. Don't get me started on her chocolate tarts. She gave so much to her food that I worried she wasn't saving enough of herself for her own needs."

So Madeline had written her a story to teach her to covet parts of herself unapologetically.

"Self-centered is not selfish. It does not necessitate that we ignore the needs of others. If we cannot take care of ourselves, if we cannot demand what we need, what do we have to offer others?"

Lulu had built her life around pleasing others. Madeline taught her to please herself. After reading the story, Lulu met Alphonse at an event for a global lifestyle company. They were celebrating a milestone that confounded Lulu, something about outreach on platforms, something intangible compared to caster sugar and Tahitian vanilla beans. The cake was to be impossibly tall, one hundred tiers for each of the one hundred goals the company had met, until the top tier was no larger than a thimble. Each time Lulu tried to build a sample cake, it would topple before she reached the top. She tried the traditional method of refrigerating the cake between tiers until it would not fit in the fridge. As always, she smoothed the buttercream icing onto each layer until it was as a level as a floorboard. She then experimented with thicker layers of icing to serve as glue. That worked better, but it compromised the taste, something she could not abide. She played with toothpicks, a plastic rod, a wooden dowel. Nothing would keep the cake upright and straight. It frustrated her in a way she'd never been frustrated before.

Lulu had been waiting to read Madeline's story until she was finished with the job. She could not afford the distraction of love while her mind needed to be entirely committed to besting this cake. At last, when she'd run out of ideas for constructing the cake, she looked to the story for a diversion. It was about a man who collected hours like they were coins, piling them away so he did not have to share them with anyone else, and as she read it, she grew enraged. What was this story of a greedy man who hoarded time, unwilling to spend it on others? How exactly was it supposed to bring her love? When she returned to her cake, she was unprecedentedly annoyed. Annoyed at Madeline for writing her such an ugly story. Annoyed at her clients for expecting her to defy physics. Annoyed at herself for accepting this job, for toiling away at something that would never work. Anger overshadowed the task before her, yet somehow, as soon as she stopped trying to solve the impossible mathematics of the cake, she assembled each of the one hundred tiers, so high she needed to stand on a chair to reach the top. It was perfect because she had stopped caring whether she could do it or not.

At the party, everyone marveled as she gingerly carried the cake toward a table at the center of the room. Everyone except one man, who was so engaged in a story he was telling that he did not notice the entrance of the cake. Gesturing wildly, he waved his drink in the air. The cake was so tall that Lulu could not see around it. She simply trusted that the path was clear ahead, that if anyone saw an impossibly tall cake coming their way, surely they would make room. Still oblivious, Alphonse began rowing his arms. As he stroked the air behind him, he caught the tail of her chef's coat, setting her off balance. The cake was rigidly tall. It had no give as she wobbled. When she managed to right her feet, the cake further tilted to a ninety-degree angle, landing squarely on Alphonse's head.

"I was so shocked," Lulu said when Madeline and Alice visited her at her industrial kitchen in Buellton, "that all I could do was laugh."

The room had fallen quiet, Lulu's wild laugh crowding the silence.

"I couldn't help it. The whole thing was just so absurd, and it reminded me of the first line of the story you wrote for me, about how outlandish truths can only be accepted in fiction. I think about that a lot, how weird life is, how much weirder than the stories we create."

This was not how Alice had read Madeline's first line. She liked that Lulu had informed it with her own meaning, that it had resonated with her at a moment that might otherwise have been devastating. After all the time she'd spent creating that cake, how quickly its perfection was upended.

Lulu's laugh persisted as the man turned toward her, his face slathered in white buttercream. He wiped it away, exposing brown eyes that sparkled. When they caught hers, he let out a laugh that matched hers, pitch for pitch, timbre for timbre. Lulu could feel everyone watching her, but they all ceased to exist. It was just Lulu in her chef's coat and Alphonse covered in her cake.

Alphonse was a tennis coach and was attending the party as the guest of one of his clients. The client who had invited him was a divorcee who never took another lesson with him again.

Alphonse taught Lulu how to play tennis. Lulu taught Alphonse how to frost a cake. Both vocations had so much technique to them. They marveled at each other's precision, at the care they devoted to their crafts, the attention they lavished on each other.

"It was like that for a while," Lulu said. Alice and Madeline were trailing her as she floated between stations, checking the progress of her bakers' creations, telling one assistant to add more vanilla to the icing, another that his cake was perfection manifest.

Over the last decade, Lulu's Cakes had grown from a one-woman enterprise to the largest purveyor of specialty cakes in the Santa Ynez Valley. "I have my husband to thank for that," Lulu said as she ushered Alice and Madeline into her office behind the kitchen. It was sparsely decorated but chaotically populated with folders, calendars, orders, and drawings of cakes. "I'm getting ahead of myself. A story must be told in the proper order. Isn't that right?" She winked at Madeline.

"As I was saying, it was like that for a while," Lulu continued.

She and Alphonse taught each other their crafts. They taught each other to love. They were the envy of all their friends, especially those who had been in relationships for so long they had lost the passion of the beginning.

"But beginnings lie and love needs more than passion," Lulu said, stacking papers on her desk so they weren't quite so haphazard. "I should have realized you were telling me that in my story."

Their passion obscured the truth of Alphonse and his jealousy. Lulu shared all of herself with Alphonse, but it was not enough. He was resentful of the hours she spent away from him, bitter about the events she had to attend for work. He would quiz her after she went out with friends on who was there, whom she spoke to, the nature of their conversations, until it was easier for Lulu to stop going out without him at all.

At first Lulu found it flattering. At first she interpreted his overbearing manner as a sign of true love. "That isn't love. It took him showing up to one of my meetings for me to see how toxic we'd become."

The irony was that it began as it had ended, with a perfect cake splattered across the floor. Lulu's clients had paid her for a sample cake before their wedding. They weren't satisfied with merely a tasting, they needed to see a replica of the cake they'd be served on their special day. Everything had to be perfect. As Lulu was carrying the cake toward a table seating the bride and groom, their parents and siblings, she spotted Alphonse through the window, watching her from across the street.

"At that point our relationship was particularly tumultuous. We both knew it. And he was so afraid of losing me that he acted out."

When their eyes met across the street, Lulu subtly shook her head no, then plastered a smile on her face as she continued with the cake. Alphonse had the footwork of a tennis player. He was fast and precise, through the door and standing between her and her clients before Lulu reached the table.

"He always talked with his hands. It was one of the many things about him that I mistook for passion when really it was posturing. Trying to make himself take up as much space as possible."

Lulu couldn't follow what he was so angry about. His ranting was incoherent. As he swung wildly, of course he caught the bottom of the cake and sent it flying, until it landed on the head of the mother of the bride. When she wiped the cake from her eyes, they were not sparkling like Alphonse's had been.

"I offered to make their cake free of charge, but there's no turning back from smashing cake in the mother of the bride's face. It's the only time I've been fired."

"I'm so sorry my story led you to so much jealousy and turmoil," Madeline said, almost like she was not sorry at all. Alice glanced over at the old woman, whose face appeared contrite. You could be two things at once, regretful and gloating. For Lulu, Madeline was genuinely sorry. For Alice, she was pleased to prove yet again that she was right. Her stories caused more harm than good. She would win their wager. Alice would be forced to stop.

"Don't be," Lulu said, leaning forward, arms outstretched across the desk as though she was reaching for Madeline. "It was unpleasant at the time. Alphonse isn't a bad man though. We just didn't know how to manage the passion and jealousy between us. Don't get me wrong, we'll never be friends, but I did bake the cake for his wedding. By then I was already with Daniel."

A few days after the cake affair, as she and Daniel had taken to calling it, Lulu got a call from a number she didn't recognize. This was not so unusual. New clients often called her. She picked up, expecting it to be a request for a job. Instead it was the brother of the bride, the son of the woman who'd suffered a face full of sticky icing.

"Immediately I was on the defensive," Lulu said, leaning back in her desk chair. "I'd already returned their deposit—unprompted, I might add. I'd emailed to apologize. I wasn't sure what more he wanted from me. Turned out he didn't want anything at all."

"Are you okay?" he asked.

"What?" she asked, confused.

"I just wanted to make sure you're okay after your boyfriend stormed in like that."

"He's not my boyfriend anymore." Lulu could hear Daniel smile through the phone.

"It took a decade to win over my now mother-in-law. Grandchildren help with that," Lulu said. "Thank you, Madeline. I never got to reach out to tell you that. Thank you for leading me to the greatest man I've ever known."

"I can't take credit for your marriage. The story I wrote, it led you to Alphonse. Everything that came after, any joy, that was your doing."

"Maybe so. I don't think it's quite so neat as that. Your story changed my life. It awakened something in me. I can't even explain it. I felt my insides reforming, taking new shape. It wasn't that you brought me to Alphonse or Daniel. You brought me to myself."

"Still," Madeline insisted, "you should not have had to endure that kind of jealousy."

"That hardly makes it your fault. Oh, Madeline, don't take my story as a sign of failure. It was a success. I'm a success. I will not let you see me as anything else."

Alice could tell from the way Madeline would not meet Lulu's eyes that she did not agree. Madeline forced a smile and told her old client, "I'm glad you're happy."

When Alice and Madeline settled into Alice's old car, Alice began speaking before Madeline had a chance to control the conversation. "Okay, before you say anything, that's not a failed story. Lulu said so herself. She credits you for the good in her life."

"You heard what you wanted to in her story," Madeline said, watching Lulu's Cakes through the passenger window.

"I heard what she said. Verbatim. Your story brought her to herself. Maybe that wasn't your intention, but it was still a positive outcome." Alice reversed out of the parking spot and headed the short distance back to the highway.

"I'm glad she's happy. But the truth is, my story caused her harm. Temporary harm is still lasting."

Alice knew better that to argue when Madeline was like this. The old woman had an intractable streak. Once her mind was set, nothing Alice said could sway it. She wondered if there was any chance of winning their wager, any amount of evidence that might convince Madeline her stories netted positive results, even when the magic faded. So far they'd seen three different outcomes: a lasting romance, a relationship that ended but that enriched life, and one that while filled with stifling jealousy guided a woman toward her husband. In the end these were all happy stories. It gave Alice hope for her stories, that even if her stories did not work according to plan, she should continue writing. For her part, Madeline refused to see it that way. Their wager was not a fair fight. Madeline was not open to being wrong. Well, Alice wasn't either. She would continue to prove to Madeline her worth until Madeline was forced to believe in it too.

23

The Complications of Love

There were two bookbinders in town, which made Alice's choice of someone else to bind her books easy. As soon as she met Howard, she realized she should have gone to Santa Barbara Bookbinders from the start. She'd been fooled by Willow Bindery's sleekness. Fooled by Duncan too.

Howard was a septuagenarian, happily married for a half century to Greta, who worked the register, keeping him company as he bound and repaired books. In the one-room storefront, the presses and paper cutters were out in the open, which made Alice realize just how secretive Duncan was. The only books on display were samples and current projects, no stationery or whimsical wrapping paper. Just a thin layer of dust on the floor and the thick smell of glue permeating the shop.

Alice could sense Howard and Greta's love the moment she walked in, even though they sat silently on opposite sides of the bindery. Greta sang old folk songs and knitted while Howard worked on his books. In the front window, a table displayed hats and scarves she had made. Alice was so rarely around old love. All her stories were new, still becoming.

Howard special ordered red leather to match the grain that Duncan used, applied the same gold leaf letters to the spine, the same font to the thick stock pages. Side by side on her shelf, the books were indistinguishable. Alice could not tell which had been bound by Duncan and which by Howard. Every time she saw them commingling, she had to shake off her sadness. It surprised her, how quickly her anger had shifted to loss.

After Coco's wedding, Duncan had left a series of messages on Alice's voicemail. His texts piled up. They all said the same thing. He was sorry. More than sorry. Remorseful. It had been unintentional. Still, he should have told her as soon as he read that very first book, which to her horror Alice realized was 127 pages of DUNCAN, I LOVE YOU. His voicemails continued. He hadn't meant for it to become a secret. He was truly, deeply sorry. He valued their connection. Could she please call him back?

She deleted his voicemails and texts, got as far as typing, Please leave me alone, then at the last minute erased her text without sending it. After two weeks of steady pleas, his messages stopped arriving. When she realized that she was still checking her phone for them, disappointed each time by his silence, she deleted his number, thinking with a hefty mix of regret and relief that this was the end.

A week after his calls stopped, Alice was sitting at her desk working on a story when someone knocked on her door. It was such an uncommon occurrence that she figured it was a volunteer collecting signatures for a local petition, a college student asking for donations to Greenpeace. Alice opened the door, prepared to politely refuse the stranger on the other side until she saw that it was Duncan.

He wove his hands behind his back as he sheepishly stared at the floor under Alice's bare feet. She hugged her body, acutely aware of her exposed legs, her flimsy cotton shorts, her father's ragged sweatshirt, her lopsided ponytail.

"What are you doing here?" she said, wishing the words had come out as a bark, disorienting him, making him cower.

Instead he looked up at her hopefully, holding out three red books. "You never came to get them, so I figured I'd drop them off."

"And you didn't think to pop them in the mail. Or just leave them on the doorstep without bothering me?"

"Alice—" He took a tentative step toward her, and she reflexively held her breath. He continued to hold out the books, but Alice refused to take them. Part of her wanted to slam the door in his face, another wanted to hear everything he had to say to her.

"I'm sorry about the bridesmaid."

Alice was about to tell him he didn't owe her a thing, that he could kiss whomever he liked. He didn't give her time to speak, time to lie.

"I've never... I'm not usually the kind of guy... I was broken when I moved here. I didn't realize how broken I was until women were stopping me at the grocery store, asking me for my number at bars, inviting me to parties. That was because of your stories. I'd be lying if I said it didn't make me feel good. That's all that bridesmaid was. As soon as she kissed me—" he lifted his eyes to Alice's, and her heart caught "—it was like the spell was broken and I knew she wasn't the one I wanted to be kissing. None of them were."

Duncan stared at Alice, trying to interpret her thoughts when she had no idea what she was feeling. She was panicked, torn, still angry, almost forgetting why. Then she didn't have time to think because he leaned forward and kissed her. She shut her eyes, letting herself get lost in his lips, slightly scratchy against hers, insistent but patient. And then she was struck, more immediately and potently than by his kiss, with the need to vomit.

Alice pulled away and grabbed the books. "Please," she barely managed to say over the bile collecting in her throat. "Just leave me alone."

She threw the door shut and sprinted to the bathroom, making it to the toilet just in time. She wondered if Duncan was still outside, if he could hear her heaving. She leaned back against the wall, shut her eyes, and steadied her breath. Dehydration, insomnia, voicelessness—she assumed she'd experienced all the turmoil her body had to offer. Vomiting was a new one, somehow more cleansing. When her stomach settled, she stood up and tossed the red books he'd given her into the back of her closet. She couldn't risk discarding them in the trash, the chance that someone might read them. Then she opened three windows on her computer and settled down to write those clients new stories. After they were finished, Alice took them to Santa Barbara Bookbinders for Howard to bind. When those books looked identical to Duncan's, when the stories immediately led to love, Alice knew she was right to avoid Duncan and the complications that came with him. She was always better off on her own.

"Alice, it's obvious you two like each other. So he kissed that bridesmaid," Gabby said, walking backward up the steep slope so she was facing Alice. She was infuriatingly fit, able to keep up a conversation while Alice struggled for breath let alone words on their hike, which made it difficult for Alice to argue back. "It's not like you haven't made plenty of bad decisions trying to avoid your feelings for someone."

"I don't have feelings for him." The words came out too forcefully on account of the physical exertion required to speak. "I don't want to at least." Alice stopped to catch her breath, looking out over her city below.

Gabby trotted down the hill and put her arm around Alice's

shoulders. "It's okay to be hurt. And confused. Just give it some time."

"There's nothing to give time to. I told him I didn't want to see him again, and I meant it."

Alice could sense Gabby's disapproval, but her best friend remained quiet. "If he hurt me this much already," Alice whispered to the vista, "imagine how much worse it would be if there was something more between us."

"You don't know that," Gabby pleaded. Alice glanced at her best friend, looking away to a crowd of hikers trudging up the hill when she could not endure the disappointed look on Gabby's face.

Alice let out a little yelp as she spotted a familiar figure charging up the hill. She never liked running into people, something that was difficult to avoid in a city as small as Santa Barbara. Small talk made her act awkwardly, and she never knew how or when to end the conversation. When she saw Skylar drawing near, her body panicked, wanting to flee. There was nowhere to go. Even if she forged ahead, eventually they would reach the top, and there was only one way back down. At some point their paths would cross. Instead she froze and clutched Gabby.

"What is it?"

"Skylar," Alice said.

"Who?"

"Remember that musician I dated a few years ago?"

"No."

"He took me to Cold Spring Tavern?"

"Oh." Although Gabby had never been a part of Alice's Sunday trips with her father, she knew all about the tradition. "You just went on a few dates. What's the big deal?"

"He's with one of my clients." Sure enough, he was hiking beside Beatriz, a woman whose fitness rivaled Gabby's. It was her obsession, an addiction really, although Beatriz did not describe it to Alice this way. She was self-conscious not about her body which was sculpted and powerful, but about the undeniable fact that her strength intimidated men, that it telegraphed all the ways she didn't need them. Love shouldn't be about need, so Alice had written her a story that taught her to want instead, and after reading it, she'd met Gavin, a former football player who had had his glory years and had no interest in joining her at the gym. Better yet, he wasn't threatened by her power. Their independence had given her a new kind of strength. Yet here she was, hiking beside Skylar. Momentarily Alice wondered if they were simply friends, until Beatriz grabbed him by the shirt and planted a decidedly unfriendly kiss on his lips.

"Oh, Alice," Gabby said, watching them make out.

"That's not who she was with after my story." It made no sense. Skylar smoked cigarettes. His tattooed limbs looked absurdly thin in mesh shorts. And was he actually wearing Converse sneakers on a hike? Meanwhile, Beatriz looked as fit as ever, rippled abs exposed between a coordinated sports bra and athletic pants. Gavin had been the perfect fit for her. How could she be with Skylar? How could Alice's story have failed?

"I can't let them see me," Alice said, turning her back to the trail as their lips unlocked and they continued their ascent.

Gabby shielded Alice so she was mostly obscured from the trail, not that it mattered. Beatriz and Skylar clung to each other as they hiked, heads nestled together, eyes only for each other and the occasional wayward rock.

"That was a little dramatic," Gabby said after they passed.

"I didn't want to have to talk to either of them."

"Yeah, but you were practically ready to jump off the bluff. Alice, should I be worried about you?"

"That's not who she's supposed to be with." Alice briefly filled her in on Gavin, how well suited he and Beatriz had seemed. Carrie, too, how she also had not found immediate and lasting love after reading Alice's story.

"Is it possible that you don't understand how your stories work as well as you think you do? Maybe it's more complicated than you think. Love always is."

But Alice had never been interested in the complications of love.

"Besides," Gabby said, resuming their hike toward the apex of the trail. "They're happy. If it was with the first person she met after your story or the second or the tenth, isn't that what's important?"

"Let's just head back," Alice said, already walking downhill. For two miles she could feel Gabby beside her, studying her every movement, wanting to press her, but knowing when to stop. Of course Gabby was right. Beatriz was happy. Carrie was happy too. That should be all that mattered. That was all that mattered. Still, after two failed stories, Alice couldn't shake the feeling that their happiness was a result of luck, and Alice knew all too well that luck was a streak, a roll, a spell destined to be broken.

But Alice could not stop writing now. There were too many people counting on her, too many souls who had entrusted her with their love. She needed to keep believing, if not for herself then for them.

24

The Purple Book

After meeting Lulu at her bakery, Alice and Madeline continued to parse through the green books, discovering more stories of jealous lovers, more relationships ruined by envy, cheating, and distrust. Jealousy did not always look dangerous. It did not always involve screaming or control. Sometimes it looked like hurt. Lovers bruised by their own expectations, by all the ways they wanted to be and were not loved. Sometimes it was earned, a rational jealousy spurred by a lover's misdeeds. Sometimes it was passionate, broken plates and shouting matches followed by sex on the kitchen floor. Sometimes it was professional, not romantic, a lover resentful of his beloved's success, a lover coming second to a job. There were as many types of jealousy as there were types of love.

Since that seemed to be what green meant, Alice reluctantly added the color to her list, writing in her spiral notepad, *Green*

= *ruined by jealousy.* It worried her to admit that, of the three colors they'd explored, two represented relationships that had come to an end. Still, almost all the former clients they encountered were happy. None of them seemed permanently bruised by the affairs they'd had in response to Madeline's books. And so many of them wound up with other partners they loved. Maybe Madeline hadn't given these souls everlasting love, but she'd taught them how to recognize it when it presented itself with someone else. Surely this supported her continued commitment to her craft.

But Madeline continued to feel vindicated. All those relationships ruined by jealousy and envy. All those clients she'd failed. As she slipped the last green book they'd investigated onto the shelf, she motioned to all the rest, "Each and every one of these is a failure." Instead of being gleeful she was resigned, as though she was at last understanding that winning their wager was not winning at all. "Face it, Alice, this is not a gift."

"I disagree." Alice refused to let her resolve waver. "Besides," she said, trying a different tactic, "we have two colors left."

"You aren't going to admit I'm right until we've looked through every book in this library, are you?"

"That was the deal."

"And when we're through? When we see how many new ways people can feel pain in these blue and purple books, will you give up?"

No, Alice thought, for she knew she would not be proven wrong. Even if many of their stories didn't last, their service bettered people's lives. "When we get to the end, we'll discover who was right," she insisted.

Madeline frowned at Alice. "Fine, but we're looking at purple next. I don't have eight hundred stories in me at the moment. I need something easier."

As if fewer meant easier. As if less could not also be more.

"Not that one," Madeline said as Alice reached for a thin

purple book. She tucked it back onto the shelf and let her fingers run along all those eggplant spines, their wails so soft Alice suspected she might be imagining them, until her fingertips electrified again.

"Not that one either," Madeline said.

This happened three more times before Alice suggested that Madeline pick the next book.

The old woman stood before the shelf staring at the twenty-eight purple books—twenty-seven from their original count and an additional book that had shifted during their studies. "I have a bad feeling about these books," she said.

"Purple is the color of royalty."

"Beheadings happen to royalty."

"You're being silly," Alice said, moving to retrieve the first book that had called to her, the slender one. As she pulled it out, Madeline ducked, prepared for the ceiling to fall on them. "Madeline, it's just a book."

"You know as well as I do that there's no such thing as just a book."

Alice found the first line in the ledger and came up with a name, Dee Raymond. "She sounds like an old-time movie star."

"Looked like one too. When she came to see me, I answered the door and thought, 'What the hell are you doing here?'" Back then, Madeline's door was an open one. There was no email. No cellular telephone. A landline, when she deigned to answer it. The only guaranteed way to reach her was to drive up the mountain and knock on the door.

She rejected as many people as she granted entry. There were all sorts of reasons for saying no—a weak demeanor, a disheveled appearance, an impatient attitude. If she got a bad feeling, she would simply close the door, no apology, no explanation, and the poor soul was left to conclude that they'd been rejected.

"Isn't that a little cruel?" Alice asked.

"Love is not for the faint of heart," Madeline told her.

There was a rumored handbook for how to approach the love

giver, as Madeline was called. Madeline never saw the handbook but she did not doubt its existence. She even heard that one of her former clients was offering consultations on how to guarantee an audience with Madeline. She did not begrudge such an enterprising person their hustle. Ingenuity, resourcefulness, these were qualities Madeline admired.

"I almost sent Dee away. I didn't trust that someone so beautiful needed my help until I saw her cower." Madeline hunched her shoulders, shrinking into herself. "It was like she was trying to make herself invisible when there was no hiding her beauty."

Dee dressed impeccably in expensive and voluminous dresses. Her face was composed yet understated, in neutral tones that matched her olive skin. Her hair fell to her waist with a natural wave and shine. The combination indicated that the woman was aware of her beauty as well as how to flatter it without calling too much attention to it. Still, her every pore emanated insecurity. It wasn't just her posture and lack of eye contact. She introduced herself as "not really a sculptor" since she hadn't sold any of her pieces to a gallery, just through word of mouth, mostly to her parents' friends. Everything Madeline said Dee accepted without question, even when Madeline contradicted herself, first saying that external accolades were not what made an artist, then testing Dee and saying, "You are not an artist until the gatekeepers embrace you." When Dee reported that she had never been loved, that she feared she was unlovable, Madeline knew that she was. She knew she could help her.

Madeline wrote her a mantra to make her brave. A mantra, not a story, for she didn't need twists and turns, fairy tales. She needed simple truths.

The purple book was seven pages long. Each page had one sentence on it.

You are a lioness.

You are an Amazon.

You are a queen.

You are all the Greek goddesses combined, and the Roman ones too.

You are courage.

You are love.

You are the only one who gets to be you.

"It was the only time I wrote anything short enough that the client could read it in front of me. She cried when she finished it. After that I never heard from her again."

Alice typed Dee Raymond's name into her phone, found no profiles on social media, no bios on LinkedIn. No pictures on the boards of nonprofits, inclusions on galleries or museum exhibitions. No death records, divorce or marriage certificates. Dee was a ghost.

"She worked part-time at her sister's diner. The name of it was a gemstone. Diamond's Diner. Or Emerald? Everyone assumed it was named for the owner, but it was really her dog."

"Ruby's Diner?" Alice guessed, not expecting to be right.

Madeline snapped. "That's the one."

Alice tucked the book under her arm. "Lucky for you, I know it well." Alice's father often took her there after school. They had the best egg creams, her father's favorite.

"You could put some of your writing proceeds toward something a little more modern," Madeline said as she climbed into Alice's passenger seat. Since that first trip to Abigail Herkowitz's, Alice had not let her drive again.

"I like my car," Alice said, putting her car into Drive.

"And do your clients like it? Haven't you learned the value of appearance?"

"Anyone who would judge me by my car is both a bad judge of character and not someone I'd want to work with."

"Fair enough."

Alice took each curve along Stagecoach Road slowly. They drove beneath the highway bridge until Cold Spring Tavern was upon them. Alice clutched the wheel. That familiar tightness took hold in her chest. She focused on deep breaths until the tavern was out of view.

"Why do you do that?" Madeline asked when they stopped at the intersection with 154, waiting for a break in traffic.

"Do what?"

Madeline gave a tiny yelp. "That noise, each time we drive by the tavern."

"Do I?" Alice said, merging onto the highway. She pressed down on the gas pedal, and the old beast flew.

"Every time. Didn't you say you used to come up here with your father?"

"Every Sunday," Alice reminded her. As soon as her mind returned to those afternoons, something released in her chest and she found herself wanting to tell Madeline more about her father and their trips to Cold Spring Tavern, the time he saved a child from falling onto the open grill, how he'd bounded on stage uninvited to sing with the band. Somehow he always won them over, even though he had at best an average singing voice. She told Madeline about their biker family of mechanics, dentists, chemistry teachers, and pharmacists, their secret society of Sunday afternoon riders. To Alice's knowledge, her father never spoke to any of them except at those outings, yet he considered them some of his closest friends. They had not attended his funeral. When her father died, Alice had no way of contacting them. Bobby had not known they existed.

"So why do you treat it like a graveyard?" Madeline asked. "If it's a vestige of happy memories, why do you hold your breath whenever you pass?"

"It scares me, I guess," Alice admitted.

"Happy memories shouldn't scare you. They are all we have." Madeline surveyed the ocean view below them, perhaps getting lost in her own happy memories.

The diner looked the same as it had when Alice was a child, right down to the metal napkin dispensers on the table and the coral uniforms the waitresses wore.

"What'll it be?" their waitress said without looking up from her pad. She was young, teenaged, but had the hardened demeanor of someone much older. Alice ordered them each an egg cream, and when the girl returned with two glasses filled to the brim with frothy white, Alice asked if they could speak with the owner.

The girl planted her hand on her hip. "Is there a problem?"

"No problem," Alice said. She pointed at Madeline. "She's just an old friend."

The girl stared between Alice and Madeline. "Dad," she shouted toward the kitchen, "someone here to see you. An old friend?"

Alice mouthed *dad* to Madeline, who shrugged. They were expecting Dee's sister.

A man with smooth sunburned skin and a hint of gray along his temples appeared from the kitchen. An apron was tied around his waist, covered with dried bits of unidentifiable food. He looked at Alice and Madeline.

"You're the owner?" Alice asked.

"Ten years now. I know, I know, we changed the chicken salad recipe. Everyone loves the old chicken salad better. It was a family recipe of Dottie's and was not a part of the sale."

"We were actually looking for the previous owner," Madeline said. "Dottie, is it?"

"She passed about a year before the sale. Her daughter was the one to sell to us."

"Any idea where we could find her daughter? We're really trying to locate Dottie's sister, Dee. It's urgent that we speak to her."

The owner stiffened. "I'm not a part of all that. I know you've all got this weird unsolved mystery cult thing, but it's got nothing to do with my diner."

When he retreated to the back, Alice whispered to Madeline, "Do you have any idea what he's talking about?"

Madeline shook her head no, staring at the linoleum floor

where the owner had just stood. She seemed dazed and perhaps a little afraid.

The waitress returned to the table, pen poised on her order pad. "You come here to eat or just to snoop?"

"Just the check," Alice said sheepishly. She drank her egg cream so quickly she got brain freeze. When the girl came back with the check, Alice left twenty dollars for the two drinks, telling her to keep the change. "We didn't mean to offend your dad."

The girl pocketed the twenty, her entire demeanor changing. "Every once in a while someone watches a clip of *The Woman Lost to the Sea* and comes in here trying to be a detective. Maybe we should have changed the name, but people would still find us. I don't get it. It's not like they found her blood here or anything. She just worked here. Part-time."

A customer at a table across the room motioned to the waitress, and she offered Alice a quick smile before skipping away.

"Blood?" Alice whispered to Madeline, who seemed to have left her body.

Outside, Alice leaned against the roof of her car, staring up at the palm trees lining the street. Although she had grown up with these impossibly tall trees, it never ceased to amaze her just how thin and high they grew, how they swayed in the wind without snapping. It was the fronds you had to worry about, which fell from the trees when they were not properly maintained.

"I remember that story," Alice said. "It was on the rocks at Carpinteria Bluffs. I always assumed it was an urban legend."

When Alice was sixteen, Gabby had convinced their group of friends to meet at the beach at midnight. She brought a candle and a Ouija board. They set up on the rocks where the police suspected a woman named Edith had been killed. Fingers poised on the planchette, Gabby deepened her voice to ask if anyone was there. "We mean you no harm," she added.

The planchette started to move, first to the *I*, then the *A*, followed by *M*.

"Iam?" one of their friends asked.

"I am," Gabby corrected, which suggested to Alice that Gabby was deliberately moving the pointer, even if she didn't realize she was doing it.

The planchette continued to move: *T-H-E-O-N-L-Y.* Gabby found a notebook and transcribed, *O-N-E-W-H-O-G-E-T-S-T-O-B-E-M-E.* They stared at the letters strung together, until someone shouted, "I'm the only one who gets to be me," before the wind picked up, throwing the planchette into the air. It crashed on the rocks a few feet from them and tumbled into the ocean. The girls screamed in unison, stumbled over the rocks to Highway One, where without speaking they hopped into their respective cars and drove away.

I'm the only one who gets to be me.

How could Alice have forgotten those words? How had she failed to recognize them when she read them in Madeline's story?

It was a balmy morning, but Alice shivered from the memory, opting not to mention it to Madeline. On her phone, she Googled *The Woman Lost to the Sea.*

"Her name was Lauren not Raymond. Edith Lauren, Dee for short. I guess that explains why we couldn't find her—she gave you a fake name. It says she went missing in 1989. Edith and Samuel Lauren lived in that big glass house on Arriba Street. The house was torn down in the early 2000s after cycling through three owners." One owner heard a woman singing at night. Another saw a flash of her white slip whenever he passed the bathroom. The third did not see or hear anything, simply felt a weight across her chest every time she lay down.

The police had found Samuel in the kitchen with a self-inflicted gunshot wound to his temple in addition to scratches along his face. Dee's dried blood caked his fingernails. A search party combed the beach for Dee. The coast guard swept the area, but nothing was found except traces of her blood on the rocky shore and a strip of her white cotton nightgown. The police concluded that he'd tossed her body into the ocean, where the tide carried her away, and then returned to the house to kill himself. Without a body, her disappearance was never classified as a murder. To her family she was still missing.

Madeline fidgeted as she listened to Alice read the story.

"You okay?" Alice asked.

"Of course I'm not okay. Would you be okay if you found out one of your clients was brutally murdered by the man you drove her to?"

"No," Alice said to the pavement beneath her feet.

"Can you take me home now?"

They followed the highway as it wound in a wide arc around the ocean toward the national forest. Madeline stared out at the lush green hills and the blue expanse of the ocean, punctuated by the Channel Islands on the horizon. Alice was thankful for the silence. Her mind reviewed Madeline's simple story, sentence by sentence, so short that Alice had memorized it. *You are the only one who gets to be you.* In the secret library those words had seemed empowering, a statement of how our inimitability gives us strength. Now they just felt isolating. No one will fully understand us. We will never fully understand anyone else either. She drove mechanically along the highway, the air pressure causing her ears to pop as they climbed higher.

It was clear and crisp up in the mountains. The sun warmed the car through the windshield, though it did nothing to quell the chill that ran through Alice. Although they had only looked at one of those twenty-eight purple books, she knew what the color meant. Violence. Bruised and hateful ends.

She pulled up the hill onto Stagecoach Road, her heart catching as they passed Cold Spring Tavern. No matter how many times she visited Madeline, she never got used to its presence, unavoidable along the drive. When she let out that involuntary gasp, Madeline observed her but said nothing.

Outside Madeline's house, they sat in the car, staring at the woods. The car idled, its engine a soundtrack to their silence.

"Do you see now?" Madeline said at last. "Do you see now why you must stop?" Unlike her previous assertions, these words seemed to bring her no joy that she had finally proven Alice wrong.

Of all Alice's fears that her stories might not work, that her clients' luck might end, that when the magic dried up they could find themselves worse off than they were before, she had never imagined anything close to murder. Dee's story was never a love story. She wasn't an example of a woman who had learned something essential from Madeline when the magic faded. At least Alice had witnessed the potential devastation before it was too late, before she'd been able to inflict violence on one of her own clients.

25

Peaches

After Alice saw Beatriz and Skylar on her morning hike, she heard whispers of other breakups. Rumors of passion that had fizzled. Heat that had tempered. Novelty that wore thin. These things happened all the time, the gossipers insisted with a shrug. Not all relationships lasted, not even those penned by the love scribe. The love-hungry of Santa Barbara were undeterred. They spoke of these instances like they were talking about devastating earthquakes on the other side of the world, fires that could never reach their hills. Once they met their soul mate, they would have the type of love others envied. It was sad, sure, that not everyone found eternal love, but Alice's stories would work for them.

Alice was dismayed each time she heard of another couple that had not lasted. She tried to comfort herself with the fact that none of these cases had turned violent or ugly, simply an example of two souls who were not meant to be together. It was startling, worrisome, but her odds were still far superior to dating in the wild. As a result, despite the stories they'd heard of love faded, her waitlist continued to grow. People still believed in her gift. Already, she'd helped so many people. So despite her fear, she knew she had to continue—until she found Stefanie waiting at her door.

Alice was just returning from a meeting with a new client. Upon first glance, Ray was a typical Santa Barbara twenty-something: board shorts, a tan, sun-shaped calf tattoo, flip-flops, shaggy hair. "I missed the memo when I moved here," Duncan would have joked about not fitting the local type. Since his visit a month ago, Alice had not heard from him again. She'd asked him not to contact her, and he'd obliged. Only her brain was not so obedient. Even if her feelings persisted, Alice was right to avoid Duncan. The mere suggestion of how she might get hurt sparked a sharp pain in her chest. She'd just have to endure his presence in her mind for a little longer. Eventually her feelings would subside. They always did.

Ray, by his own estimation, was a philosopher. He worked at one of the tasting rooms, pouring glasses of wine as he recited memorized notes on the legs and the bouquet, but his mind was existential. He went on so long about freedom and existence that Alice had to stop him. "Sorry, I'm just passionate," he explained, knocking back a tiny cup of espresso with his pinky pointed out. "It intimidates women." His problem wasn't that he was passionate. Rather, he confused self-absorption with passion. No one wanted a man who didn't listen, particularly not one who Alice suspected did not own a proper pair of pants. Clients like Ray were her least favorite. They were also her simplest cases. Her dislike made it easy for her to diagnose their problems, to crank out a story and be done with them. Within steps of the coffee shop, an image came to her, a pie slamming into Ray's face. She'd have to massage it a little, but she saw it repeatedly, pie after pie across his pensive brow.

When she reached her driveway ready to write the story, a woman was sitting on her doorstep with her head resting on her knees, her long dark hair obscuring her face. She looked up as Alice rolled into her parking spot—one eye crystal blue, the other swollen shut, ringed by purple so dark it looked like makeup. Stefanie Bloom was one of her more recent clients. She'd been so sad when she first came to see Alice. Not sad as in lonely or heartbroken. Something deeper. Something that neither love nor Alice could fix. Sadness was her natural state of being. So Alice had written her a story about embracing all the beauty and strength her sadness afforded her. Now she didn't look sad so much as pissed. Fed up. She stood and blocked the door.

"Is this what you call love?" she shouted as Alice approached, shoulders hunched like she wanted to disappear inside herself. Alice paused, unsure what to do. While visibly upset, Stefanie did not seem volatile or dangerous, just wounded and scared. "I have a black eye, Alice. You think this is the kind of love I wanted?"

Gabby had prepared Alice for countless scenarios that had yet to arise. They'd rehearsed responses if people wanted their money back, if they wanted follow-up stories to make their partners better lovers, better cooks, better listeners, better shaped. Gabby had prepared her for clients looking for fertility, for fortunes, for health and aging well, never for this.

Stefanie stared at Alice, waiting for an answer she couldn't provide. "Let me make you some tea," Alice offered.

As soon as she invited the woman inside, she realized her mistake. Other than Duncan's brief appearance at her door, no one had been to her apartment in months, not even Gabby. In that time she'd allowed dishes to remain unwashed in the sink, mugs to collect on the desk beside her computer. Her bed was unmade, sheets crumpled at the bottom. At least she'd managed to clean out Agatha's litter box each night, but that was more on account of her cat's antipathy to mess than hers. If Alice waited too long to clean the litter box, she would return home to urine on her sheets, something she could never abide even as she allowed the rest of the apartment to go neglected. She had no problem leaving dirty clothes like a trail of breadcrumbs from where she discarded them to when she flopped into bed. As she followed Stefanie's eyes, she could imagine the story the woman would tell her friends about the love scribe who could not tend to her own space let alone other people's hearts.

Alice halfheartedly cleared the coffee table of its piles of magazines and notes for stories, stacking them on top of her bookshelf.

"I'll just make us that tea," Alice said as Stefanie lifted a ratty afghan with two fingers and dropped it on the other side of the couch.

In the kitchen, as she set the kettle to boil, Alice recalled the story she'd written for Stefanie, the love she'd reported to Alice after she read it. The story was about a peach orchard, a farmer who grew unsightly peaches that no one would buy, even though they were the most delicious peaches, if only anyone would try them. The farmer attempted to make them beautiful. She dyed them. Glossed them with simple syrup. Massaged them until they were round. The deformity persisted. Finally she piled all the peaches in a barrel and stuck a Free sign on top. When they were free, no one saw the blemishes, the discoloration. All they tasted was the sweet flesh inside.

After Stefanie read the story, her mouth went dry with desire for a juicy peach, the kind that would drip down her chin. She ventured down to the farmer's market and walked the aisles, dismayed to discover that they weren't in season. What about an orange? Or a tangerine? No, it had to be a peach. She paced the market in growing despair. It seemed vital that she eat a peach, but no one had peaches for sale. As she walked home, forlorn and defeated, she passed a bakery, one she'd never noticed before, with cute teal and white tile. Through the window she saw a single peach pie glistening in the case.

She waited in a modest line, her stomach tensing as the boy behind the counter helped one person then another, relieved when they ordered cupcakes and cookies. Soon there was one customer left between her and that perfectly bronze pie. And then he ordered it.

"Excuse me." She tapped him on the shoulder until he turned. "I was going to order that."

"Should have gotten here first, then." He motioned to the boy behind the counter, who was boxing up the pie, and asked, "Will it keep until tomorrow?"

The boy assured him it would.

Tomorrow? If he wasn't even going to eat it until tomorrow, surely he could come back the next day when there were new pies.

She tapped him again, and he turned again, annoyed. "You don't understand. I need that pie."

"Your life depends on it?"

"No, but I need it."

"You're going to a funeral, and it's in honor of the deceased?"

"No." Her voice was growing weaker.

"It's your mother's birthday and she just found out she's got cancer? Peach is her favorite?"

Stefanie shook her head, unable to muster any voice at all.

"Or you promised to bring it to a potluck wedding? No? Your nephew's birthday, then? You're having marital problems, and your husband loves peach pie, so you're hoping if you bring it home, he'll remember how much he loves you?"

"I'm not married," she said.

"Well, what is it? Tell me why you so desperately need this pie and it's yours."

"I was reading a story, and it made me want a peach, except peaches are out of season. Then I saw this bakery and thought, yes, a pie." Why was she telling this stranger all that? She twisted the onyx ring on her index finger.

"Must have been quite the story." His tone had changed, and she noticed that his eyes were the same color as her favorite ring. She should have known that a man with onyx eyes would bring trouble. At the time she was struck by how shiny those eyes were, staring intently at her.

They stood in the small shop, talking about poetry as customers skirted them to order. Stefanie had never met a man who liked *The Death Notebooks* before. The pie rested untouched on the counter. Eventually, when they were the only customers left, the boy behind the counter cleared his throat and asked if they needed anything else.

"Being inspired by a story seems the best reason of all." He lifted the pie off the counter and held it out to Stefanie.

She hesitated. "What if we split it?"

She meant divide it down the middle, each taking their respective half, but he asked the boy for two forks and led her to a nearby park where they found a bench and over the next two hours proceeded to eat the entire pie.

Alice sighed. It had been six weeks since Stefanie called to tell her about Keith. Theirs had quickly become one of Alice's favorite love stories, the way they shared a pie like teenagers in old films shared milkshakes. Except this was not love. Even before Stefanie told her the details, what she saw on Stefanie's face was not love at all.

The kettle whistled, and Alice fetched two mugs. She'd wanted Stefanie to see the beauty in her sadness, but she must have given her the wrong story. No, this wasn't love. It wasn't an example of a woman who had learned from the wrong relationship. This was violence, and Alice couldn't stomach any part of it.

She brought their tea into the living room, where Stefanie sat on the couch, staring vacantly at the smudged glass coffee table.

She took the mug from Alice, warming her hands on its sides. Alice waited for Stefanie to tell her what happened.

"My dad, he would… I watched it for years. I swore I would never let anyone do that to me. Keith wasn't…he didn't seem like the type. Then again, my father didn't either." She blew on her tea. Then she looked up at Alice, one eye wide, the other swollen shut. "Why would you write that for me?"

There was no sufficient explanation or apology, so Alice simply said, "You didn't deserve it."

The women sat side by side, sipping their tea. Alice considered offering to return her money but sensed this would offend her.

Suddenly Stefanie stood, put the tea on the table, and wiped the single tear that had escaped her good eye. "I just figured you should know what sort of story you wrote me." With that, she walked out.

Alice surveyed the spines on her bookshelf until she located Stefanie's story. Throughout the story, the peaches, while blemished, were never bruised. In over seventy pages there wasn't a single thing that could be viewed as violent. There wasn't any discordant diction, any foreboding imagery. The story was sad, sure. Melancholy even, but there wasn't a moment of violence in it. It would have made sense to Alice if the story was filled with battered, bleeding peaches, angry metaphors. Then she would at least understand how Stefanie's tragedy could have happened. Instead she was left with the unsettling realization that her stories could be dangerous and she had no idea why. At last she was convinced. A million love stories were not worth this one.

26

Closed for Business

Alice waited for the backlash, an exposé in the local paper, a scathing review on Yelp, calls from former clients asking if one of her matches had turned violent. But nothing happened. There were no cancellations from present clients, no names removed from the waitlist. If anything, new requests grew at a more vigorous rate. Alice stopped answering her emails and voicemails. Books recently bound remained on the shelves of Santa Barbara Bindery. Works in progress languished. No more names were added to the waitlist, and those already on it were holding out hope for something that was never going to happen. Alice was done. Oh, Alice Productions was closed for business. At least she hadn't quit her catering job.

She picked up five shifts a week, more than she ever had, even when she'd really needed the money. After three consecutive nights her wrists required icing. After four she added the heating pad to her nighttime routine. After five she poured Epsom salt into the bathtub and soaked until her skin raisined. Her body ached in places she didn't realize it could ache. This level of work was not sustainable, yet it was better than returning to the page. Plus, the physical punishment felt deserved. It was nothing compared to a black eye, a bruised heart, or worse.

While Alice had cut writing from her routine, Gabby was not about to let her quit any of the other new adjustments to her life. The regular hairstyling continued, the well-tailored clothes, the nude lipstick and nail polish, the morning hike. Now that Alice was no longer a love scribe, everything about this altered identity seemed even more like a lie.

"That's guilt talking," Gabby said as they barreled down the hill on a new hike. After seeing Skylar and Beatriz, Alice had decided she didn't want to press her luck. She bribed Gabby with coffee to wake up twenty minutes earlier and venture to a less popular trail on the outskirts of town.

Throughout the hike Gabby had not mentioned Alice's stories. They'd talked around them the way they would talk around an ex-lover, carving a giant arc so wide as to pretend the relationship had never existed. Still, Alice could sense the questions on the tip of Gabby's tongue.

It wasn't until they were sitting in Gabby's car outside Alice's apartment that Gabby cautiously said, "You're sure you want to quit?"

Alice knew she was done writing. Even if she'd wanted to, she couldn't free her mind to the muse, couldn't craft stories for people as though she wasn't aware of the consequences.

The moment reminded Alice of med school, when Gabby had asked her the very same thing. That was Alice. A quitter. It was not surprising that she was quitting writing. The true surprise was that she'd kept it up for so long, oblivious to the real damage she caused. Oh, sweet irony. In med school she could not handle the phantom injuries she might inflict on people. With her stories she did not recognize the harm she did.

"It's too risky," Alice said.

"Love is always risky," Gabby said. "You aren't responsible for what happens after people connect."

"Why not?"

Gabby studied Alice's Victorian, the bay window of her studio apartment. "It's horrible what happened to Stefanie. It's worse than horrible. The guy who did that to her should be castrated. Or at least in jail. There's nothing we can say that will make what happened to her okay. But it's not your fault. *He* hurt her, not you."

The paint on the house was chipping along the scales and sticks. If you squinted, you could see the life it had once lived, before it was carved into apartments, before it was neglected.

"She never would have met him if it weren't for me."

"You don't know that."

"Well, if she was destined to meet him anyway, then there's no point to my stories."

"That's not what I meant. Alice, you have a gift."

"Look, I appreciate what you're trying to do, but I contributed. Whether it was my fault or not, I'm part of the worst thing that's happened to her. I don't want to be part of the worst moment in anyone's life."

"So the answer is to give up? What about all those people who are counting on you?"

"You think if they knew, they'd still want my help?"

"Maybe not everyone. Most people believe they're too strong to be with someone who would abuse them. That they'd never let it happen."

"Is that supposed to make me feel better?"

"It's supposed to be honest."

Alice wiped sweat off her brow. The car was suddenly very hot. "Well, what if it was Oliver?"

"What the hell is that supposed to mean?" Gabby's defensiveness was startling.

"I just mean, if something happened with Oliver, if he hurt you or something—"

"Why would you even say that? He would never hurt me." If they were outside, Gabby would have stormed off. Instead, trapped in her car, she leaned against the window, creating as much space between them as possible.

"Of course he wouldn't. I just meant that if my story had led you to the wrong person, would you want me to keep writing?"

"Is there some reason you don't like Oliver? I know you two haven't gotten to spend that much time together. He's just been so busy preparing for his show."

"This isn't about Oliver. Oliver's great."

"He is. And he isn't going anywhere. Besides, if it came to it, I could take him in a fight. His idea of working out is walking to and from the fridge. I tell him all the time that he's lucky he's naturally fit."

They both forced a laugh. Alice felt unsettled, like she hadn't gotten at the essential truth she needed to convey to her best friend.

"I'm sorry I brought up Oliver. It was only meant to be a hypothetical. I just, I'm wondering why you want me to keep writing stories, knowing that some of them aren't destined to work out."

"You can't promise that every relationship will be candlelit dinners and roses. That's not what people want from you though. They want the love to be theirs. They just want you to make it appear." Gabby fiddled with the switch for the window, sending the glass up and down an inch as she spoke. Was she right? Was this all her clients wanted from Alice, a beginning, a fighting chance rather than a guarantee of everlasting love? No one could guarantee that, not even Alice. Maybe her gift was more complex than she realized.

"Don't doubt yourself," Gabby added.

"You make it sound so simple," Alice said.

"Well, it isn't easy, but it is simple. It's a choice, Alice. You're stronger than you think. Believe in your strength."

Alice wasn't sure if they were talking about her stories anymore or something else entirely.

"Have you talked to Duncan?" Gabby asked.

"That's over," Alice insisted. She could hear everything Gabby didn't say, everything Alice didn't want to hear.

After six messages from Greta about the books waiting for pickup at Santa Barbara Bindery, Alice ventured to the shop with no plans of delivering the books to their intended recipients. Howard took pride in his work. Leaving the books to molder would be as great an offense as she could inflict upon him. The problem was not his books. The problem was the nature of her gift. The problem was love itself.

Greta was sitting in the front window when Alice arrived, knitting a scarf from multicolored alpaca wool with shiny strands of copper woven throughout, her long silver hair dangling over her right shoulder. The scarf was so long that it had collected at her feet and started to grow around her legs. It was the type of image Alice had only seen in stories, a never-ending scarf that could warm all the cold souls of the world. It would have been a perfect image for her client James, who—no, Alice would not let her mind go there. She was finished with her stories. Even if she could bring James love, it would not compensate for the violence she'd imposed on other lives. She hated that her mind thought in stories, that she could not control the images, the chill down her arms beckoning her to write. But Alice was stronger than her gift. She had to be.

"Alice," Greta exclaimed when the bell rang as Alice entered. "We were beginning to worry that something had happened to you."

"I've just been really busy."

Greta rested the knitting needles on the windowsill, the bottom half of her body cocooned in color. She studied Alice. "You sure everything is okay?"

"Why is your scarf so long?" Alice asked, pointing to all that alpaca obscuring her legs. "It seems like it would be hard to wear."

Greta shrugged. "It just hasn't felt finished yet. The scarf will tell me when it's the right length. Besides, I rather like the idea of a scarf so long I could wrap it around my entire body. Come—" She unfurled her legs from the scarf and stood. "Your books are waiting for you."

Alice followed Greta to the back of the store where Howard's printing press was.

"Howard's on a delivery, one of those hoity-toity Montecito folks who can't be bothered to drive into town. I shouldn't complain though. They keep us in business."

Greta found Alice's eight cherry red books on the shelf, two copies of each, and handed them to Alice. As always, her mind drifted to Duncan when she saw Howard's books. They looked identical to Duncan's. The whole point of switching binders was to forget him, yet every interaction she had with Howard and Greta and their books just made him more present in her mind. If she couldn't prevent herself from thinking in stories, from being inspired to write, she couldn't keep herself from missing Duncan either, from wanting to forgive him. But Alice was stronger than her desires. She had to be.

Alice thanked Greta and started to leave with the heavy pile of books when Greta stopped her. "Oh, I almost forgot. Our distributor discontinued the cherry you use." She held up three different colors of red leather, one burgundy, one amaranth, the other carmine. "Will one of these work instead?"

They were lush, deeply saturated colors, deserving of stories that brought people lasting love. Bound in any of these colors, the books would look different from Duncan's. In their difference she would still be reminded of him.

"I'm actually taking a break for a bit," she said.

"Good for you." Greta put the leather away. "Your generation works too hard."

Alice didn't correct her.

Greta motioned for her to wait one moment. Alice watched as she crossed the shop to her knitting display, riffling through several hats until she found one toward the bottom of the pile and lifted it out. It was red, like Alice's books. A beret.

"I knitted this a few years ago, but I knew the moment I met you that I was keeping it for you." Greta set the beret on Alice's head, angling it left and right until she was pleased with its arrangement. "We'll be here when you're ready to get back to it."

In early December, it was still too warm outside for wool, but Alice wore the beret under her bike helmet all the way home. In her back pocket, her phone buzzed repeatedly. It had become a steady rhythm to her ride until she almost didn't notice it anymore. By the time she arrived at her apartment, she had four messages from unsaved numbers and four missed calls from Gabby. Gabby never left messages, never called multiple times in a row either. Briefly Alice wondered if something was wrong, but she was running late for work—a wedding of course—and frankly she didn't want another lecture from Gabby about Duncan. As close as they were, Gabby would never understand that it wasn't some conquerable fear that Alice was running from. It was something deeper, something dispositional that she could not change about herself. When Gabby called again, Alice silenced her phone and dashed into her apartment to get ready for work.

27

The Reverse Pilgrimage

The requests kept coming. People offered more money, hard-to-get reservations, free housing. To them all, Alice gave the same response: she was no longer in business. One man proposed a sum so grand she would never have to work again, as a scribe or anything else.

It has come to my attention, she explained to him over email, that not all my stories lead to everlasting love. Some have ended in cheating and violence, heartbreak. It's too dangerous to continue.

Almost immediately, he wrote back. Everyone found love before the heartbreak?

Yes, Alice admitted, but it wasn't lasting.

I'd be happy to take that risk, he declared. When can you start?

She did not write back. She stopped engaging with the other requests entirely. The phone continued to ring at all hours. Her voicemail box filled. Even on silent she could hear her phone pinging with new texts. One day, when she couldn't take it anymore, she decided to go for a walk, hoping to clear her head.

She walked north on State, away from the ocean. The symbolism was not lost on her, this reverse pilgrimage on the same street but in the opposite direction from all those pilgrims who had followed the hummingbird to the ocean and found love. She imagined that with each step she was erasing her love stories, the ones she'd written, the ones she would never write, all the love and danger she might manifest in the world.

All around her the scenery presented images for clients whose stories she'd abandoned. A streetlight. A phone pole. A Rottweiler. A leaf. They struck her as forcefully as ever. She walked faster, which exposed her to more material. When she arrived at the shopping center that housed her favorite bookstore, she dipped inside, hoping the holy presence of all those books might save her from her gift.

The familiar layout of the store calmed her, the burgundy carpeting, the tight aisles, the calligraphy signs dangling from the ceiling, designating the different sections. She shut her eyes and breathed in the smell of paper, of bodies, of calm.

"Alice Meadows?" a familiar but not quite identifiable voice called from behind her. "Alice, is that you?"

She opened her eyes to find a stranger smiling at her. Immediately she panicked. Was he one of her clients? It was reckless, how quickly she passed along their stories, then allowed them to vanish from her mind. Clearly she had never respected her gift, never afforded it the care and attention it required.

"I thought that was you." He shook his head in disbelief. "Alice, Alice, Alice, is it possible that I haven't seen you since you were fourteen?"

Fourteen. Fourteen had stopped being an age, a year of life, anything other than the before and after of her father's death. Alice studied this man, who was clearly pleased by their chance encounter and who remembered that time differently than she did, a time not bleached by her father's death. As he smiled, she saw through his wrinkles, furrows, and an unfamiliar shock of white hair.

"Mr. Thomas," she said remembering. He was her eighth grade language arts teacher. Alice had always enjoyed reading, but Mr. Thomas had made it into a religion for her, something to believe in. All that was before. After, her teachers never mentioned the papers she did not submit, the books she did not read, the tests where she wrote nothing more than her name at the top. Her grades for every class remained the same as they had been before that last month of finals. When her report card arrived, Bobby decided they should celebrate her near perfect average. Alice saw nothing celebratory in those grades, the way they pretended that nothing had changed.

"I'm surprised you recognized me," Alice said breathlessly.

"At the risk of sounding foolish, you look the same. Older of course, but you look like you. That's refreshing these days. Don't worry," he laughed. He had a generous laugh. It was part of what made him such a compelling teacher. He seemed to genuinely revel in his students' discoveries. "I'm not expecting you to tell me I look the same too."

"Well, you look enough the same that I recognized you." Alice's body relaxed. For Mr. Thomas, her time in his class was just another year of teaching.

"I suppose that's something." He shook his head. "Well, I would ask you what brings you here. I suppose it's pretty obvious. I'm so glad you're a reader. I know I can't take credit for that. It always makes me feel like I've done my job though when I discover that any of my students is a reader or writer."

"I'm definitely not a writer," Alice blurted. She tucked her hair behind her ears, embarrassed.

"Oh, I'm not so sure about that. I still remember the story you wrote for my class when we were reading *Animal Farm*," Mr. Thomas said.

"We wrote stories for your class?" She had no memory of the assignment. In fact, she'd been certain the story she wrote for Gabby was the first one her mind had ever concocted.

He nodded like a proud father. "I asked everyone to write an allegory, and you came up with this story about a tortoise and a tricycle. It was delightful. I was reading it when I first met my husband."

This got Alice's attention.

He rubbed his hands together like he had in the classroom when he wanted to make sure he had a rapt audience. "I used to do all my grading at this diner not too far from here. It closed years ago. On Saturday mornings I'd sit at the counter and grade as I ate my breakfast. I was so focused on your story that I didn't notice the man who sat down next to me. I sensed his presence, but I couldn't have told you the first thing about him, so absorbed was I. When he cleared his throat I looked over to see golden brown eyes watching me. 'Must be quite the story,' he said, and I followed his eyes to the counter where syrup was dripping off my plate onto my pants. I startled and jumped up, managing to knock the whole plate into his lap. I expected him to be pissed off. He just laughed and said, 'Well, now I need to see what was so interesting that we're both covered in your French toast.'

"At some point," Mr. Thomas continued, "our *coincidental* breakfasts became planned. I'm not sure why either of us felt the need to be coy. Maybe it made everything seem more fated, like the kind of love story you'd read in a book." He stared at Alice with the look she'd come to know well from her clients. She could hear *Oh, Alice* on the tip of his tongue.

Mr. Thomas leaned forward like he was about to tell her a secret. There were dark circles engulfing his eyes, his complexion ghostly white. "This might sound a little woo-woo—it felt like your words bonded us. Like the story was ours."

Alice tried to smile in the way that was fitting for when someone told you how they met their partner, only she was still coming to terms with what it meant that he'd read her story, spilled some maple syrup, and fallen in love. Gabby's hummingbird hadn't been her first. And if this story had led Mr. Thomas to love, did her lab reports and history essays help her other teachers find their special someone? Maybe there were dozens of educators out there on whom she'd unknowingly bestowed love. Maybe her emails made people brave. Maybe every word she committed to the page was magic. Maybe her gift had been part of her since birth, not hers to control, something she couldn't stop now even if she tried.

"Really, Alice," Mr. Thomas said. "I can't tell you how happy it makes me to see you. Wait until I tell Joe that I ran into *the* Alice Meadows. You're a bit of a celebrity in our house."

"Are you still teaching?" she asked, hoping to steer the conversation away from herself.

His smile lines disappeared into the loose skin around his mouth. "I had to retire last year."

All at once, Alice saw that he was sick. His pallor wasn't fatigue but illness, lurking below the surface of his skin.

"Enough about me. Tell me what you're up to."

"Well, okay. After college I enrolled in med school. It really wasn't the right fit for me. It was too much pressure, so I moved back here and started catering." This was not the story of her life that she wanted to tell her former teacher. Before she could take it back, she heard herself saying, "I have been writing a bit."

His face flushed with life. "Tell me more."

"I've been writing these stories, they aren't magic—" She had to swallow the *or anything* that threatened to follow. "When I meet someone who wants to fall in love, an image or lesson comes to me, something concrete yet abstract, and I write it down for them. Then they meet someone. Or did. I led a few good people to bad ends, so I stopped writing. I didn't want to be involved in anyone's heartbreak."

Mr. Thomas nodded throughout her ineloquent speech. Then, at "meet someone," his expression changed as he realized this was exactly what had happened at the diner with Joe. "Do you think," he whispered, "is it too greedy to ask if you could write another one for me?"

Before Alice could fumble through an awkward explanation of how she couldn't support infidelity, he said, "It's for Joe, actually. You see, I've got cancer. Pancreatic. It's why I had to stop teaching." Alice did her best to keep her composure as he told her the bare facts of his situation.

"Mr. Thomas," Alice began, relieved when he interrupted her, because she wasn't sure what to say next.

"It's Hank," he said. "I never liked being called Mr. Thomas—the school insisted. But I digress." Mr. Thomas had always been full of digressions. Half of what Alice had learned from him, the many books she'd read at his recommendation, was the product of his digressing and his complex mind.

Mr. Thomas—Hank—explained that he had been diagnosed a year ago. There'd been signs, issues with back pain and nausea. When the doctor told him, he was strangely calm on account of an innate knowing. What he hadn't expected, what caused his calm to descend into panic, was the timeline the doctor gave him.

"I wish there was something I could do." Alice meant that she wished she could write a story that could stop cancer like it could start love.

"Alice, don't you see? You are the only person who can help me. The doctors are worthless at this point, and I'm not about to die with dignity. I'm going to hold out until the very last indignant breath, but Joe, he refuses to accept that my time is ending. And this will be so much harder on him if he doesn't prepare himself."

Alice fidgeted, picking at her fingernails as Hank continued.

"Joe is the kind of person who needs someone. Don't get me

wrong, our love isn't about need, but he won't be happy alone. He has too much love to keep it all to himself. I'm afraid he'll never let himself love again. And he needs to. I want him to. If he'd let me, I'd pick his next partner. He won't, so maybe you can. I want him to find someone deserving of his love."

That familiar itchiness overtook Alice's body, this time from seeing too much desire in someone. His love was rawer than his cancer. To Alice it seemed just as dangerous.

"I've never written a story like that before."

"Only one way to start."

"I'm really not writing anymore. It's too risky." She proceeded to explain all the ways her stories had gone wrong. She would never be able to forgive herself if she brought someone violent into Joe's life.

Hank clicked his tongue as he considered her words. It was a sound he used to make in class, one that had always made her feel like her adolescent interpretations of *To Kill a Mockingbird* and *A Yellow Raft in Blue Water* were not just insightful but essential.

"Look, forget the story." He waved it off like it was in the past. "What would you say to dinner? Joe would kill me if he knew I ran into you and didn't invite you over to meet him."

"Sure," Alice said. "Dinner I can do."

28

The Vanity Room

Alice lifted the ring of the brass lion knocker and waited nervously for Hank to answer the door. Although he'd said to forget about the story he'd asked her to write, it was all she could think about, how she could do him this small favor before he died, if she might be able to help him in a way no one else could.

"Well, well, well, you must be the notorious Alice Meadows," said the man who opened the door. Joe, obviously. He was tall and thin, with warm brown skin and a head so bald it shone. His chin was hidden by a neatly trimmed beard with a white patch shaped like a heart. When he caught Alice staring, he rubbed his palm against the spot.

"Some people wear their hearts on their sleeves. I wear mine on my face." Joe invited Alice inside. "Hank's just setting up the porch. I hope you don't mind eating al fresco."

Alice stepped into the living room of the renovated Craftsman. From the low-profile couch to the midcentury banquette and the built-in bookshelves, every piece of furniture was a statement. The scuffed wood floors were overlaid with Persian rugs, the walls covered to their last inch in paintings. It was the kind of house where you could be yourself. Alice had never considered a house in this way before, not even the one she'd grown up in. She wondered what the house would feel like in a month or a year when Hank was gone, if the ease would be replaced by something else.

As they walked toward the kitchen, Joe narrated the paintings in the hall. "This was from my Cubist phase." He pointed to the elongated face fashioned from shapes Alice didn't have names for. "And that—" he motioned toward a pastoral scene "—that's when I thought I was a landscape artist."

Alice peered into the dining room, where the walls were covered in portraits. A child seated on a swing, laughing at the sky. Overlapping heads facing away from the viewer with different haircuts. A composite of feet that somehow all clearly belonged to the same person. The largest painting on the far wall was a portrait rendered entirely in shades of blue: a sky background, a teal chair, cobalt pants, cornflower skin with cerulean and indigo wrinkles etched into it. Despite the lined skin, the veiny backs of hands, Hank looked boyish, with perfect posture and a robust chest that made Alice realize just how emaciated he had become.

"Hank calls this the vanity room," Joe said in a tone that revealed that all the portraits were of her old teacher. Joe frowned at the blue portrait, the only one where Hank's face was identifiable. "If I'd known he was going to get sick, I never would have chosen blue."

Alice almost asked him why he didn't just take the portrait down. That would be its own kind of death. It was easier to avoid the room, especially when avoiding it had the undeniable advantage of dining al fresco.

Hank was as inspired a cook as he was a language arts teacher. "You're too flattering," he said when Alice complimented the perfect flake of the halibut even though she'd never considered the flake of halibut before. "Cooking has been a good place to channel my energy since I stopped teaching."

"It's a blessing and a curse," Joe said, tapping the small bulge of his belly.

"Were you this superficial when I met you?" Hank teased.

"Were you this expressive with butter? That will be your lasting influence on me, a tire around my middle."

Alice laughed politely, although she had trouble finding their repartee funny. There was a fourth presence at their dinner, Hank's illness, which they ignored like a guest who had had a bit too much to drink. Alice never got to joke about her father's impending death. She never got to avoid it either, to pretend that she was prepared for life without him. Were they better for this time, Hank and Joe, for knowing just how precious and fleeting life was?

After dinner Hank walked her to the door.

"Oh, Alice," he said. "It was so good to see you." Alice waited for him to ask again about a story for Joe. Instead he smiled forlornly. There was a finality to his words. It had been twenty years since she'd seen him. Suddenly the idea that this was likely the last time was simply too much.

"I'd like to help," she heard herself saying. "I just, I'm not sure I can write another story. Not just for Joe. For anyone."

"Use that fear. If you're afraid of a story, that means it's one you need to write."

"What if I write Joe a story and it brings him someone dangerous?"

"Joe's never liked dangerous men. After all, he married me."

Alice didn't laugh. "It's not your job to worry about the consequences. You write the story. The rest is up to the reader."

"I don't know how to help him, though." The story Hank had asked for wasn't about love so much as grief. Hank wanted to rush Joe's grieving process. Joe seemed to want to avoid it altogether. Grief was an essential part of losing someone you loved. Alice did not want to spare Joe this. She wasn't sure how else to help him. And she felt none of that electric energy coursing through her, telling her the muse was close.

A mischievous look overtook Hank's face. "I have an idea, but you aren't going to like it. Will you come by tomorrow?"

The following afternoon, when Alice arrived at the house for Hank's mysterious plan, Joe was there alone, standing outside the garage.

"Hank's at the store," he said. "buying ingredients to make some baked good our midsections don't need. So, are you ready?" He unlocked the door to garage.

"Ready for what?"

Joe laughed. "Of course he didn't tell you."

If you wanted to get to know a hairdresser, you would have them cut your hair. If you wanted to get to know a chef, you would eat their food. If you wanted to know a comedian, you would listen to their jokes. If you wanted to know a bookbinder, you would—no, no more thinking about bookbinders. If you wanted to know a painter you would sit for them.

Joe's studio was musty and damp, with tapestries loosely hung over the unfinished walls. He approached Alice, nudging her face upward. "You have a confident jawline."

"Thank you?" Alice could hardly take credit for the confidence of her jawline, the ways it seemed to belie how utterly uncomfortable she felt at being observed.

"Hold still." He shifted her face again, then stepped away and resumed sketching.

"Do you do a lot of portraits? I mean, other than Hank, do you do portraits for hire?"

"This will be easier if you stop talking." He flipped page after page in his sketch pad, filling it with renderings of Alice's chin and profile, which he would not let her see when she asked.

"They're just studies. They're for me, as the artist. Better to wait until I have a finished portrait." Joe stepped back and looked at her. "Actually, let's try standing up. Good. Now turn to the left. Okay, the right. Straighten your spine. Yes, and do something with your hand. No, don't put it on your hip. I'm not asking you to pose. I want to see you naturally."

Alice was standing so straight, her back muscles clenched. Her tailbone hurt from the unforgiving stool. No matter where she put them, her arms felt heavy and in the way. Nothing about this was natural.

"Knock, knock," Hank said without knocking. He'd just gotten back from the store and carried a tray with a pitcher of lemonade and plate of almond biscotti.

"Hank tries to convince me that biscotti aren't cookies, but I'm on to him."

"They are twice-baked bread," Hank said with mock innocence.

"Still carbs. Besides," Joe said as his charcoal continued to scratch the sketch paper, "who ever heard of lemonade and biscotti? It's not a thing."

Hank placed the tray on the drafting table. "You won't drink coffee after noon, so I had to improvise." He looked over Joe's shoulder at his sketch pad in the same way he had studied student essays in the classroom. "Her eyes aren't right. They are wider, more doe-like."

"Yes, thank you, I realize that." Joe's eyes bounced between the sketch pad and Alice's face. "Hank, if you don't step away, I'm going to make a sketch of just how I'm seeing you right now. Trust me, it won't be pretty."

"Fine, no need to get all bent out of shape." Hank shot Alice a devilish look before departing. It was easy to forget, in moments like these, that this could not last.

"Alice, you're fidgeting," Joe said, although her unconscious movements didn't seem to keep him from ceaselessly sketching.

"Can we call it a day?" Alice stretched. Seeing Hank and Joe together renewed her guilt at being unable to help them.

"It's more challenging than it looks, isn't it?" He flipped the cover of his sketchbook closed and set it on the table. "We want other people to see us, but we don't truly want to be seen."

Alice smiled awkwardly. "I need to get going." Her knees wobbled as she tried to walk.

"Before you go—" Joe held out the plate of cookies "—you must try Hank's biscotti. They're heavenly. And if you tell him I told you that, I'll draw you with horns."

29

A Visit to the Tavern

Alice did not return to Madeline's house for over a month. Over that month she felt the loss of Madeline as acutely as she felt the loss of her scribedom. It went without saying that their bet was over, that Alice had lost. Sure enough, Madeline had proven to Alice that their stories were more curse than gift. As promised, she would stop writing, but she was too humiliated to face Madeline, to confront how wrong she'd been.

As more time passed, her mortification waned when her mind drifted to Madeline. Why should Alice's pride keep them from spending time together? So she hopped in her car to see her friend in the woods.

Alice rapped with the lion knocker, listening as the sound echoed through the dark house. Eventually alabaster feet appeared on the stairs, the bottom hem of a white nightgown, then a veiny hand clutching the banister, a face so ghostly and weathered it was almost unrecognizable. Their journey had given Madeline so much vitality. Now it was gone, drained from her emaciated figure. When she opened the door, she nearly collapsed into Alice's arms.

Alice helped the old woman to the parlor, settling her into one of the chairs before the fireplace. Cold air whistled down the chimney, causing Alice to shiver as she realized that the fireplace had not lit up on its own the way it normally did when they entered. The room was dimmer than it had been before, and a thin layer of dust coated the coffee table. On the mantel, Alice spotted a clock, one that not only ticked but had three hands, rattling off each second. There were also new paintings on the walls. Cubist portraits and monochromatic scenes of children reveling.

Alice found a pile of kindling beside the fireplace and a newspaper. She tore off the front page, rolled it into a ball, and tucked it between the logs with some twigs.

Once the fire was roaring, she joined Madeline in the other chair facing the heat. The flames reflected off Madeline's glazed eyes as she stared vacantly into the hearth. Currer, Ripley, Ellis, Acton, and Poirot wove through their legs, the cats' names reminding Alice that you can never vanquish stories, not entirely.

"I can't stop thinking about Dee." Madeline scooped Ripley up and stroked him deliberately. "When she showed up on my doorstep, my first thought was, *not you*. I wanted to turn her away, but I ignored my intuition. As writers, we should know better than to deny our instincts."

"You can't blame yourself for her death," Alice said.

"I don't." Madeline's fingers disappeared into Ripley's fur as he purred. "I've had a lot of time to think since you've been gone." There was no resentment in these words. "I've spent my time reading. Not my stories, the books that inspired me. The books that belong to me as a reader. My Highsmith. My Brontë sisters. My Christie." She used her chin to point to the cats. "Stories don't belong to their writers, not once they're complete. This is especially true for our stories. They have to belong to their readers. That's what makes the magic work." In long, graceful movements she continued to comb Ripley. "Do I feel guilt over what happened to Dee? Of course. But I now see that doesn't make it my fault."

Alice bent down to cradle Poirot, stroking him mindlessly as she mulled over Madeline's words. Once a story was written and delivered, it was no longer the writer's to control. That seemed another testament to why they should stop writing.

"I've been thinking about you too, how we are united in tragedy. We both lost the men we loved most. You've let that love stunt you. You've convinced yourself that it taught you never to love anyone else." Suddenly galvanized, Madeline stood, swooped Alice's keys from the table, and walked toward the door.

"Where are we going?" Alice's voice faltered.

"You forced me to confront the past I feared. In doing so, I learned to let go. Now it's your turn." Madeline threw open the door and stepped out into the brisk afternoon with Alice's keys.

"You're in your nightgown," Alice protested as she followed Madeline outside.

Madeline shrugged. "One of the benefits of growing old is that people hardly notice you. I could walk naked, and no one would bat an eye."

Madeline adjusted the seat, so it was closer to the wheel, which she rotated a few times for good measure before starting the car. Her nightgown blended into the off-white upholstery, almost as if she had no body at all.

Alice hesitated at the passenger door. Madeline revved the engine a few times to taunt her. When that didn't work, she began honking, gently at first, until she laid the heel of her hand into the horn. It let out an incessant cry. When Alice couldn't take it anymore, she hopped into the passenger seat. Before she could put her seatbelt on, the car was already in motion, thumping down the dirt road.

Alice involuntary gasped as Madeline pulled over across from the tavern.

"There it is again," Madeline said, unbuckling her belt. "Let's go see what exactly you've been so afraid of."

At two on a weekday only a few of the outdoor tables were populated. The car filled with mountain air smelling strongly of grilled meat and pine when Madeline opened the door. She was a strange sight as she walked toward the bar, her bare feet crusted with pine needles, the hem of her nightgown dirtied, her body so thin it was formless beneath the cotton. Even as Alice watched her disappear inside, she wasn't quite convinced that the moment was real.

Alice waited in the car, prepared to outlast Madeline. The afternoon grew colder as it inched toward the winter night. The parking lot filled. The tavern opened for dinner. Patrons at the bar spilled out onto the picnic tables. Conversations crowded the air. Still Madeline did not reappear. Alice had no choice but to go inside, unless she wanted to sit shivering in the car until the bar closed.

The wood-paneled bar looked just as she remembered, right down to the deer heads on the walls, the taxidermy bear lurking in the corner. The license plates above the liquor display, the scent of beer and Lysol, it all came rushing back to her. The space had always been a little dark, worn, old-timey.

Madeline sat on a stool at the far end of the bar, chatting with a middle-aged bartender spilling out of an overly tight tank top. She spotted Alice hovering by the door and waved her over.

"I was wondering when you were going to buck up," she said as Alice slipped onto the barstool beside hers. Above the array of taps for beer, a moose head watched over them. Madeline signaled to the bartender. "Shirley, a beer for my friend, please."

Shirley sloshed the beer as she placed it on the slick bar. She pulled a rag out of her back pocket and wiped up the spill.

"Alice used to come here every Sunday with her father as a kid," Madeline said.

"Is that right?" Shirley said indifferently. "What's his name? Maybe I know him."

A moment passed before Alice said, "Paul Meadows."

Shirley's face grew animated. "No shit. You're Paul's kid? I remember you." Alice wasn't sure she believed her until Shirley said, "You had matching brown leather jackets. What was it he used to call you, Big Al?"

"Tall Al." No one had called her Tall Al in years. As with her height, Alice had hated the nickname. "Don't try to change the things you dislike about yourself," her father would tell her. "They might end up being the things you like most." Alice had learned to love her height, which was the same as her father's. It allowed her to see the world from his altitude.

"I always wondered what happened to you two." Shirley wiped the rag over the bar again. "One day we just never saw you again. Lot of disappointed folks, I'll say that."

Madeline watched to see how Alice would respond. "He passed away. That's why we stopped coming."

Shirley's eyes misted. "I'm real sorry to hear that." She laughed. "I'll never forget this one time, the bar was slammed and I was here on my own. Some drunk guy broke a glass, and it sliced me." She held out her palm to show Alice a cut like a love line across her palm. "I mean it was gushing. One of the regulars was a doctor. He bandaged it real tight so I could finish my shift. Meanwhile, the place is going wild. I look over and your dad's behind the bar, pouring this and that into pint glasses then sliding them over to customers. When my hand was good and bandaged, I saw him pouring Sprite and grenadine into a mixer. I said, 'Paul, what the hell is that supposed to be?' And your dad's all innocent, 'That's not what's in a Manhattan?' And you know what? The guy he made it for said it was the best Manhattan he'd ever had." She laughed again. "He was a good man, your dad."

"He was," Alice said.

Shirley said she'd be right back and returned with three shots of tequila. She raised her glass. "To Paul."

Alice and Madeline lifted their glasses to hers.

They stayed long enough for Madeline to drink another beer and the effects of the shot to leave Alice's bloodstream. The bar grew busy, and whenever a longtime regular came in, Shirley pointed Alice out. Some of them Alice recognized. Others she wanted to recognize. They all had stories about her father, how he did this magic trick with a quarter that they could never figure out, how he settled fights before they started, escorting troublemakers out without their realizing he was doing it, how he could get any band that rolled through to play "Honky Tonk Women," even those who claimed not to know the chord progressions.

Alice grew dizzy with the past, stories she half recollected, others, like the magic trick, that she doubted were true. Her dad had thick, clumsy hands. Still, she believed these regulars recalled the trick because her father could make any moment magical, even kicking a guy out of his favorite bar.

When Madeline's head drooped, Alice decided it was time to leave. Outside, the mountain air invigorated her. She wanted to run through the woods, to twirl among the spindly oak trees. Instead she ran to her car and lay on the hood, looking up at the starry sky.

"Oh, Madeline. Thank you," she said when Madeline joined her on the hood. "I needed that."

"Your father's death was a tragedy," Madeline said to the stars. "Don't let that define all the good times that came before it."

The sky was dark in the mountains, making the few constellations Alice knew easier to find. For her eighth birthday her father had bought her a star. He called it Alice Minor. It came with a certificate and a star chart to locate it in the vast sky. On the night of her birthday it was too foggy to see any stars. They had to wait three nights, and when it was finally clear, they still couldn't identify Alice Minor among the stars above. For a week they scanned the sky fruitlessly. Alice Minor was nowhere to be found. "I think you've been had," Bobby said to Paul. "Those companies are all scams. Only the International Astronomical Union can name stars." It was like Bobby to look this up. It was like Paul not to.

"That just means the whole sky is yours," he told his daughter. "You can look up and know any one of those stars might be yours." Alice didn't want the whole sky. She wanted her star.

After her father died, she forgot entirely about Alice Minor. When she looked up at the night sky, she just saw a marker of another day that had passed without him.

How had she forgotten about the star her father bought for her? How had she let the tavern become a relic of his death rather than a monument to his life? Madeline was right. She had allowed his absence to consume everything that came before it.

"What about you, with Gregory? You cut yourself off from everything after he died."

"On the contrary, I'm living the life we always planned to live together. The house we shared, the library Gregory built for me, that was his dream. Maybe it isn't the life others would want, but it's everything to me." Madeline closed her eyes.

Alice watched as the contours of the old woman's face blurred into the darkness surrounding them until she could not tell where Madeline ended and the night began. Eventually it got too cold to stay outside, so they retreated to the car and drove to Madeline's house. Alice pulled to a stop outside and looked over at Madeline, whose head bobbed in and out of the porch light, there and then gone. There and gone again.

"I won't forget this night," Alice told her.

In the morning Madeline's door was closed. Not wanting to wake her, Alice tiptoed downstairs, surprised to find no thermos of coffee waiting on the counter. She searched the cupboard until she found a French press and ground beans. As she waited for the water to boil, she surveyed the fridge for something to eat. What little food remained on its shelves had grown moldy.

Carrying her mug, Alice slipped outside to watch the fog dissipate. The morning was chilly, and she pulled her thin sweater around her. When she finished her coffee and went inside, Madeline was still asleep.

Alice wasn't sure how to be in this house without their quest. Perhaps a book would distract her while she waited for Madeline to rise. Upstairs, she checked the heart-shaped knob, surprised to find it unlocked.

The library was downright icy. Alice opened and closed the door, hoping to initiate whatever process had in the past triggered the fire to ignite, but the fireplace remained dark and ashy.

Against the far wall the candelabrum was tipped over, the door to the secret space ajar. Inside, Madeline's books were strewn across the floor, piles they'd explored, blue tomes they had yet to read. The ledger sat open in the center of the room, flipped to Dee Lauren's page. As with the other stories, the first line was inscribed here. *You are a lioness.* Alice couldn't believe this story, one rife with bravery and pride, had led Dee to a man who killed her. But Madeline was right. You couldn't control where stories lead people.

Alice found Dee's thin purple book and returned it to the shelf with the other purple stories. Scanning the library arranged by color, she couldn't leave Madeline's books this way. Better to return them to their initial chronological order, as if Alice and Madeline's journey had never happened.

With the ledger to cross-reference, she began the laborious task of putting the books back in order. She twisted a curl as she worked. When she drew her hand from her hair, one long, completely white strand was woven around her forefinger.

Alice reorganized the oldest books first. The grandfather clock continued to tick away. Madeline did not disrupt her. Above her, the top rows were already in their written order, for Alice and Madeline had never found a way to reach them. The first book on the top shelf, the very first story Madeline had written was the same purple as Dee's. Last time Alice saw it, it was red. Madeline had never talked about her first story, and Alice had never asked who her first client was, whose story had signaled the beginning of her gift.

Alice was wondering about the color change when a tower of blue books careened and fell to the floor, knocking Alice down. Her head spun. The room vibrated, and the floor rumbled beneath her feet. The shaking intensified, and by the time she realized what was happening, the earthquake was over. It was more threatening than destructive, the earth reminding her how much devastation it could cause.

Immediately Alice got up to check on Madeline. As she made her way toward the outer library, something moved in her periphery. She turned in time to see the first purple book float to the ground, gentle as a feather. It was thinner than it looked on the shelf, no more than a dozen pages bound together. Unable to resist her curiosity, Alice opened it, skimmed the first paragraph and gasped, dropping the book to the floor. It fell open to a description of a hummingbird whose wings shed crimson confetti hearts when they fluttered, faster than a heartbeat.

Alice stared down at her hummingbird tale, encased in purple leather. How did Madeline have the story Alice had written for Gabby? A fear coursed through her, one she had not experienced since she walked into her dining room at fourteen and saw her father slumped on the table. Gabby's book was purple. Gabby had to be okay.

Alice tore through the library, leaving the door wide open as she barreled downstairs and out of the house. She needed to find her best friend.

30

Babe

Alice raced toward Gabby's building, dread souring her stomach. As she sped across downtown, she cut off an angry truck driver, nearly ran over an old lady crossing the street, and ran a stop sign. Her heart raced in her eardrums. Why had she avoided her friend's calls?

When she pulled up outside Gabby's apartment, Gabby was waiting on the steps, hair perfectly curled, body clad in a sleek red dress. As always, her makeup was flawless. Alice was in what Gabby called the "old Alice" clothes, baggy sweatshirt and ripped jeans, no makeup, hair as obstinate as ever.

"Well, well, well, look who's alive. I was beginning to think you were avoiding me." Gabby stood and smoothed her dress as she walked over to the car. She raised an eyebrow when she saw what Alice was wearing. "I know it's a comedy show. That doesn't mean you have to dress like a comedian."

"Are you okay?" Alice asked breathlessly. Gabby looked confused. Alice wasn't sure how to explain. "I had like a dozen missed calls from you."

"None of which troubled you enough to call me back," Gabby sniped as she climbed into the car.

"I've been…busy."

"Look, I'm sorry if I pushed you too hard about Duncan. It's your life. If you want to be on your own, that's your choice. Just don't run away from me too, okay? I need you."

Alice promised she wouldn't. "You're sure you're okay?"

Gabby swatted away Alice's worries. "Oh, yeah. Oliver has just gone complete oversensitive artist. The condo looks like a tornado hit it because he couldn't find his lucky shirt. I mean, what is a *lucky* shirt anyway? For Oliver, it's some ratty old flannel he's had since his first open mic. He's literally worn it to every performance. Can you imagine? And it was hanging in his closet. Now he's wearing it and pacing the apartment, interpreting everything I do as a sign I think he'll bomb. When I tell him he's going to do great, that he's funniest person I know, he accuses me of being insincere and patronizing. I couldn't take it anymore. I told him we'd see him at the show. Can we get a drink first? I'm dying for a margarita." Gabby pulled down the mirror and traced the line of lipstick along her bottom lip with a pointy nail.

"But you're okay?"

Gabby's attention remained on her reflection. "He was just driving me crazy."

Alice heard a mix of sentiments in her best friend's tone. Annoyance, amusement at her sensitive artist. Somewhere beneath those immediate feelings was pain. Whatever Oliver was going through, he didn't know how to share it with her.

After two margaritas Gabby's irritation amplified to nervousness.

"I mean, he's going to do great," she said as they stumbled out of the cantina toward the brewery that was hosting Oliver's showcase. "It's just a really important show for him. He's been preparing for months. Did I tell you agents and managers are going to be there?"

"You may have mentioned it," Alice said, steadying her friend against her side. Gabby had told her this at least a dozen times tonight alone.

"It's weird," Gabby said, the ocean air sobering her. "I'm seeing this new side of him. I'm realizing that I don't know him as well as I thought."

They'd only been together for nine months. Even when you rush a relationship, you can't rush how people reveal themselves over time. Not that Alice said any of this. "Is that a bad thing?" she asked instead.

"Actually, it's great. He's more complicated than I realized. More human."

When they got to the brewery, it was brighter inside than Alice would have liked. Classic rock bled from the speakers. The smell of fried food filled their nostrils. A stage had been set up against one wall with the tables angled toward it. A half hour before the show was due to begin, the brewery was filling up. Oliver wasn't there yet.

"Did Oliver reserve a table for you?"

Gabby shook her head no. She spotted a small empty table in the middle of the room and walked toward it. "I guess we should have gotten here earlier. Will he be able to see us all the way back here from the stage?"

Alice suspected not but didn't say so.

"It's probably better if he doesn't," Gabby decided. "I don't want to make him nervous."

It seemed unfair, this pressure Gabby was putting on herself for Oliver to succeed. "Let's try to have fun," Alice suggested, offering to buy her a drink.

"Club soda," Gabby shouted over the music. "I don't trust wine at breweries."

Alice was perched at the bar, waiting to place their order with the bartender, when Oliver arrived. She watched him scan the room. Gabby waved eagerly to him as his eyes passed over her, settling on a table of men dressed in similar plaid shirts and boot-cut jeans seated beside the stage. Oliver joined them. Alice took in the scene, dread settling in her stomach, as Gabby self-consciously brushed her hair with the hand she'd just used to wave and scanned the room to see if anyone had noticed the slight.

Oliver gave a few of the scraggly-haired men high fives and clapped others' shoulders. Alice's attention switched between Oliver and Gabby, alone at the table, pretending not to watch him. Eventually, he got up and walked over to Gabby's table. He kissed her cheek, gently massaged her shoulders as he sat down. Gabby glowed, nodded too forcefully. When he stood, Gabby stood too, giving him a dramatic kiss that seemed to embarrass him. He returned to the men.

At last Alice ordered herself a cider, Gabby a club soda, and made her way back to the table. Gabby was focused on her cuticles, which she was picking, even though she was not the type to pick or bite her nails.

They sat quietly for a few minutes as Alice searched for the right thing to say. Everything reassuring sounded like a lie. Everything else seemed like a distraction. Fortunately the lights dimmed, and one of the men sitting with Oliver bounded onto the stage.

"How's everybody doing tonight?" he breathed into the microphone, pacing the small stage as he heckled the audience. He wore a Santa hat even though it was still a couple of weeks until Christmas. The emcee told some benign jokes about the holidays with family and a few softballs aimed at a table of women who revealed themselves to be on a bachelorette weekend, made quips about first dates before pronouncing it time for someone funnier to take the stage. The first comic started her routine with the myriad questions guys asked her about being a redhead.

"You know what they never ask me?" She stopped pacing to

cast a no-nonsense gaze at the audience. "Whether my kids are redheads."

The crowd laughed more enthusiastically than the joke warranted, which continued to be the case throughout the next two sets. It's not that they weren't funny. They were just your-funny-friend funny. Not stand-up-in-front-of-a-room-and-make-a-career-out-of-it funny. Alice felt a new dread, one she hadn't considered before—what if Oliver bombed?

When it was his turn, Gabby clenched Alice's hand. Oliver kept his head down as he climbed onto the stage, looking a bit sheepish.

"Oh, God, he's nervous," Gabby said.

He cleared his throat and tentatively looked up. "How's everyone doing tonight?" he said weakly.

Gabby gripped Alice tighter. "He's so nervous."

"So, my girlfriend says I tell jokes like her grandfather." He used the microphone as the top of a cane and pretended to be hunchbacked, launching into a harmless story of an old man talking about kidney stones. Everyone laughed. Gabby's grip loosened. Oliver returned his microphone to the stand and began his routine in earnest.

"Actually, my girlfriend is here tonight, and it's the first time she's seeing me perform." Oliver mimed biting his nails, and the audience made various sounds of encouragement. "Gabs, where are you? There she is," he said when the spotlight found Gabby, who was blinded momentarily. The light returned its attention to Oliver. "I know what you're all thinking, how did someone like me land *that*."

Alice did not like the way he said *that*. Gabby's hand flinched in hers.

Oliver proceeded to make a few self-deprecating jokes about how he didn't have any money, wasn't particularly well-endowed—Gabby flinched again—wasn't a gifted dancer or cook. In bed, as in most parts of life, he was only a little better than average. "So how, you may ask, does a slightly above average man like me lock down a woman like that?" Alice braced herself for patter about her gift and the hummingbird story, a joke at her expense. And then he said, "Vanity."

After a few moments of relief that she was not his target, she understood that it was far worse. Gabby's grip continued to tighten as Oliver told a joke about how it took Gabby ninety minutes to get ready anytime they went anywhere. "Even when she's just going downstairs to get the mail. I'm lucky if I remember to put on pants to get the mail. But my girl, she's dressed in Gucci and stilettos before she steps foot in the hall. So my question is, what exactly is in the mail that's so important it requires club attire?"

He launched into a few seemingly innocuous jokes about how Gabby could rationalize anything involving numbers: unusual weather patterns ("I didn't realize I was living with a meteorologist"), the need for chocolate ("I'm already taking cover by the time the words *low* and *blood sugar* exit her mouth"), bad tipping ("Only monsters and people who have never worked in the service industry tip on the total before taxes"). His jokes didn't seem particularly funny, but everyone was laughing as he turned Gabby into a caricature of herself. Her grip was making Alice's fingers throb from constricted blood circulation. Alice knew better than to look over at her. Whatever facade of calmness Gabby was wearing would crumble the minute she locked eyes with Alice.

"You know what it doesn't take her ninety minutes to get ready for? Going to the dry cleaners. That's 'cause she's all like, *Babe*, and I'm down the block before I even know what hit me. You guys know what I'm talking about, *Babe*, *babe*, *babe*." Each time he said the word, he gave a coy little shoulder shrug, placing his hand on his hip. "What it is about that word *babe*?" He made the awful motion again. "It's like hypnosis. It's a more powerful weapon than withholding sex. *Babe*, will you stop by my mom's house and walk her dog. *Babe*, I think I may have thrown out my favorite lipstick. Will you rummage through the dumpster and find it? *Babe*, will you drive to LA to get me that smoothie I really like? Oh, and will you make sure it doesn't get too warm on the way home? Then can you drive to Ojai to get that lotion that makes my skin smell exactly like the lotion they sell at the drugstore here except it has to be the one from Ojai that's artisanal and costs three-point-three repeating times as much. Rounded down, not up." Oliver laughed with the crowd and then his face grew serious. "All jokes aside, I love this woman. Gabs, will you come up here? Just try not to take ninety minutes, because I have to be off the stage in about thirty seconds."

The light found Gabby again. She stood, gave the crowd a Miss America wave, and sauntered up to the stage. This was not the response Alice expected. It wasn't that Gabby didn't have a sense of humor or was unwilling to make fun of herself. Oliver's routine wasn't funny. It was laced with too much truth, too many ways only someone who knows you intimately can turn your quirks into failings.

Oliver went to kiss her on the lips. Gabby offered her cheek instead and whispered into his ear. He continued to smile as she spoke to him, but his eyes went a little dead. Gabby, Alice understood, was furious.

She held Oliver's hand as they walked off the stage together. Then she dropped it and walked steadily toward Alice. The smile on her face vanished. Her eyes were watering slightly, but she wouldn't cry.

"Let's get out of here," Gabby said, heading for an exit sign in the back.

"What did you say to him?" Alice asked once they were outside.

"I told him that if he isn't out of my apartment by tomorrow morning, I'm going to have my cousin Raul come over. He's a professional boxer, and trust me, if I call him, he won't take ninety minutes."

"I didn't realize Raul boxed." As far as Alice knew, Raul was an immigration lawyer in San Francisco, more than an hour and a half away.

"He doesn't, but Oliver doesn't know that." A smile flitted across Gabby's face before it was replaced by a distant stare. "I've never been so embarrassed in my entire life."

"That wasn't you up there he was making fun of," Alice said.

"Yes it was." Gabby leaned against the brewery wall, breathing deeply as she tried not to cry. The alley smelled of stale beer and garbage. "All I did was love him and be supportive. Why would you do that to someone who loves you so much?"

Alice guided her friend toward her car, parked a few blocks away. It went without saying that Gabby would stay at her apartment that night.

"Jesus, Alice. What happened in here?" Gabby said as she took in the unwashed dishes on the counter, the dirty clothes draped across the room.

"I told you I've been busy."

"This isn't busy. It's insane. Come on." Gabby lugged her best friend into the kitchen and pulled the dishwasher open. "I'll load, but you're scrubbing. There's no way I'm going near whatever that is." She pointed to a bowl with a layer of cereal congealed to the bottom.

Dish by dish, the two friends cleaned the kitchen. Gabby found a shopping bag under Alice's sink and used her thumb and index finger to lift individual articles of clothing from the floor, barely deigning to touch them.

"I get you to buy silk, and this is how you treat it," she said forlornly, setting the bag of clothes by the door. "I'll be taking these to my cleaners tomorrow. Clearly you can't be trusted."

"Glad to see you're feeling like yourself," Alice teased as she turned off the faucet.

Alice and Gabby worked in silence until Alice's apartment resembled its natural state, cluttered yet clean.

"I'm not okay," Gabby said as she settled into Alice's double bed, "but I'm going to be." She reached over Alice to flip off the light.

The old friends talked best in darkness, when talking to each other became talking to themselves. After Alice's father died, Gabby spent a week with her. During the day, Alice insisted that talking didn't help. Then the second the light went out and they were lying beside each other in Alice's twin bed, she admitted things she hadn't even allowed herself to think in daylight, like about how she didn't get to say goodbye. She wasn't sure that would have made it easier, but the unexpectedness of it didn't feel real, and yet it had to be real because she was never going to see her father again.

She told Gabby how her father had taken care of her mother in ways neither of them fully recognized and now she didn't know how to take care of her mom in his place. Her mom knew how to love her, she just didn't know how to parent, not in the groceries-in-the-fridge, clean-clothes-in-the-dresser sort of way. It was selfish, but Alice didn't want to have to learn to do these things for herself. Not yet. She didn't want them to not need her father. Gabby never said anything as Alice spoke about all the ways she didn't want her life to change. Sometimes, Alice feared her friend had drifted to sleep until Gabby's grip on her hand tightened, squeezing at appropriate intervals.

It was no different in Alice's bedroom tonight, other than it was Gabby who did the talking, detailing all the changes she planned to make in her life. First she was going to put her apartment on the market. After two failed relationships, she simply couldn't live there anymore. She calculated the hit she'd take on it, how she could recoup some of the loss through taxes. Alice let her get lost in the numerical minutiae, until she had no idea what Gabby was calculating.

"I'm sorry," she said when Gabby grew quiet. "I'm sorry I brought him into your life."

Gabby sat up. "Did you know something? In the car, is that why—"

"No," Alice said a little too quickly. "Not even an inkling. I guess I'm not as good at understanding people as I thought. He seemed like a good one."

"It's not your fault."

"If it weren't for my story, you never would have—"

"I'm getting a little sick of this. This happened to me, Alice. Not you. You didn't make him an egomaniac comedian any more than I did. Please don't make this about you."

Alice had no reply.

"Sorry," Gabby continued. "I'm just so embarrassed. Mortified, really. I've never had anyone do anything like that to me before. Don't get me wrong, I'm heartbroken too, but I've been heartbroken. I've never been completely humiliated."

"None of it was true."

"It was all true." Gabby got out of bed and walked over to the window, opening the thin curtains that looked onto the street. The streetlamps shone into the room, outlining her figure, curvy even in Alice's baggy pajamas. "You know what? I love who I am. Someone else will too. It just isn't Oliver. It would have been nice, though, if it hadn't required public humiliation to find that out."

Gabby walked back to the bed and perched on the edge. "Look, if you're really done writing, I'm not going to pressure you, but don't use me as an excuse." She wove her hair into a bun, collecting her thoughts.

When she spoke again, her voice was softer. Insistent, yet loving. "I was always going to meet Oliver. This was always going to happen to me. I believe that as much as I believe in your story.

You didn't bring Oliver into my life, you just made it happen in a way that felt magical. Not felt, it *was* magical. Even now, after everything that's happened, that moment when we met, the beginning—I wouldn't give that up for anything."

Gabby crawled into the bed and burrowed under the covers, snuggling up to Alice. The room was light enough that Alice could see Gabby's large eyes, so close to her own. In that moment, Alice knew her best friend was going to be okay. But was that enough to convince Alice she should keep writing?

"I love you," Gabby told her.

"I love you too," Alice said. If only it was that easy. If only this was the kind of love people wanted. The kind of love Alice wanted. Again, her mind drifted to Duncan, the pressure of his lips against hers, how much she wanted to kiss him again. And why couldn't it be that easy? Why couldn't Alice let herself fall? A fall. A leap, a jump, a crash. There was that language again. The dangerous vocabulary of love. No wonder Alice felt the risks so acutely.

In the morning Alice made them coffee in her French press. When she looked out the window, Oliver was standing across the street with a dozen red roses. To his credit, his eyes were bloodshot and he was wearing the rumpled lucky plaid shirt from the night before. The expression on his face was contrite, pleading. It sent a chill down Alice's spine. She had no idea how he knew where she lived. She shut the curtains.

An hour later when Gabby left for work, he was still there. Gabby paused at the doorstep and watched as he darted across the street to talk to her. Alice was standing behind her in the open doorway, but Gabby asked her to give them a second. She shut the door and peeked out through the curtains, listening, ready to run out with her father's bat at the slightest threat.

Oliver said everything predictable. He was sorry. Beyond

sorry. He was trying to be funny. He had no idea his jokes would hurt her that much.

"You didn't think that having you stand up there for fifteen minutes making me the butt of your jokes would hurt?"

"It's just comedy," he said pathetically.

"Well, I hope you and your comedy are very happy together. Now, if you don't leave, I'm calling the cops. And if I see you anywhere near me or Alice, I'm going to file a restraining order against you, *babe*." She shrugged her shoulder like he had in his routine and flipped him the middle finger.

31

The Walk

Gabby was not the only one who had been feeling neglected by Alice. Without registering it, Alice had not seen her mother in over a month.

"If I don't see you this weekend," Bobby threatened into Alice's voicemail, "I'm alerting the authorities."

Alice hadn't meant to avoid her mother. She hadn't meant to avoid Gabby either. She'd just retreated so far inside herself, her failures, that she'd lost track of her old routines. And Bobby had been spending so much time with Mark that Alice didn't need to check up on her constantly. Her mother was happy. Alice had wrongly assumed that happiness had kept them apart rather than her own hibernation.

Alice met her mother by the sea lion statue in Carpinteria for a morning walk. They'd never walked together as an activity. This was part of her mother's new routine, one she'd created with Mark. As she approached the familiar figure seated on the lip of the statue, facing the ocean, Alice couldn't shake the disappointment that they'd grown apart, that her mother's happiness came at a cost to their relationship.

Bobby wove her arm through her daughter's. In the early morning hours the beach was empty save for surfers carving the waves. Alice and Bobby kept to the narrow wooden boardwalk, each waiting for the other to speak. Alice could not remember a time since her father's death when there had been such weighted silence between them. She felt the need to apologize, except she wasn't certain what to apologize for.

"So," Bobby said, leaning against Alice as a gust of wind rolled off the ocean. "Renata told me about Oliver. How's Gabby holding up?"

"Okay, I think."

Gabby had stayed with Alice for three nights while she put her apartment on the market and devised a plan for getting over Oliver. First she signed up for a week-long meditation retreat in the mountains. This was very uncharacteristic of Gabby, who hated silence the way other people hated blasting music, but that seemed to be the point. Alice hadn't heard from her since she'd left for the retreat, which was a good sign.

"It really is horrible what he did to her and just around the holidays," Bobby continued as she marched through the wind. "It's good that she found out what he was like before they got too serious."

"It was already too serious," Alice said, trying to block her eyes from the hair that twirled around her head. She'd forgotten the first rule of curly hair and the ocean, always bring a ponytail holder. "I just wish there had been signs earlier. Or maybe there were and we missed them. He really did seem like one of the good ones."

"He might be, for someone else, someone who doesn't mind the public spectacle, someone who finds it funny."

"His jokes weren't funny though. They were mean."

"Gabby is strong. She'll survive this, and she'll be better for it."

Alice looked out over the ocean, trying to decide if she agreed. "Are you better for surviving Dad?" she asked.

Bobby stopped walking and faced Alice. The freckles on Bobby's face had morphed into sunspots, but she still had a girlish look about her. "I'm not sure how to answer that. Do I wish he was still with us? Of course. Am I certain we would have been happy growing old together? I can't say for sure." She motioned Alice back toward downtown. "Come on," she added casually, as though she had not just said something that jolted Alice, that rearranged her world order. "I'm starving."

Alice planted her feet firmly on the wood planks of the boardwalk. "What are you talking about? You two were perfect."

Bobby frowned. "Alice, c'mon." Alice didn't budge. "No relationship is perfect," Bobby said.

"You two were," Alice argued, feeling childish. Her mother brushed Alice's hair away from her face, awaking a forgotten memory of Alice screaming as Bobby brushed out the permanent tangle of knots in her thick hair. She always remembered her father caring for her as a child, but there were ways her mother tended to her too.

"I think we've both remembered your father as we needed to. As I've opened myself up to Mark, to the possibility that we might be together for a while, it's made me revisit how I've idealized your father."

Alice marched past her mother. "I have to go," she said. She was being petulant, immature, but that familiar tightness had intensified in her chest, making her feel closed in despite the cool ocean air.

"Alice, stop," Bobby said, scurrying to keep up. Alice had inherited her height from her father, and her legs were a good deal longer than her mother's. "Let me finish. You need to hear this."

"It's fine. I just, I have to go." Alice walked faster, and Bobby ran to keep up until she blocked Alice's path.

"Look, I'm sorry to upset you. You need to hear the truth.

I loved your father. He was the greatest love of my life. Nothing will change that. But romanticizing our relationship wasn't helping me. And it's not helping you either."

Bobby stood her ground, forbidding Alice to pass her. Mother and daughter stared at each other until Bobby said, "Come on, let's get some breakfast."

Bobby did not give her daughter time to agree, just started lugging her the short distance back to Linden Avenue toward Ruby's Diner where Alice used to go for egg creams with her father. She'd forgotten that she and her mother went there sporadically through the years too.

Inside Alice shuddered as she recognized the metal napkin dispensers on the table, the coral uniforms. A waitress escorted them to a table in the back, then offered each of them a laminated menu.

Bobby hummed softly as she surveyed the menu.

Alice shuddered. "This place is so creepy. It hasn't changed since I was a kid."

"I would think you'd find that reassuring," Bobby said, not looking up from her menu.

"Maybe, if it wasn't connected to a gruesome murder."

Bobby glanced at her daughter perplexed.

"The Woman Lost to the Sea?" Alice added.

"Right," Bobby said neutrally. "I forgot how obsessed you and Gabby were with that story. It was just an urban legend."

"It wasn't," Alice pressed, the emotions the story stirred rising again. "She was murdered by her husband in the name of love." Love, Alice scoffed. Who could dare to call it that? No, it was hate disguised as ardor, a reminder of what could happen when the wrong people were paired together. "It's terrifying."

Bobby closed her menu and fixed her gaze on her daughter trying to infer everything Alice hadn't said aloud. "I'm sorry I upset you earlier. I've been wanting to talk to you about this for years now, and until recently, until I talked it over with Mark, I haven't known how."

"Please don't bring Mark into this," Alice said.

The waitress arrived at their table. "What'll it be?" she asked, without looking up from her pad.

"Nothing for me," Alice said, handing her menu back to the waitress.

"I'll have a coffee and the veggie scramble, and she'll take an egg cream and a corn muffin," Bobby said, ordering for them both. After the waitress left, Bobby frowned at Alice. "Like I would let you come here and not get an egg cream. I'm not asking you to forget him or let go of any traditions, I just—you're old enough that you need to see the past clearly. Your father and I loved each other very much, but there were times when it wasn't pretty. Like me going to med school."

The waitress returned to their table with a steaming mug of coffee for Bobby and a frothy egg cream for Alice. The fizzy sweetness hit Alice all at once. She hated how good it tasted, how much it evoked those afternoons with her father.

"I assumed he'd be supportive," her mother continued, "so I didn't tell him when I applied. I figured I'd wait to see if I got in first. I couldn't imagine the idea of his disappointment in addition to my own if I got rejected."

Paul had come home early that day, Bobby could not recall why, and checked the mail even though that was usually her job. When she got home, she saw the large envelope on the hall table.

"It was so strange," she said. "When I saw it there, it didn't even occur to me that a big envelope meant I got in. I was panicked that he'd seen it. I expected him to be angry that I'd applied in secret, that I hadn't let him share that moment with me. Instead he was in disbelief that I still wanted to be a doctor. A job was fine, necessary even, but a medical degree? For one thing there was the cost, and then there was the undeniable fact that I would outearn him, which challenged the values he was raised with.

"He came around in the end. And you know better than anyone how well he took to being your primary caretaker. I will always love him for that. It strained our relationship though, me being the breadwinner, the fact that he always felt I owed him something for allowing me to follow my dream."

Alice's face grew hot. That was not how it happened. It was one of her favorite stories, the way her father encouraged her mother to go to medical school. "Where is this coming from? Dad was always supportive of you. He brought you the applications. He practically filled them out for you."

"No, Alice. That's what I mean about glorifying him. I applied on my own. He always wanted to be supportive. It was hard for him sometimes. He had dreams too, dreams that never quite came to fruition."

Alice jiggled her straw up and down in the egg cream, unable to take another sip. During her mother's story, the waitress had dropped off her corn muffin, cut in half and toasted, butter melting on each side. "I don't understand why you're telling me all of this now."

"Maybe it's being with Mark or just that I always get a bit retrospective around the holidays, but I realized how much this has all been holding me back. You helped me break free of how tightly I was latching on to your father's memory, and I realized that's what you've been doing too. You've constructed this image of him that no other man can live up to."

"That's not what I'm—"

"No relationship is perfect. It can't be, not if human beings are involved. But that's the beauty of love. Even if someone's not perfect, you can still love them. You can love them more for it. That's what you've given me with Mark. It's what I want for you too."

Alice wanted to be mad at her mother. She wanted to do something immature like throw that nostalgic egg cream in her face or just storm off. Her mother was right though. Her father was never perfect. As her mind drifted back to all those dinners where her mother spoke of her patients, she could see the look on his face. At the time she hadn't understood it. Now, now she realized that it was frustration over her mother's career, the way she provided for their family when he'd expected to be the patriarch of his home. And there were Saturdays on the beach when it was cold and her father would get after her for whining, or Sunday afternoons at Cold Spring Tavern that turned to evenings when Alice had homework, and her father would ignore her continued requests to go home, snapping when he said for the tenth time that they'd leave soon. No, her father wasn't perfect, but she'd loved him. She still loved him.

"So it's love then, with Mark?"

"It was always love. I just didn't view it that way because it has such a different tenor than I had with your father. It's quieter. Calmer. We never fight. Instead we negotiate. And when we want different things, we give each other space. We aren't trying to be everything to each other." Bobby's food arrived, and she pushed it around her plate, absorbed in her thoughts. "Love won't break you," she finally added. "Even if the worst happens, you'll survive it."

Alice wasn't sure she agreed. She could see how much her mother needed to share this wisdom with her, to think that in renewing her belief in love, she might be able to compel the same from her daughter.

So Alice just said, "I'm sorry I got mad earlier." She nibbled her corn muffin, relieved when it was just as buttery and grainy as she remembered.

32

The Blue Book

Alice could not stop thinking about Gabby's hummingbird tale, shelved in Madeline's library. How was it there? What did it mean that it was purple? In her notebook Alice had written, *Purple = Violence. Bruised and hateful ends.* Yes, Gabby had been emotionally lacerated. Yes, Oliver was not a good partner for her, but he was more careless than violent. It seemed he never considered that his routine would hurt Gabby. Alice truly believed this, that he hadn't meant it viciously. So had she been wrong about the meaning of the purple books?

This question, while pressing, was not as troubling as the inexplicable presence of Alice's hummingbird tale among Madeline's stories. One thing was perfectly clear. Madeline was still keeping something from her. So she ventured to the woods again, this time to demand answers.

When her car careened to the left, turning sharply onto Stagecoach Road, her thoughts were with Madeline, so much so that she did not register passing Cold Spring Tavern until it was in her rearview mirror. As it grew smaller, a warm sensation rose in Alice. Those hours she and her father spent there weren't perfect, but they were good. Maybe that was better.

Alice banged on the brass knocker. There was no answer. She walked around the back of the house, where she was surprised to see the patio covered with leaves and debris as though no one had used it in some time. She pressed her face to the French doors and peered inside. The recessed lights were on, casting the kitchen in unnatural yellow. Alice tried the handle. It clicked open.

"Madeline?" she called. Only the ticking of the grandfather clock responded. As Alice walked down the hall, the ticking grew louder. Upstairs Madeline's door was closed.

Alice stood outside, debating whether to barge in. Despite her frustration, her desire to confront Madeline about how and why she had Gabby's story, Alice could not bring herself to open the door. She was scared of what she might find on the other side, Madeline's lifeless body, perhaps no one at all. She marched down the hall toward the library. Madeline was not the sole source of answers in the house.

In the secret library everything was just as Alice had left it. Door thrown wide, piles of books across the floor, Gabby's open at the center of the room. The cats circled the books, stalking them, braving a sniff, before settling onto the piles. Acton nestled into the small space on the purple shelf and fell asleep. Alice lifted Gabby's book from the floor. In the warmth of her hands, it shifted to red again. Did this mean Oliver was not the end of her story? That her best friend was not about to give up on love?

Alice looked up at the shelves that remained out of reach. The books no longer seemed inaccessible. She spotted footholds and ledges she could use to scale her way to the top. When she climbed onto the first shelf, it creaked in protest, bowed slightly, but didn't give. The sound roused the cats. They stood tall, spines arched, hair raised.

They remained on guard as she ascended shelf after shelf until she could reach the top row of books where Gabby's hummingbird story had been. She stretched out her arm to push the books off the shelf, and they crashed to the floor below. It felt like a physical blow, the violence of it, the reckless way she treated the books. The cats jumped back, then inched forward, inspecting the objects like they were birds fallen dead from the sky.

Alice laid these books from the highest shelves in a circle around her. Sure enough, they were stories of sea glass, natural pools of mud, unsightly peaches. They were here, all the stories she'd written.

Among her books she spotted one that was blue. It was the only color she and Madeline had not investigated. In the other colors they'd seen lasting love (red), love that ran its course (yellow), love destroyed by jealousy and envy (green), and love that was fueled by hate (purple). They'd seen so many ways for love to end; there had to be other ways for it to persist.

Alice sat on the floor with the blue book in her lap, noticing several enlarged veins spidering up her bare calves. Even before she opened it, she knew its first sentence would describe an aisle that never seemed to end, a butterfly betrothing a bride to herself. She thought of her mother and Mark, the love they'd found with each other later in life. Theirs was a love more affectionate than passionate, a companionship more than a romance. Without investigating the other blue books, she wrote *Blue = a cool and steady love* in her notebook.

Across the library floor there were far more blue books than there were red. Before becoming a love scribe, Alice would not have considered that cool steadiness a form of love. Now it seemed like the most natural kind, one steeped in respect and admiration. She was glad she'd written a story for Bobby, glad she'd chosen to believe in her gift. Love would not break her mother. It wouldn't break countless couples in these stories either, but she wasn't convinced that meant she should continue writing. Even if there weren't very many purple stories, even if most of the green tales had further chapters that weren't about jealousy or envy, even if the heat of yellow had tempered without an explosion, she did not want to be part of anyone's pain. No, Madeline had won their bet. Alice would honor the deal they made.

A chill like a feather tickled the back of Alice's neck, and she expected to find the old woman standing in the doorway, a twisted smile across her face as though this had been her plan all along. Alice could feel her presence, yet when she glanced up, there was no one there. At that moment, she knew with full certainty that Madeline was gone.

33

The Water That Isn't There

Before Alice sat down to be painted, Joe had her do acting warmups. They spoke of Peter Piper as fast as they could and tossed an invisible ball back and forth with growing intensity. Joe had her shake out her limbs, and Alice flopped awkwardly.

"You call that a shake?" Joe said. "Pretend you just crawled out of a vat of termites. Good, now when I say stop, don't think, just sit."

"Will you turn around?" Alice asked, waving her arms like she was trying to dance. "I want you to see me comfortable, but I don't want you to see me getting comfortable."

Joe looked away, and just when her movement was starting to have a rhythm to it, he called, "Stop."

Alice dropped to the stool, crossing her right leg over her left even though she usually crossed her left over her right. Her left hand disappeared beneath her right forearm as her right hand dangled.

"Okay," she called, and he spun around, his face glowing like she'd just tried on the perfect wedding dress.

Joe disappeared behind the canvas, the crown of his shiny bald head visible above the easel. The sound of his paintbrush against the canvas echoed softly through the garage as Alice focused on her breathing, trying to ignore the discomfort. She was hyper-aware of the unnatural position of her limbs, of the sweat collecting above her lip, which she fought the urge to wipe away.

"How's the writing going?" Joe asked.

"The writing?" Alice asked, returning to the garage, the awkward positioning of her limbs.

"Oh dear, I hope I didn't overstep. Don't worry, I won't ask you what you're working on. It's always seemed so intrusive to me when people ask writers what they're working on. Describing a book that's not fully formed is like asking a pregnant woman what her unborn child is going to look like. It sets her up for disappointment when that perfect creature comes out wrinkled and alien."

Alice laughed.

"Don't laugh. It changes your face. Well, you don't have to scowl either. Just be."

"You know how hard that is, to just be?"

"Not the Buddha on the mountaintop type?"

"Did I have you fooled?" Alice asked hopefully.

Now it was Joe's turn to laugh. "Not for a minute."

They were quiet again, and Alice realized that Joe was waiting for her to tell him about her writing.

"Did Hank tell you about my writing?" Since Hank had set her up with Joe on these portraits dates, he hadn't mentioned the prospect of a story again. This led Alice to regard that the matter as settled, both silently agreeing it was a bad idea. If he'd mentioned it to Joe, that meant he was holding out hope that she would deliver. She felt a swell of guilt as she wondered if she may be disappointing Hank.

"Yes and no. You know Hank. He prefers to talk in abstractions. He's excited about whatever it is though. Alice, you're frowning again."

"Sorry," she said, trying for a neutral expression.

"I've written a few stories," she said evasively, "I don't think I have the stomach to be a writer."

"Spoken like a true artist. I know we're all supposed to pretend we're immune to criticism. I've been painting for forty years, and it still kills me every time someone doesn't like my work. But every time you get a little stronger. Every time you trust your gut a little more."

It sounded nice, following your gut, except Alice's always directed her to quit, to give up, to run. She didn't know how to feel through that doubt to something deeper that would encourage her to continue.

"Knock, knock." Hank opened the door without knocking.

"Why do you always say that when you could just actually knock?" Joe asked.

"I'm simply here to inform you that it's quarter after five, which means we are fifteen minutes late for happy hour. Palomas are waiting on the deck."

Joe added a few final brushstrokes, then loosely covered the canvas. "This one can't be trusted not to peek," he said, pointing to Hank, who shrugged.

Alice followed the two men through the house to the deck, where Hank had put out a pitcher along with chips and guacamole. She listened politely as Joe and Hank debated the merits, or lack thereof, of a film they'd seen earlier that week, zoning out as their disagreement continued. They were another example of one of her successful stories, one she hadn't even realized she'd written. Would they have met without her tale of the tortoise and the tricycle? She hoped so, but she could never really know because the story was an inextricable part of their love.

"Okay, let's not make this personal," Joe said, pretending to be hurt.

"My artist," Hank said, rubbing his back. "I forget how thin his skin is."

Joe stuck his tongue out at him, and Hank laughed. Below them something rustled in the waterless riverbed, startling them. It was only a squirrel darting up the opposite side.

"Was there water when you moved in?" Alice asked. Judging from the overgrown bougainvillea and moss snaking the rocks, the riverbed looked like it had been dry for a long time.

Joe gave her a peculiar look. "There's still water. You're telling me you can't see the water?"

"Stop." Hank swatted at him. "You're confusing the poor girl."

"I just want her to see it. Right there." He leaned over the deck railing and pointed to a spot in the dry basin. "See the trout? Sometimes, when Hank forgets to go to the store and we have nothing to eat, we cast a rod and that guy's dinner."

"You don't have to play along," Hank said to Alice.

"Ignore him," Joe said. "He isn't an artist. He can't see the water unless it's right in front of him. You and me, Alice, we see the water that isn't there. We see it and we bring it to life."

Alice stared at the debris, the bushes rustling in a gentle breeze. The breeze picked up until it was not a breeze but a current. A single water drop trickled down to the center of the basin. Then another and another until a thin stream flowed. The hair on Alice's arms stood up as that familiar electricity invaded her body.

"I see it." She clapped as the water filled the riverbed in a gentle flow. She leaned over the railing. "I see it."

She glanced at Hank, whose mind drifted elsewhere. She watched him retreat until he sensed her staring at him and smiled.

On her bike ride home Alice crossed an empty creek bed thick with brush. She'd never paid much attention to the dried-up tributaries in her city. As she biked by bed after bed, she imagined them filling with water until they overflowed, making the entire city an extension of the ocean it lived beside. She felt alive with the rush of the water, the current of the muse.

Alice managed to fight the tingling until she got home. Once inside her apartment, she lunged toward her desk and offered herself to the mercy of the writing gods. As with the invisible river flowing through the basin behind Joe and Hank's house, the words poured out of her once she started writing. When her phone rang, she ignored it. When Agatha rubbed against her leg, she nudged her off until she realized the poor cat must be hungry. She set out enough food to last her the day, then decided she should nourish her own body too if she wanted it to fuel her into the night.

For days her life narrowed to the distances between her kitchen, desk, and bed. Light pestered the curtains, reminding her that time was passing, but she lost track of how many dusks called her to eat, how many dawns beckoned her to the desk again. She was vaguely aware of her phone's pinging, of her upstairs neighbors trotting off to work in the morning and home again at night. She wrote and wrote until she'd reached the end.

The story was about a man with no descriptors, not a height, a skin color, a weight. A man who could be Hank or Joe or someone else entirely. He had lost his lover, a lover with no descriptors either. The man himself was not the protagonist. His grief was, a grief too big for his neither tall nor short body, too vast for his airy home. Grief arrived at his door and let itself inside, where it pressed down on him, squeezing the water from him in the form of tears. So many tears they filled the house and poured out, flooding the dry river bed behind his home. The man always knew the water would return, he just didn't think it would come from his own body.

Then, when the current was strong, he wrestled Grief off him and threw it into the water. Grief screamed for help. It flailed as the water carried it away. With Grief gone, Fear knocked at the man's door. As Fear approached, the man dove into the river to escape for he could not defeat Fear, not in the same way he had tackled Grief. The current took hold of him, the white water like a roller coaster bobbing him up and down. The man loved roller coasters. He loved amusement parks. At heart he was a thrill seeker, he'd just forgotten.

He let his body relax into the current, the water carrying him past neighborhoods and borders, beyond the edge of the land, until he was no longer swimming in a river but in the ocean. Schools of tropical fish circled him. He dove with dolphins. He hunted with sharks. It was a life he'd never imagined. Grief was still everywhere. Here, beneath the surface of the ocean, it was part of a larger ecosystem, a predator that could be avoided. Eventually he learned to love this life as much as the last, not to distinguish between the two lives because his beloved had brought him here to the bottom of this ocean, vast enough for him to live alongside his grief. To live alongside his happiness too.

When Alice typed the last period, something didn't seem quite right. It was an inexact feeling, vague but potent. She scrolled to the beginning of Joe's story, trying to pinpoint what was off about it. Only as she read it, it was perfect. The imagery, the language, the message. It had taken shape on the page exactly as her mind had intended. Yet the hesitancy persisted.

She went for a walk to clear her head. The inspiration was gone from her body, and she felt calm. She'd written a story for Joe and it was beautiful, even if something about it still seemed off.

As she wandered beyond her neighborhood to the hillside streets, past large Spanish Revival homes and yards too green for the drought, she could hear Hank arguing that her doubts were good, that the conflict she felt about the story meant that it mattered. And it did matter. Not just to Alice. Not just to Joe. It was as much for Hank as it was for Joe. Like the first tale she'd scribed for him, the one he'd shared at the diner with Joe, this story was for both of them. For it to work, Hank had to read it too. He needed to be present on the page, informing every scene, permeating every word.

At half past five, when Joe and Hank were drinking caipirinhas or Manhattans on their porch, Alice skulked up to their doorstep and left her manuscript, wrapped in brown paper. *For HANK,* she wrote on the front, *(that means NOT YOU, Joe).* She liked that she knew their routine. She liked that she knew Joe would want to read it but would never disrespect the request of another artist. She liked that she knew them so well, she knew what their story needed to be. She skipped down the steps with a confidence she hadn't experienced for months.

Later that night, as Alice was drifting to sleep, her phone buzzed.

The text was from Hank: It's perfect.

34

The Perfect Story

Hank invited Alice over to celebrate just how perfect her story was.

When he opened the door, the circles around his eyes had darkened or maybe the skin of his cheeks had paled. Along the short walk to the living room couch, Hank walked unsteadily. Pretending not to notice, Alice surveyed Joe's paintings on the living room walls. The room smelled strongly of fir needles although there was no Christmas tree in the room, no debris left on the floor. For some reason that stung Alice most of all, that another holiday had passed for Hank and Joe, possibly their last.

On the wall, amidst all those familiar abstractions, there was a new painting, a Cubist portrait of two men in black tuxedos, holding hands.

"It was Joe's Christmas present to me," Hank panted between words. "He realized that he'd never painted our wedding."

"It's stunning." It was also devastating. Alice's heart panged in her chest. "Where's Joe?" The house was quiet in the way only empty houses were.

"I made a playdate for him," Hank laughed. The laugh was mostly a dry cough with a little uptick at the end. "He hasn't seen friends in so long, and I wanted some uninterrupted time with you to talk about your story."

Hank crossed his legs and gestured toward the plate of biscotti resting on the coffee table. They were store-bought. Uniformly sized. Perfect distribution of cherries and flakes of dark chocolate. Alice wasn't hungry, but she took one anyway, politely nibbling. The manuscript rested on the table, overturned so a blank page stared up at her.

"Alice," Hank croaked. He reached for the glass of water on the coffee table. "Alice, Alice, Alice. You've outdone yourself."

"Really?" She knew her story was good. Why did it surprise her that he might consider it to be good too?

"Joe's going to hate you, it's so perfect. And I know it will bring him the perfect partner."

"Doesn't that hurt you, though, thinking of Joe with someone else?"

"What hurts me is the idea of him spending the next twenty years alone and unhappy. Or worse, being one of those partners who dies six months after because they cannot bear to be alive. I just want him to have a chance to love again. And for that, I'm eternally grateful to you."

Alice took the manuscript from Hank and held it in both hands, feeling its power. She didn't know where it would lead Joe, but she knew that if she gave it to him, it would guide him to a place he needed to go.

"Look," Hank said, "I hope you don't have to give your story to him for a long time. You'll know when the moment's right."

As he walked Alice to the door, he took her arm. "Alice." Hank cleared his throat and blinked repeatedly, trying to stem the tears. "I can't tell you what a joy this has been. I always knew you were gifted." He tapped the door frame. "I'll see you soon."

From Hank and Joe's, Alice headed straight to Santa Barbara Bindery only to find it closed for the holiday season. She put her face to the window. Inside, it looked more like an exhibit, a display of a workshop rather than a workshop itself. She slipped an envelope holding her cat flash drive into the mail slot, with a note explaining that she wanted this one in a natural undyed leather, as though without the red it was not one of her love stories. The envelope made a soft tap as it hit the floor. However this story might affect Joe, it was the last one she would write.

35

A Sleeve of Many Colors

Howard bound Joe's book in record time, calling Alice two days later to report that it was ready.

"Figured if you dropped it over the holidays, it must be pretty important." Howard held out her book, cloaked in a multicolored sleeve knit from yarn of red, blue, green, yellow, and purple. The colors organically interwove in a pattern that looked like spines on a shelf. "It was so bland, Greta wanted to give it a little beauty."

As always, the pride they took in their work reminded her of Duncan. It had been two months since he appeared on her porch, and she could still feel his lips on hers, the way they were chapped, that detail almost more intimate than the kiss itself. Then she remembered that the bridesmaid had felt the pressure of his lips too, and the sense of betrayal rose to the surface again. It wasn't that he'd kissed the bridesmaid, it was that there would always be a bridesmaid, a writer with a book to bind, an event planner with a special order who had their eye on him. No matter how much she missed him, she needed to protect herself.

"It's perfect," Alice said, holding out her credit card. Howard waved it off.

"This one's on the house. Happy holidays, Alice." Alice's eyes stung, and Howard laughed. "Now, now, don't get all sentimental. I'll be charging you for the next, don't you worry." Only there wouldn't be a next.

As Alice was walking out of the shop, he called to her. "You sure you don't want another copy of that one?"

"I'm sure," she said.

Alice unlocked her bike from the streetlamp. Her phone buzzed in her back pocket and she reached to retrieve it. As soon as she saw Hank's name, she knew. Fate had an ironic sense of timing, so cruel it would have been unrealistic on the page.

She hesitated before she picked up. When she heard Joe's voice, her intuition became certainty.

"Alice," he half whispered. She wanted to hang up, to throw her phone into the street where a car could run over it, but she stayed on the line. "I'm sorry to call from Hank's phone. I didn't have your number in my phone. I guess we've never exchanged numbers. If we had, I would have added you to my text yesterday. Maybe it's a cop-out, I couldn't imagine conversation after conversation, saying the same thing. But you weren't in my phone, so—" As he continued to ramble, he found new ways to talk around Hank's death.

"When's the funeral?" she asked.

"Saturday. No funeral. Just a gathering at the house. I hope you'll come."

"I'll be there. Joe? I'm so, so sorry." Alice wanted to say more. From experience, she knew that no other words mattered. People had a way of comparing loss, as if the fact that their spouses or parents or siblings had died would make you feel better about your own tragedy. Over time, Alice realized that her father's death could unite her with others who had suffered a similar loss, but not because the deaths were the same. The bond lay in the fact that no one else could understand precisely how you felt, not even your own family. Although Alice imagined Joe must be confused, overwhelmed, and empty, the reality of how his life would change not yet settled in, she could not actually empathize with him. Only sympathize, and who ever wanted someone's sympathy?

"I'll see you Saturday," Joe said, hanging up.

Alice found Joe and Hank's book, still tucked into that too bright sleeve in her messenger bag. The yarn was slightly scratchy. She took the sleeve off. The smooth book was cooler than her skin. She held it to her until she could not distinguish its temperature from her own.

Her back pocket buzzed again. Hank's name lit up on the screen. I forgot to mention it's a luau. Hank never did meet a Hawaiian shirt he didn't like. See you around five.

Alice responded simply with okay, no punctuation, for a period seemed too cold, an exclamation mark too perky, an emoji of any kind too false. Once she saw that he'd received her text, she deleted both, so that the last one she would ever receive from Hank's number was when he finished reading her story: It's perfect.

36

A Synonym for Birth

Up and down Hank and Joe's street, every parking spot was taken. A chorus of voices greeted Alice as she approached their house. Inside, the front room was crammed with people in jeans, sundresses, and brightly colored shirts. She recognized a few teachers from her middle school, a handful of fellow graduates whose names she'd forgotten. Alice wasn't about to wear a bikini top or a grass skirt, so she'd selected the most floral dress she owned, a pink wraparound with white lilies that she'd bought at Gabby's behest. As she scanned the crowded living room, searching for someone she knew, she pulled at the bottom hem self-consciously. She hadn't realized the dress was quite so short.

After some polite conversation with her former life sciences teacher, she spotted Joe alone on the back deck, leaning over the railing as he stared into the waterless riverbed below. She clutched her bag with the tan book and walked toward him.

"Alice," he said, throwing his arms open to embrace her. Joe was wearing a fuchsia flowered shirt. "He always did love me in pink." He smiled, finding two drinks on a tray, and giving one to Alice. It had a slice of pineapple and two maraschino cherries in it.

There were a million words of condolence Alice wanted to say, but that wasn't what Joe wanted from her. Instead she held her glass to his. "To pink," she said, wincing at the sweetness of tropical drink. It was worse than Gabby's blue ladies.

"It's terrible, isn't it?" Joe puckered. "What would you say to some of the good stuff?"

She followed him through the house as he greeted several guests and said he'd be back in a minute. Outside, the front porch was crowded with more people who wanted to talk to him. He just kept saying the same thing, "I'll be right back," the smile on his face waning. They jogged toward his studio where he unlocked the door and slammed it behind them.

Once he caught his breath, he smiled at Alice, exhilarated. "We survived," he said.

Alice reached for the tan book peeking out of her bag, but a voice inside pulled her back, telling her not yet.

As always, Joe's easel was faced away from the door, the last layer of protection against curious eyes. He winked at Alice before venturing to the back of the garage, where he opened a chest Alice hadn't noticed before.

The good stuff turned out to be a vodka that tasted as close to water as any vodka Alice had imbibed, not that she was much of a vodka drinker. They leaned against an unfinished wall, not talking, sipping their drinks, deciding whether to share their art. When Alice's glass got low, Joe refilled it. On the second pour she tasted something earthy and nutty, not altogether unpleasant.

"If I'd kept this in the house, Hank would have used it for cocktails, which would be sacrilege." He took a sip, contemplated the vodka, then swallowed. "I've been dreading this day for so long. Now that it's here, I'm surprisingly Zen. Don't get me wrong, tomorrow when I wake up alone, or the next day when I discover the last toothpaste Hank and I shared is gone, or a week from now when I finish this bottle—" he held it toward Alice "—I'm guaranteed to fall apart. For now, calm waters."

Calm waters. It made her think of the story she'd written for him.

"Refill," he asked. Alice was already more lightheaded than she liked and declined. He filled his glass again. The bottle was nearly empty. "So much for this lasting a week."

He drained the glass in one long sip, then leaned back against the wall, in no rush to return to the party. They'd spent so much time together in this converted garage, but there had always been the portrait distracting them from the simple act of being together. Alice reached for the tan book again. It was now or never.

"This is something I wrote for you. At Hank's request." His eyes widened and she debated outlining how her gift worked. It was better if he figured it out on his own. Her job was to write the story and get him to read it. After that, the rest was up to him.

"Hank wrote a little letter to you in the front. It explains why—well, I'm not sure what it explains, really. I didn't read it. It wasn't for me." This was half true. Rather, she hadn't realized she was reading it until she got to the part about their inside jokes. Then, although she knew it was wrong, she kept reading. Maybe the same had been true for Duncan when he read her stories, that he couldn't help himself.

Alice tapped the book for effect. "It was important to Hank that you read it."

For the first time that afternoon Joe looked like he might cry. Instead he laughed. "Hank was always trying to get me to read more. He left copies of *Letters to a Young Poet* under our bed, on the driver's seat of my car, on my easel, which really pissed me off because he wasn't supposed to come in here without my permission. He must have bought fifteen copies of that book, all different editions. And you know what? I read it and loved it, but I pretended I hadn't. Ever since Hank got sick, whenever I see a copy I buy it. Even if it's an edition I already have." He took the tan book from Alice. "You know, you were the last friend

Hank made. He had no reason to let anyone new in. He chose you. He wanted you to be a part of our lives. I'm so glad he did."

"Me too," Alice said.

Joe kept staring at her until it made her uncomfortable. Even after she looked away, she could feel his gaze on her. It wasn't the same as when he observed her to paint her portrait.

"I have something for you too," he said. "I've been going back and forth, adding a little color to your cheeks, then removing it. Adding more blue to the background, then deciding it made you look washed out."

"I am washed out," Alice said, and Joe laughed.

"Well, you aren't in my painting." He studied her again, somberly. "To be honest, I wasn't entirely sure I was going to show you the portrait until just now. I try not to control what I paint. The image comes to me, and I honor it. I don't overanalyze it or try to understand why I see people the way I do. An artist's job is to create, and an audience's job is to interpret. God, if Hank were here, he'd tell me to stop being so pretentious."

"He *is* here." It was very unlike Alice to say this. "He'll always be here."

Joe looked down at the floor. Exactly as Hank had predicted, he didn't want to confront the idea of Hank being absent while still being present. That was the whole point of the story she'd written.

"People assume the brave part of making art is creating," Joe finally said. "The bravery is in finishing. Saying nothing else I do will make this piece better and it's time to send it into the world. Creating is a synonym for birth, but it's as much a death. An ending. Because once it's out there you can't take it back. You have to let it be complete."

Now it was Alice's turn to stare at the cement floor. At a loss, she did what she imagined Hank would do in this situation. "Now, that really is pretentious," she said even though it wasn't.

Joe walked over to the canvas and looked between it and Alice. "You may hate it. It's how I see you, and I think it's beautiful." He motioned her over. Alice's heart raced. It wasn't often you got to witness how other people saw you. She suspected that how Joe saw her was how she really was.

On the canvas an old woman stared back at Alice. The painting was a composite of different shades of blue, red, and yellow veering into purple and green. A long, jagged line traced the woman's cheek, a scar or a shadow. Her wild blue-white hair was a halo of corkscrew curls around her head. A tingling crept up Alice's arms. She felt like she'd seen this woman before, like she knew her, and she did. The tingling intensified into an electric shock, surging through her body. The woman in the painting was Alice. Not as Alice was but as she could be.

"You're an old soul, Alice," Joe said, studying her for a response. "You have so much more wisdom in you than you know. You need to let people see your wisdom. Don't fear it. Let it define you."

The woman in the painting was very old and very beautiful. She looked powerful. Confident. Wise. She could survive anything. Even love. The physical sensation coursing through Alice was the strongest yet, stronger even than when she'd needed to write a story for Joe. It wasn't a dump truck of inspiration. It was an earthquake, a mudslide, a tectonic shift. Of course there was another story she needed to write, one that would force her to decide if she should continue to be a love scribe.

"I have to go," Alice said as she raced out of the garage. "I love it, thank you. I'll come by and get it tomorrow. Right now I really have to go."

Alice ran toward home. Her shallow heels slowed her down, so she took them off, sprinting barefoot past dried tributaries, Victorian houses, palm trees, the physical world that had inspired so many of her stories. Like all her other stories, she had an image and a purpose. Only this time, the story was for her.

37

In Which Another Envelope Arrives

Alice could feel, as distinctly as she'd felt her father's absence, that Madeline was gone, but she needed to find out for certain. So she left the secret library a mess of books and made her way down the hall toward Madeline's closed door.

At first she knocked tentatively, then more assertively, until it grew absurd to continue knocking on a door when you presumed no one was inside. She creaked the door open to find the bed neatly made, the poppy wallpaper a mix of blooming orange flowers and buds not yet opened, just as it had been the first time she saw it. On the night table beside the ceramic bowl with the two wedding rings and the antique key was an envelope with *Alice* written in practiced cursive on the front.

The envelope was sealed with the same red wax stamp as the letter Madeline had left under Alice's door, the start to their journey. Alice fingered the initials, observing their symmetry.

A mirror hung above Madeline's dresser. In its reflection *MA* became *AM*, her own initials. Beside the envelope Alice caught her own image. The few strands of white she'd recently found in her mane had spawned. Her hair was now more white than brown. Humidity hung in the air, tightening her curls into a halo around her head.

Alice sat on the bed, slipped her finger beneath the wax seal, and pulled out the card. She expected to know what the letter said. The words, like so much of Madeline, were unfamiliar.

My Dear Alice,

By now I trust you know our connection, how we're bound, how we reflect one another. Don't be mad at me for this deception. It's something you've kept from yourself, something you needed to embrace slowly. In the end it wasn't a deception at all. I did call you here to write me a story. Only the story was for you.

By now you've also discovered what the colors mean—red for lasting passion; blue for a cooler, steadier love; yellow for fleeting romance; green for relationships ruined by jealousy and envy; purple for a hate too profound to call love. Except stories are never just one thing. In love we find loss. Humor is so often laced with sadness. In lies you'll see truth. In every ending we can find a beginning. Take Dee Lauren, for instance. When her niece sold the diner, she used the money to open the Dee Lauren Women's Shelter. It's housed hundreds of women, saved dozens of lives. This doesn't undo Dee's tragedy, but her death is only one part of her story.

You're at a critical moment when you must decide if it's worth the risk to continue to be a love scribe. I won't tell you to stop writing or to keep going. Just promise you won't let fear guide you. And don't be so distracted by the way relationships end that you miss the middle. That's where life exists, the moments we build into memories that shape who we become.

Though our time together has ended, your story isn't over. You have so much love still left to give, Alice. To yourself and to others. Be brave, my dear. Discover who you truly are.

With gratitude,

Madeline

Alice's eyes returned to the beginning to reread letter. As she retraced the words, the ink faded, word by word, line by line, until just the last two sentences were left: *Be brave, my dear. Discover who you truly are.* Then they vanished too. The card began to age, crumbling in her hand until it was just a pile of dust. A wind wafted in from a window that blew open, catching the bits of powdery paper and scattering them across the room.

Alice remained seated on the bed, revisiting Madeline's words, which she realized came from somewhere deep inside herself. She wanted to be brave. It was time for Alice to let her stories belong to their readers.

As she stood from the bed, the white eyelet comforter began to yellow until it disintegrated along with the sheets and the mattress. The mahogany frame desiccated into sawdust on the floor. The other wood furniture suffered a similar fate, the wallpaper curled away from the wall, the curtains frayed until there was nothing left of the room.

Alice made the familiar journey to the library and slipped through the crack into the secret space behind it. The books were just as she'd left them, scattered across the floor. Book by book she filed them away. She stepped up toward the top shelf before her other foot was firmly planted below and slipped. Her elbows took the brunt of the fall. Pain radiated through her arms to her neck and head. Her cheek stung where she'd landed on a book. Hearing the commotion, the cats raced in, nosing her as she lay on the floor, panting through the pain.

"I'm okay," she told the cats, noticing one more encircling her than there'd been before. It was her own cat, Agatha. Agatha had never been outside Alice's apartment. Alice buried her face in her fur. "Aggie, how did you get here?"

Agatha jumped away from Alice and joined Madeline's cats, becoming part of their clowder. Alice touched her right cheek where the book had left its impression. When she pulled her fingers away, they were covered in blood. She was surprised a book could draw blood, but books drew blood all the time.

The book she had fallen on belonged to Stefanie, Alice's most violent case. She could see the rim of purple around Stefanie's left eye, the brutality of it an affront to love. Yet here the book was red. Stefanie's story wasn't over. She was a survivor. She would be alright. She still believed in love.

Alice let the blood congeal on her cheek. The cut was deep. It would scar. Alice found she didn't mind. She stood and continued to work until the books were shelved in their original chronological order.

When she tucked the last book onto the shelf, a white light exploded into the room. Alice covered her eyes until the sparks died out and when she opened them every book in the library was red again. It was impossible to determine which ones had been blue, which purple, which were her books, which were Madeline's, although Alice now understood they were all hers. The stories she'd written. The stories she might write if she chose to continue. They all looked the same, though they housed a thousand different endings, just as they housed a thousand different beginnings, a thousand middles too.

Alice herded the terrified cats into the main library. As she pushed the secret door shut, Alice watched the red books quickly dissolve. The now-empty shelves collapsed, then the secret library itself disappeared. She shoved the wall shut, locked the candelabrum into place. In the main library, the fireplace was again ignited, flames flickering up the walls emblazing the books, reds, yellows, greens, purples, and blues flaring wildly.

The cats followed Alice into the hall, breaking into a run when the floor trembled. Alice shut the door and flipped the key back and forth in the lock until the woman's parasol pointed to one. As she pulled the key from the brass plate, the house began to quake violently and the walls began to crumble. Alice and the cats raced downstairs. Outside, they watched the house collapse to rubble.

The clowder skulked toward the debris to investigate. Alice scooped Agatha up and said, "Not you," carrying the cat to her car. As they drove away, the dirt road dematerialized in the rearview mirror inch by inch until all that stood behind them was the forest.

38

A Story of One's Own

Inch by inch until all that stood behind them was the forest. Alice jumped back from her desk, nearly landing on Agatha, who screeched in protest. Timidly Alice leaned forward and tapped her laptop screen to sleep. The buzzing sensation had abated, and Alice knew she'd reached the end of her story. *Her story.* She'd never imagined writing anything for herself. Then again, she'd never imagined writing anything for anyone else either.

This story was not like the others. It felt real. Not metaphorical or symbolic but lived. Alice stroked her cheek, surprised to find it smooth instead of scabbed. When she looked in the mirror, her curls were loose again, falling to her shoulders with the same chestnut brown shade she'd always known. She could hear her future self, calling to her to be brave.

"Alice, I'm not going to read that," Gabby said, looking down at the pages Alice had printed. It had been five days since she'd written the story for herself. It did not belong to anyone. As soon as she read it, it would be hers, something she'd never experienced. She wasn't sure how the magic would work when she read her own tale.

Alice and Gabby were at the beach bar they'd taken to regarding as their bar, with its white leather couch and the library in the back, complete with poppy wallpaper and candelabra on the bookshelves. They came here almost every week, drinking those blue ladies that turned their tongues an electrifying shade. Gabby wasn't looking for her ex, Brian, anymore, and Alice was fairly certain that Gabby liked the bar for the same reason she did. It symbolized how far they'd come from those first blue ladies, from that hummingbird.

Since Gabby returned from her silent retreat, she'd been staying with her mother while she looked for a new condo. At eighteen, she had sworn she would never spend another night under the same roof as Renata. In adulthood, however, they proved to be good roommates. Renata had taken over as Gabby's primary hiking partner—"Just for now," Gabby promised Alice, who pretended to be disappointed—and they'd started going salsa dancing together, her mother the perfect foil for anyone who tried to hit on Gabby.

"I just want to know if it's good." Alice nudged the pages toward her best friend.

"You don't need me to tell you it's good. Besides, what would you do if I said it wasn't?"

"Burn it," Alice sulked, as though Gabby had read it and hated it. This was why she never talked to anyone about her stories. From the way they cocked their heads or their eyes drifted as she spoke, she inferred judgments that weren't there. In this way writing was a lot like love.

As a New Year's resolution, Gabby had decided to take a year off dating. Alice didn't believe she would last that long, but she'd already rejected three suitors, one of whom Alice thought she should have pursued. "If he's around a year from now, maybe. If it's going to happen, it will happen," Gabby said.

In the eleven months since Alice wrote Gabby's hummingbird tale, all five relationships it inspired had run their course. Gabby's sister, Maria, had ended things with Claudia when she realized she hadn't been single in a decade and had just run from girlfriend to girlfriend, slipping into domesticity before she could decide if the home they created together was one she wanted to live in. She and Claudia stayed friends, both admitting they'd rushed too quickly into something more—or less—than what they wanted. Who was to say that romance was a more serious relationship than friendship? Alice had certainly given more of herself to Gabby than she ever gave to anyone romantically. The others who'd read the story—Erica, Sal, and Cat—all decided that they needed time alone and separated amicably from partners who weren't meant for the long term. In the end Alice had brought each of them love, just not with someone else. They'd followed the hummingbird to the ocean and learned to lead themselves.

Gabby pushed the pages back to Alice. "This one is for you."

Alice sighed and put the pages back in her bag. "I'm just, I'm afraid."

"It's okay to be afraid. A lot of important parts of life are scary. Just imagine if you didn't run from fear. What if you embraced it instead? Maybe it wouldn't be so bad."

Alice had always run from fear. Fear was a hurricane, a tornado, a mudslide, something you sought shelter from. She didn't know how to think of it as a steady wind you could catch in a sail, a storm that might produce a rainbow, a downpour to dance in.

The days mounted as Alice avoided her own story, ignored calls from potential clients, erased increasingly frustrated and frantic messages about works in progress. She couldn't stop thinking about Madeline, who still seemed so real to her. She couldn't believe that the old woman wasn't waiting for her in the mountains. It made her realize that she had one more journey to make, one she'd confronted on the page but not in real life.

Alice's heart beat faster the moment she started up the incline to Stagecoach Road, pounding as she wound around each hairpin turn. When she pulled up to that familiar tavern and bar along the road, the buildings looked smaller than she expected. Alice parked her car and followed the gravel walkway.

It smelled just as she'd remembered, Lysol and beer, stone and wood, but so much about its appearance was different. She'd spent enough afternoons here that she was certain its contours had been imprinted on her just as they really were. The ceiling was lower, the small bar almost claustrophobic. It held a few tables, and while deer heads and skulls lined the walls, there was no taxidermy bear, no moose heads. Above the fireplace a metal plate displayed a quote about how the clock was the eternal soul of a room.

"Get you something?" the waitress asked Alice, wiping down the bar with a towel. She was not Shirley of Alice's story, but she was around the same age.

Alice ordered a beer and leaned against the bar since it was too narrow for stools. When the bartender plopped a disposable plastic cup of beer before her, Alice sipped it slowly, taking everything in. It was the same bar from her youth, only like everything about her childhood, Alice had preserved it as she'd wanted it to be rather than as it was.

When the waitress asked if she wanted to order any food, Alice declined. "Just the beer. I used to come here all the time as a kid. I haven't been here in nearly twenty years."

"Is that right?" the waitress said.

"On Sundays I'd ride up with my dad. His name was Paul Meadows. Maybe you knew him?"

The waitress looked squarely at Alice, breathing her in. "I've only been working here a few years," she said regretfully. There was no one else around to ask about her father, no one to confirm that those trips to the mountains had been as adventurous as Alice remembered.

Alice finished her beer, thinking not of her father but of her mother. Bobby was right. Alice had glorified the past. It still scared her to let go of all the ways she'd made her father infallible, their time together perfect. Except it didn't need to be perfect to be special. He didn't need to be perfect for Alice to love him. Alice didn't need to be perfect for someone to love her either.

Alice took the long way back to town, like she and her father used to do. The road dipped beneath the overpass of 154 and continued to wind through the dense forest. At some point Alice had passed the spot where Madeline's house had been, but the roadside was all steep, sandy hills. There was nowhere for any other road, marked or unmarked, to branch off into the woods.

The trip back to the highway was much longer than Alice recalled. It gave her time to think. She was ready to read her story, ready to confront all the ways her gift scared her, ready to confront all the ways life scared her too. By the time she got home, she knew what she needed to do.

39

Just Breathe

The sign on the door to Willow Bindery was turned to closed. Alice peered through the window. The shop looked exactly the same as it had on her last visit. She wasn't sure why she'd expected to find the card display gone or the wrapping paper wall displaying different prints, concrete alterations conveying that too much time had passed without her. In back, she could see light bleeding from Duncan's workshop. She pounded on the door.

He emerged, looking slightly miffed at the intrusion. His hair was falling from his ponytail, and he had ink on his cheek. Relief washed over his face when he saw it was Alice. He unlocked the door, stepping back to create a physical distance between them.

"Alice," he said, with too many emotions—wariness, hope, confusion, perhaps a touch of fear—fleeting across his face for Alice to isolate one and intuit what it meant for him to see her after two and a half months.

"Here," she said, holding out the cat thumb drive. Her heart was racing so fast she feared she might collapse. She leaned back against the door, gasping for air. This pain was familiar to her body, but it wasn't any easier to endure now that she accepted it signaled a phantom danger.

"Hey." Duncan reached for the drive and set it on the counter beside the register. He put both hands on her shoulders. "It's okay. Just breathe."

He brought her behind the counter, sat her down on the single stool, and told her to stay put as he disappeared into the back. A distant faucet ran. Alice could barely hear it above the throbbing in her ears. This was not how she'd imagined their reunion.

By the time Duncan returned with a glass of water, Alice's heart had slowed and her nerves had settled to her stomach where they felt sour and heavy. She brought the water to her lips. Its coldness soothed her throat. Duncan watched as she finished the glass. When she looked up at him, she expected him to make a quip about how that was quite the entrance or how he often had that effect on people; he just stared at her, concerned.

"You're okay," he said after a moment, and she realized she was. She'd just experienced the kind of panic her body knew well, nerves shouting at her to run, but she hadn't run. She'd endured it, and she was okay. She would be okay.

"Sorry," she said. Duncan leaned against the counter, his legs crossed at the ankles. They were so close, Alice perched on the stool and Duncan standing above her, that their thighs touched. There was a searing at the point of contact, at least for Alice. She wondered if Duncan felt it too.

"I'm glad you're here." Alice waited for him to continue. Instead he pointed to her empty glass. "More?"

Alice nodded because she could use another moment alone. She handed him the glass, their fingers grazing.

Alone, Alice breathed deeply. She gave herself a pep talk that mostly consisted of insults. *What are you doing? Can't you act like a normal person? You're going to make him think you're a complete and total freak.* Perhaps it was not a pep talk at all.

"Say, Alice?" Duncan called from the back. "Come here for a sec. I have something for you."

Alice held her breath as she walked through the curtain that blocked off his workshop. Inside, it was immaculate. Not a speck of dust anywhere. It smelled like a mix of leather, ink, and glue, a piquant scent she inhaled deeply, wanting to make it part of her. It was the perfume that often wafted off Duncan's body. The center of the room hosted the printing press and several vises. One wall was completely magnetic, holding metal rulers, brushes, scissors, spools of thread, and small tools that Alice did not recognize. A large linoleum counter spanned the length of the room in front of a window overlooking the alley beside the shop. Boxes of flowers lined the sill, making what would have been a view of concrete into a garden. Right away Alice knew that Duncan had planted them, that when he stood at the counter, working on his desktop computer, the paper cutter, he could see a little beauty beyond. It was the sole window in the studio, yet it let in enough light to make the room golden.

Along the back wall finished books were stacked by customer's last name above several drawers labeled in neat handwriting that she assumed was Duncan's, indicating the types of leather, muslin, and cotton within. It struck her then that she was not familiar with Duncan's handwriting, and that he didn't know hers either. They'd shared so many words but not the hands by which they were composed.

Duncan stood at the counter with his back to her. When she cleared her throat, he motioned her over. On the perfectly clean linoleum rested a gold book. It was large, like a cookbook.

"What's this?"

"I made it a while ago, before we stopped…before I messed everything up." Duncan lifted the book off the table and showed her the pages, which were lined with columns for clients' names, hours logged, fees accrued. "You probably already have a system for keeping track of your stories."

Alice took the book and flipped through it. It was the ledger of her dreams. Rather, the ledger of her story, Madeline's ledger. "It's perfect," she said, deciding then that she would use it, that she would continue to be a love scribe.

The phone rang in the store, but Duncan ignored it. As it continued to ring, he sighed and told her he'd be right back. She heard him answer, heard him detail the binding services he offered and estimate that it would take two weeks to complete the job. She heard him give the person on the phone his email address. As she listened, she wandered around the room, letting her fingers touch everything. She liked the idea of leaving her mark on his private space.

When Duncan returned, he introduced her to his tools and printing press, which he called Hercules. He showed her vises that held the books as they dried, others that stretched the leather around the cardboard covers.

"I wasn't sure I'd see you again." Duncan picked up a spiral brush and stroked it against his palm. "I hope you know how sorry I am."

"I know," Alice said. "I'm sorry too."

Duncan snorted. "What are you sorry for?"

"For letting my fear win." Her heart pounded again, threatening to overtake her. It was good fear though. It meant she knew what she wanted.

"Well," Duncan said, reaching out to twist a strand of her hair, "you're here now." He whispered her name, *Alice.* It was such a simple name. In Duncan's mouth it became exotic. Ornate.

Alice stroked his cheek, scratchy with stubble. Without thinking, she leaned down and kissed him. As she pressed harder into him, he opened his mouth. She wasn't worried about whether he liked what she was doing or what might happen if he pulled her shirt over her head. She didn't keep kissing him because she was afraid of it ending. She kept kissing him because at that moment there was nothing else she wanted to do more.

When Duncan pulled away, she wasn't filled with dread. He held her face, the smooth skin of her cheeks against his calloused fingers and looked into her eyes. His were green with brown flecks, something she hadn't noticed before. He tipped her head so their foreheads touched, their faces so close that they could commune without words, without movement.

"I don't know how to do this," Alice told his dirty sneakers.

He laughed. "You think anyone does?"

Certainly some people knew how to do this. Most people knew how to do this better than she did. Maybe each time, though, no matter how many loves you'd had before, maybe each time you had to learn again. In that way love was a lot like writing.

"What I mean is, I've never been—" She wasn't prepared to use the L-word in front of him. "Whenever I start to feel something, I try to mess it up."

"Then stop trying."

"I'm not sure it's that easy."

"It doesn't have to be easy," he said, kissing her again. They kissed until their lips were sore. Alice didn't want to stop, but she had one more thing to do.

She strode through the workshop into the store and found her cat drive on the counter. She hadn't read the story she wrote. She wouldn't, not until Duncan bound it, but it had worked its magic. It had made her brave.

When Alice returned to the workshop, she offered Duncan the drive. "I'm hoping you can bind it for me."

"I can't promise I won't read it," he said.

"I want you to read it." Alice held the drive out to him. He needed to understand what it meant for her to stay put, to face her fear.

"Okay then." He took the drive, twirled it. "I'll get to it."

She smiled and waved goodbye. In a moment she would worry that she'd left too soon, that whatever spell had settled over them broke the moment she walked out. In a week she would stress if she hadn't heard from him, certain the story had scared him away. For now though, she felt a foreign comfort in not knowing what would happen. He'd bind the book, return it to her. Then it was time for their story to begin.

★★★★★

Acknowledgements

Writing acknowledgements always makes me a little sentimental. They are a marker of a transition. The drafting is done, and at last, it's time for this manuscript to begin its journey toward becoming a book. There's still so much ahead, yet I can't help but look back, grateful to everyone who has helped me get to this pivotal point.

First, thank you to everyone at The Gernert Company and Park Row Books for enabling me to pursue my lifelong dream of writing books. It never gets old, and I feel so lucky to have such an amazing team behind me. Thank you to my agent, Ellen Coughtrey, who always goes above and beyond, even on leave. To Anna Worrall, for jumping in so enthusiastically and quelling all my last-minute nerves. Thank you also to Will Roberts, for tending to foreign rights, and to everyone at Gernert for lending your expertise throughout.

Thank you to my editor, Laura Brown. Your careful eye and wise notes have made this book a million times stronger. To Natalie Hallak, for suggesting I write a love story—and not flinching when I came back with this idea. To Leah Morse, the best publicist a book could ask for, and to everyone else behind the scenes at Park Row, who helps get my books into readers' hands.

Thanks to my small but mighty group of first readers: Jess Cantiello, Amanda Treyz, Julie Clark, Laura Herstik, and Joy Johannessen. It's a lot to ask someone to read a draft of your novel, then it's even more to ask them to read it in a matter of days. I don't take your help or time for granted. Thanks for seeing issues both big and small that I was too close to spot on my own.

One of my favorite parts of publishing has been gaining a new community of writers, booksellers, librarians, and readers. A writing career has its fair share of doubts and anxieties, both real and phantom. I'm grateful to have met so many kind and open-hearted writers over the course of three books and to call you all my friends. A special thank you to Christi Clancy, who is always so supportive and encouraging. To the many booksellers and librarians who have championed both my books and books in general—I will never meet a nicer and more generous bunch. And finally to all my readers, those in the bookstagram world, those who have invited me to visit their book clubs, those who write to share their experiences reading my books (it makes a writer's day to get a note from a reader), and those who quietly read and enjoy. It is still surreal to me that anyone besides my family reads my books.

Speaking of family, I started out with a pretty great one and have inherited even more. To the Meyersons, Perrottas, Chans, and Taners, thank you all for being in my corner. A special thanks to Alice for lending your name to this character that, other than being lovable, is nothing like you. I can't wait for you to find your name on the pages of this book. And thanks to Jessica for yet again answering my many—often morbid—medical research questions.

Finally, to the family I've created with my husband, Adam, and our little ones, Wesley and Ruby. Ruby was born two weeks before I finished drafting this book. While that has brought added challenges to the already difficult task of writing a book, it has also made this book particularly special to me. Ruby, we are so excited to see who you become. And to sweet Wesley, who forced me to take breaks when I didn't know I wanted or needed them. I definitely cried the first time you saw my picture on the back of a book and said, "Mommy." And I'm not a crier. At least I wasn't before becoming a parent. Children open up so much emotion and creativity. Although this isn't a book about parenthood, being a parent has informed this story and transformed how I think about love.

See, I warned you I was feeling sentimental.